## Praise for Patricia Davids and her novels

"Davids' deep understanding of Amish culture is evident in the compassionate characters and beautiful descriptions."
—*RT Book Reviews* on *A Home for Hannah*

"Davids writes with credibility that puts you right in Amish country."
—*RT Book Reviews* on
*An Amish Christmas Journey*

"*The Amish Nanny* is a quick, enjoyable read."
—*RT Book Reviews*

## Praise for Jan Drexler and her novels

"Drexler has delivered a pleasing read with touches of romance, suspense, drama and faith. This story also touches on the theme of deliverance and how prayer is critical to faith."
—*RT Book Reviews* on *A Home for His Family*

"The interaction between family members serves to entertain."
—*RT Book Reviews* on *A Mother for His Children*

"This is an interesting blend of gangsters and Plain folk."
—*RT Book Reviews* on *The Prodigal Son Returns*

After thirty-five years as a nurse, **Patricia Davids** hung up her stethoscope to become a full-time writer. She enjoys spending her free time visiting her grandchildren, doing some long-overdue yard work and traveling to research her story locations. She resides in Wichita, Kansas. Patricia always enjoys hearing from her readers. You can visit her online at patriciadavids.com.

**Jan Drexler** enjoys living in the Black Hills of South Dakota with her husband of more than thirty years and their four adult children. Intrigued by history and stories from an early age, she loves delving into the world of "what if?" with her characters. If she isn't at her computer giving life to imaginary people, she's probably hiking in the Hills or the Badlands, enjoying the spectacular scenery.

# PATRICIA DAVIDS

*An Unexpected Amish Romance*

&

# JAN DREXLER

*The Amish Nanny's Sweetheart*

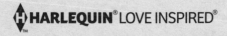

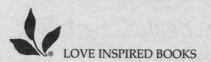

LOVE INSPIRED BOOKS

Recycling programs for this product may not exist in your area.

ISBN-13: 978-1-335-47008-9

An Unexpected Amish Romance and
The Amish Nanny's Sweetheart

Copyright © 2019 by Harlequin Books S.A.

The publisher acknowledges the copyright holders
of the individual works as follows:

An Unexpected Amish Romance
Copyright © 2018 by Patricia MacDonald

The Amish Nanny's Sweetheart
Copyright © 2018 by Jan Drexler

www.Harlequin.com

**Printed in U.S.A.**

# CONTENTS

# AN UNEXPECTED AMISH ROMANCE

Patricia Davids

This book is dedicated with boundless love to my granddaughter Shantel Widick. You are a smart, beautiful young woman of many talents, a lover of animals, a keen-eyed photographer and the person I most enjoy laughing with on a late-night sleepover. Remember to put down the phone and experience life firsthand. Oh, and never drive the four-wheeler that fast in front of your great-grandfather again. Ever.

Love you always.

MeMa Pat

Whoso findeth a wife findeth a good thing,
and obtaineth favour of the Lord.
—*Proverbs* 18:22

# Chapter One

Mark Bowman lifted his straw hat off his face and sat up with a disgruntled sigh. Trying to sleep on a bus was hard enough, but the sound of muffled weeping coming from the seat behind him was making it impossible. He turned to look over his shoulder. The culprit was an Amish woman with her face buried in a large white handkerchief. She was alone. Should he say something or ignore her?

Normally he avoided meddling in the affairs of others, but he recalled his uncle's advice to him before he'd left Bowmans Crossing four days ago. A business owner needed to be a good listener as well as a good salesman. Success wasn't always about numbers, it was about making people feel you cared about them and their concerns. It was about building friendships. Isaac had asked Mark to make an effort to be more outgoing on this trip.

There was no one Mark respected more than his uncle. Isaac Bowman had achieved everything Mark was working toward. He had a successful furniture-making business and a large happy family. Isaac was well respected in his Amish church and in the community and with good reason. He was always willing to lend a helping hand.

Mark didn't have to imagine what his uncle would do in this situation. He would ask if he could help. Taking a deep breath, Mark spoke softly to the woman. "Fräulein, are you all right?"

She glanced up and then turned her face to the window. "I'm fine."

It was dark outside. There was nothing to see except the occasional lights from the farms they passed. She dabbed her eyes and sniffled. She was a lovely woman. Her pale blond hair was tucked neatly beneath a gauzy, heart-shaped white *kapp.* He didn't recognize the style and wondered where she was from. "You don't sound fine."

"Maybe not yet, but I will be."

The defiance in her tone took him by surprise and reminded him of his six-year-old sister when she didn't get her way. Experience had taught him the best way to stop his sister's tears was to distract her. "I don't care much for bus rides. Makes me queasy in the stomach. How about you?"

"They don't bother me."

"Where are you headed?"

"To visit family." The woman's clipped reply said she wasn't interested in talking about it. He should have let it go at that, but he didn't.

"Then someone in your family must be ill. Or perhaps you are on your way to a funeral."

She frowned at him. "Why do you say that?"

"It's a reasonable assumption. You'd hardly be crying if you were on your way to a wedding."

Tears welled up in her eyes and spilled down her cheeks. With a strangled cry, she scrambled out of her seat and moved to one at the rear of the bus, effectively ending their conversation.

Confused, he stared at her. Somehow he'd made things worse, and he had no idea what he'd said that upset her so. He shook his head in bewilderment. Women could be so unpredictable. Fortunately, the woman he planned to marry was sensible and level-headed. He couldn't imagine Angela drawing attention to herself by weeping in public.

He noticed a few of the nearby passengers scowling at him. He shrugged and settled back to finish his nap. He should have gone with his first instinct to mind his own business. His brother Paul claimed most women were emotional creatures who enjoyed drama and making mountains out of molehills. Clearly she was one of those. He was fortunate she had moved to the back of the bus and wouldn't trouble him again.

Helen Zook squeezed her eyes shut to stem the flow of fresh tears brought on by her nosy and insensitive fellow passenger. His beardless cheeks told her he was a single man. She didn't want to talk to anyone, let alone a handsome dark-haired Amish fellow who was brash enough to strike up a conversation with a woman traveling alone. Perhaps he had meant to be kind, but his words stung. He was half right. She wasn't going to a wedding. She was running away from one.

Today should have been her wedding day, but all her dreams of the happy life ahead of her had come crashing down when her fiancé announced three weeks ago that he had changed his mind. He wanted to marry her sister Olivia instead. Today had been their wedding day.

How could Joseph betray her like that? How could her own sister deceive her by seeing Joseph behind her back? They were questions without answers that tumbled around in her mind like leaves in a whirlwind. Helen refused to admit that some of the blame rested squarely on her shoulders. She was the victim.

The shock and the shame had been more than Helen could bear, although she tried to pretend it didn't matter. She was so angry with them. That was wrong. She knew it, but she couldn't change how she felt. The two people she trusted most in the world had betrayed her and made her a laughingstock in the community.

The morning of her sister's wedding, Helen had realized she couldn't remain at home and watch Olivia wed Joseph. Without a clear idea of what she was going to do, she'd taken her savings and purchased a one-way bus ticket out of Nappanee, Indiana, with the intention of staying with her aunt Charlotte. She hoped she could find a job and get a place of her own soon. She prayed her aunt would take her in. She hadn't had time to write and explain that she was coming nor had she told anyone where she was going.

Helen had met her father's youngest sister a few times over the years when they came to visit at Christmas and such, but she didn't know her aunt well. Charlotte was something of an odd recluse and not overly fond of visitors, but Helen would make herself useful. She was fleeing to her aunt's home because Charlotte lived the farthest away of any of the relatives. She had never married, choosing to stay at home and care for her aging parents until they were both gone. She had a small income from the rental of farmland her father had left her near Bowmans Crossing, Ohio. According to the letters she wrote to Helen's parents, she lived happily with only her pets in a little house by the river.

It seemed like the perfect hideaway to Helen, but as the miles flew by she was learning distance alone didn't diminish a heartache.

Mark roused as the bus slowed and jolted to a halt. "Berlin, Ohio," the driver announced over the intercom. He opened the door with a loud whoosh.

Mark stretched and rose to his feet. After pulling his duffel bag from the overhead bin, he made his way down the aisle and got off the bus. It would be wonderful to sleep in his own bed after having stayed in motels for the past four days, but at least his trip had been a success. He looked forward to telling his uncle that they had two new stores in Columbus willing to sell the handmade furniture produced in his workshop.

Berlin didn't have an actual bus station. They had stopped in a parking lot in front a local restaurant that was already closed for the evening. A single floodlight provided the only illumination, with moths and other insects fluttering around it.

Several other Amish passengers got off the bus including the weeping woman who seemed to have recovered her composure. She pointedly avoided looking at Mark and kept her eyes downcast. There were several buggies parked along the roadway. Various passengers gravitated to them. The woman spoke to the bus driver, who was unloading luggage. He pointed toward a white van at the edge of the parking lot. She nodded and crossed to the vehicle where she spoke to someone inside and then got in.

Not much more than a wide spot in the road, the village of Berlin was still fifteen miles from Mark's destination of Bowmans Crossing. He looked around for his uncle or one of his cousins but didn't see them. They knew he was coming in on this bus, so he expected they would be along soon.

The driver of the white van approached. Mark recognized Abner Stutzman. The wiry gray-haired man was one his uncle's English neighbors who earned extra money by providing taxi service to the Amish folks in the community.

"Evening, Mark."

"*Guten nacht,* Abner."

"Your uncle arranged for me to pick you up and take you home tonight."

Mark grinned. That meant he'd reach his bed all the sooner. "I'm grateful for Onkel Isaac's thoughtfulness."

"I hope you don't mind me taking on another fare. There's a young lady needing a ride, too. She's going past Bowmans Crossing, so it won't hold you up any."

"That's fine." Mark hoped she wouldn't start crying again when she saw he was sharing her ride.

Abner rubbed his hands together. "Okay, let's get going. The missus came along to keep me company, but she doesn't like to stay out late."

Since Abner's wife was seated up front, Mark had no choice but to get in the back. The woman from the bus was already seated in the second row. He had the option of sitting beside her or behind her in the third row of seats. Would she start crying again if he sat beside her? Riding in the back of Abner's van might trigger Mark's motion sickness. Which would be worse? He put his duffel bag on the rear seats and sat down beside her without a word. She kept her face averted.

"All set?" Abner asked, looking at them in the rear-view mirror.

The woman nodded slightly. Mark said, "We're ready."

Abner pulled out of the parking lot and onto the narrow highway headed toward Bowmans Crossing. After a few long minutes of awkward silence, Mark decided perhaps he should apologize. He leaned toward her. "I'm sorry I upset you earlier."

"It wasn't you," she murmured. He had to strain to hear her.

She kept her face turned toward the window. He wished he could see her better. "*Goot*. I'd hate to think I added to your troubles."

"You didn't." Her clipped reply wasn't encouraging.

"If no one is ill or has died, why were you crying?"

"My reasons are my own."

He shifted uncomfortably on the seat, feeling out of his depth but sure that his uncle would want him to try and aid her. "Some people say it helps to talk about your problems."

"Well, some people are wrong."

He sighed inwardly with relief. She didn't want to pour out her troubles any more than he wanted to hear them. "I find that's true. I'm glad you don't wish to discuss it with me."

Her eyes widened. "Then why did you offer?"

"My *onkel* tells me I need to work on my communication skills. He says it's important for a business owner. I'm supposed to practice showing interest in people and become a better listener."

"So you chose me to practice on?"

He caught a hint of anger in her tone. "No need to ruffle your feathers."

"My *feathers* are not ruffled," she said through gritted teeth, her eyes snapping with irritation.

"I'd say they are getting more ruffled by the second."

"You are a rude man. We're done talking." She folded her arms tightly across her chest and turned back to the window.

She had no idea how glad he was to hear her say that. Still, he couldn't help wondering what had made her cry in the first place. She stirred his curiosity, and that was unusual.

Twenty-five silent minutes later, Abner pulled to a stop in front of Mark's uncle's home. Mark tipped his hat to the woman and got out. She didn't even glance his way. To his mind, she was the one being rude.

His uncle's advice was harder to put into practice than he expected it to be.

The following day, Mark stayed busy in his uncle's workshop until early evening. Although he had been put in charge by his uncle and oversaw the day-to-day operations of the business, it was carving that Mark enjoyed the most. He was putting the finishing touches on a mantelpiece depicting foxes at play in the woods when his uncle stopped beside him.

As Mark had hoped, his uncle had been pleased with the success of his trip. He had omitted telling him about the woman on the bus, although he wasn't sure why. Maybe it was because he hadn't been successful in that endeavor. He kept going over their conversations trying to pinpoint what he'd done wrong, but he couldn't put his finger on it.

"Time to close up shop, Mark. Ah, I see you're almost done with the mantel. This is *goot* work. If you decide not to open your own business, I'd be happy to keep you on here. You have a rare God-given talent."

"*Danki*, but I will stick to my plan."

"I felt sure you would say that. Don't let your supper get cold."

"I'll be along in a few minutes." Mark ran his hand along the surface of his project, satisfied with the way it had turned out. All that was left was to stain the oak wood the color the customer wanted. It was one of his better pieces, although he was a long way from being a master carver the way his cousin Samuel and coworker Adam Knepp were.

A short time later, he entered the front door of his uncle's home and saw his brother, Paul, waiting with a big grin on his face.

"Your fair Angela has written you another love letter, *bruder*. Will you read it aloud to us tonight?"

Mark ignored his brother and picked up the letter addressed to him from the top of the mail piled on the end of the kitchen counter. Despite his foolish younger brother's suggestion, Mark knew it wasn't a love letter. Angela was too practical for such nonsense. Their relationship was based on respect and the knowledge that their marriage would be mutually beneficial to both their families.

He slipped the letter into his pocket to read later and hung his straw hat on one of the pegs by the kitchen door. Seven identical Amish hats were already lined up. His uncle, his five cousins and his brother had come in earlier. Mark had lingered behind making sure the lights were off in the workshop, checking on the orders for the next workday and making certain the generator had enough fuel to start up again when they needed it. His uncle had placed Mark in charge of the business for the last three months of his apprenticeship. He was determined to show his uncle his faith wasn't misplaced.

"Leave off teasing Mark and sit down for supper,"

Anna Bowman said, carrying a steaming pot of roast beef and vegetables to the kitchen table using her folded black apron as a hot pad for her hands.

"I can't leave off teasing him, Aenti Anna. It's *Gott's* will that I annoy my big brother since Mark annoys the rest of us. He has become a tyrant."

"I never ask anyone to do more than I can do myself." Mark pulled out a chair and took his place at the long table. His uncle Isaac sat at the head of the table with his oldest son, Samuel, at his right hand. The rest of Isaac's sons were arranged according to age down the length of the table with Mark and Paul taking up the last two chairs. The wives and daughters of Mark's cousins were seated on the opposite side, all in plain Amish dresses with their black work aprons and white prayer *kapps*. It made a big family gathering when everyone was home. The room was filled with chatter and the clinking of dishes along with the pleasant aromas of the stew, cornbread muffins and hot coffee.

Anna surveyed the table and then took her place at the foot. The noise died away. Isaac bowed his head, and everyone did the same, reciting the blessing in silence. When Isaac raised his head, signaling the prayer was finished, the business turned to eating. The talk was minimal until the meal was over.

After finishing his peach cobbler, Isaac leaned back in his chair and patted his stomach. "It was a *goot* meal."

"*Danki*, husband. What time do you expect to start the frolic in the morning?"

"I imagine most workers will be here by eight o'clock as long as the rain holds off."

All the members of the Bowman family had arrived to help with the work party set for the following day. The women had spent the day cooking and cleaning since Isaac and Anna were hosting the party. Most of their Amish community would come to help clear the logjam beneath the only bridge into and out of the valley on the far side of the river. While the men worked, the women would usually visit then serve coffee and a hearty lunch, but tomorrow there was to be a quilting party for the women, too. As the rest of the men went into the living room, leaving the women to clean up, Mark went upstairs to his room at the back of the house.

His window was open, and the evening breeze fluttered the simple white curtains his aunt had in all the upstairs bedrooms. Outside, the spreading branches of a huge ancient silver maple tree kept the room cool, but it obstructed the view of the river from this room. Mark didn't mind. It was more practical to have a cool place to sleep in the summer than a view.

His uncle had been talking about cutting the tree down. The old thing was past its prime, having as many dead limbs as live ones branching off its enormous trunk. Silver maples were notorious for breaking in wind storms. Two large limbs had come down in the last storm, fortunately on the side away from the house, but it was only a matter of time before one fell on the roof. Mark's aunt was the reason the tree hadn't been taken down already. She had an irrational, sentimental attachment to it because Isaac's parents had planted it the year Isaac was born.

Mark pulled out his letter and sat on the edge of his bed. Angela's letters came like clockwork every Tuesday, and today was no exception. She normally wrote about the weather and the people back home, about her father's lumber milling business and about what changes she hoped to make to the farm when she and Mark were married. Unlike with the overly emotional woman on the bus, he knew exactly what to expect from Angela.

His letters to her were about his work and the ways he saw he could incorporate his uncle's teachings into the business he would own one day. The day was fast approaching when he could put his plan into effect.

It had been her father's business and the location of their farm that first gave Mark the idea to build his future workshop there. Otis Yoder's small farm had poor, rocky soil, but it fronted a busy road in an area where tourists flocked to gawk at Amish folks and buy Amish-made goods. The fact that Otis could supply almost all the raw lumber Mark would need cinched the plan in his mind.

When Mark had approached Otis about buying some of his land, Otis wasn't interested. He saw value in Mark's idea but wanted his farm and business to go to Angela, his only child. Mark persisted, and eventually Otis made a surprising counteroffer. If Mark would marry Angela, then Otis would enter a partnership with him. Angela was a widow a few years older than Mark. She was quiet, hardworking and practical. To his amazement, she agreed with her father's proposal.

Getting a wife along with the land was a bonus in Mark's eyes. He'd never had the time or the inclination to date women, but he did want a family one day. He wanted sons to carry on the business he would build. The idea of romance and falling in love to achieve that didn't make sense. Why base one of the most important decisions a man could make on something as flimsy as a feeling? In his mind, it was much better to base it on mutual respect and shared goals than love.

He and Angela had settled on a long-distance courtship while Mark apprenticed with his uncle. Mark sent her a portion of his paychecks each month as a down payment on the land.

Little by little he had been accumulating the machinery and tools he would need and had them stored in his father's barn not far from the Yoder farm. Isaac had put him in contact with people who were interested in purchasing Pennsylvania Amish–made furniture. Things were almost ready for him to open his business.

He slipped his finger under the envelope flap and tore it open. He quickly skimmed through her short letter. It didn't contain any of the usual news. Mark couldn't believe his eyes. He read the note again. Angela wanted to end their engagement.

For almost two years he had been working toward a goal that would provide them with a lifetime of security and now, two months before he was due to return home, she was tired of waiting for him?

They had talked about this before he left, and she had assured him that two years would pass before they knew it. Angela agreed they had to stick to a plan if they were going to succeed. He read her words again. She was sorry, but she no longer wished to marry him.

What was the plan now? What about the land? What about his partnership with her father? What about the money he'd sent? He had no idea where all of that stood. He crumpled the note into a ball and threw it toward the wastebasket in the corner. It bounced off the rim.

The door opened, and Paul stuck his head in. "What did the fair Angela have to say? Did she send you a hug and kiss with an *x* and *o* ?"

"My business is my own, Paul," Mark snapped. He wasn't ready to share this news, certainly not with Paul.

"Hey, you look a little funny. Is something wrong?" Paul took a step into the room.

"Your harassment is what's wrong. I'm tired of your jabs."

Paul held up both hands. "*Bruder*, I never mean you harm. I hope you know that. Forgive me if I have offended you."

Mark rose from the bed. "Please forgive me also. I'm tired tonight, that's all."

He took Paul by the shoulders and turned him to the door. "I need my sleep and so do you. We'll have a hard day tomorrow."

"You might. I intend to have fun."

"When do you have anything else?" Mark gave him a friendly shove out into the hall and closed the door behind him. He bent to pick up the crumpled letter. Instead of throwing it into the trash, he smoothed it out. He had planned a future with her for so long that he wasn't sure how to plan one without her.

If she didn't want to marry him, that was fine, but what about the land? All she said was that her feelings toward him had changed. How was that possible if they hadn't seen each other? Although their intentions hadn't been made public, he saw her request as a breach of contract. With a few strokes of her pen she upset his carefully thought-out plan and left him twirling in the wind like a new-fallen leaf.

He needed to consider all the ramifications of what this meant. He didn't have enough information. He sat down to write and ask for more details. Even if Angela's father still intended to sell Mark the land, he now faced the distasteful task of finding another woman to marry. In his opinion, courting was a waste of a man's time.

Unbidden, the memory of the woman from the bus slipped into his mind. She was the perfect example of why he dreaded looking for a mate. All he had done was try to help. In the first instance, his words had sent her fleeing in tears. In the second, they had made her spitting mad, and he still had no idea why.

Who was she? Why had she been crying? Abner had said she was going beyond Bowmans Crossing. The chances of seeing her again were slim.

So why couldn't he get her tear-stained face out of his head?

# Chapter Two

Two days after arriving unannounced at her aunt's home outside of Bowmans Crossing, Helen Zook sat in the buggy beside her aunt Charlotte wishing she had thought to plug her ears with cotton before leaving the house. The woman had been talking nonstop for the past two miles. Her basset hound had been barking loudly for almost as long.

"Remember, Helen, as far as anyone knows, you are here to visit me for the summer. The less said about your unfortunate incident, the better. In fact, don't say anything about it. Unless you are specifically asked, then you mustn't lie. Liars never prosper."

"It's cheaters."

"What did you say, Helen? Clyde, do be quiet."

"I said cheaters never prosper."

"Of course they don't. I'm sure you have never cheated anyone. I know I haven't. The truth is the best defense, Helen, but there's no point in telling people everything. Bowmans Crossing is a wonderful community, but there are those among us who like to spread gossip. I shouldn't name names, but Verna Yoder and

Ina Fisher are the worst offenders. Clyde, get down, can't you see I'm driving?"

Charlotte gently pushed aside the overweight brown-and-white hound dog trying to climb onto her lap. Helen took him by the collar and tugged him back to the floor. He gave her a mournful look before settling all seventy pounds of his wrinkles and flab on her left foot. Gritting her teeth, Helen tried to move him, but he refused to budge another inch.

Charlotte slowed the horse as the buggy rounded the curve beside the district's one-room school. The playground and swings were empty now. The students were home for the summer, but Helen couldn't go home.

"Are you paying attention to me, dear? I feel as if I'm talking to myself."

Helen freed her foot, but her shoe remained under Clyde's slobbery chin. "I'm paying attention, Aenti Charlotte. I'm visiting for the summer. Don't mention that my fiancé humiliated me in front of all our family and friends when he threw me over because he wanted to marry my sister *one week* before the banns for our wedding were to be announced. Bowmans Crossing is wonderful, except for the gossiping pair Ina Fisher and Verna Yoder. Cheaters never prosper, but they can get married and live happily ever after, but I don't have to watch them moon over each other. How could my own sister do this to me? How could Joseph?"

Helen didn't share the part she had played in the disaster. Why should she? She was the one suffering now.

It was all so horrible. She might have been able to bear the pitying looks and well-meaning comments that only served as salt in the wound. The real thing she couldn't tolerate was seeing how happy they were together.

"You girls will make up, and this will all be forgotten in time."

"I don't see how. She stole the man I wanted to marry." Helen's voice crackled.

Joe should have stood by her. If he loved her, he would have. Helen raised her chin. It was painful, but it was better to know how shallow his affections had been before they wed.

"You must not look at what you have lost for it is not your will that is important. It is His will."

"His will was to marry my sister, and he did just that."

Charlotte cast Helen a sidelong glance. "I'm not talking about that young man's will. It is *Gott's* will you must accept. You must forgive your sister and her husband as is right."

"I forgive them." Helen spoke the words, but they didn't echo in her heart. The pain was too new and too raw.

"That is *goot*. Forgiving blesses the forgiver as much as the forgiven." Charlotte clicked her tongue to get the horse moving faster.

The road straightened, and a covered bridge came into view. The weathered red wooden structure stood in sharp contrast to the thick green trees that grew along the roadway and along the river in both directions. Wide enough for two lanes of traffic, the opening loomed like a cave. A new community awaited Helen beyond the portal. What would she find? Hopefully employment.

Charlotte pointed with her chin. "Just the other side of the river is Isaac Bowman's home, but you have to go about a quarter of a mile farther down the road and turn the corner to reach their lane. That's where the frolic is being held today. He and his wife, Anna, have five sons. I'm sorry to say the young men have all married, but Isaac has two nephews from Pennsylvania living with him now and they are unwed, although one has a girl back home."

It had been dark when the van stopped to let her rude companion out, but Helen was almost certain the Bowman house had been his destination. They hadn't exchanged names so she couldn't be sure of his identity. She hoped and prayed he wouldn't be at the frolic. Her behavior hadn't been the best but neither had his.

"Isaac also employs a number of unmarried fellows in his furniture-making business. You will have plenty of young men to pick from."

Helen rolled her eyes. "You make it sound like I've arrived at the husband orchard."

"The husband orchard. How cute. It should be the title of a book. I'd read it. Oh, that's very clever."

It hadn't taken Helen long to realize her aunt was an avid reader. Her living room held stacks of dog-lover magazines and heaps of novels, from an extensive collection of the classics to some popular romance stories the bishop might raise an eyebrow at if he knew she had them.

Charlotte chuckled and looked at her dog. "Isn't Helen a clever girl, Clyde?"

He took it as an invitation to climb into his mistress's lap. Helen used the opportunity to grab her damp shoe.

"Not now, Clyde, I'm driving." Charlotte pushed him aside. Helen quickly drew her knees up and wrapped her arms around them to give the hound more room to spread out on the floorboards. He locked gazes with her but didn't test her patience by trying to climb in her lap. Instead, he started barking at the roof. Scrabbling overhead accompanied by a chittering sound proved her aunt's pet raccoon was still safely riding atop the buggy.

"Did we have to bring Juliet?"

"Her feelings would be hurt if I took Clyde along and didn't take her."

"We could have left them both at home." The buggy rolled into the dark interior of the bridge. The horse's hoofbeats echoed back from the rafters. Helen stared through the slatted sides at the Bowman house on the hillside across the river. She could see tables had been set up on the lawn, and groups of people were already gathered there.

"Honestly, Helen, I don't think you like my little friends. Please remember they had made their home with me long before you arrived, and they'll be with me long after you have gone back to Indiana."

"I'm not going back to Indiana." Helen had no idea where she was going, but she would make her own way in the world. As soon as she found the means to support herself.

Charlotte's brow wrinkled with concern. "You are welcome to reside with me for the summer, but you never said anything about staying permanently."

"Don't worry. You won't be burdened with me for long."

"That's the spirit. Things will work out for you and your sister. You'll see. Oh, Clyde won't be happy until he can look out the windshield. Helen, take the reins."

Helen grabbed for the lines her aunt dropped as she scooted over to make room for her dog. The horse veered sharply to the right as they came out of the dark bridge into the bright sunlight. A man standing on the edge of the roadway was forced to jump backward to avoid being run down.

Helen managed to stop the horse. Clyde, now taking up more than his fair share of the front seat, started barking wildly. Helen leaned out the door to look back to see if the man was injured. He appeared unharmed as he got to his feet. "I'm sorry," she called out.

Her breath caught in her throat. The man picking his hat up off the road was the fellow from the bus. She knew by the way his eyes widened that he recognized her, too. His brows snapped together in a fierce frown. "If you can't drive any better than that, you should give the reins to the dog," he shouted at her.

Of all the nerve. As much as Helen wanted to tell him exactly what she thought of his rudeness, she held her tongue for her aunt's sake. It wouldn't do to start her time in Bowmans Crossing by embarrassing Charlotte in front of her friends, for several women were walking along the roadway with hampers and baskets over their arms. The women all waved or called a greeting to Helen's aunt. Charlotte waved Clyde's front paw at them. Helen slapped the reins on the horse's rump, and the mare trotted forward.

"Who was that rude man?" she asked, glancing in her rearview mirror.

Charlotte turned to look behind them. "The one standing by the bridge? That's Mark Bowman. The nephew. He has a girl back home. I admit he's a nice-looking young man with those striking green eyes, but handsome is as handsome is."

"As handsome does," Helen said, glancing back again. He wasn't bad-looking, but she didn't think he was particularly good-looking. Okay, maybe he was mildly attractive.

"As handsome does what, dear?"

Helen took note of her aunt's faintly puzzled expression and sighed inwardly. She'd only been at her aunt's home for two days, but it was already shaping up to be a trial. "Never mind."

"You'd do better to try and attract the attention of the younger brother, Paul, although Anna tells me Mark is the more hardworking of the two."

"I'm not here to attract a man." She wouldn't make that mistake again anytime soon. If ever. And certainly not with a rude, arrogant fellow like Mark Bowman or his brother.

Mark raked a hand through his hair as he stared after the buggy. That had been a close call. If he hadn't been so preoccupied with thoughts of Angela's letter, he might have seen the horse veering his way sooner. It wasn't like him to be distracted. He grew angry with himself for allowing it to happen.

"Are you all right?" His brother, Paul, came up the steep bank, his eyes full of concern. His cousin Noah rushed up behind Paul.

"I thought you were going to be wearing hoofprints up the front of your shirt. Who was that?" Paul demanded.

"Charlotte Zook," Noah said. "I recognized the raccoon on her roof. The woman is a little *ab en kopp*."

Mark shook his head. "Charlotte may be off in the head, but she wasn't driving. I don't know the woman's name, but I saw her get off the bus when I did the other night." He decided not to share the conversation they'd had.

"Another mystery woman." Paul craned his neck to see down the road.

"What does that mean?" Mark asked.

Paul grinned. "Haven't you heard? We've got nearly

a dozen new single girls visiting folks in the area. They are all unknown to me and waiting to be discovered. Was the girl driving Charlotte's buggy pretty?"

His brother was always on the lookout for an attractive girl. He was four years younger than Mark, and he hadn't yet learned that looks didn't matter. A man needed a steady, strong, levelheaded woman for a helpmate. He thought he had that with Angela, but he had been wrong. "I didn't notice. I was trying not to get run down. Let's get this frolic under way."

The *frolic*, a word the Amish used for almost any kind of work party, had been called by Mark's uncle Isaac Bowman to clear a logjam from beneath the covered bridge. The recent rains and flooding had wedged an unusual amount of debris there, which was acting like a dam. Although the county was responsible for maintaining the bridge, the public works department was swamped with other repairs and couldn't bring in their heavy equipment for another two weeks. With the forecast calling for more rain, flooding could threaten farms and homes on both sides of the river.

Men with chainsaws and teams of horses had been arriving for the past half hour and were now gathering on the roadway. Isaac strode up to Mark and surveyed the men around him.

"I reckon we have all the help we need to get started. I sure appreciate you coming," Isaac said, addressing the group. "Samuel and I will oversee the men pulling logs free and getting them up to the roadway. Noah, Paul and Mark will cut and stack the usable wood beside our barn to be divided among our families. The Lord has supplied us with free firewood for the taking. We shouldn't let it go to waste. My sons Timothy and Luke will flag down vehicles heading for the bridge to warn them we are working here." Both men he spoke of were wearing their volunteer firefighter jackets and pants with bright fluorescent yellow banding.

Isaac turned to Mark. "There is more rope in the barn loft. Bring it with you. We may need it." He turned back to the men. "Are there any questions?"

Everyone knew what was expected of them. The group split up, and Mark headed with his brother and his cousin toward his uncle's barn, where the family's draft horses were hitched to two large hay wagons. Noah looked over at Mark. "Aren't you going to miss us?"

Mark knew what he was referring to. "Sure, I'll miss all of you when I leave. Your whole family has been good to me."

"But you won't miss us enough to stay."

"Staying here isn't part of my plan." Mark had learned the business of woodworking and furniture making from the ground up working alongside his uncle and his five cousins, but it was almost time to return home and put his knowledge to use and open his own business. He realized he was more upset about the uncertainty facing him now than he was about Angela's decision not to marry him.

"Plans change," Noah said with a wry smile. Mark knew Noah's desire to play professional baseball had been changed by the neighbor girl across the road. Fannie and Noah had wed last fall.

Paul laid a hand on Mark's shoulder. "My brother's plans don't change. He's been talking about starting his own furniture-making business since he could talk."

"I'm guessing it's the girl back home that has Mark pining to leave us. Fair Angela. Paul, is she fair or is she dark-haired? Mark never talks about her."

"I like to keep my personal life private," Mark said before Paul could comment.

"I can respect that." Noah nodded solemnly but couldn't keep a straight face.

Paul chuckled. "Don't let my brother fool you, Noah. He doesn't have a personal life. With him, it's all work, work, work."

"Hard work and strong faith will supply a man with the best rewards in this life and in the next." They were words Mark believed in.

"But will it put a pretty woman in your arms?" Paul asked, wagging his eyebrows.

Noah chuckled. "Are you ever serious?"

"Not if I can help it. Mark and Angela are the serious ones. I'm not sure I've ever seen them laugh."

Mark scowled at his brother. "Not everyone is a jokester like you."

"Fannie makes me laugh all the time. I love that about her." Noah's gaze shifted toward the house where the women were working. A gentle smile curved his lips. It was easy to see the newlyweds were still madly in love.

Love was okay for some men, but it took more than that frail emotion to build a future. Mark wanted the security of a home and a business where he could support a family. He never wanted his children shuttled from one temporary home to another the way he had been passed from relative to relative when his father was out of work. God willing, Mark's younger sisters and his children would never know the kind of fear he had known wondering if his father would come back for him each time he left.

Mark glanced back toward the bridge. The first logs

were already on the roadway. "We should get moving. They have started without us. Where is the extra rope?"

He wouldn't tell his brother and his cousins about Angela today. He'd wait until he knew exactly where he stood with her father.

A quarter mile past the bridge, Helen and her aunt reached the stop sign on the main road between Berlin and Winesburg. An enormous oak tree stood near the intersection. Dozens of gaily painted gourds hung from its branches. Helen stared at them in amazement. "Look at all the birdhouses. How lovely."

Smiling, Charlotte murmured her agreement. "Very pretty. I believe Luke Bowman makes them. Turn here, dear. The Bowman lane is up ahead."

A sign proclaiming Amish-made gifts and crafts fronted the highway in front of a low blue building. There were several cars and buggies in the parking lot dotted with mud puddles left over from the recent rain. Helen glanced at her aunt. "Do the Bowmans run a gift shop?"

"Anna does. Isaac runs the woodworking business in that building up ahead. He employs almost two dozen young men along with his sons. He ships his furniture to *Englisch* businesses across several states. I understand his work is much in demand. The community is grateful for his efforts to keep our young men employed, since not all of them can farm these days."

It was a common problem in many Amish communities. Cottage industries were needed where farmland was too expensive, or urban encroachment had gobbled up land that once supported small farms. "Does Isaac hire women in his factory?"

Helen needed a way to support herself. She'd been serious when she said she wasn't going home.

"I believe he has hired one or two for office work."

"Full-time jobs?" Helen didn't know anything about woodworking, but she was willing to learn.

Charlotte shook her head. "I don't think so."

Helen eyed the gift shop. Maybe she could find employment there. She had worked in a fabric store for a while back home. She had retail experience.

"Park by the barn, Helen, and try to stay out of the mud. Clyde loves it. I'm delighted you will have a chance to meet so many people at this frolic. I do enjoy them, but sometimes I feel guilty visiting with my friends while we watch the men work."

The grounds were dotted with puddles, but Helen saw a dry place to let her aunt get out. She drew the horse to stop. "Aenti, you and I have been up baking since before dawn. We have already done our work. I hope the men know it."

"How could they? I wouldn't want a bunch of men watching me at work in my kitchen. It's much too small. I guess they could stand outside and look in the window."

Helen sent up a quick prayer for a job and a place of her own as soon as possible.

Her aunt took Clyde's face between her hands. "I'm sorry, dear friend, but you are going to have to stay on your leash until you calm down and mind your manners. I can't have you jumping on everyone you see. Helen is going to look after you. I'll take the hamper to the house."

Helen got out, keeping a tight hold on the dog's leash after noting his interest in the puddles. She glanced at the buggy top. "What about Juliet?"

Charlotte put the hamper down and stepped back to survey the top of the buggy. "Come here, dear one. She doesn't jump on people, so she has no need for a leash."

The plump raccoon scrambled down. A bright pink collar marked her as a pet. Charlotte picked her up and settled her in the crook of her arm, where she began purring loudly. After a moment, she climbed to the top to Charlotte's shoulder and began patting her face and *kapp*.

A trio of women walked past, carrying baskets and boxes. Clyde nearly jerked Helen's arm out of the socket as he tried to leap at them, woofing in his deep tone. Charlotte greeted the woman and walked off with them.

Helen bent to pick up the hamper of baked goods her aunt had left on the ground. As she switched Clyde's leash to her other hand, he spotted a new victim and launched himself at a man stepping out of the barn door, ripping the lead from Helen's hands. Her shriek wasn't enough warning. Clyde hit the man in the back of knees and felled him like a scythed weed. Right into a puddle.

"I'm so sorry." Helen rushed to snag Clyde's leash before he could do more damage. Loud guffaws of laughter erupted from the two men who came to help the poor victim to his feet. When he turned around, Helen wanted to sink into the mud herself. It was Mark Bowman, the rude man from the bus. The one she narrowly missed running down ten minutes ago.

He stood and shook the mud from his hands. His eyes widened when he caught sight of her. "You! I might have known."

"I'm sorry. He got away from me. He's very strong." She pulled Clyde to her side, where he sat happily with his tongue lolling, looking as innocent as only a dog can.

The men with Mark were trying to stifle their laughter without much success. He glared at them and then at her. "Has anyone told you that you're a menace?"

Helen's mouth dropped open. It wasn't like she had planned to humiliate him. She fisted her hands on her hips. "Let me think. *Nee*, no one has mentioned it, but I'm sure someone has told you that you're judgmental as well as rude."

She spun on her heels and yanked on Clyde's lead. He ambled happily beside her, occasionally stepping on his own long ears.

When she rounded the corner of the house and was sure she couldn't be seen by *him*, she stopped and stared at Clyde. "This was not how I wanted to start out in a new community. I'm going to have to apologize."

She peeked around the corner of the house. Mark was still standing with his friends. She jerked back when he looked her way. She pressed her head against the side of the house. She didn't have the courage to return and face him.

"I don't need to apologize, I just need to avoid him. How hard can that be?"

## Chapter Three

Mark stared after the woman as she vanished around the corner of the house. He couldn't remember the last time someone had made him so angry. "I think she did that on purpose. Who is she?"

Paul continued to chuckle. "What did you say that upset the *madel* enough to set her *hund* on you?"

Mark wasn't proud of his earlier comment. "Nothing."

"The truth now, I heard you shout something at her when the buggy flew past you. What did you say, *bruder*?"

"After she almost ran me down, I said if she couldn't drive any better than that to give the reins to the dog."

"Ouch." Noah grimaced.

"I know. It was not my best moment." He could see now that he'd been too harsh. Both times. He rubbed his hands on his pants. They would be dirtier than this before the day was over anyway. Hopefully, she and her mutt would stay out of his way from now on. He'd sure keep an eye out for the pair. Looking toward the house, he wondered how long she would be staying in the area.

Noah combed his short beard with the fingers of one hand. "She's a good judge of character."

Mark picked up the rope he had dropped. "What makes you say that?"

"I know that you can be judgmental and rude, but I've worked beside you for two years. She's only just met you."

"I'm not judgmental." He looked at his cousin and his brother. "Am I?"

They both nodded. Mark tossed his rope in the wagon. "I like to see things done the right way. Stop laughing like jackals and get to work."

Paul climbed to the wagon seat still chuckling. "I wonder if she will rent out her dog. I'd love to have a way to take you down a peg or two when you get short with me."

"If you did your work, I wouldn't get short with you, and if I never see that mutt again, it will be too soon." Mark hauled himself up beside his brother.

"I like him. He's a cute dog. Fannie adores him." Noah boarded the other wagon and picked up the reins.

"He's a ridiculous animal. His legs are too short, his ears are too big and he smells bad."

Paul unwound the reins from the brake handle. "Careful, your rude and judgmental character is showing."

"Go soak your head." Mark glanced toward the house again, but *she* was staying out of sight. Who was she?

Helen found Anna Bowman directing the placement of tables and benches that would be used when the noonday meal was served. Charlotte was standing beside her. She caught sight of Helen and motioned her over.

Clyde tried jumping on Anna when she came within range, but Helen was prepared and held on tightly.

Charlotte swept a hand toward Helen. "I've brought my niece along. Helen is visiting me for the summer. That's the only reason she is here, and I'm not going to say another word about it."

Anna chuckled. "And a very good reason it is. It's nice to meet you, Helen. I'm Anna Bowman." She turned and beckoned to a young woman at one of the tables. "Fannie, will you show Helen where we are setting up the food? Fannie is married to my youngest son, Noah. She'll introduce you to everyone and make you feel welcome."

"Oh, I see Grace and Silas Yoder. Let's go say hello, Juliet." Charlotte and Anna walked away to visit with an older woman in a wheelchair and the man standing behind her. The couple called a greeting to Clyde, who barked and wagged his tail.

Her aunt was quickly surrounded by a group of children who wanted a closer look at Juliet. The raccoon seemed delighted with the attention, moving from shoulder to shoulder and patting each child's face in turn.

"Your aunt is quite a character," Fannie said.

Helen judged Fannie to be near her own age. Twenty-two or twenty-three perhaps. She had a contagious smile, red hair and more than her fair share of freckles. She turned aside to avoid Clyde's leap and said, "Bad dog. Sit."

To Helen's amazement, he did. "I don't believe it."

Fannie laughed. "I've had a lot of experience training animals. My husband and I train horses. Let me take the hamper. Where are you from, and how long will you be staying with us?"

"I'm from Nappanee, Indiana, and I'll be staying with Aenti Charlotte until I can find a job and get a place of my own." Helen walked beside Fannie toward the house. Clyde trotted happily at Fannie's side, sending her adoring glances.

"You're planning to settle here permanently?" Fannie walked beneath the branches of a large tree near the door at the rear of the house. She held the door open.

"That will depend on what kind of job I can find. Any suggestions?"

"My husband mentioned something about his father's business needing help the other day, but I don't know any details. What kind of work are you looking for?"

"One that pays a salary. I'm not picky."

"We don't have many businesses in this area. Besides the woodworking shop, there is only Anna's gift shop and a hardware store up the road that's run by Luke Bowman and his wife. I'll introduce you to Emma after we put this food out, but I'm sure they aren't looking for help. Emma has two younger brothers."

Helen followed Fannie to the kitchen and started to unpack her hamper. Clyde raised his nose to sniff the food already laid out on the counters. Fannie put a foot on the leash as he tried to jump up, foiling his effort to snatch a tidbit.

"Down." The single stern word from Fannie made him plop on the floor. She praised him sweetly. He wagged his entire rear end but stayed put.

Through the open kitchen window, Helen could see the operation below the bridge as logs were hauled out. An older man with a long gray beard was directing the operation. Mark Bowman and the two other men Helen had seen earlier stood conferring with him as several of the bigger logs were being hoisted onto a wagon. Why hadn't she kept her mouth shut instead of calling him rude? He must think she was a sharp-tongued woman without an ounce of meekness, and he would be right.

She drew herself up straight. Maybe she was. She didn't have to be meek, but she did have to find work. She studied the older man beside Mark.

"Is that your father-in-law, Isaac Bowman?" Helen would ask him about a job as soon as the opportunity arose.

Fannie glanced out the window. "It is. The good-looking fellow with the short beard is my husband, Noah. The other two with them are Mark and Paul Bowman. They are Isaac's nephews."

"I almost ran into Mark earlier and then Clyde did. It wasn't pleasant."

Fannie grinned and took a step closer. "That sounds intriguing. Do tell."

Something about the sparkle in Fannie's eyes prompted Helen to confide in her. "On our way here, Aenti Charlotte dropped the lines and I grabbed them as we came through the bridge. The horse veered sharply and almost ran into Mark as he stood at the side of the road. He suggested that I let the dog drive if I couldn't do any better."

"He didn't?"

Helen nodded. "He yelled at me."

"Mark can be gruff, but I'm sure he was sorry he shouted at you."

"That wasn't the worst of it. A short time later, Clyde jumped on him from behind and laid him out in a mud puddle in front of your husband and Paul."

Fannie giggled and clapped both hands over her mouth. "That I would have liked to see. Mark is the stuffy sort. It's odd that Clyde should pick on him."

"I haven't noticed that Clyde is particular about who he jumps on."

"He can be. Mark is all business. I imagine my husband was laughing, but I'll guess that Paul was roaring. He has a...large...sense of humor."

"I was so embarrassed that I barely noticed. Mark was not laughing. He called me a menace."

Fannie smothered her grin. "He shouldn't have done that. He owes you an apology. It was an accident. Everyone knows Clyde isn't exactly well trained." Fannie glanced at the dog lying quietly at her feet.

"I'm afraid I'm the one who owes Mark an apology. I told him he was rude and judgmental, and then I fled."

Repeating her comment aloud made her ashamed of her behavior. She bowed her head. "I'm afraid I showed a serious lack of *demut*."

Fannie slipped an arm around Helen's shoulders and gave her a squeeze. "Humbleness is something I struggle with, too. Don't worry about it. I will say you hit the nail on the head about Mark. Don't get me wrong. I like him, but he's not the friendly sort. He's hardworking, diligent and thrifty, all fine traits, but not much fun. I think underneath there is a happier man waiting to emerge."

Helen appreciated Fannie's understanding and knew she had made her first friend in Bowmans Crossing. "Would it be forward of me to ask Isaac about a job today?"

"You'll have to ask Mark. Isaac put him in charge of hiring new workers a few months ago."

"Oh, dear." Helen closed her eyes. How much worse could this get? So much for not caring what Mark Bowman thought of her. He wasn't likely to hire her after the way she had spoken to him, even if he had been rude first. "Are you sure you don't know of anyone else looking to hire a maid or a nanny, a gardener, anything?"

"I don't. I'm sorry, but there will be lots of people here today. Maybe someone will have better news for you."

"If you hear of anything, please let me know." If nothing else was available, she would have to apologize and soon. What could she say that would make up for her stinging comments to him?

Fannie lifted a container of pastry from Helen's basket. "These cream horns look yummy. Did you make them?"

"I did. Have one and tell me what you think. It's a new recipe. I've added something special to the puff pastry."

Fannie bit into the cream-filled treat and her eyes widened. "Oh, Helen, these are amazing."

*"Danki."*

"I hate to admit it, but I'm not much of a cook. I'd rather be taking care of the horses outside instead of doing anything inside."

"Baking is a pleasure, not a chore. I love finding ways to improve on things I've made or try out ways to add different flavors and textures to breads and cakes."

"My mother always told me that the way to man's heart is through his stomach. At least that is how she claims she won my father over."

Helen stared out the window where Mark had climbed out onto the mass of debris to loop a rope around a tangled root mass. Two men in a small rowboat on the river surveyed the mass and called out directions. Mark moved confidently, but it looked like dangerous work. She waited until he was safely back on the bank. "I'm not looking for a way to his heart, only a way to apologize."

"For a plateful of these, I'd forgive you just about anything."

"Even a dog-assisted tumble into a puddle?"

*"Ja."* Fannie nodded as she licked some of the filling from her fingers. Helen prayed Fannie was right.

"Then I'll set aside a half dozen and brace myself to grovel with them later if I have to." If she found work with someone before the men came in to eat, she might be spared the pain.

As it turned out, she came up empty while getting to know many of Charlotte's friends and the likable young women of the Bowman family. Clyde had been turned over to some of the children who were wearing him out with a game of fetch. Juliet was occupied with getting a grape from Charlotte, carrying it down to the river to wash and then eat it before racing up the hill to beg for another.

When the men came in, Mark took a seat beside Isaac without so much as a glance in Helen's direction. Before the meal was served, everyone bowed their heads for silent grace. After that, she kept a close eye on the men and noticed Mark took three of her ham and cheese-filled crescent rolls and managed to snag the last of her cream horns when the plate was passed. When he licked a smear of filling from his fingers, she knew he liked them. She'd been smart to keep some back.

She rushed to the house and took the half-dozen pastries outside as she rehearsed her apology. To her chagrin, Mark was already on his way back to the river. She hurried after him and called out, "Mark Bowman, may I speak to you for a moment?"

He stopped and looked back. She saw the indecision cross his face, but he nodded. "I reckon."

*Smile. Don't look intimidated.*

"I've brought some of my cream horns as a peace offering." She lifted the plate just as her foot encountered Juliet racing past. The outraged raccoon squealed. Helen hopped over her to keep from tripping. Clyde, who until that instant had been fetching a ball for one of the children, leaped on Helen from behind, knocking her forward. She plowed into Mark as he tried to catch her. Horrified, she looked down at the plate of pastry sandwiched between them and then back to his darkening brow. Clyde danced around them, barking excitely.

"What was it that you wanted?" Mark asked in a cold, calm voice as he held her away. The remains of the smashed cream horns covering his shirt began dropping to the ground. Clyde darted in to snatch them up.

"To apologize," she answered in a small voice. She still had the empty plate in her hands.

"I'm sorry, but I don't know your name. Who are you?"

"I don't think I want to tell you." She began plucking the stuck pieces off his shirt.

He grabbed her hand. "Miss?"

"Zook. Helen Zook. I'm visiting my aunt for the summer, and that's all I'm going to say about it." She turned away and walked back to the tables, aware of the snickers of laughter from the onlookers. She passed them with her head down and went to her aunt.

Charlotte was trying to coax Juliet out of the tree next to the house. Juliet hissed when Helen stopped beside Charlotte and went up to the top of the tree. "Aenti, I'm going to walk home."

"That's a *goot* idea, dear. Poor Juliet is very upset with you."

"I'm afraid she's not the only one." Helen didn't

bother looking to see if Mark was still watching her. She could feel his eyes boring into her back.

"I have told Juliet you aren't staying with us long, but I'm not sure she understands me. She isn't fond of company."

"Please tell her I'm sorry I stepped on her." Helen kept walking and didn't look back. She guessed her chance of being hired by Mark Bowman was now about zero or less thanks to Clyde. Things could get desperate if her aunt chose her pet's happiness over her niece and asked Helen to leave.

She wasn't going home, so where would she go?

Paul walked up to Mark, swiped his finger through a clump of cream filling and stuck it in his mouth. "She and that dog together are a menace, but you have to admit she makes a fine dessert."

"Go away."

Paul held out his finger. "Just one more lick?"

"Paul." Mark bit out the name with as much threat as he could manage.

"Okay, okay, I'm going. It's sad to say, because today has been mighty entertaining, but I don't think we will see much of Helen Zook for a while."

"I hope not."

Fannie came down with a wet napkin in her hand. "I thought you might need this."

He took it and began wiping the front of his shirt. "I've never met anyone like that woman."

"I know. Clyde has taken a shine to her and to you. Isn't that *wunderbarr*?"

He looked up in amazement, but Fannie was already heading back up the hill chuckling to herself.

The rest of the afternoon passed quickly and uneventfully, for which Mark was grateful. The work was hard, but it was satisfying when the jam finally broke free and washed under the bridge. They had gathered enough wood to keep a good many homes warm during the coming winter.

Exhausted and determined not to think about the outspoken and annoying Helen Zook or the troubling letter from Angela, Mark went up to bed not long after supper. With a cool evening breeze blowing through the open window beside him, he fell sound asleep just minutes after his head hit the pillow.

Until the howling began.

# Chapter Four

Charlotte entered the kitchen the morning after the frolic and sniffed the air appreciatively. "Something smells *wunderbarr*. What are you making?"

After a sleepless night, Helen had been up mixing, kneading and watching her dough rise for over three hours already, and it was barely seven o'clock. "I'm making chocolate almond crescent rolls."

Because she was unsure if the oven temperature was accurate on her aunt's ancient propane model, she had put only four rolls on her baking sheet to test them first. They were done to a beautiful golden brown. She slid them onto a plate on the table and set the pan aside to cool while she rolled up another dozen. Now if only her decision to see Mark Bowman later today would turn out half so well. She wiped her damp brow with the back of her arm and then rolled up her sleeves.

"May I have one of these?" Charlotte took two from the plate on the kitchen table without waiting for Helen to answer her.

"Help yourself. I'm taking them with me when I go to ask for a job today. I hope Mark Bowman likes them, and I hope he doesn't end up wearing them."

It had occurred to her a little before 3:00 a.m. that it was highly unlikely that today could turn out worse than yesterday, but at least she wouldn't have Clyde or Juliet to hinder her. She planned to go alone to the Bowman workshop.

If Mark would see her, and if she made a sincere effort to apologize, and if she could convince him that she desperately needed a job, he might offer her employment. And if he liked her chocolate almond pastry as much as he had seemed to like her ham and cheese rolls yesterday, she wasn't above using them as a sweetener. It was a lot of ifs, but what choice did she have?

"Why would Mark Bowman want to wear your baked goods?"

Helen drew a deep breath and smiled fondly at her aunt. "I have no idea, but I desperately hope he will offer me a job. He should. I've had experience working in the fabric shop in Nappanee. I worked in a hardware store for a summer, but I didn't care for the man who ran it. He was creepy. I'm conscientious. I'm hardworking. I'm a quick learner. I would be an asset to any business, even one run by a rude, judgmental and annoying fellow like Mark Bowman."

"I don't think he's annoying. Did you let Clyde out this morning?" Charlotte stood in the middle of the kitchen turning in slow circles. She bent down to look under the table then moved the trash can to look behind it as if the dog might have become paper thin overnight.

"I did not."

"He isn't in the house. I've looked everywhere, and Juliet is missing, too." Charlotte opened the door to the cellar and called down the steps, "Clyde, come here, boy."

Helen placed her batch of rolls in the oven, wound the

kitchen timer and set it beside the stove. "I'll go outside and look for them in a few minutes. I'm sure they are playing in the yard. You mentioned that Juliet can open a door when she wants to. Was the back door open?"

"I believe it was. I'll look, you finish what you're doing." Charlotte went to the back of the house. She returned a few minutes later. "They aren't outside. I called and called. Clyde never misses a meal, and neither does Juliet. Something is wrong."

"I'm sure they are fine." Helen realized she hadn't heard or seen the dog and raccoon all morning. That was unusual.

Charlotte's eyes widened. She pressed both hands to her cheeks. "Someone has stolen them."

Helen caught herself before she laughed aloud. She struggled to speak in a reasonable tone. "Aenti, calm yourself. Who would want to steal your pets?"

"I've read that the *Englisch* people make hats out of raccoons, and Clyde is a very valuable animal. Why, the bishop's wife remarked on his amazingly long ears just yesterday. Oh, the nerve of that woman to take him from my house. Well, she can't have him. I'm going right over there and tell her so."

Helen caught her aunt by the arm as she marched toward the kitchen door. "*Nee*, you are not going to accuse the bishop's wife of dognapping. She said his ears were foolishly long for such a squat-bodied *hund*. I was standing right beside you when she said it."

"I heard her say his ears were luxuriously long, and she deeply admired such a dog."

Clearly her aunt heard only what she wanted to hear when people were talking about her pets. "Even if she admired him, she wouldn't steal him."

"You don't know that woman. Her family is from Nappanee."

"So is your family."

"Exactly!"

Helen caught the sound of distant barking. "I think I hear him."

"You do?" Charlotte rushed to the door and pulled it open. "Clyde! Where are you?"

Helen moved to stand beside her aunt. Dawn was turning the eastern sky a pale gold color beyond the tree-covered ridge to the east. "I'm sure it was him."

The barking started again, closer now. Charlotte pressed her hands to her chest. "I hear him, too. It is Clyde. Come here, baby boy."

She rushed outside just as a horse and buggy turned off the main road and rolled up her lane. The barking, louder and more frantic now, was coming from the buggy. Helen stepped out onto the porch but almost turned and scurried back into the house when she saw Mark Bowman was driving. What was he doing here? The barking was definitely coming from his buggy. Why did he have Clyde with him?

Mark started to step down, but her aunt planted herself in front of him with one hand on her hip as she shook a finger in his face. "How dare you! I never would have suspected a Bowman of such dastardly behavior."

"What?" He looked utterly confused. Helen knew exactly how he felt.

Charlotte folded her arms over her ample chest. "Stealing is a sin and beneath you, Mark Bowman, but I forgive you, since you have returned him."

Mark looked at Helen. "What is she talking about?"

"She thinks that you stole Clyde."

His puzzled expression snapped into a fierce scowl.

"I did no such thing. Your miserable mutt began howling outside my window at three o'clock this morning. I couldn't make him leave. He woke the entire household. I almost returned him then, but I decided to wait until a reasonable hour."

Charlotte already had the rear buggy door open. Clyde was smothering her with doggy kisses as he struggled against the makeshift leash preventing him from jumping out. "Untie him at once, and I won't mention your deplorable behavior to Bishop Beachy."

"I didn't steal your dog!"

Helen patted his shoulder. "I think I can help. Aenti, listen carefully. Mr. Bowman didn't take Clyde. Your poor dog became lost in the woods last night. Mr. Bowman found him and took time out of his busy morning to bring your precious pet home because he knows how much you love Clyde. Mark is a mighty *goot* fellow."

Charlotte eyed him suspiciously for a long moment and then looked at Helen. Her eyes brightened. "He's a hero just like in the book I'm reading. He rescued poor Clyde from a terrible fate. Bless you, my boy."

"I wouldn't go that far," Mark muttered under his breath. He untied the rope holding Clyde in the buggy.

The overweight hound tumbled out the door and immediately jumped up on Charlotte. She toppled to her backside and hugged him close as he climbed into her lap. "My poor fellow. You are safe at home. *Danki*, Mark. Do come in and join us for breakfast."

"I can't. I must get home." Mark helped Charlotte to her feet.

"Nonsense. I insist. I must reward your efforts on behalf of poor Clyde. My niece makes the most delicious rolls. Where is Juliet?" She rose on tiptoe to try and see the top of his buggy.

"Who is Juliet?" Mark asked, looking to Helen for an explanation.

"Her raccoon."

Charlotte bent to pet her hound. "Juliet is Clyde's dearest friend. They go everywhere together."

"She'll be along shortly," Helen said to appease her aunt.

"Oh, *goot*." She shook a finger at Clyde. "You were a naughty dog to wander off."

Helen leaned toward Mark and whispered, "You haven't seen her, have you?"

He shook his head and leaned closer. "*Nee*. Why are you whispering?"

She jerked her head toward her aunt, who was busy making a fuss over the squirming dog. "I don't want to upset her. She'll start worrying again that someone has made a hat out of her pet."

"Why would she think— *Nee*, never mind. I've been told she's a bit strange. I just didn't realize how strange."

"She's odd, but she's harmless." Odd but oddly endearing, as Helen was learning. She'd never met anyone like her aunt. It was hard to imagine she was related to Helen's stoic father.

"If you say she is harmless, I must believe you." Mark started toward his buggy.

This wasn't how Helen had visualized their meeting, but she wasn't one to let an opportunity slip by. She would ply him with coffee and rolls, apologize and ask him about a job. "Do come inside. I wanted a chance to speak to you about—"

Mark cut her short as he pointed behind her. "I see smoke. Something's burning." He started toward the house.

"My rolls!" Helen dashed around him and up the steps and into the smoke-filled kitchen.

He followed her inside. "Where's your fire extinguisher?"

"I don't know where my aunt keeps it."

"The best time to locate one is before a fire."

"Thanks for the tip." Helen grabbed her hot pads and jerked open the oven door. More smoke billowed into the room. She started coughing, but she managed to pull the pan of charred rolls out and head for the door. He opened the other kitchen window and then followed her outside, coughing and wheezing, too.

Helen plunked the pan on the porch railing and stared at the charred remains through watery eyes. Charlotte came up beside her. "I believe your last batch was better, dear. These look overdone. She'll bring some better ones when she comes to see you later today, Mark."

"See me about what?" he asked.

"Helen desperately wants you to give her a job. You should. She's conscientious. She's hardworking—"

Helen cut in quickly. "Aenti, he doesn't need to hear this."

"Of course he does. She's a quick learner. She would be an asset to any business, even one run by a rude, judgmental and annoying fellow like you, but I still don't understand why you want to wear her baked goods. That doesn't seem right."

Helen closed her eyes and bowed her head in defeat. She tossed the burned rolls on to the grass. "I was wrong. Today is worse than yesterday." Her voice cracked, but she raised her chin and continued. "I'm so very sorry for your trouble, Mark. Thank you for bringing the dog home. He means a great deal to my *aenti*."

She started into the house. Mark caught her by the arm. "Wait until the smoke clears."

She looked down in surprise at the warmth of his hand on her bare forearm and then looked at his face. She hadn't noticed much about him before except his scowl.

He wasn't a bad-looking fellow. Not as handsome as Joseph, but he had a strong face with a broad forehead, high cheekbones and blond hair that wanted to curl from beneath his hatband. He had a dimple in his left cheek and a small scar in his right eyebrow. His intense green eyes, beneath thick eyelashes, gazed intently at her. They widened slightly, and his pupils darkened as she looked into them. A shiver skittered across her skin.

Mark noticed the smudge of flour on Helen's cheek. The white powder stood in high contrast to the bright blush staining her face. Her gray eyes held specks of blue in their depths, and they glistened with unshed tears of humiliation. She blinked and looked away. Her shoulders slumped. He withdrew his hand and rubbed his tingling palm on the side of his pants. He took a step back. "Find where she keeps the fire extinguisher."

"I will." She sniffed once but didn't look at him.

He took another step back and bumped into the porch railing. "I didn't mean to be rude yesterday."

After a long pause, she nodded slightly. "You had just cause."

He should get going. He didn't understand why he had this urge to linger, except that he didn't want to see her cry. "My brother and my cousin say that I can be overbearing. If I was, I'm sorry."

"I don't know what's the matter with me. Why can't a single thing go right? Everything used to be so easy."

She covered her face with her hands, and her shoulders started shaking.

He stepped closer. "Please don't cry over a few burned rolls."

She made a sound like a strangled sob and fled around the corner of the house, leaving him feeling foolish and brutish at the same time. Every time he tried to help, he seemed to make things worse. She managed to fluster him, and he didn't like the feeling. He turned to her aunt. "Will she be okay?"

"*Ja*, we have plenty of flour."

"Flour?" He didn't follow her.

"To make more rolls for you so that you will give her a job." Charlotte smiled sweetly.

"I don't need a baker. I need an inventory clerk and a general office worker. Has she had any experience?"

Charlotte held her hands up and raised her eyes to the sky. "I shudder to tell you the experiences that child has had. I'm amazed at how well she is handling it."

"Handling what? Never mind. I need to get going. Tell Helen to come by the shop tomorrow, and I will interview her for the job, but I can't promise anything." He didn't want to know more about Helen, and he didn't want to try and stay in a conversation with Charlotte Zook. It was an impossibility.

"All right. Do send Juliet home directly when you see her."

"Juliet? Oh, the raccoon. Sure." He nodded and made his escape.

As he turned his horse and buggy toward home, he glanced over his shoulder, but Helen remained out of sight. He felt a stab of pity for her. Living with Charlotte Zook couldn't be easy. The woman was odd to say the least. He might pity Helen, but he wouldn't hire her unless she was right for the job. So far, he hadn't seen anything that suggested she would be.

It had been a mistake to tell the aunt he'd discuss a job with Helen. He'd spoken in a moment of weakness, and that wasn't like him. Something about Helen left him feeling off-kilter.

Besides which, her assessment of his character continued to go downhill. He'd gone from being rude and judgmental to annoying, as well. He was confident Charlotte had been repeating what Helen had said about him.

He chuckled as he recalled the look of horror on Helen's face when her aunt started listing her qualifications. She knew what was coming. It served her right for her less-than-charitable comments about him. A man looking for a humble, modest and mild-mannered wife wouldn't find those qualities in Helen Zook.

Leaning back in the buggy seat, his smile faded as he imagined interviewing her. He'd already interviewed a half dozen people for the job, and none of them had been right. His brother said he was too picky, but his uncle's business was important, and hiring the wrong person was worse than working shorthanded.

Mark glanced back at Charlotte's house. Unless he was sadly mistaken, Helen wouldn't be right for the position either, but he would do her the courtesy of giving her a chance. If she showed up. From the way she had rushed off in tears, he didn't imagine she would find the courage to face him again anytime soon.

# *Chapter Five*

Helen came out of her room a few minutes after she heard the buggy drive away. She stopped in the bathroom to splash cold water on her face and erase the marks of her tears. The burn of humiliation would linger much longer. How would she ever face Mark again?

She stared at her pale face in the mirror. Perhaps this was part of God's plan to make her a humbler person. If that was the case, it was working.

She had always taken pride in her accomplishments and in her intelligence, although she knew they were gifts from God. She'd been the brightest scholar in school. *Englisch* customers in the fabric shop often commented on how friendly she was. Many of the young men she walked out with before settling on Joseph had said she was the prettiest young woman in her community. Prettier and smarter than her sister.

Helen was the better cook, the better quilter, the better seamstress. Olivia never truly excelled at anything. More than once, Helen had heard her referred to as the simple sister in the Zook family. Olivia wasn't simple. Things just didn't come easily for her.

Helen sighed. There had been pride in her heart because of Joseph, too. He had been the most sought-after and eligible bachelor in their community. She had set her sights on winning him even after she knew her sister was in love with him. When he asked for Helen's hand in marriage she had been overjoyed, but look how that triumph had turned out for her. She became a laughingstock when Joseph broke their engagement to marry the "simple" sister.

No doubt this morning's adventure along with yesterday's disaster would be recounted to the entire Bowman clan and beyond for many more laughs at her expense. She wouldn't be able to look anyone in the eye. Her summer would be spent living off the charity of her aunt and avoiding the community as much as possible. And then what? When the summer was over, where did she go? Home? She couldn't go there. Was she destined to travel to yet another distant place and start over somewhere new?

She turned away from her reflection. Despair wasn't an expression she wore well.

Her aunt was seated at the table with a cup of coffee in front of her when Helen entered the kitchen. The room was clear of smoke, but the smell of burned bread lingered. Clyde lay on the floor beside her aunt's feet. He looked sadder than usual, with his heavy jowls spread over his front feet and his eyes half-closed.

"He hasn't touched his food," Charlotte said, staring down at him.

"Perhaps Mr. Bowman fed him before he brought him here."

"I expect you're right. That Mark is a mighty nice fella. It's a shame he has a girlfriend back home. Clyde and I think he'd make an excellent match for you."

"*Nee*, he would not. I can't abide men with green

eyes." Or one with a dimple in his left cheek, thick dark eyelashes and a sour expression whenever he looked at her. Helen crossed to the oven and turned it off.

"Have you decided not to make more rolls?"

"There isn't much sense in wasting more of my time and your supplies." Helen began cleaning up.

"I guess that's true. You don't need to tempt Mark with sweets since he has given you the job."

Helen spun around. "What did you say?"

"You don't have to tempt him with sweets, although I'm sure he would enjoy them."

"He told you he is willing to hire me?"

"*Ja*, something like that."

Helen sat down opposite her aunt and took her by the hand. "Tell me exactly what he said, Aenti. This is important."

"Exactly?"

"Word for word."

Charlotte closed her eyes. "Let me think. I believe he said he didn't need a baker, but he did need an inventory clerk and a general office worker. I'm sure that's what he told me. Clyde certainly has taken a liking to him. I have, too."

"But what did he say about *me*?"

"He said to tell you to come by the shop later today and start work. He couldn't promise that you would like the job, but he did promise to tell Juliet to come home as soon as he saw her."

Helen was almost afraid to hope. Could it be true? "He is giving me a job? Aenti, are you sure that's what he said?"

Charlotte smiled and gave Helen's hand a quick squeeze. "People often accuse me of not listening, but

I hear well enough. Sometimes I even hear what isn't said. You want a job. Mark needs help."

She patted Helen's hand, took a drink of coffee, rose and carried the mug to the sink. "You must hurry if you are going to get another batch of crescent rolls done and get to work on time. You should take my bicycle. It will be faster than walking."

"He actually said I had the job?" Helen's spirits rose like a kite in a strong wind.

"Honestly, Helen, I'm beginning to think you are the one who doesn't listen. I'm sure your sister and your fiancé told you many times that they were falling in love with each other even though they struggled against it."

Helen's bright mood plummeted. "*Nee*, they never mentioned it. They went behind my back and met in secret."

"I thought Olivia was working for Joseph's mother? They would have had a reason to see each other every day. I'm sure I read that in one of your mother's letters. I keep all my correspondence in boxes. I can look for it."

"Joseph's mother had to have surgery, and Olivia went to help with the housework and nurse her for a few weeks. I couldn't do it. I had to help Mamm get ready for the wedding."

"Olivia has always had a sweet and caring nature. I'm sure she was glad to help."

"She helped herself to my fiancé," Helen said bitterly. "I don't want to talk about it."

"Pain is part of life, but it's hard to heal in silence. Talking helps. I shall pray for your sister. I'm sure she has been hurt by your actions."

"My actions? What did I do?"

"You turned your back on her and cut her out of your life just when she most needed your forgiveness. Well, it can't be changed. Water under the bridge as they say. I've always wondered who *they* are, but I guess I'm one of *them*, for I just said it. The Lord has a plan for us all, Helen. Including you. Now I must go look for Juliet. What time will you be home from work?"

"I'm not sure." Grateful that her aunt had changed the subject, Helen turned the oven back on. After her aunt had gone out, Helen started on a new batch of rolls. She was determined not to think about Olivia and Joseph, but it was impossible in the quiet house with only the ticking of the timer to fill the silence.

Joseph had tried to tell her about his growing feelings for Olivia. Helen had refused to listen. She knew she could make him forget her sister in time. None of that excused his betrayal. It might be water under the bridge because their marriage couldn't be undone, but she wasn't ready to forgive him or her sister.

Strangely, her anger toward them didn't burn as brightly as it once had. It was giving way to sorrow. She missed her sister and her parents.

An hour later, with a basket of still-warm rolls in an insulated bag over her arm, Helen rode her aunt's bike the two miles to Bowmans Crossing and entered the front door of the workshop a few minutes before nine. The large room was already bustling with activity as a half-dozen men operated various machines. The smell of wood shavings, diesel fumes and the loud hum of engines filled the air.

Off to her right, she noticed an interior window into what appeared to be an office. A young dark-haired woman dressed in jeans and a bright yellow and red print blouse sat at a desk. Helen stepped inside, and the noise dropped away when she closed the door behind her. The woman looked up from a computer and smiled. "Welcome to Bowman's Amish Furniture. I'm Jessica Clay. How may I help you?"

"I'm Helen Zook. Mark Bowman is expecting me."

Her eyebrows shot up. "He is? He didn't mention he had a client appointment."

"I'm not a customer. I'm here to start a new job. Inventory clerk and general office worker. I'm guessing that means I'll be working in here with you."

Jessica's smile widened. "Awesome. I could sure use the help. Mark's gone to arrange for a special order of hardware from John Miller, the local blacksmith. He should be back in an hour or so."

Helen sat on the edge of a small upholstered bench and tried to still her racing heart as she clutched her basket. Jessica seemed pleasant enough. The office was small but neat, with a wide exterior window that let in the sunshine as well as the interior one that overlooked the work area. She was surprised to see a number of modern devices. "The local bishop must be very progressive to allow phones, a fax machine and a computer in an Amish business."

"We get questions about it all the time from our customers who are familiar with Amish ways. Isaac Bowman has a silent partner named James Carter. He's a furniture dealer in Cincinnati, and he isn't Amish. James had the computer and phone installed and even had a website built for the business. We now have satellite phone and internet. It was actually Mark who suggested it as a way to make the business more productive."

"But I didn't see any electric lines to the building."

"The business is powered by a diesel generator, in keeping with the rules of Isaac's church. Because of that, we are able to have a limited amount of technology, which I run since I'm not Amish, either. The Bowmans do have permission to have a phone in here so they don't have to use the phone shack up the road that the other Amish families use. We also have a few solar panels for charging cell phones and pagers for the volunteer firemen who work here."

"I have heard of Amish churches who are this progressive but I've never met anyone from such a church." She wondered what other rules were different from the ones her congregation had.

Jessica returned to her computer but soon said, "Something smells delish."

Helen smiled and placed the basket on the corner of the desk. "I've brought some treats as a thank-you for Mark, but help yourself. I made plenty."

Jessica moved her chair closer. "Are you sure?"

"Absolutely." Folding back the red-and-white napkin, Helen unfastened the insulated bag and offered the basket to her.

The door opened, and a tall blond Amish man leaned in. "Jessica, has Mr. Barker decided if he wants six or eight chairs with his dining set, because I'll have to special order more walnut if he wants eight."

"Let me check our email again, but I don't think so. Samuel, this is Helen Zook. Mark hired her."

"He did? He never mentioned it to me." He stepped inside and closed the door.

"It was only this morning," Helen said.

His surprise was apparent. "This morning? Mark hired you this morning? Wait. Zook? Are you the one with the dog?"

Helen wished everyone didn't look so shocked by the news that Mark had hired her. Why hadn't he told anyone? "My aunt owns the dog. I'm sorry if he disrupted your sleep."

"He sure enough did that. I'm Samuel Bowman. My father Isaac owns this business. Didn't I see you at the frolic?"

"I was there for a little while." Helen clenched her lips together. The less said about that day the better.

"These rolls are amazing." Jessica licked her fingers. "Try one, Samuel."

"Please do," Helen said quickly offering him the basket.

*"Danki."* Samuel took one. "The email, Jessica?"

"Right." She spun back to the computer and started typing. "He did reply. Says here he only wants six. Problem solved."

"These are *wunderbarr*," Samuel said taking another bite. "I don't suppose you brought enough to share with everyone. I feel a little guilty enjoying this while the men working out there get nothing."

"I made three dozen. There's plenty to go around. Is there *kaffee*?"

"In the break room," Jessica said. "I'll go make some. Cream or sugar?"

"Just black." Helen quickly folded a half-dozen rolls in the napkin and then handed the basket to Jessica. "Take these with you so the men can enjoy them on their break."

Jessica went out the door. No sooner had it closed behind her than the phone started ringing. Samuel smiled and nodded toward it. "Might as well get started."

"Me? Oh, *ja*, I reckon so." Helen went to the desk and picked up the phone. "Bowman's Amish Furniture, this is Helen Zook. How may I help you?"

She quickly wrote down the customer's order and his contact information as Samuel stood at the counter listening to her end of the conversation. When she hung up, she handed him her notes. "Mr. Fielding in Akron wishes to order three bedroom suites for his furniture showroom. He has sold the ones he purchased before. He says you'll know which styles he wants. Is there anything else I should have asked him?"

"*Nee*, this looks great. He didn't by chance say he needed a custom fireplace mantel, did he?"

"He didn't. Should I have asked that?"

Samuel gave her a wry smile and shook his head. "We had a customer cancel his order for one after Mark finished carving it. Since Mark isn't here, why don't I give you a quick tour. We have our main workroom out there where you came in. The break room is the next door down."

Helen followed him as he crossed the office to a door opposite the one she had entered. "Through here is our showroom. We keep a few dozen pieces on display and for sale, but most of our work is shipped to furniture stores in different parts of the country."

In a large room, well lit by numerous skylights overhead, Helen saw dining tables and chairs, bedroom sets, armoires, benches, side tables and even butcher-block islands. She admired the workmanship in the solid wood pieces. One in particular caught her eye. A beam almost six feet long sat on a pair of sawhorses. A forest scene with cavorting foxes in carved relief covered the entire length. "Is that the mantel you were talking about?"

"It is. It's still raw wood. Mark hasn't chosen a finish for it yet. Foxes aren't as popular as wolves or deer, but I'm hopeful we can sell it." He glanced at the memo she had taken. "I'll check if we have any of these in stock. I think we do."

"Should I wait for Mark to give me my instructions?"

"I'm sure Jessica can keep you busy until Mark returns. Have her tell the fellas to take an early break and enjoy those rolls. And tell her to save one more for me." He walked to the far end of the room.

Helen returned to the office to find Isaac Bowman conferring with Jessica over a ledger. Outside, a pickup pulling a horse trailer turned into the parking lot and stopped. A middle-aged couple in riding clothes got out and came inside. Isaac left Jessica's side to welcome them. "How may we help you?"

The man held out his hand. "I'm Vern Jenks, and this is my wife, Theresa. We've just come from the Stroud Stables where we mentioned we were looking for some authentic Amish-made furniture, and Connie Stroud suggested we stop in here."

Isaac nodded. "Noah, my youngest *sohn*, works for Connie. She is a *goot* neighbor."

"And a fine horse trainer," Theresa added. "We've just picked up a new hunter for our daughter."

"What type of furniture are you looking for?" Isaac asked.

"Rustic," Theresa said. "Reclaimed barn wood, unusual pieces. I'm redoing our hunt club meeting room in American primitive."

Isaac pulled on his long gray beard. "I don't believe we have what you are looking for, but we do custom work. If you can give us an idea of what you want, we can make it for you."

Theresa's expression fell. "I'm not sure I want to wait for custom pieces to be built. If I change my mind, I'll let you know."

Helen could tell the couple wouldn't be back, but she couldn't let them walk away without at least trying to make a sale. "Is there a fireplace in the room you are redecorating?"

Theresa nodded. "There is."

"Then there is something you might like in our showroom. It's a hand-carved primitive fireplace mantel that would go beautifully in a hunt club setting. The wood is unfinished and could be stained or painted, if you like, or left raw under a clear-coat finish."

Isaac grinned. "I'd forgotten about Mark's piece. Right this way, folks. *Danki*, Helen."

Jessica clapped softly when the door closed behind them. "Nice going, newbie. Let's hope they buy it. Now I have some filing for you to do."

Helen smiled and breathed a sigh of relief. She was going to enjoy working with these people.

Mark entered the front door of the workshop and stopped in his tracks. Where was everyone? The machines were all sitting idle. He glanced into the office. It was empty except for an Amish woman in a blue dress and black apron standing behind the desk at the file cabinet. She had her back to him, but he knew it had to be the wife of one of his cousins. They sometimes came to help out.

He opened the office door and stepped in. "Where is everyone?"

She squeaked and spun around. It was Helen.

So she did have enough pluck to face him again. He was surprised and a little pleased, but he couldn't let that show. He scowled at her. "What are you doing?"

"Filing."

"Filing what?"

"Paid invoices. Jessica asked me to do it."

"Where is Jessica? Where is everyone?"

"In the break room."

He glanced at the clock on the wall. "It's not break time."

"I'm afraid I'm to blame. I brought some rolls, and everyone seems to like them. Isaac and Samuel thought the men might enjoy them while they were still warm. I saved some for you."

She picked up a red-and-white checkered napkin bundle and held it toward him. "I'm so very grateful for this job. You won't regret hiring me. I won't disappoint you."

He tilted his head to the side. "When did I hire you?"

"What do you mean?"

"It's a pretty simple question. When did I hire you? *Nee*, let me rephrase that. I haven't hired you. I haven't even interviewed you."

She pulled her arms to her chest and clutched the bundle tightly in both hands. "But Aenti Charlotte said you wanted me to start work today."

"Well, Aenti Charlotte got it wrong. I'll hazard a guess that's not the first time that has happened."

The office door opened. Mark turned to see Jessica and Samuel enter. They were both grinning. Samuel clapped a hand on Mark's shoulder. "Mark, you picked a winner. The men love your crescent rolls, Helen."

Jessica took her seat. "Not only does Helen have typing skills and a pleasant phone voice, and she knows how to file, but she also knows how to use the fax machine. I'm impressed with your choice, Mark."

"I learned to use a fax machine at my last job, but that was before I was baptized. I'm not sure how your bishop would feel about me using it now unless it was an emergency."

Helen pushed a slip of paper across the desk. "Jessica, here are your phone messages. The receipts are filed and

Samuel, Mr. Barker says Mrs. Barker has changed her mind and wants eight chairs. I took the liberty of calling several local lumberyards. The one in Berlin says they have the type of walnut you're looking for.

"*Goot*. Order it. I'll have Luke pick it up tomorrow."

"I will," she said as Samuel went out and closed the door behind him.

"*Nee*, you will not," Mark said. "You are not an employee here."

"She acts like an employee to me," Jessica said. "Besides, I'm tired of doing the work of two people because you can't make up your mind and hire someone."

"Hiring the right worker takes thoughtful consideration. I won't be rushed into a decision."

"Well, you'd better hurry, or you'll be giving thoughtful consideration to hiring two people instead of one. I can get a job anywhere. I happen to like working here because it is close to home and Isaac is so very sweet, but I'm not married to this job."

Helen stepped up beside Jessica. "Please, don't quarrel because of me. My aunt misunderstood. She's a little eccentric, and she got it wrong."

Helen lowered her eyes and clasped her hands together in front of her, wringing the napkin into a tight ball. "If you would grant me an interview, I would be deeply grateful."

He gave a dismissive wave of his hand. "I don't see you working out. I'm sorry."

Jessica folded her arms across her chest and gave him a sour glare. "You should reconsider."

"I'm not going to change my mind. She isn't right for the job."

The outside door opened again, and Isaac leaned in. "Helen, we're happy to have you with us. I would have let a sale walk right out the door today if not for your quick thinking. She sold your mantel, Mark. You made a *goot* choice when you hired her. I was beginning to worry about your ability to know the right kind of worker when you met one. I'm pleased my faith in you wasn't misplaced."

Mark swallowed the denial that rose to his lips. How could he argue with his uncle? This was his business after all. "*Danki*, Onkel."

Isaac closed the door, and Jessica burst out laughing. "I can't wait to hear you tell him why you fired her."

Mark pressed his lips together. "I can't fire someone I haven't hired."

Helen took a step closer. "I will go explain to Isaac what has happened."

He shook his head. "Never mind. Come with me. I'll show you where we store our inventory and go over our ordering practices."

She squealed and grinned, her pretty gray eyes sparkling with happiness. "*Danki*. I'll do my best for the company. I'll work hard every day. You won't be sorry."

He already was. "This is a trial period only. One month. Your work will have to speak for itself."

"I won't let you down. Here, these are for you." She forced a smile and handed him the napkin. He unwound it. Inside was a pile of chocolate-covered pieces of bread.

She pressed a hand to her lips. "Oh, I guess they got a little squished, but they should still taste fine."

"I'm not hungry. I'm worried."

"About what?"

He handed the napkin back to her. "About the next disaster you'll bring down on our heads."

# Chapter Six

Helen quietly followed Mark as he detailed the jobs he expected her to do. She'd had the forethought to bring a small notebook and pencil, so she was able to take notes as he went along.

He pushed open the swinging door of a room off the main woodworking shop. "This is where we keep most of our non-lumber supplies."

Helen saw three sides of the room were lined floor to ceiling with bins in different sizes, all neatly labeled. The other side of the room held a large pegboard where various types of tools hung, also neatly labeled.

"You will need to keep an accurate inventory of parts, tools and hardware. Notify me when any items are running low. Each bin has the name of the item on the front and the minimal count number. For instance, this is our most popular cabinet pull." He opened one of the drawers. "The lowest the count should ever be is sixteen."

"Will I order more or simply notify you?"

"Notify me to start with. After you've been here awhile, I may let you take over ordering. If you make it past your probation."

"What type of inventory counting system do you use? A computer program or ledger?"

He eyed her closely. "Ledger."

"How often will I do cycle counts?" She scribbled a note to herself.

"Weekly on Mondays. You've done this before, haven't you?"

"I worked in a small fabric shop for several years. Our inventory was fabric, buttons and threads, not hardware and wood. We did monthly cycle counts." Helen saw the beginnings of respect in his eyes. She could handle this job, and she would prove it.

He slipped his thumbs under his suspenders. "A lot of inventory issues stem from improper employee training."

She nodded. "I agree. Inventory inaccuracy, damage and misidentification can usually be traced to mistakes made by people."

He frowned slightly. "As I was saying, proper training increases a business's efficiency and cuts down on inventory issues."

She resisted the urge to laugh at his pompous demeanor. Instead, she clasped the notebook in front of her and tried to appear the eager pupil. "I look forward to learning all I can from you. May I see the ledger so I can familiarize myself with your inventory?"

"It's on my desk."

She looked around. "Will I be working in here or will I be in the office?"

"Where would you like to work?"

"Out front with Jessica to begin with. I know I'll have a lot of questions, and it will save running back and forth if I'm out there where I can ask someone without interrupting you needlessly."

"I'll have a desk put up front for you."

"Who are your main suppliers? We should send them a card or letter letting them know I'll be placing orders when my training is over."

"Your concern should be making it past the thirty-day mark." He turned on his heels and left the room.

Helen took a deep breath and sent up a quick prayer that she could do just that.

She made it through the rest of the day without subjecting Mark to a new disaster, in spite of his concerns. When he left to meet with one of their local wood suppliers, Helen was handed over to Samuel and Jessica. Her head was spinning with all the information poured over her in a single day, but she took copious notes and remained convinced that she could do the job.

When she arrived home just after five o'clock, she found her aunt pacing in the kitchen, distraught with worry. Her shoes were muddy. Her dress was torn at the hem, and her *kapp* was missing. Juliet hadn't come home.

"I don't know where she can be. I've called and I've called. I have searched everywhere." Charlotte paced the floor of the kitchen, returning again and again to look out the door.

Helen hadn't spared a thought the entire day for her aunt or her aunt's missing pet, and her conscience smote her. She slipped her arm over her aunt's shoulders. "I'm so sorry. I'll help you look for her."

"Will you? Bless you, dear."

"Sit down for a few minutes and catch your breath. Let's think about where she might have gone. Have you had anything to eat today?"

"Not since breakfast. I'm just so worried."

Helen steered her aunt to the table. "Sit and I'll make you a cup of coffee. When you've had a bit of a rest, we can put our heads together and figure out what to do next."

As the coffee perked, Helen fixed a couple of chicken salad sandwiches from leftovers in her aunt's propane-powered refrigerator. She set a plate in front of Charlotte. Taking a seat, Helen folded her hands and said a silent prayer of grace. When she was finished, she took a bite of her sandwich.

Charlotte glanced over her shoulder toward the door, where Clyde lay on his rug with his head on his paws and his eyes fixed on Juliet's empty bed. His food remained untouched in his bowl. "He's so sad. I worry about him."

"Aenti, has Juliet ever disappeared like this before?"

"Only once. She was gone for an entire day but not overnight. That was weeks ago. She's been content to be with us ever since."

"That should make you feel better to know she came back once before."

"I reckon it should, but it doesn't." Charlotte's tone was so dejected that Helen's heart went out to her.

Helen got up to pour them both a cup of freshly brewed coffee. "Do you know where she was when she stayed away before?"

"I saw her follow another raccoon into the forest."

"Another raccoon? So perhaps she has a friend she has gone to visit. That seems the most likely possibility."

Charlotte pushed her half-eaten sandwich aside. "You don't think some terrible person made her into a hat, do you?"

"I do not. She wears a pretty pink collar. That would tell anyone she's a pet." But it wouldn't prevent Juliet from returning to the wild if the instinct was strong enough.

"She could be caught in a trap."

Helen shook her head vigorously. "It's not trapping season. That takes place in the winter. Please try not to worry. Finish your sandwich, and we'll go look for her together."

"You must think I'm a *narrish* old woman to go on so about a raccoon."

"I don't think you're crazy."

"I raised her from a baby. Clyde found her in the forest and brought her home to me. He seemed to know she needed help. They've been devoted to each other ever since and to me. Clyde and Juliet don't care that I'm absentminded. They don't mind that I talk to myself or that I'm different. They don't make fun of me behind my back as some of the children do. They just love me. They are kinder than many people."

Helen reached across the table to lay her hand on Charlotte's forearm. "Your family loves you, Aenti Charlotte."

"I know, but they are far away, and letters can't give me a hug when I'm lonely. Listen to me prattle. I'm sorry, Helen, I haven't even asked about your new job today. How was it? Did you enjoy it?"

Helen shook a finger in mock annoyance. "I have a bone to pick with you about that."

Charlotte folded her hands as her gaze shifted from Helen to the ceiling. "With me? Whatever for?"

"Mark Bowman didn't tell you he wanted to hire me."

Charlotte sighed and reached for the sugar bowl. "He didn't?"

"He did not."

After spooning two lumps of sugar into her cup, Charlotte stirred it slowly. "Did I get that mixed up?

Well, it doesn't matter. You were hired, weren't you? I knew you'd do an excellent job, and I'm sure Mark quickly saw what an asset you are."

"I'm not sure he would call me an asset yet, but I did get the job." Although not because Mark wanted her to have it.

"And you like it?"

"It's okay. I have a lot to learn. It's not permanent yet. I was hired on a thirty-day trial basis."

Charlotte raised her cup to her lips and peeked at Helen from beneath her lashes. "And you like Mark?"

Helen drew back. "I most certainly do not like him."

"Oh. I thought you might have changed your mind. He does have nice eyes."

"But he has terrible manners." Helen opened her mouth to list his flaws but quickly changed her mind. It wouldn't do to have her aunt repeating her comments, even if they were true. Helen suspected Mark would welcome an excuse to fire her.

"Did he enjoy the crescent rolls you baked for him?"

Helen chuckled. "He never got to try them, but at least he didn't end up wearing them."

"Will you bake something again tomorrow for him?"

Helen turned the idea over in her mind. She enjoyed baking more than just about anything. "I think so. The people at the business gobbled up what I took in today. I think I'll make cinnamon rolls."

"That sounds *wunderbarr*. With raisins and icing?"

"Is that the way you like them?"

"*Ja*. Lots of icing."

"Then that's what I'll make, and I'll leave plenty here for you."

"*Danki*. Can we go look for Juliet now?"

"Of course. Did you take Clyde with you when you searched earlier?"

"I did."

If Clyde with his keen nose couldn't locate Juliet, Helen doubted they would be able to find her, but she didn't voice her thoughts.

It was fully dark when they returned to the house, having searched up and down the river and woods in both directions without success. Clyde had cast about continually for a scent, but Helen had no idea if he was searching for his friend or a rabbit to chase.

Helen closed the door and lit the lamp over the kitchen table. "If she doesn't come by morning, we'll ask the neighbors to help us look for her."

"Whatever am I to do if I don't find her?" Charlotte wailed. She covered her face with her hands and sobbed.

Helen gathered her weeping aunt into her arms. "Don't give up. It's only been a day. I'm sure she'll come home tonight. If she doesn't, tomorrow we'll spread the word that she is missing. I'll tell the Bowmans and the people at the workshop. Someone may have seen her and not realized we are looking for her. The more eyes we have helping us the better."

"You are so practical, Helen. You know just what to do."

After helping her exhausted aunt to bed a half hour later, Helen turned on the battery-powered night-light that sat on Charlotte's dresser. Clyde was curled in his dog bed in the corner, snoring loudly. Helen started out the door but stopped when her aunt spoke.

"I wasn't happy when you first arrived and told me you were staying for the summer," Charlotte said in a small voice. "I like living alone, but now I'm very glad you are with me."

"I'm glad that I'm here, too," Helen said quietly and closed the door.

In her room, Helen unpinned her *kapp* and hung it from a peg on the wall. She let her hair down and rubbed the top of her scalp where it sometimes got tender by the end of the day. After donning her nightgown, she sat on the edge of the bed and started brushing her hip-length hair.

So much had happened, it was hard to believe it had only been one day since the frolic. Like a child on a teeter-totter, she had gone from the low of her early-morning baking calamity to the high of getting a job and proving her worth to her new employer.

She chuckled as she remembered the look on Mark's face when Isaac praised her and complimented Mark for hiring her. Clearly, his uncle's approval meant more to him than getting rid of her, otherwise she would have been out the door in short order. Would she be able to earn Mark's respect and keep her job? It surprised her how much she wanted to do so. He'd seen her at her worst. She wanted him to see her at her best. It'd be good to have him look at her without disgust or anger in his eyes. His "pretty green eyes," as her aunt was fond of saying. He did have nice eyes, and he might have a sweet smile if he used it once in a while.

The high point of her day had given way to a new low again upon seeing her aunt's anguish over her missing pet this evening. Helen was deeply touched by Charlotte's admission that she was glad to have her here at such a time. She'd never thought much about her father's odd sister except to wonder why she hadn't married. To Helen that had seemed like a fate worse than death and yet, by her own admission, Charlotte was happy living alone. Perhaps that was true, but people needed people to care about them.

Helen finished brushing her hair. As she braided it, her thoughts turned back to Mark. What would he have to say to her tomorrow? Hopefully, he'd find some time to enjoy one of her cinnamon rolls and their day would get off to a better start. It was hard to imagine getting off to a worse one. Still, her morning's difficulties had ended in a job, so it wasn't a total loss.

She had never had to work so hard for something in her life.

Now, if only Juliet would see fit to come home tonight and take one worry off her shoulders.

Helen tied a ribbon to the end of her braid and knelt to say her prayers. It suddenly occurred to her she hadn't thought about Joseph once since early that morning.

Mark sat bolt upright in bed as the hound's baying reverberated through his open window. "Not again!"

A glance at the clock on his wall showed it was four thirty. He jumped out of bed and headed to the window. He could just make out Clyde's white face pointing to the sky at the base of the tree through the foliage below. "Go home, you foolish dog!"

Clyde rose on his back feet, planted his front feet on the tree trunk and howled louder. The whole house would be awake in no time. Mark thrust his feet in his slippers, pulled a robe over his pajamas and rushed toward the stairs. His uncle looked out from his bedroom door as Mark went past. "I'll take care of him, Onkel."

"Why doesn't she keep him at home?"

"I don't know, but I'm going to make certain Helen understands this isn't acceptable."

"It's Charlotte's dog, not Helen's." Isaac closed the

bedroom door, and Mark went downstairs. It might not be Helen's dog, but she was going to have to control him if Charlotte wouldn't.

Mark opened the back door. In the moonlight, he saw Clyde was still standing with his front paws on the tree trunk, gazing upward. Another mournful howl rent the air. Mark grabbed him by his collar and pulled him away from the tree.

"Enough. Go home. Get." He pointed toward the bridge.

Clyde wagged his tail happily and woofed, but he didn't get.

"Come on. It's this way," Mark clapped his hands and walked a few feet toward the road. *"Goot hund."*

The dog darted back to the tree, stood on his hind legs and howled a long, lonesome cry.

Mark jumped to grab his collar again. "Bad dog. You are going home, and this time I'm not waiting until a decent hour to return you. We'll find out if Helen and Charlotte like being rousted out of bed in the middle of the night."

He turned around to see Paul standing in the open doorway without his usual grin. He rubbed his face with both hands and headed toward the barn. "I'll go hitch up the buggy and take him back this time."

"Hitch the buggy, but I'll take him." Mark couldn't wait to see Helen and tell her exactly what he thought of her crazy mutt.

The dog climbed in the buggy willingly and scrambled onto the front seat when Paul opened the door for him. "He looks eager to go home."

"I wish he would stay home." Having dressed for the day, because he knew he wouldn't be getting any more sleep, Mark climbed in and picked up the reins. Clyde tried to crawl into Mark's lap. He pushed the dog away, muttering under his breath.

"What was that?" Paul asked, a grin pulling at one side of his mouth.

"If you still want to drive him home, you can because I have better things to do."

Paul held up both hands. "*Nee*, he chose to serenade your window. I think he likes you."

Clyde licked Mark's ear and woofed. Paul burst out laughing. "See. He does like you. Shall I open the shop for you?"

Mark wiped the side of his head with his shirt sleeve. "I'll be back to do that. Just make sure the generator is fueled."

"I will, *bruder*. Enjoy your buggy ride."

Mark clicked his tongue to get the horse moving. As they pulled away from the house, Clyde hung his head out the window and howled a long, lonely note. Once they passed through the covered bridge, the dog lay down on the seat with his head on his paws.

When Mark turned in Helen's lane, he saw light pouring out the kitchen windows. Someone was already up. So much for his intention to rouse Helen from a sound sleep to see how she liked it. He pulled his horse to a stop at the hitching rail and got out. The dog tumbled out after him and waddled to the front porch. Mark followed.

Through the window, he saw Helen, wearing a dark blue dress and a black apron, standing at the kitchen table with her back to him. Her hair hung down in a long blond braid the color of ripe wheat in the sun. Instead of a prayer *kapp*, she wore a white kerchief tied at the nape of her neck. She was humming as she mixed something in a large bowl. The movement sent her braid swinging back and forth. He wondered what it would look like unbound. In his mind he could see it spread out like a cape of golden ripples shimmering in the light.

He shook off the fanciful thought and knocked on the door. She spun around, her eyes wide. She had another smudge of flour on her face, this time above her left eyebrow. He opened the door and stepped inside. Clyde squeezed past him and rushed to her, dancing about her legs with his tongue lolling and his tail wagging so fast it was almost a blur.

Her astonished gaze went from Mark's face to the dog and back again. He folded his arms over his chest and glared at her.

## Chapter Seven

The wonderful smell of baking bread filled the kitchen, making it hard for Mark to maintain his ire. He'd barely eaten any supper last night, and he hadn't had breakfast.

Helen's look of astonishment changed to one of defeat. "Not again."

"My words exactly when he woke me from a sound sleep. Again."

The dog ambled to his dish and began eating.

Helen met Mark's gaze, her eyes filled with remorse. "I am so sorry. I thought he was still in my aunt's bedroom. I wonder how he got out."

"I don't know, but could you make sure it doesn't happen again?"

"I'll certainly try." She glanced toward the doorway into the living room and lowered her voice. "At least you brought him home before Aenti Charlotte woke up. I thank you for that. She was so upset last night over Juliet's disappearance that I was worried about her."

He heard the genuine concern in her voice, and his conscience stabbed him. His intention hadn't been to do something kind. Just the opposite. "Her raccoon hasn't returned?"

Helen shook her head. "*Nee*, she hasn't yet. Aenti Charlotte is beside herself."

"Is that unusual?" he asked, letting his sarcasm slip out.

She pinned him with a pointed look. "My aunt may be a trifle odd, but she loves her pets. They are like her family."

Looking down, he shifted his weight from one foot to the other. He deserved the rebuke in her tone. Few Amish looked upon dogs as anything but working animals to guard the farms or herd livestock, but he had no right to judge Charlotte Zook harshly because she felt differently. "The raccoon might not come back. She's a wild animal for all your aunt treats her like a child."

"That was my thought, too." A ringing sound came from behind Helen. She spun around, sending her braid flying out like a rope as it swung over her shoulder. She picked up a kitchen timer and turned it off, then donned a pair of oven mitts and pulled a tray of cinnamon buns from the oven. They smelled and looked wonderful. His stomach growled loudly.

She shot a quick smile his way. "You're welcome to one of these as soon as I frost them. Would you like some coffee? It should be ready." She set the pan on a wire rack to cool and flipped her braid back over her shoulder with a careless gesture that was strangely endearing. He resisted a shocking urge to catch it in his hand and see if it was as soft as it looked.

She seemed different this morning. Not scatterbrained or desperate to please. She moved about the kitchen with confidence and a simple grace he found appealing. Maybe he had misjudged her. He'd heard only praise about her from his uncle and cousins yesterday at supper.

He needed to get going, but something held him in place. "I wouldn't mind a cup."

She looked surprised but nodded toward the cupboard. "Help yourself while I finish these."

After locating a pair of cups, he poured them both some coffee from the pot on the back of the stove. "Are you making those to take to work?"

"I am." She looked at him, her eyes full of quick concern. "Do you mind?"

"I see no harm in it. If it makes our workers happy, all the better. My uncle says a happy man does the best work."

She smiled. "I think he is right."

He took a seat at the table. It pleased him that he had made her smile. "You know you already have the job. You don't have to impress anyone by supplying us with food."

She drizzled icing over the cooling buns and put one onto a plate. She put it in front of him. "I may not need to impress you, but I do need to apologize for yesterday morning. I'm sure you know my aunt was repeating something she heard from me."

"Do you mean the part when she said I was rude, judgmental and annoying?" He took a bite of the roll.

Helen's cheeks blossomed with bright red spots of color. "*Ja*, that part."

"This is *wunderbarr*," he said with his mouth full. The bread was warm and stuffed with plump, sweet raisins—just the way he liked it.

"*Danki.*" She waited with her hands clasped together. "I hope you can forgive my impertinence. It was mean-spirited of me."

"I might forgive you if you give me a half dozen of these." He took another bite.

Her mouth dropped open. She snapped it shut and huffed, actually huffed, at him. Then a reluctant grim curved her lips. "Rude, judgmental, annoying and greedy. I'll fix you a box to take them home in." She turned away and missed his smile. He liked the way her eyes crinkled at the corners when she was amused.

"*Guder mariye*, Mark Bowman," Charlotte said from the doorway. "What has the two of you grinning like a pair of cats licking the cream?"

The easy comradery Helen was enjoying with Mark vanished under her aunt's questioning gaze.

Charlotte clasped her hands together. "Mark, have you found Juliet?"

He shook his head. "*Nee*, I've not seen her."

"He brought Clyde home again," Helen said. "Did you let him out of your room last night?"

"Did I? I don't think so."

"How could he get out of the house unless you let him out? Perhaps you forgot that you opened the front door for some reason," Mark suggested.

Charlotte pressed her lips together and shook her head. "I didn't open the front door, and I didn't open the back door. I did open my bedroom window. He must have gone out that way."

Helen looked at Mark. "The window is much too high for him to jump out."

"He got out somehow." Mark took another bite of his delicious roll. They were about the best he'd ever had.

Charlotte smiled at Mark. "I'm mighty glad Clyde fetched you here in time to join us for breakfast. He's a very sociable fellow. When he likes a person, he can't keep it a secret." She moved to the cupboard and took down a cup and plate for herself.

Clyde left his empty bowl and sat beside Mark with

his eyes fixed on the remaining half of the cinnamon roll on Mark's plate. He woofed once then planted his front feet on Mark's leg and tried to grab it. Mark yanked the prize away before Clyde's teeth made contact.

"See how much he likes you," Charlotte said in delight.

Mark scowled as the dog sank back to the floor with his eyes still fixed on the plate in Mark's hand. "I see how much he likes my food. He has mighty poor manners."

Clyde seemed to sense he wasn't going to get anything from Mark. He padded around the table to Charlotte's chair. She bent to take the dog's face between her hands and rub his wrinkled face. "You are a fine *hund*. Even Mark says so."

Helen caught Mark's look of disbelief and shrugged. "Aenti, would you like a cinnamon bun, too?"

Charlotte clapped her hands like a delighted child. "*Danki*, I dreamed about them all night long. It's so kind of you to make them for me. I could bake them myself, but I think food always tastes better when someone else makes it with love. Don't you agree, Mark?"

"If the same recipe and the same ingredients are used, I don't see how the taste could vary." He rose and pushed in his chair. "I have to get to work. Please make sure that Clyde stays at home tonight."

Charlotte glanced at the clock on the wall. "It is getting late. Helen, you must hurry and get ready. You don't want to keep Mark waiting."

"Waiting for what?" he asked, a perplexed look on his face.

"Why, to give Helen a ride to work, of course. That's why you stopped by, isn't it? So very thoughtful of you."

"You don't need to wait for me," Helen said quickly.

Charlotte rose from the table. "Of course he does. How can he take you to work if he doesn't wait? Hurry along, dear. I'll box up your rolls. It was very sweet of you to go out of your way for my niece, Mark. I'll be sure and mention to Isaac and Anna what kindness you've shown her." She opened a cupboard and pulled out some plastic containers.

Mark sighed heavily. "I'm happy to do it. If Helen will hurry up."

She pulled off her apron and dashed toward her room at the back of the house. In record time, she had her hair in a bun that wasn't quite straight but would have to do. Pinning her *kapp* in place, she pulled on a clean white apron and hurried back to the kitchen. Mark wasn't there.

A sharp stab of disappointment surprised her. It couldn't be that she was eager to spend more time with him. That was ridiculous. She didn't even like him.

Okay, she liked him a little. "I guess he got tired of waiting and left without me."

"*Nee*, I had him carry the rolls out. He's waiting for you in the buggy. Have a nice day, dear, and do ask everyone to keep a lookout for Juliet. I can't imagine why she hasn't come home."

Tears shimmered in her aunt's eyes. Helen gave her a hug and kissed her cheek. "We'll find her. Don't give up hope."

"I won't, for I know the Lord cares for all His creatures. Run along. I don't think Mark likes to be kept waiting. If I didn't know better, I'd think he was annoyed with us."

Helen hurried out the door, knowing her aunt was right for a change.

\* \* \*

Mark drummed the fingers of his left hand on the armrest of his door. His buggy horse tossed her head, sensing his eagerness to be off, but he held her in check. Finally, Helen climbed in on the passenger's side. He slapped the reins, and the mare lunged ahead. Helen fell against the seat back with a tiny shriek.

"Sorry." He guided his horse down the lane and onto the highway, taking the corner fast enough to send Helen toppling against him.

"Sorry," he said again as she righted herself and scooted away. He urged the horse to a faster pace.

Helen straightened her *kapp*. "You can stop here."

"Why?"

"Because we are out of Aenti Charlotte's sight and I'd like to get to work in one piece."

He scowled at her. "Are you criticizing my driving?"

Helen braced her hands against the dash. "I know you're upset, but please slow down."

"Why would I be upset? Because that ridiculous dog woke me in the middle of the night two nights in a row? Because your *narrish aenti* has decided to play matchmaker between us?"

"Matchmaker? What are you talking about?"

"Anyone with half a brain could see what she was doing. She practically forced me to take you up in my buggy."

"She did not."

"If we are seen riding together there will be talk."

"Now you are being ridiculous."

"Am I? You and the dozen other single women who have descended on Bowmans Crossing this summer are husband hunting and everyone knows it."

"I can't speak for anyone else, but I am not. I repeat,

I am *not* looking for a husband." She smacked her fist against her chest. "I intend to earn my own living."

"Ha!"

She crossed her arms and glared at him. "What's wrong with a woman wanting an independent life?"

"Nothing, if she can't get a man to marry her."

She sucked in an audible breath and turned her face away. He'd hit a nerve. "Oh, I see how it is. You had a beau but he decided he was better off without you. Smart man."

"I don't wish to discuss it."

"I imagine he's celebrating his escape."

"Did it ever occur to you that maybe I called it off?" The catch in her voice stung his conscience. She was on the verge of tears, and he was being a lout.

He slowed his horse and brought the buggy to a stop. She had been crying the first time he saw her, and he didn't believe it was because she had broken it off with some fellow. "I'm sorry, Helen. My words were cruel. I don't know what came over me. I'm not normally like this."

She cleared her throat. "Lack of sleep might be the culprit. That would make me grumpy."

"You are kind to offer me an excuse, but I'm in the wrong, and I beg your forgiveness."

She wiped her cheek with one hand and sniffed. "You are forgiven."

He sat quietly for a long moment, wondering what to say next and how to regain the ease that had existed between them earlier. He glanced at her, seated beside him with her head bowed. "Your aunt is eccentric."

That coaxed a smile from her. "Tell me something I don't know. Now you understand why I must have a job. I want to get a place of my own, and the sooner the better."

"Are you sure she doesn't have matchmaking on her mind?"

"She has informed me that you have a girlfriend back in Pennsylvania, but your brother is free, so I don't think matchmaking between us is her intent. However, I can't be sure of anything where she is concerned except that she loves her silly dog, and she is worried half to death about Juliet."

He didn't have a girl back home anymore. He was tempted to tell Helen about Angela's letter, but he squashed the impulse. "Any thoughts on how to find the raccoon?"

She glanced at him. "I hoped you would have some ideas."

"I think I can come up with a workable plan. First, you should ask the folks at the workshop to keep a look-out for her. All of them live in this area. Then, I will have Jessica make some lost-pet flyers. We can post them around the neighborhood and at other businesses."

"That's a fine notion."

"Where was she last seen?"

"At my aunt's house the evening after the frolic."

"We should concentrate our flyers and searches at the houses closest to yours and then work outward."

"*Danki*. From the bottom of my heart, I mean that."

"For what?"

"For taking Juliet's disappearance seriously."

He clicked his tongue to get the horse moving again. "Don't give me too much credit. I have a selfish motive. If we find Juliet, then maybe Clyde will stay home and let me get a good night's sleep."

"I promise I will do everything in my power to see that he stays home from now on."

"I'm going to hold you to that. Why do you think he keeps coming to my uncle's house?"

"Who knows? Maybe he truly likes you and wants your attention."

"If that's the case, I'll have to prove to him that I'm not a likable fellow."

"How do you intend to do that?"

"I have no idea."

They rounded the curve by the school, and the bridge came into view. He slowed the horse. The ride was almost over, but he wanted to know more about Helen Zook. He'd never met anyone quite like her. "Are you planning on staying in this area?"

"That depends if I can support myself here."

"My uncle pays a fair wage."

"He does. I'm not complaining."

"But you would like to earn more."

"If I continued to live with Charlotte, the pay would be more than adequate, but she doesn't want me there. She says she enjoys living alone."

"So there's a good chance that you'll return home?"

"*Nee*, I will not be going home."

"That sounds final. Were things really that bad?"

She was silent for a long time. He waited, hoping she would confide in him.

She sighed deeply. "I was engaged to be married. A week before the banns were to be announced, my fiancé told my family in front of our bishop that he wanted to marry my sister instead of me. They were married a few days ago. As long as they are there, I won't go home."

It pleased him that she trusted him enough to share

her story. Now he understood her tears. "That must have been a difficult time for you."

"You can't imagine how humiliating it was."

"That's the reason you were crying on the bus."

She nodded. "It should have been my wedding day."

"I reckon that was as good a reason as any for tears. Do you still love him?"

"Honestly, I'm not sure how I feel about him except to say I feel betrayed. By both of them."

"Have you forgiven them?"

"I want to say that I have, but I can't. Not yet."

It was a very honest answer, and his respect for her grew. "The time will come when you can say it and mean it."

"I pray that is true."

They came through the bridge and out the other side. He had been wishing the ride could be longer, but perhaps it was best that it wasn't. He was starting to like Helen Zook a little too much.

To his chagrin, Paul was standing beside the front door when they pulled up. His brother's eyebrows rose sharply when Helen stepped out of the buggy.

Helen turned to thank Mark and was taken aback by the deep scowl on his face. He hadn't been angry a few seconds ago. What had changed?

"Good morning, *bruder.* I see you got the dog home safely. Good morning, Helen."

The hint of suppressed laughter in Paul's voice made her realize why Mark was upset. He suspected that Paul would jump to the wrong conclusion because she was riding alone with Mark, and it appeared he was right.

She raised her chin. "Good morning, Paul. You brother was kind enough to give me a ride to work after he returned Clyde this morning. I'm sorry Charlotte's dog is raising havoc. It won't happen again."

"If Mark doesn't mind, I don't." Paul's smile was a bit too flirtatious for Helen's liking.

"I do mind, and I've made that clear, haven't I, Helen?" Mark's stern tone marked an end to the pleasant ride.

"Very clear." She was sorry she had confided in him only a few minutes ago. The sympathetic man who had listened and understood her hurt had vanished. Perhaps he'd only been practicing his listening skill again, and now he was back to his normal self.

"I'll be in as soon as I put the horse and buggy away," Mark said and drove off without a backward glance.

Paul's teasing smile vanished. "I hope my brother wasn't too hard on you."

"Not at all."

"He can be single-minded, and he sometimes forgets other people have feelings, but he has a good heart. I'm happy he didn't scare you away from us. I think you'll enjoy working here."

Would she? With Mark blowing hot and cold, it might not be a comfortable position to be in.

She walked into the office and put her container of rolls on the corner of the small desk that had been moved in since she left last night. It wobbled beneath her hand. The desk had seen better days. It was well-worn with deep scratches in the top surface and scuff marks on the legs. When she tried to open the only drawer, she found it stuck, and she had to use both hands to pull it free.

"A temporary desk for a temporary worker. Message received, Mark Bowman," she muttered drily.

"Are you talking to yourself?"

Her pulse took a jump at the sound of Mark's voice. She spun around to see him in the doorway.

"I was," she admitted.

"You'll have to be careful or some people will think you're as odd as your aunt."

"Some people might be right. I thought you were putting the horse away."

"Rebecca, my cousin Samuel's wife, caught me before I unhitched. She needed to go into town this morning. I see Paul found you a desk." He leaned against it and noticed the wobble. "In a shop that makes furniture, you'd think Paul could find something better than this."

Inordinately pleased that Mark hadn't chosen it for her, she shrugged. "It's fine. I can put a piece of cardboard under the foot to keep it level."

He took a step back. "*Nee*, I'll find you another one."

She picked up her container of cinnamon rolls. "While you are doing that, I'll take these to the break room."

"Wait, I get six of them, remember?" His eyes sparkled with mischief.

She smiled, happy to see the return of the friendly Mark but worried the wrong word from her would have him frowning again. She decided she would treat him as she would anyone else and not worry about his moods. She raised her chin defiantly. "Why should I save six for the greedy man who hasn't said he forgives me?"

He nodded in acknowledgment. "You're forgiven. Hand them over before Paul gets into them."

She opened the plastic container. The aroma of fresh-baked bread filled the small office. "Where shall I put them?"

He reached over and took one. "Put them all in the break room. I was only teasing. Let the men enjoy them.

Everyone's been working long hours. They deserve a treat."

Helen smiled as she left the office. He wasn't such a bad fellow after all. The fact that he cared about the men working under him proved that. She put the container on the table in the break room and started the coffee before coming back to the office. Jessica had arrived and was wiping down the counter. Mark was licking his fingers.

Helen chuckled. "Did you even taste it or did you swallow it whole?"

Jessica swept a few crumbs into her palm. "He swallowed it whole and didn't even offer me a bite."

Helen giggled. "I left more in the break room, Jessica."

Mark licked his lips. "I tasted it, and it was *wunderbarr*. Have you considered selling some of you baked goods at the farmers' market in Berlin?"

"This is the first I've heard about a farmers' market." Helen wondered if this was something worth looking into.

Jessica dumped the crumbs in the waste basket. "They hold it every Friday afternoon from three o'clock until seven during the spring, summer and fall. In the winter, they hold it every third Friday of the month. There's also a weekly market at Apple Creek although it's smaller. It's held on Tuesday afternoons from three until eight."

Helen turned the idea over in her mind. If she could supplement her income with her baking, that would be wonderful. "The Berlin market, is it big? Is it well attended?"

Mark shrugged. "It's not as large as some of the ones

I've attended in Pennsylvania, but it draws a fair-sized crowd. A lot of *Englisch* come each week."

Helen walked to the calendar hanging on the wall. If she started cooking as soon as she got home tonight, she could have plenty of goods to sell. "Every Friday afternoon. Would I be able to get off work to go?"

"If we aren't busy," Mark said. "You could make up your hours by coming in early a couple of days a week or by staying late, if you didn't want to lose pay."

"Count me as a customer," Jessica said with a broad smile. "I always swing by there on my way home and stock up on fresh produce and baked goods for the weekend."

Paul came in and leaned on the counter. "What are we talking about?"

"The farmers' market." Helen turned to Mark. "May I have tomorrow afternoon off?"

He cupped his hand over his chin and tapped his index finger against his lips. "This Friday? Maybe. I'll have to check our freight schedule."

"Okay. Well, I should get to work. I'm only here on probation for a month."

Jessica laughed. "If Mark fires you, come back in two months' time. He'll be long gone to Pennsylvania, and I'll make sure Isaac hires you again."

"You're leaving?" Helen stared at Mark, unable to keep her surprise hidden.

# *Chapter Eight*

So Mark was leaving Bowmans Crossing. Helen wasn't sure how she felt about that. On the one hand, it would be nice to work without him frowning at her every move. On the other hand...

She gave herself a mental shake. There was no other hand. She liked him a little, although she didn't know why. He was gruff and rude, and he had a girl back home. That put him off-limits as surely as if he were married. She would never do to another woman what her sister had done to her. She wasn't interested in a new romantic relationship anyway, not after the way Joseph had treated her. She wasn't sure she could trust her heart to another man after that.

Paul moved to stand beside her, his flirty smile once again in place. "My brother may be leaving, but I intend to settle down here and make my home in Bowmans Crossing."

"Then I may have to move," she replied with marked indifference and hoped he got the message that she wasn't interested. She caught Mark's eye as he smothered a grin.

He sobered quickly. "That put you in your place, little brother."

Jessica giggled. "You are wasting your time, Paul. She is too smart to fall for the likes of you."

Paul clasped his hands over his heart. "You wound me, Jessica. If you were Amish, you'd be the only one for me."

"I've seen you go out with non-Amish girls. I'm too smart to fall for the likes of you, too."

Someone cleared his throat, and the group turned to see Isaac standing in the doorway. "If I'm not mistaken, there is work waiting to be done."

Jessica sat down at her computer and turned it on. Paul squeezed past his uncle and went out the door. Helen glanced at Mark and saw his face was beet red. "Forgive my slacking. It was my intent to have the men start on the Fielding projects, but I was…"

"Sidetracked. I can see that," Isaac said, with a pointed look at Helen. "Why don't you help with the Fielding project, Mark, and I'll shadow Helen today."

"I'll do that." He nodded to his uncle and went out.

"I didn't mean to keep the men from their work. It won't happen again," Helen said earnestly.

Isaac chuckled. "It will happen again. Jessica loves to chat."

"True, very true," she said from her desk.

Isaac's smiled fondly at her and shook his head. "Paul finds any excuse to delay getting started in the workshop. He's a slow mover except when he's working as an auctioneer. Then, he's amazingly quick. I fear furniture making isn't his calling. I admit I was surprised to see Mark visiting in here instead of working."

Helen didn't know how to respond. She hadn't meant to distract anyone. "I am going to put these cinnamon rolls in the break room, and then I will be ready to get started. Mark was going to show me how to inventory the different types of wood used here."

Isaac held up a hand to stop her. "Before you go, I'll take one."

"Of course." She opened the plastic container and held it out to him. He took his time selecting which one he wanted.

"I'm not a great fan of raisins."

"The next time I make them, I'll remember that and bring some plain ones."

"You don't have to feed us," he said.

Helen shrugged. "Mark said the same thing. I like to bake, and it's nice to bake for people who appreciate what I make."

"Then far be it for me to discourage you." He stepped aside, and Helen went down the hall to leave her rolls in the break room. Mark was coming out of the supply room with a new circular saw blade in his hand. He passed her without speaking.

"Mark, I'm sorry," she said to his back. She had apologized more to this man than anyone in her life. Was God still trying to teach her a lesson in humility?

Mark stopped. "It wasn't your fault."

"He's not angry with you."

"I disappointed him. It won't happen again." He walked away without looking at her.

Later in the morning, Helen was making notes as Isaac went over the different types of plywood they kept on hand and their uses. After counting the stacks of three-ply, five-ply and cabinet-grade plywood, she finally had to say something.

"If you feel that Mark is distracted because of me, I can look for employment elsewhere."

Isaac scratched his beard. "Are you distracting Mark?"

"Not on purpose, but we have had some unusual encounters."

"Such as?"

Helen was sorry she had broached the subject. Should she mention they had met on the bus? Had Mark told anyone about her? "My aunt's dog has been annoying Mark in the middle of the night. Twice he has had to bring the dog home."

"Charlotte's dog has been annoying the entire household."

"I know, and I'm sorry. Mark feels he disappointed you this morning, and I wanted you to know the reason why Mark brought me to work with him today."

He tipped his head to the side. "I wasn't aware that Mark brought you to work."

"My aunt forced him to bring me. It's a long story. Perhaps I should stop talking now and go back to counting types of plywood."

"Your desire to defend Mark is admirable. I certainly am not disappointed in Mark. I was pleasantly surprised to see him socializing. He is normally something of a loner."

"He values your opinion. If you are not upset with him, I wish you would let him know that."

"I will, and thank you for the reminder. I seldom praise the men here for a job well-done, and I should do so more often. It's almost lunchtime. We can resume this count after we eat. My wife has asked that you join us for lunch."

"I would be delighted."

"Then I will see you up at the house, but first I must speak with Mark."

As they went back through the workshop, Helen saw all the men, save Mark, had turned off their machines and were heading outside to enjoy the lunches their wives or mothers had packed for them. One man rode off on his bicycle. Helen assumed he lived close enough to go home for lunch.

Isaac crossed the room to speak with Mark. Helen went into the office and found Jessica texting on her cell phone. She grinned at Helen and held the device in the air. "This is the number one reason I could never be Amish. I don't know how you do without one."

"I can't miss what I have never had."

"I guess that's true. Are you eating here, or are you going to go home?"

"I've been invited up to the house."

"Have you met Anna?"

"Briefly, at the frolic." Helen would rather forget about that day. She was glad Jessica hadn't been in attendance.

"You will like her. She's a hoot."

"I wanted you to know that I was leaving." Helen waved goodbye and stepped out into the workroom. Isaac was already gone. Mark was shutting down his machine. She started to leave, but he called her name.

She waited for him to catch up as a flock of butterflies took flight in her stomach.

Mark reached Helen's side and held open the door for her to go out ahead of him. He wanted to thank her, but he wasn't sure how to put into words what he was feeling. They walked toward the house in silence until they reach the front door. He caught her arm before she went in. "Why did you tell my uncle I felt that I'd let him down?"

"I knew you were upset, and I wanted to make it right since it was partly my fault. Your uncle told you he wasn't disappointed, didn't he?"

"He's not a man who gives compliments freely, so when he tells you that you have done a *goot* job he means it." For Mark, the warm glow of his uncle's praise was still centered in his chest. He knew he had been working hard, but to hear his uncle express his admiration was akin to winning a hard-fought race.

"I'm glad." She gave him a shy smile that made his pulse jump a notch higher. Why did she have this effect on him? He scowled as he tried to understand what it was that she was doing. Her smiled faded, and she rushed through the door.

During the meal, he found it hard to keep his eyes off Helen. She conversed easily with Anna and Rebecca. The tale of Juliet's disappearance had everyone speculating about what could have happened to the raccoon. The consensus among the men was that she had returned to the wild, but most of the women disagreed. Twelve-year-old Hannah and her mother, Mary, promised to keep an eye out for Juliet when they were out in the rowboat fishing on the river, an activity they both enjoyed. The story of Charlotte accusing the bishop's wife and then Mark of dognapping had everyone chuckling.

Occasionally, Helen glanced his way, and he noticed a slight rise in the color of her cheeks each time she met his gaze. He had never been interested in a woman enough to want to find out more about her until now. There were many things he wanted to learn about Helen. Did she have a big family? What kind of books did she enjoy? What kind of man had been engaged to her and chose another woman instead?

She smiled at something Samuel said, and Mark noticed the color and shape of her lips for the first time. Try as he might, he couldn't recall Angela's lips. Were they narrow or full like Helen's? Were they the color of pink rosebuds, or were they pale?

Paul kicked the side of Mark's foot. He glared at his brother. "What?"

"You're staring," Paul whispered.

"I was not." Mark looked down at his plate. "Did she notice?"

"I don't think so."

He glanced at Helen once more. She was talking to his cousin Timothy's wife, Lillian. Helen happened to glance his way, but he quickly looked down. He folded his napkin and rose to his feet. "I forgot something in the shop."

"Don't you want some gooseberry pie for dessert?" Anna asked. "It's your favorite."

"Save some for me. I'll have it later." He walked away without looking at Helen, until he reached the front door. When he glanced back, she was watching him. He ducked his head and left the house.

Ten minutes later, Paul stopped beside him in the workroom. "Is there something you want to tell me?"

"I need another sheet of three ply," he said without looking up from the dresser he was building.

"If I didn't know better, I'd say you are smitten with Helen."

"Have you seen the hand sander?"

"Samuel is using it, and you are trying to change the subject."

Mark sighed loudly and looked at Paul. "What subject would that be?"

"Whether or not you are smitten with the very attractive Helen Zook."

"I'm not. Do you think she's pretty?"

"Very. Don't you?"

"I hadn't noticed. Are you gonna get me that three ply, or do I have to get it myself?"

"I'll get it. Just be careful, that's all I'm saying."

"I'm always careful around power tools."

Paul leaned in to look Mark in the eyes. "I wasn't referring to power tools. A broken heart can't be fixed with nails and glue."

"You're being ridiculous. I've only just met her. No one's heart is in jeopardy. Least of all mine."

"For your sake I hope that's true." Paul walked away.

Mark laid down his hammer. Paul had it all wrong. Even if he was attracted to Helen, which he wasn't, he told himself sternly, she was not the kind of woman he needed. She made him feel as if his skin was too tight. How could a man be comfortable with a woman like that?

For the first time since receiving Angela's letter, Mark considered trying to win her back. It would solve so many problems. Her father would sell him the land he wanted. He wouldn't have to start over and find a new place to build his business. He wouldn't have to deal with dating women to find one who would suit his needs.

He would write Angela's father and ask if he knew why she had changed her mind. He would get his plan back on track, and then he would forget about Helen Zook.

The moment she got home from work, Helen pushed all thoughts of Mark out of her mind as she threw her heart and soul into baking. Charlotte, although disappointed that there wasn't any sign of Juliet, joined Helen in the kitchen, and the two of them were soon elbow deep in dough. By midnight, they had eight loaves of bread, three decorated cakes, two dozen assorted crescent rolls, three dozen frosted cupcakes, six dozen cookies and four pies. Two peach and two gooseberry, because Anna had said it was Mark's favorite.

Happily, Clyde stayed at home that night, so there was no early-morning visit from Mark. Helen slept later than she intended and had to rush to get to work on time. Charlotte promised to pack up the food and a table to display it on and pick Helen up at one o'clock. That would give them enough time to get to Berlin, pay the booth-rental fee and get set up before the market opened at three.

At work, Helen was eager to share her idea with Mark, but every time she approached him he took off in another direction. He seemed so busy she started to wonder if he was avoiding her. She settled for discussing her plans with Jessica, who was wonderfully supportive.

Keeping busy until it was time to leave wasn't a problem. A shipment of hardware came in at ten o'clock and it took her the rest of the morning to put it away in the assigned drawers. Twice, Mark came in to get something but didn't speak to her.

To her utter relief, Charlotte showed up as promised and without Clyde. Helen had persuaded her that it would be hard to keep the dog safe with so much traffic in town. Rather than risk losing another pet, Charlotte had shut Clyde in her bedroom.

They found where the market was to be held and located the man taking booth fees. Because she was the last person to pay for a spot, Helen was given a booth at the far end of the grassy lot. After rushing to get set up and get her wares on the table, Helen was finally able to take a deep breath and relax for a few minutes after three. The tree-lined green space at the park was lined on both sides with tents and colorful awnings. Fresh fruit and vegetables were displayed in wooden cases stacked on bales of straw or on tables. People strolled down the avenue with bags for carrying their purchases or even small wheeled carts.

As she scanned the approaching shoppers, she noticed Mark sitting beneath the shade of an oak tree across the way. He rose and strolled over to her table.

She smiled brightly. "Good afternoon. Can I interest you in some baked goods, sir? All fresh from the oven."

"So, what is your plan? What business model are you working from?"

Her smile slipped a little. "My plan is to sell all my baked goods and go home with extra money in my pocket. I don't know what a business model is, and I don't want to know. Would you care to buy a pie? I have gooseberry."

"Maybe later. I'm going to look around first, and I don't have a place to leave a pie. Are you giving away free samples?"

"*Nee*, if you want to see what it tastes like, you'll have to buy it."

"That might be a mistake."

Her patience vanished. "If you aren't going to buy anything, please move along so others can see what we have."

He tipped his hat and walked away. She turned to Charlotte, who was sitting on a folding chair behind the table munching on a cookie. "Aenti, those are for sale, not for snacking."

"I forgot." Charlotte slipped the half-eaten cookie back underneath the plastic wrap and returned the package to the table.

When Helen was sure Mark was out of earshot, she spoke to her aunt. "Do you know what a business model is?"

"I believe those are the women who wear tiny swimsuits and have their pictures in a magazine. Shameful, if you ask me. You don't want to be one of those. The bishop would forbid it."

Helen was sure that Mark hadn't been referring to women in swimsuits. "Why don't you finish your cookie?"

"Oh, may I? *Danki*, my dear." She snatched up the package and unwrapped it.

Helen fixed a smile on her face and waited for the patrons to make their way to her end of the market. She had made one sale, a dozen chocolate chip cookies, by the time Mark returned an hour later. It wasn't enough to cover her booth rental.

"How are you doing?" he asked.

"If things don't pick up, I will lose money instead of making it. Good food should sell itself."

"Does anyone here know you're a good baker?"

"I do," Charlotte said, waving her hand in the air.

"Besides your *aenti*?" He covered his mouth with his hand.

Helen's patience was wearing thin. "What are you doing here?"

"Moral support. I suggested this, and I wanted to see how it worked out for you. I was afraid you hadn't had enough time to adequately prepare."

"It's working out just fine. You may go home now."

He pointed toward the far end of the market. "There

is a bakery booth down there that's doing a brisk business."

She let out a huff of disgust. "Pour salt in my wound why don't you."

"I'm telling you this so you can see your mistakes and correct them. If you had done a little research—"

"Go away."

He shook a finger at her. "That was rude. I'm trying to help."

"Please go away."

"All right. I'll be over there if you need me." He turned and walked off. Helen was tempted to throw a gooseberry pie at him but thought better of it. Such a display of temper was sure to turn potential customers away.

Three hours later, Helen stared at everything she had to pack in the buggy again. Besides the cookies, she had sold one loaf of bread and one pie to Jessica. No one had purchased her beautifully decorated cakes and she'd sold only one dozen cupcakes. Discouraged didn't begin to describe how she felt.

And to have Mark witness her failure made it even worse. He left his shade tree and came over. "Can I help you pack up?"

"If you must."

Charlotte carried a box with a cake in it to the buggy. "Look at it this way, dear. We won't have to bake anything to take to the church service on Sunday. We can spend the entire day tomorrow looking for Juliet."

"Let's hope we have more success at that than I had today."

"Your cookies were delicious." Charlotte had consumed a half dozen.

Mark folded the table and slid it in the back seat of

Helen's buggy. "What did you learn about selling at a local market today?"

"That it was a waste of time and money. I wish you'd never said anything about it." Helen climbed in the buggy and jiggled the reins to get the horse moving. She couldn't wait to put this unsuccessful experience behind her.

Anna Bowman was working in the kitchen when Mark came in the house after returning from Berlin. He set two jars of jam that he had purchased at the market on the counter. "I thought you might like these. The little jar is lavender jam, and the tall pink one is rose-petal jam."

"How interesting. Would you like to try some now?"

"I'd rather not be the guinea pig. Ask Noah. He'll eat anything."

Anna laughed softly. "I like this change in you, Mark."

He leaned against the counter beside her. "What change?"

"You never used to joke around. You were always so serious, even as a little boy when you stayed with us that year."

It had been the summer after his mother died. Mark's dad hadn't been able to care for him and had sent a sad, lonely little boy to live with Anna and Isaac, the aunt and uncle he'd never met. Fortunately, he soon fell in love with the entire family. They were everything his family wasn't. "Maybe Paul's antics are beginning to rub off on me."

"How did Helen fare at the market?"

"Not well, and I feel responsible. It was my suggestion, but she took the idea and ran with it without any kind of plan or forethought. She wasted her time and money. She wants to get a place of her own, but it won't happen if she keeps on the same path. She's so impulsive. I don't know what to do with her."

"That's too bad."

"What do you think about Helen selling some of her goods in your gift shop?"

"I don't see why not. We already sell jams and candy and other food stuffs. Some homemade Amish bread might sell well if we pair it with a discounted jar of jam. It's nice of you to try and help Helen."

He shifted from one foot to the other. "I'm not sure she thinks so."

"Perhaps her pride is getting in the way."

"She thinks she has to succeed on her own."

"No one succeeds without help along the way, both from Heaven and from our friends and family on earth. You like her, don't you, Mark?"

"Maybe. She leaves me feeling all tied up inside."

"And Angela?"

"Angela doesn't make me feel like a fool or a brute or both at the same time."

Anna cupped his face between her hands. "You are neither a brute nor a fool. I'm going to miss you when you go back to Pennsylvania."

"I'll write and come visit often."

"*Goot*. I look forward to meeting your Angela."

If there was anyone he could confide in, it was Anna. "She may not be my Angela anymore."

"What? Why is that?"

"Her last letter said she has decided she doesn't wish to marry me."

"Mark, I'm so sorry. Did she say why?"

"*Nee.*"

"What are you going to do? You must go home at once and find out what is wrong. The two of you have been corresponding for ages. I thought the matter had been decided between the two of you."

"I wrote to her father."

"That's not the same as talking to her face-to-face. She has faithfully written to you every week as you have written to her. You should go see her."

"My apprenticeship with Isaac is almost finished. I will stick to my plan and speak to Angela when I go home."

"I pray you know what you are doing."

"I have thought it out, and I believe that's the best course for me."

"Matters of the heart seldom follow the plans *we* make, for it is *Gott's* plan that leads us to our soul mate. Do you pray for His guidance?"

"I do," he answered, but he wondered if he spoke the truth. God hadn't been at the forefront of Mark's life for a long time. His focus was on what he wanted and how he could achieve that.

His aunt's words stayed with him all evening and even after he said his prayers and climbed into bed. In his determination to fashion the life he had dreamed of as a child, he'd lost sight of the importance of prayer. What if God had a different plan for his life? How would he face that? Could he accept it? How did he know what God wanted him to do?

After a fitful first half of the night, Mark had finally drifted off to sleep when a mournful howl brought him wide awake. Fuming, Mark sat up and looked at his clock. It was three thirty. "That miserable dog! I'm not hauling him home again!"

He flopped back and covered his head with his pillow, but it didn't help. The deep baying penetrated even that barrier.

Mark threw back the covers and noticed his slippers at the side of the bed when he sat up. He snatched one and crossed to the window. He spied movement in the darkness below.

"Go home!" he shouted and threw the shoe.

"Ow!"

Startled to hear a woman's voice, he leaned farther out the window. "Helen?"

# Chapter Nine

 $\sim$ 

Sitting on the ground beside Clyde's tree, Helen held both hands over her stinging left eye, trying not to cry.

"Helen, are you okay?" She heard Mark's voice above her.

The pain was so intense she couldn't open her eyes. "*Nee*, I can't see."

"Stay still. I'll be right down."

"Oh, great," she muttered. This was exactly what she had hoped to avoid. Clyde proceeded to lick her ear and bark eagerly. She pushed him away. "Stop. This is all your fault."

By the time Mark reached her side the pain had eased some, but she still couldn't open her eyes without the discomfort returning, so she kept them tightly closed. He grasped her by the shoulders. "What's wrong, Helen?"

"Something hit me in the eye."

"I'm afraid it was my slipper. What are you doing here?"

His slipper? "Why did you throw your slipper out the window?"

"I was aiming at the dog. Not aiming exactly, but I was trying to scare him into going home."

She peeked with her good eye. Clyde was dancing around them, happily wagging his tail and darting in to lick her ear then trying to lick Mark, who pushed him away. "He doesn't look scared to me," she said drily.

"Helen," Mark said slowly. "What are you doing here in the middle of the night?"

"I was trying to stop Clyde from waking you, but I got here too late."

"Why don't you start at the beginning."

"I heard a commotion outside my aunt's home. When I looked out my window, I saw Clyde disappearing into the woods in this direction. I got dressed, grabbed his leash and got on my bicycle to try and get here before him. I didn't know he could run so fast. I mean, look at him! He's all flab, and he has little stubby legs, but he got here first and started howling before I could grab his collar. I heard you yell, and I looked up. The next thing I know something hit me in the eye."

"I'm so sorry."

Helen struggled to her feet. "I know it was an accident. We seem to have a lot of them, you and me."

"That is an understatement. I'll get the buggy and take you home."

She managed to keep her eye open for a few seconds before she had to squint again. "I don't need a ride. My bicycle is up on the road. Would you snap the leash on Clyde, please?"

"You can't ride a bike and manage Clyde, too." He fastened the lead and handed it to her.

"I'll walk him home. The sound of a horse and buggy driving up to the house might wake Charlotte. I'd rather avoid that." Helen climbed up the slope leading to the road with one eye open. She looped Clyde's leash around the handlebars and started for the bridge. He wasn't in the mood to go and nearly jerked the bike out of her hands as he tried to dart back to his tree. "Clyde, please, I just want to go home."

"Let me have him." Mark had followed her and stood with his hand out.

She sighed and untied the dog. "Okay."

Mark took it, and Clyde immediately sat beside him looking up with what she could only describe as an expression of doggy admiration. She cupped her hand over her stinging eye again. "I think Charlotte is right. He likes you."

"I'm so honored."

Helen had to chuckle at his sarcasm. "Imagine how boring this week would have been without Clyde. I wouldn't have almost run you over with a buggy."

"I wouldn't have taken a dive into a mud puddle."

"And you wouldn't have been wearing my delicious cream horns on your shirt front."

"You wouldn't have tried to burn your aunt's house down. Did you locate the fire extinguisher?"

"I did. Without Clyde, I wouldn't have a shoe print on my face." The pain was almost gone. She could keep both eyes open if she squinted.

"Let me see." He leaned forward to see her face by the light of the moon. "Your eye may be red for a while, but I don't think it will leave a mark."

"If it does, I'm telling everyone at church on Sunday that you stepped on my face."

"You wish to get me shunned?" he asked in outrage.

"*Nee*, I wouldn't. I'm only teasing."

"I know, so am I," he said with a grin. She smiled softly in return and started walking again.

He stared after her. He'd never teased or been teased by a woman before. He'd certainly never spent a moonlit night walking a girl home. Helen's presence had become comfortable in a way he hadn't thought possible. Maybe it was because she wasn't looking for husband. He didn't have to worry that his attention would be mistaken. He liked the idea of having her as a friend.

Clyde jerked on the lead, forcing Mark to stumble forward. As soon as he caught up with Helen, Clyde stopped pulling and walked quietly beside him.

Mark stared at the dog and stood still again. Once Helen was a few steps ahead, Clyde started pulling on his lead. When Mark caught up with her, Clyde ambled quietly beside Mark, occasionally bumping against his leg, forcing him to move closer to Helen. "This is a strange dog."

"He gets it from Charlotte. She talks to him like he understands what she is saying."

"Do you think he does?"

She shot him a look of disbelief. "He's a dog, Mark."

"Yeah, you're right. He's just a dog." Wasn't he?

Clyde wagged his tail and woofed once.

"What are you going to do with your leftover baked goods?" he asked to change the subject.

"I will take some to church on Sunday and freeze some. I'll take the rest to the shop on Monday. Charlotte and I can't eat them all."

"Aenti Anna said you are welcome to sell some baked goods at her gift shop."

"I'll think about it."

"You are giving up too easily."

"I'm not giving up," she insisted. "I know I can turn a profit if others can. I need to start small and work my way up."

"You failed to make a profit on your first attempt, but that isn't unusual for a new business venture. You made some beginner mistakes." Mark found himself on familiar ground. He knew the ins and outs of business, and he didn't mind sharing that knowledge.

"And now you're going to tell me what they were?" Helen asked. "It might have been helpful if you had told me beforehand."

"I didn't tell you because you didn't ask. You have enthusiasm, but your approach lacks common sense. You overestimated the amount you could reasonably sell because you didn't do your research. You failed to identify who your customers are, and you failed to study your competition. A well-thought-out business plan is important before you take the first step of investing time and energy. That's why you didn't do well."

She started walking faster. "I can't thank you enough for pointing out my shortcomings."

"You're quite welcome. We can all learn from our mistakes."

"My mistake was letting you walk me home." She sounded angry, and he didn't know why.

"I don't understand."

Helen stopped in her tracks. "I don't need a lecture from you."

"I thought you wanted my advice."

She fisted her hands on her hips. "You thought wrong. Since you seem to know so much about business, why don't you come up with a plan that will work?"

"For you?"

"*Ja*, for me. I'd like to see you figure out everything I need to do to turn a profit. Since you are a furniture maker and not a baker, I don't believe you can do any better than I did."

"It would be difficult to do worse."

She made that huffing sound that told him he should've stopped talking a while back. She got on her bike and began to pedal away from him. He had to jog to catch up. She pedaled faster.

He was winded by the time they reached her aunt's house. He bent over with his hands braced on his knees to catch his breath. Clyde flopped to the ground, panting heavily.

Helen took the dog's lead from Mark's hand. "Thank you for escorting me home. Good night."

"I'll do it," he wheezed.

"What?"

"I'll come up with a business plan for you," he said between deep breaths, wondering why he felt compelled to help someone who clearly didn't want it.

"Don't bother." She tugged Clyde up the porch steps.

Mark straightened, ignoring the stitch in his side. "It's no bother."

She entered the house and shut the door without answering.

Sunday, after the three-hour church service and a midday meal, Helen sat beside Fannie and Rebecca Bowman, watching the young people enjoying a game of volleyball. Helen had given up playing after her baptism. She missed the friendly competitions, but she was happy in the company of her new friends. It was nice to relax and have a conversation with young women near her own age.

Fannie nibbled on one of Helen's cream cheese–stuffed crescent rolls. "How is your job going? Do you like it?"

Helen shrugged. "It's okay. I'm learning a lot about wood and tools."

Rebecca held the hand of her toddler as the boy walked with shaky steps to Fannie. "Samuel tells me you're catching on quickly."

"I'm happy someone thinks so. I'm afraid Mark isn't of the same opinion. He's the most arrogant man I have ever met!" Helen rubbed her left eye. It was better, but Mark's comments about her shortcomings still rankled.

"Don't take Mark's cool attitude personally," Rebecca said. "Samuel said he's been like that all his life. He thinks it's because Mark's mother died when he was so young, and his father had trouble taking care of him. Mark ended up being shuffled from one family to the next while his father searched for work. The poor child never stayed anywhere more than a few months until he came to live with Isaac and Anna. They refused to send Mark back to his father until he had a steady job. Mark lived here for two years. His father eventually remarried and settled down, but by then Mark didn't want to go back."

"Did he stay here?" Helen asked, more interested than she cared to admit.

"His father insisted he come home. Isaac and Anna gave in but not before a lot of tears were shed."

"What about Paul?" Fannie asked.

Rebecca held out her hands to her son. He grinned and bounced on Fannie's lap. "Paul and Mark aren't related by blood. Paul's mother was a widow with a young son when she married Mark's father. They had five children together, so Mark and Paul each have five younger half siblings."

Fannie held the baby's fingers while he took steps back to Rebecca. "Paul and Mark act like brothers."

"They do," Helen agreed. She looked across the lawn to where Mark stood in conversation with Bishop Beachy, Samuel and Isaac. Mark's story gave her a little more insight into his personality. Had a childhood of insecurity produced a man who craved order? It made sense. Maybe she needed to be more tolerant of his quirks instead of taking offense.

On Monday, Helen resolved to be pleasant to him, but she had little opportunity to put her resolution into effect, for he worked on carving a new mantelpiece the entire day and left her to manage the supply room alone.

She walked out of the shop a little after four o'clock in the afternoon. Isaac had closed early because many of the men were traveling to a wedding the next day. Mark was sitting in an open-topped buggy outside the front door. He nodded toward the passenger side. "Get in."

She arched one eyebrow. "You forgot to say please."

He closed his eyes and took a deep breath. "Please get in."

She smiled. "See how much more pleasant you sound when you use that one small word?"

"Are you going to get in or not?"

"There's no need for you to take me home. I rode my bike to work."

"I'm not taking you home. I'm taking you to the farmers' market in Apple Creek to see what you did wrong."

His pointed reminder of her failure at the last market crumpled her new resolve. "I didn't bake anything, so I have nothing to sell." She walked past him to where her bicycle was parked.

Mark clicked his tongue to make his mare move up beside her. "You challenged me to come up with a business plan for you."

"And you haven't said a word about it. You barely spoke to me today."

"I was busy. I'm willing to talk about it now. The first rule of business is to know your customer. The second is to know your competition. You have a good product, but you don't know what the demand for it is. You don't know the price point you should set, and you don't know what sells best at a farmers' market."

She folded her arms across her chest. "It was glaringly apparent that I did not know these things. I thought good food would sell itself."

"One way to learn the business without so much painful trial and error is to observe your competition in action. Come on. I can develop a plan for you, but I can't implement it for you."

"Did anyone ever tell you that you don't talk like an Amish person?"

He tipped his head to the side. "What does that mean?"

"You use big, hard-to-understand words."

"I have furthered my education. I'm sorry you don't like the tone of my speech. What words didn't you understand?"

"Implement."

"It means I can't start the plan for you."

"Why don't you say that?"

"Come along with me. Don't you want to see what you did wrong?"

"Maybe."

"I think I know you better than that. I think underneath that I-don't-care exterior, you're dying to give it another go."

How did he know she was itching to try once more?

Maybe she wasn't as good at pretending indifference as she thought she was. "You're right. I am."

She rushed around the back of the buggy and climbed into the passenger seat, ignoring the self-satisfied grin on his face.

"That's the spirit." He slapped the reins against the horse's rump and guided her out onto the road. She trotted along at a brisk clip.

Helen gradually relaxed and began to enjoy the ride. It was a lovely spring afternoon. The sun was shining, but a north breeze kept it from becoming too hot. She stole a glance at Mark. "I have to ask. What prompted you to offer me this help?"

He met her gaze. "Your determination. Anyone else would have given up trying to get a job with me after the abject failures you had. It was dogged determination on your part, and I admire that."

"Desperation not determination."

"I don't agree. You encounter a dilemma, and you attack it. Your sister steals your fiancé. You don't hide at home, you set out to make a new life for yourself in another state. You don't want to continue living with your odd aunt. You decided you needed a job, and you kept at it until you were hired."

"Aenti Charlotte was responsible for that."

"Perhaps, but few people would have come to face me after the humiliation you suffered. You wanted to earn extra money, so you decided on a course of action based on sound principles. You enjoy baking, and you're very good at it. Then you put your idea in motion. Your vision suffered a setback, but I don't believe you'll let that stop you. You will try again, and ultimately I think you will succeed."

"You do? You think I will succeed at my own business?"

"We all have a different idea of what success is, but I think you will reach your goal of being able to move out of your aunt's home."

Helen folded her hands together and raised her eyes to heaven. "Please let that be what happens. I love Charlotte, but she and Clyde are a trial to live with."

"Has she always been strange, or is she getting worse because she is getting older?"

"She's always been different, but her obsession with her pets is getting worse. I think she is lonely, but she claims she enjoys living alone."

"Sometimes people say one thing and mean another."

Was he talking about himself or her aunt? She wondered if he was as indifferent to her as he tried to make out. "I have been guilty of that in the past."

"I take it the flyers have not been successful in locating Juliet?"

"One *Englisch* man stopped by to say that he had seen her by the side of the road on the way into town, but he couldn't say for sure that it was Juliet. He wanted to know if there was a reward. I'm not sure he saw anything, but it could've been another raccoon."

"Surely by now your aunt is ready to accept that Juliet might not return."

"*Nee*, she isn't ready to give up. She says she has a hunch that Juliet will turn up."

"A hunch is just a guess," he said softly.

"Or a wish."

Helen had a hunch that Mark was interested in her. Was it a guess or a wish? The last thing she wanted to do was to steal another woman's fiancé. No matter how much she might like Mark, she could never act on those feelings. He wasn't free. She had to keep a lid on her emotions until he left in a few weeks. If she could. He was much too good at reading her feelings.

The ride in the countryside was beautiful. Farmhouses along the way had flowers blooming in abundance in the yards, including colorful tulips and daffodils. The fruit trees were in bloom, and the cattle stood knee-deep in bright green grass.

It wasn't long before the outskirts of the town came into view. Small houses with small lawns gave way to businesses that lined both sides of the streets. He slowed the mare and stopped at a red light. Helen looked around in amazement. "The traffic is much heavier today."

"It will stay this way most of the summer and into the fall. This community is a tourist destination. Bowmans Crossing is still far enough off the beaten path to avoid much of this, but I don't think it will stay that way for long."

He found a place to park and, after leaving his horse with feed and water, he reached up to help Helen get down. The touch of his hand on her arm sent a thrill spiraling through her midsection. He quickly pulled his hand away as if he felt the sensation, too. She pretended to admire the array of tents and canopies that had been set up.

"If I do continue, I will need a canopy."

"Why not a tent?"

"Because I want my food to be on display. I don't want people to walk by because they don't know what's inside."

"*Goot*. Now you are thinking like a businesswoman. Write it down in your notebook."

"How did you know I brought a notebook?" she asked as she extracted it from her bag.

"During your orientation at work, you kept writing in one. I assumed you would want to take notes today."

"I'm not sure I like the way you seem to know what I'm thinking."

"I observe people, and I learn things about them. It's no secret."

"Maybe not, but it's a little creepy."

They walked together down the grassy aisle between the booths. Everything from woven baskets to carved wooden toys and fresh honey was for sale. The booth that was selling baked goods was doing a brisk business.

"What do you see that you like about their setup?" Mark asked.

"The displays are beautiful, and they are tipped at an angle so people can see them better. I had my things arranged flat on the table. I see they are giving out samples, too. I didn't want to give away my product, but I see now that if people like what they taste, they will purchase more. I also see that my prices were high."

"Folks come to a farmers' market for bargains. Notice what people are buying and what they are eating." Mark tipped his head toward an *Englisch* mother with two small children. The children each had a cookie in their hands.

"Things they can carry and eat as they shop." She noticed cookies and muffins in the hands of several other patrons. No one was carrying two-layer cakes.

"Shall we see what the other food vendors are doing?"

"*Ja*, I'd like to do that. Did you know all these things before you suggested I try selling my goods at a farmers' market?"

"I noticed them while I was watching you last Friday. You weren't selling much. I know your product is good, so there had to be a reason people weren't buying."

"I should have done that instead of being hurt and humiliated that no one wanted my cooking."

"You're doing it now."

"I reckon you can teach this old dog new tricks," she said with a chuckle, and he grinned.

She had made him smile. The satisfaction she felt was far out of proportion to her accomplishment. Movement across the way caught her eye.

"Mark, look, there is another basset hound. Isn't she cute?" Helen walked toward the *Englisch* couple holding the dog's leash. The dog was following her mistress's commands and showing off some tricks, earning treats from a plastic bag.

"I'm not sure I would use the word *cute*," Mark said drily.

"I think she is. I'm going to talk to them."

"Of course you are." Mark tagged along behind her.

She stopped in front of a couple. "Hello. I just had to say what a pretty basset hound you have. What is her name?"

The woman smiled. "She has an AKC-registered name, but we call her Bonnie."

Helen laughed. "My aunt's dog is Clyde."

The woman chuckled. "That is too funny. Bonnie and Clyde. We absolutely must get them together someday for a playdate. Does your aunt live nearby?"

"She lives just past Bowmans Crossing. What is a playdate?"

"It means getting together to let the dogs have some fun. We make a date to let the dogs play together. A playdate."

"Now I've heard of everything," Mark muttered. "Making a date for your dog."

"I think it's a great idea." Helen squatted on her heels

to pet Bonnie. "She's so well trained. My aunt's dog is…not so well trained."

Mark pushed the brim of his hat up with one finger. "He's a self-taught terror."

Helen grinned at him. "I'm afraid Mark is right. Clyde is very stubborn, and my aunt spoils him something fierce."

"Is he play motivated or is he food motivated?" the woman asked.

"He's mischief motivated," Mark answered.

Helen ignored him. "I'd say he is food motivated."

"Then you might try training him with some of these." She held out her baggie with a few remaining dog treats in it. "Bonnie will do just about anything for one."

Helen stood and took the bag from her. "What are they?"

"Peanut-butter flavored, all-natural, low-calorie dog snacks. I make them myself."

"Really? Clyde does enjoy peanut butter." She hadn't noticed before but many of the *Englisch* shoppers had their dogs with them. Had that been the case at the Berlin market, or was this something that Apple Creek encouraged?

"I can write out the recipe, if you like. It's simple," the woman offered.

Helen smiled her thanks. "That would be very kind. I have a notepad and pencil."

The woman scribbled out the recipe and handed it to Helen. "I use a cookie cutter to make them bone-shaped, but small flattened balls will do just as well."

"*Danki*, thank you." Helen placed the notebook in her pocket, gave Bonnie one last pat on the head and walked off with Mark. Together, they strolled along the row of tents and booths until they came to a baker's display.

Mark took his time deciding on a cream horn while Helen chose a raspberry scone. They moved away to eat their purchases.

"Yours are better," he said after he popped the last bite in his mouth.

"These scones are *wunderbarr*." Helen kept her eye on what people were buying from the baker as she nibbled. Although there were two beautifully decorated cakes in the display case, people were buying items that were easy to carry, and the baker was handing out order forms for special-occasion cakes to customers who expressed an interest. Packages of cookies, scones, cinnamon rolls and cake pops sold the best. Occasionally, someone bought a loaf of specialty bread.

"What do you see that you could incorporate into your booth next time?" Mark asked.

"Pretty tablecloths. I can easily invest in another table and an awning for shade. I wonder how much those acrylic display cases are."

"Why would you need them?"

She swatted at a fly buzzing around her face. "To keep the insects off the food. I'm going to ask the baker where he got them and how much they are."

She took a step toward the booth, but stopped and turned around. "Mark, I have to thank you. I don't know how long it would have taken me to figure this out by myself."

"You would have done it," he said, and she knew he meant it. The warmth that settled in her chest had little to do with his compliment and more to do with the admiration in his eyes.

*Am I falling for him? I can't be.* She turned away quickly. Their buggy ride home suddenly loomed large in her thoughts.

# Chapter Ten

Only a few minutes into the trip home, Mark noticed that his talkative companion had grown strangely silent. "Is something the matter, Helen?"

Her bright smile looked forced. "Why should anything be the matter?"

"I don't know. You look worried."

"I was just thinking about everything I've learned today." She stared off into the distance.

"It might seem overwhelming now but if you break it down into small sections, you can implement the changes you need little by little."

She turned to look at him. "When did you become interested in how a business works? The Amish men I know want to farm as their fathers and grandfathers farmed and if they own a business, they want to run it as their father and grandfather did."

"You aren't giving us enough credit. We may look like we are farming as our grandfathers did with horses or mules, but we aren't. A lot has changed. Fertilizers and pesticides that our ancestors never dreamed about are now commonplace. Organic produce has become popular, so some farmers adapt and use the old ways to manage pests. Soil health is something that can be studied and improved. It's the same with any business. There are men who want to do a better job and improve their product even if it is the same product their grandfather sold. Unlike many *Englisch* businessmen, the Amish aren't in it to earn a lot of money. If we make enough to get by, that's our measure of success."

"Okay, but what inspired you?"

He glanced at her and saw she truly was interested. He wasn't used to talking about himself. "My father didn't own a farm. He was the oldest son. Isaac was the youngest, and he inherited grandfather's farm. Daed could have stayed and worked the farm with Isaac but he wanted his own business. He tried a number of different enterprises, and none of them worked out. After a while, he worked odd jobs for other people, but he was never content to stay in one place. Because of that, we moved around a lot."

"Rebecca told me that your mother died when you were young and that you came to stay with Isaac and Anna." Her sympathetic tone gave him the courage to share his story.

"I was eight. During the time I stayed with them, Isaac realized that farmland was becoming too expensive for all of his sons to eventually own their own land. He knew that to keep his family together he would have to have work that would provide a living for them. That's when he started his furniture-making business. Unlike my father, Isaac was able to grow and expand the business he started. Anna, too, had good business sense and opened her gift shop. By the time I was ten, I had realized that it wasn't chance or fate that made them successful. It was understanding how a business should be run."

"Perhaps it was because the Lord favored them."

One side of his mouth lifted in a half smile. "The Lord brings the rain and sun that makes your garden grow, but you must still pull the weeds if you want a good harvest."

"That was one of my grandmother's favorite sayings."

"It's one of Isaac's, too. That's why I came to apprentice with him before I open my own furniture-making business. I have invested two years to learn all I can from him."

"And those two years are almost up. Where will you go after that?"

"Back to the village where my family lives in Pennsylvania. I have the land picked out where I will build my shop." He hoped that land was still available to him. He had not heard from Angela's father, and the uncertainty gnawed at him. Helping Helen gave him something to work toward and kept his mind busy.

He glanced her way. That wasn't the whole truth. Helping Helen made him feel good. Just being with her was somehow soothing and exciting at the same time. "Are you planning to stay in Bowmans Crossing?"

"I'm not sure. I have a good job, so I may stay. I'm fond of Charlotte even if she is a trial. Eventually, she will need someone to watch over her."

"You mean someone other than the dog?"

"Exactly. Clyde is already five years old, and his breed normally lives to be ten or twelve. When he's gone, I worry that Charlotte will have difficulty adjusting. She doesn't have any close family other than my parents and my sister in Indiana."

"The church will take care of her if need be."

"That's true. She has friends, too. I may be concerned about nothing."

"Isn't your goal to lead an independent life? I hope you know I respect that choice."

"I am leading my own life," she declared. "But sometimes plans change."

"Mine won't."

"What would you do if you couldn't purchase the land you wanted back home?"

"I won't think in terms of failure. I can't." He hoped Helen didn't notice the hint of fear that crept into his voice.

She laid a hand on his arm. "Then I pray God allows you to fulfill your dream."

Helen pulled her hand away and clasped her fingers tightly together. She didn't want Mark to think she was bold. Something in the sound of his voice told her how critical the success of his plan was to him. She sensed there was more to the story than a desire to start a business in Pennsylvania. Something about it was vitally important to him. Perhaps it involved the woman waiting for him back home. Maybe he didn't want to marry until he could support a wife and children. It made sense that Mark was that kind of man.

She remained silent for the rest of the ride home. Mark didn't seem to notice, or at least he didn't comment. When they reached the workshop, he stopped beside her bicycle, and she got down. "*Danki*, Mark, I will carefully consider all the things you have told me."

"I hope I have helped."

"You have. I once thought you were arrogant and judgmental, but I was wrong. You have been both a good teacher and a friend. *Danki*."

He inclined his head. "I don't have many friends. I'm honored you count me as one of yours."

She watched him drive away, wishing there was some way she could pay him back for all he had done for her. Perhaps the day would come when she could.

Paul was standing just outside the front door of the building. Mark waved to him, and Paul waved back as he ambled toward Helen as she was getting on her bike. "My brother has been taking you up in his buggy often these days."

"He has been very kind to me considering what a problem Clyde has been." She didn't want to discuss her relationship with Mark.

Paul folded his arms over his chest and leaned one shoulder against the wall of the building. "I thought maybe I should tell you a few things about my brother. Things I figured you might not know. He doesn't like to talk about himself."

"I don't listen to gossip."

"It's not gossip. I love my brother, and I want him to be happy. I have a feeling you want the same thing."

She glanced at him and saw he was watching her intently. She hadn't given Paul enough credit. He was more than a jokester. "Your brother has told me quite a bit about himself."

He arched one eyebrow. "Now that is surprising. I don't want you getting your hopes up where he is concerned. He's a good catch, but he has an understanding with a girl in Pennsylvania."

"I know. My aunt told me that the first day I came here."

"I guess I didn't realize it was common knowledge."

"It is. I also know Mark is committed to running his own business someday."

"*Committed* is a good word. He doesn't compromise. He sets his mind to something and works until he has achieved it."

"Why are you telling me this?"

"I have the feeling that he likes you. Even admires you."

"I like and admire Mark, too. There's nothing wrong in that."

"Maybe not, but if you expect him to change his mind about his plans to return to fair Angela and his dreams back home, I'm here to tell you that you are wasting your time. Call it friendly advice, or call it a warning if you will. I like you, too. I don't want to see you get hurt, either."

"Then I thank you for your friendly advice, but it isn't needed. Mark and I are becoming friends, that's all. He's a good teacher, and I'm a willing pupil. Besides, I have plans of my own, and they don't include starting a romantic relationship with anyone, if that's what you're hinting at."

"It's good to know where you stand." He straightened, touched the brim of his hat and walked away.

Helen watched him go then got on her bike and pedaled for home. She had two uninterrupted miles to consider her feelings for Mark Bowman. By the time she reached her aunt's home, she had come to the decision that they might remain friends, but she would guard her heart against any deeper feelings. She wouldn't come between him and the woman named Angela.

During the rest of the week, Helen made a point to avoid Mark as much as possible. When she couldn't, she maintained a friendly demeanor. She wondered if Paul had spoken to Mark about his concerns for the two of them. She had no way of knowing. She certainly couldn't bring herself to ask Mark outright.

With Mark's suggestions for her business in mind, she got ready for Friday's market. She asked Samuel to make her some wooden holders that would allow her to set her display trays at a slight angle for easier viewing. He offered her the loan of a canopy, which she gladly accepted. She had Jessica help her pay for her booth space online and order acrylic cases and domes from a bakeware website. The cases hadn't arrived by Thursday morning, and she resigned herself to doing without them for this week's market.

When Helen came home from work, she found Charlotte had spent the afternoon making a mountain of dog treats for Clyde from the recipe the *Englisch* woman with the bassett hound had given her. Clyde was snoring in the corner, and Helen wondered how many he had sampled.

To Helen's further surprise, Rebecca, Anna and Fannie showed up on Thursday evening to help her bake. Apparently, Mark had mentioned her project, and the women of the family were eager to see that Helen had a successful second day at the market. They were soon mixing, baking and sampling a variety of cupcakes, cake pops and even pie pops at Rebecca's suggestion. Rebecca donated a jar each of homemade peach, cherry and pumpkin pie filling. Charlotte happily joined in, but Helen noticed that she had trouble remembering how to seal the edges of the pie pops. Helen had to go back and reinforce all her efforts.

The kitchen was full of delicious aromas and cheerful chatter as the Bowman women regaled Helen with stories of their husbands and children. Good-natured teasing and a genuine interest in Helen's project soon had her feeling as if she had known these women for years. Surrounded by her new friends, Helen missed her mother and her sister even more. They would've enjoyed being part of the frolic. In spite of her sister's recent actions, Helen realized she had many fond memories of their times together while they were growing up. Perhaps she could forgive Olivia one day. Maybe she could forgive herself, too.

As the women were getting ready to leave that evening, Charlotte went out onto the porch and started calling for Juliet and clapping her hands. Charlotte turned to Helen, who had come outside with her. "I can't understand why Juliet is out so late this evening. She should've come in for supper before now."

Helen laid a hand on her aunt's arm. "Juliet has been missing for over a week now."

Charlotte looked puzzled for a few seconds then her gaze cleared. "That's right. How silly of me to forget that. I'm just so used to having her here with me."

She patted Helen's hand. "You and Mark are looking for her. Clyde certainly has taken a liking to you and to Mark. Dogs know things about people. I think I will go to bed now. I'm very tired. Come along, Clyde. Good night, all."

The dog trotted after her, his long brown ears occasionally getting in the way of his feet and causing him to stumble, although he didn't seem to mind. The dog hadn't made a single visit to his tree since the night Mark hit Helen in the eye with his slipper. Hopefully, the dog's nocturnal visits were done for good.

Helen followed Anna out to her buggy. "Does my aunt seem more confused to you?"

Anna shook her head. "Charlotte has always been

a little scatterbrained. She's fine. I know she is happy to have you here."

"Really?"

"She was just telling me yesterday when she stopped in for coffee what a blessing it has been having you stay with her."

"That's good to know. She has been a blessing to me, as well. I'm afraid I have been a self-centered person for much of my life. I didn't always consider how other people felt."

"We have seen none of that in you," Rebecca said from the front seat of the buggy.

"I hope I am improving. The good Lord has given me a lot to think about in these past weeks." Foremost among her thoughts was Mark and her growing feelings for him, but she didn't share that with anyone.

"Mark mentioned you wished to sell some of your baked goods in my store. Bring them by whenever it's convenient."

"Whatever I don't sell tomorrow I'll bring over." Helen waved goodbye to her company and went inside.

That night she sat down to pen a letter to her parents. She didn't want them to fret about her any longer. She had worried them enough.

After finishing her letter, she went to bed and tried to sleep, but her eyes wouldn't stay shut. She was too excited for the coming day. Would she earn enough money to make all her work worthwhile? Would she remember all that Mark had taught her? Would it rain?

She rolled over and hugged her pillow. She was dying to know one certain thing. Would Mark be there again?

Mark sat up and glanced at the clock beside his bed. It was five thirty in the morning. He listened closely, but heard only the wind in the tree branches, the murmur of the river and the chirping of night insects. Clyde had failed to show again. Mark flopped back against his pillow with a big grin and stretched. Maybe the foolish dog was howling under someone else's window for a change, or maybe he was home sleeping as he should be.

Today was the day Helen was going to try selling at the farmers' market again. Mark was eager to see how much of his advice she took and how much her sales would improve because of it. He did want her to succeed.

Helen's resiliency in trying again so soon was admirable. He didn't know how she could shake off her humiliation so easily and get right back into the fray. She was a remarkable woman. Not at all like his first impression of her. Or his second. Or his third. He chuckled to himself at the memory of their meetings and her abject failures in her attempts to ask him for a job.

Helen Zook was persistent if nothing else. She would succeed at her baking business or go down in smoke and flames trying.

After breakfast, Mark, Paul, Samuel and Isaac went down to the workshop. The rest of the crew soon arrived. Mark kept a lookout for Helen. The surge of happiness that hit him when he saw her took him by surprise.

His uncle handed Mark the clipboard with the daily announcements. Mark read them off and assigned men to each task. The last note on the page took some of the joy out of his day. He'd have to meet with clients this evening.

He looked at Helen. "We are expecting a shipment of lumber and assorted items later today. Helen, why don't you help Jessica in the office until they arrive. Samuel,

I want you to make sure we get the right grade of wood. The company sent us a cheaper grade last time, and I had to send it back."

"What did you bring us to eat today, Helen?" one of the men asked. It was Adam Knepp, Isaac's master carver.

"A box of nails and wood chips," Jessica quipped.

Adam laughed. "Those gingersnaps the other day were as good as my Grosmammi Stutzman used to make."

Helen inclined her head. "*Danki.* It was my grandmother's recipe. Maybe my grandmother and your grandmother knew each other. I didn't bring anything today as I am selling my goods at the market in Berlin this afternoon. You are welcome to come and *purchase* some of those gingersnaps."

Adam shook a finger at her. "I see what your plan is. You ply us with sweets until we expect them, and then you say, "Come buy them,' thinking we will spend our hard-earned money to enjoy your cooking."

Mark opened his mouth to defend her but before he spoke, she said, "Exactly. Is it working?"

"It is," Jessica said, and the men laughed. "My mom and I really enjoyed the oatmeal bread I bought from you last week. Can I buy it from you here?"

Helen smiled at Mark. "Anna says she has room for some of my baking in her gift shop. You should be able to get what you want over there. If you would care to give me your orders, I can make certain I fix what you like."

Several of the men crowded around her, listing items they wanted. Mark stepped in and raised his voice. "This can wait until break time. She isn't going home to make up a batch of cookies for you today. We have work to do."

As the men moved away to get started, Helen remained beside Mark. "I didn't mean to be a distraction."

"I would be a poor boss if I couldn't get them to order baked goods on their own time. Are you ready for this afternoon?"

She nodded. "Anna, Rebecca and Fannie all came over to help me bake last night. I have nearly as much stuff to take as I did that first day."

He leaned close enough to smell the scent of fresh-baked bread that seemed to cling to her. "That must mean you have some confidence in my advice."

"I have a lot of confidence in the things you taught me, and I have baked things I think the market customers will enjoy." She looked down at her hands clasped in front of her. "Will you be going?"

"I wish I could, but don't count on me. I'm meeting with a couple of clients this evening who want to order a custom bedroom suite. I'm afraid I won't finish in time to stop by and see how you're doing."

She looked up at him with a sweet smile that warmed him clear through. "I have every intention of doing well, God willing. Is it all right if I make up some of my time tomorrow? Jessica has said she has filing I can do."

"That will be fine. I will be working on that new mantelpiece for a while tomorrow. You can tell me all about your success or failure then."

"I refuse to think about failure." She spun around and went into the office.

Mark hadn't intended to work on the project but if she were going to be here, he would use it as an excuse to spend a little time with her. He liked Helen and enjoyed her company.

He realized he was still staring at the office door that she had vanished through. He spun around and got to work before anyone else noticed that he had a hard time taking his eyes off Helen Zook.

Charlotte arrived at the right time with the buggy Helen had loaded before she left that morning. The only thing Helen was upset to see was that she had Clyde with her. The dog woofed happily and wagged his tail. He tried to lick Helen's ear as she climbed in, but she managed to hold him off.

Mark came out of the building and waved to Charlotte before heading around to the lumber storage area. Charlotte turned to Helen. "Isn't Mark coming with us?"

"He has to meet with some customers."

"But he came last time."

"He didn't go with us. He went on his own." Helen took the reins and soon had the horse trotting at a brisk pace on the road.

"Clyde would rather have Mark along." Charlotte looked behind them.

"Clyde and me both," Helen muttered.

The occasional car or pickup shot around them. One car passed them and then slowed down beside them in the oncoming-traffic lane so that a woman could lean out the car window and snap a picture with her phone. Helen turned her face aside and held up her hand. The car sped on. She turned to see Charlotte also had her hand in front of her face and was holding one of Clyde's ears over his face.

"They are gone, Aenti," Helen said, choking back a laugh. She couldn't wait to share the story with Mark.

Charlotte lowered her hand and dropped Clyde's ear.

"Rude tourists. I have no idea why they feel the need to take pictures of us."

"They think we are quaint."

"Then they are silly, and they need to find better things to do."

"Let's hope they are on their way to the farmers' market and will buy our baked goods."

Helen was prepared to do whatever it took to make a profit this afternoon. More than anything, she wanted to prove to Mark that she could succeed. Tomorrow morning couldn't come soon enough.

# *Chapter Eleven*

A loud howl followed by deep quick barks pushed aside Mark's pleasant dream and brought him to the edge of wakefulness. He stared at the dark ceiling, wondering if the sound might have been part of his dream. He closed his eyes and tried to slip back into sleep where Helen waited for him with a sweet smile on her lips and her arms out to welcome him.

The howl came again.

Not a dream.

"Unbelievable." Mark sat up.

He should have been annoyed, but he wasn't. Clyde's arrival meant Mark would get to spend an extra hour with the real Helen, not the confusing woman of his dreams who never let him close but who seemed ready to welcome him.

Knowing it wouldn't do any good to yell at Clyde, Mark got dressed, picked up his boots and went downstairs to open the back door. Clyde came padding in without being called. He woofed once and launched himself at Mark. Prepared for the impact, Mark managed to stay upright but had to drop his boots.

"Why can't you come calling at a decent hour, Clyde?

This is so rude. And now I sound like Charlotte talking to a dog as if you can understand me."

Mark rubbed Clyde's big soft ears and then nudged him to the floor. Frisking like a puppy around Mark, Clyde followed him to the front door. Mark opened it and pointed to the road. "Go home."

Clyde flopped to the floor, put his head on his paws and whined.

"Is that a no?"

Clyde whined again.

"Want to go for a buggy ride?"

Bounding to his feet, Clyde wriggled eagerly. Mark rubbed the sleep from his eyes. "You know what 'go for a buggy ride' means, don't you? I sure wish you would learn 'go home.' It's almost time to get up anyway. Let me get my boots on."

He sat on a chair against the wall and smoothed his socks. Clyde came to smell his feet. The dog sneezed, making Mark laugh. "Can you keep a secret? I'm making a carved wooden spice rack for Helen. It was going to have solid doors, very Amish, very plain, but I have just now decided to decorate the doors with basset hound carvings. Do you think she'll like it?"

Clyde wiggled eagerly and woofed once.

"I think she will, too. Something to remember us by." He sobered as he considered the possibility that he might not see her again after he went home.

"Mark, who are you talking to?" Anna asked from the kitchen doorway.

"Charlotte's dog," he said without looking up.

She chuckled. "Is he answering you?"

"Not yet, but we are working on some sign language." He pulled on his left boot.

"Did you pick some of my tomatoes last night or this morning?"

"Nope. Clyde, are you stealing tomatoes now?"

The dog sat down and whined. Mark looked at his aunt. "I think that means no."

"Well, someone helped themselves to three big ripe ones I planned to pick this morning. Your breakfast will be waiting for you when you get back."

"Don't bother. I'm sure Helen has something to feed me."

"She is a *goot* cook, *ja*?"

"Not as fine as you but pretty close." He pulled on his right boot.

"Not married, pleasant, a baptized member of our faith and a *goot* cook. Charlotte even said she is glad Helen has come to visit. You could do worse."

He figured that he and Helen would become the subject of discussion after the church service tomorrow if he didn't put a stop to it. He stood and brushed his hands together. "She isn't looking for a husband. She wants an independent life. Her words, not mine."

"So, you have discussed this. That's a fine start."

He put his hands on his hips. "The start of what, Aenti Anna?"

"Courting."

"We aren't courting. We are simply friends. I'm taking her dog home to her. Again."

"And having breakfast there. Again. Tell Charlotte I said she has a very smart dog."

He shook his head at his aunt's nonsense and left the house with Clyde ambling behind him. At least he didn't have to drag the dog away anymore. After hitching up the buggy, he climbed in and Clyde scrambled up after him. The dog happily sat beside him during the ride and jumped out as soon as Mark pulled to a stop in front of Charlotte's house. He ran to the front door and started barking.

There was a light in the kitchen. Mark assumed someone was already up. A few seconds later, the door opened and Helen looked at the dog in amazement. "I don't believe it. How did you get out?"

She looked at Mark. "How is he getting out of this house?"

"My guess is that someone is letting him out."

Outrage filled her eyes. "Are you accusing me?"

He held up both hands. "I was thinking of your aunt."

Helen stepped aside so he could come in. "I can't believe she would willingly put him out in the middle of the night. She barely lets him out of her sight during the day."

He hung his hat on one of the pegs by the front door. "What's for breakfast?"

"I was about to make some oatmeal."

He made a face. "I was never very fond of it myself."

"I have some day-old croissants."

"Sounds great, if you have a cup of coffee to go with it." He sat down at the table.

She put her hands on her hips and glared at him. "I was just about to brew some. Make yourself at home, Mark Bowman. Don't mind me."

"I figured since I was already here, you would want to tell me all about your success at the market yesterday. Am I right?"

She raised one eyebrow. "What makes you think I was successful?"

He leaned back in his chair and grinned. "Because I taught you all that you needed to know."

"Oh, you did? How strange. I thought it was my

hard work and my fine baked goods that won over the customers."

"So, you did have a successful day?"

"I did." She carried the coffeepot to the sink and filled it. "I sold eighty percent of the goods I took. The pumpkin pie pops were the biggest hit. I had several repeat customers throughout the afternoon for them and sold out before five."

"Where was your booth?"

"I had Jessica purchase it on the computer for me instead of waiting until I got there, so I was located near the middle of the grounds instead of down on the end."

"Good thinking. I'm sure a better location helped. How did the other bakery do?"

"Fair, I think. Several people commented that my bread prices were higher than his."

"And how did you respond to that?"

She giggled. "I told them the quality was higher, as well."

"Did they walk away?"

"They didn't, because I reduced my price to match his. It was near the end of the day, so I figured it was better than not making a sale. It was still within my profit margin for bread, so I didn't lose money on the loaves."

"You have the makings of a real businesswoman, Helen. I'm impressed. Can you duplicate your success? That's the next question."

"I think I can, but you won't believe what brought in the most people."

"Had to be your cinnamon rolls." He wished she had saved him one.

She brought a plate with a croissant and several

pieces of cheese and set it in front of him. "Nope, it was Clyde."

He slanted a glance at the dog sitting by his feet. "Clyde? Explain."

She added coffee grounds to the pot and put it on the stove before coming to sit at the table. "He was absolutely adorable. Charlotte sat out front of our booth on her chair, and he did trick after trick for her. Each time she gave him one of the treats she'd made, he'd sit up on his hind end and fall over with a smile of bliss on his face. I am not making this up."

Mark pointed to the hound at his feet. "This dog did tricks?"

"I'll show you." She went to the cupboard and took out a plastic bag full of small brown cookies. "Clyde, do you want a treat?"

He immediately woofed.

"Beg for one."

He sat back on his haunches, wobbling a little, and then waved his front legs together. She gave him a cookie. It disappeared in one gulp. Then he sank over sideways and rolled to his back. Mark had to admit he did look like he was smiling.

Helen was grinning from ear to ear. "Isn't he adorable?"

She was adorable. He realized he'd never seen her so happy. Her eyes sparkled with mirth. Her lips were parted in a sweet smile. Her excitement was infectious. He had trouble thinking about why he was here. "He's not adorable when he's barking outside our house in the wee hours of the morning."

Her grin faded. "You have a point."

Charlotte came into the kitchen from the hallway. "Helen, did you let Clyde out of my room? I can't find him. Oh, there he is," she said when she spied him. "Mark, how nice to see you. Have you come to give Helen a ride to work?"

"I've come to return your dog. He was howling outside my window again."

"How strange." Charlotte stared at Clyde. "What are you doing visiting the Bowmans at such an hour?"

He lay on his back, wagging his tail.

Helen passed out the coffee mugs and poured them all into a cup. "Are you sure you didn't open the door for him last night, Aenti?"

"I didn't open the front door, and I didn't open the back door for him. He must be getting out through my window."

Mark rose to his feet. "I'll take a look and secure it so he can't get out again."

Helen followed him down the hall. "I can't believe he can get out that way."

He opened the door to Charlotte's room. The window ledge was three feet off the floor and the sash was only up a few inches. There wasn't any furniture the dog could climb on near it. Mark was as baffled as Helen. "You're right. I don't see him getting out this way. I can cut a length of wood to act as a stop so he can't push the window open wider if he is getting up here."

They walked back to the kitchen where Charlotte sat sipping her coffee. "Did you figure it out?"

"We didn't," Mark admitted. "I can build a kennel for him to stay in at night."

"Absolutely not." Charlotte plunked her coffee mug down. "I will not keep him in a kennel. He has been raised in this house. I wouldn't put either of you in a cage."

"Aenti, he can't keep waking up the Bowman family in the middle of the night. We have to be better neighbors."

Charlotte blinked back tears. "He would hate a kennel. If only Juliet would come home, he wouldn't be wandering around in the middle of the night looking for her."

The last thing Mark wanted was to make a woman cry. "I won't put him in a kennel."

She sniffed once. "You won't? I'm sure he won't get out again. I'll talk to him," Charlotte assured Mark.

Like that would help. He turned to Helen. "Are you ready to go to work?"

"Give me a minute to get my things together, and I'll be ready."

"I'll be in the buggy, waiting." He paused at the door and looked back. Charlotte had Clyde's face between her hands as she whispered something in his ear. He remembered what his aunt had said. "My *aenti* Anna says to tell you that you have a smart dog."

Charlotte looked at him. "She figured that out, did she? Anna was always a bright one."

Unsure of what she meant, he left the house and waited for Helen outside. It didn't take her long to join him. "Sorry to keep you waiting."

"That's okay. There isn't any rush. It will be just you and I at the workshop this morning."

"I'm glad you are letting me make up my lost hours. That's very kind of you."

"It's my *onkel's* rule. He doesn't want his workers to feel cheated. They have the opportunity for overtime work if they wish it."

"Will you have the same management style at your business?"

"Most likely. It may be a year or two before I can hire

an extra worker, but I want to help support the community as my *onkel* is doing."

"That's a fine goal."

"It isn't about making money. It's about making a living for my family and others."

"You put me to shame."

"Why do you say that?"

"Because my only goal is to move out of my aunt's home before I tear my hair out."

"You would look odd bald. It's a worthwhile goal."

Helen regaled him with more stories of her day at the farmers' market. He listened to her with only a few comments, enjoying the sound of her voice and the undercurrent of excitement she couldn't contain. He couldn't remember the last time he had enjoyed a buggy ride so much.

When they finally reached the workshop, he got out and turned to help her. She rested her hands on his shoulders as he grasped her waist and swung her down. She was so close his mind stopped functioning. He couldn't release her, couldn't step away. Her upturned face was so close to his. All he had to do was lean forward a little and he could kiss her.

Helen held her breath as Mark's hands lingered on her waist. She gazed into his beautiful green eyes and wished with her whole heart that she could move closer. Her fingers rested lightly on his shoulders, and she could feel his firm muscles through the fabric of his white cotton shirt. She wanted to be kissed. And she had no right to wish such a thing. She looked down and stepped back. He released her and rubbed his hands up and down on his pant legs.

"What are you working on today?" she asked as she walked toward the workshop door.

"The people that I met with yesterday want a reproduction piece made to match the antique dresser that they have."

She couldn't be sure, but she thought his voice sounded strained. "I thought you were doing a mantelpiece."

"It can wait. These people are willing to pay a premium for a rush job."

"How soon do they want it?"

"Two weeks."

"Are you serious? Can you do it in two weeks?"

"If Samuel and I work on it together, we can."

Helen saw the antique dresser wrapped in plastic sitting in the middle of the work area. "This is what you have to copy?"

"That's it." He stopped beside it and began unwinding the protective sheeting.

"I shall leave you to it." She reluctantly walked away and entered the office. When Mark was being nice, he was a very attractive man. She liked him much more than she should. Keeping a guard on her heart wasn't as easy as she thought it would be.

An hour later, Helen had filed everything Jessica had set out for her. She cleaned and dusted the office area, including the shades on the windows, and mopped the floor. There was nothing left to fill her time, so she went out to find Mark. He was bent over a large drafting table where he was making a full-size, detailed drawing of the dresser. It sat beside him. He got up to measure the width and height of the legs. She didn't want to disturb him, so she turned to go.

"Leaving already?" He pulled his pencil from behind his ear and made a notation on the paper.

"I've done everything Jessica left for me. Unless you have some work that needs doing, I'm going to go home."

"Can you give me a hand with this for a few minutes?"

"Of course." She hurried to his side.

He held out his tape measure without looking up from his drawing. "Check to see that the drawer heights are the same on all three drawers. They don't look quite even."

"Sure." She took the tape measure, being careful not to touch him.

After checking and rechecking the drawers, she handed the tape back to him. "The bottom drawer is one-quarter inch shallower than the others." She read off the measurements, and he jotted them down.

He tapped his lips with the eraser end of his pencil as he stared into space. "I've been thinking."

"About what?"

"Clyde."

"I honestly don't know how to keep him in without putting him in a locked kennel or a dog crate, and I don't think Charlotte will stand for that."

"You are right about the window. I don't see how he can get out that way. Charlotte has to be letting him out."

"She is adamant that she isn't."

"I hate to call her a liar, but she must be." He spun around on his stool to look at her. "Maybe she sleep-walks. I have a little sister that does."

Helen shrugged. "I guess it's a possibility. How would we tell unless we saw her doing it?"

"I can't expect you to sit up every night all night."

"I'm the last person you want for that job. I can fall asleep at the drop of a hat."

"So you won't be any help."

"I could ask her if she sleepwalks. Your aunt might know. Some of her friends might know if she does, but I would hate to start a lot of speculation if I started asking questions. Charlotte is a very private person."

"We could ask Clyde. If he says no, then we don't have to ask anyone else."

"Ha-ha. Very funny."

"When the answer is no, he lays down on the floor and whines."

"Are you trying to tell me that you speak dog now?"

"Clyde and I are reaching an understanding." He wagged his eyebrows.

She looked down and giggled. "Be serious."

"Believe me, my sleep is serious business."

"I'm sorry he is making such a pest of himself."

"Me, too." He turned back to his drawing.

Helen hesitated. The desire to stay and watch him work was strong, but she forced herself to start toward the door.

"Helen, I have an idea."

She turned around to see a mischievous grin on his face. This was not the Mark she had met on the bus or even later. This fellow with his sparkling green eyes and infectious smile was downright dangerous for her heart. "Let's hear it. How do we find out how he is getting out without watching the house all night?"

"That's exactly what I intend to do. Would you care to join me in some detective work?"

"I should hear your entire plan before I agree, but *ja*, count me in."

After hashing over the details of their plan, Helen went home, and Mark went up to the house. The family was gathering for lunch. The men had come in from the fields and were taking their places at the table. The women were busy in the kitchen. Paul hopped up from his seat and waved an envelope at Mark. "Another letter for you."

"From Angela?" Had she changed her mind? Part of him wanted her to and yet part of him didn't want that.

"It's from her father." Paul handed it over.

Mark took it and stared at Otis Yoder's spidery script. Inside was the information Mark had been waiting for. Was the land still available, or had Angela's change of heart ruined all his years of planning?

# Chapter Twelve

On Monday night, Helen waited until after midnight, then she quietly opened Charlotte's bedroom door and peeked inside. Clyde was snoring on his blanket in the corner. Her aunt was snoring, too. The curtain on the open window waved gently. The sash was up a foot. Enough for Clyde to squeeze through if he could get up there. Helen closed the door and liberally sprinkled flour on the wooden floor in front of it. She did the same outside the back door and outside the front door, then she slipped out of the house and crossed the yard to the buggy that was parked in the yard. She gave a squeak of surprise when Mark reached out to help her up.

"Shh." He held one finger to his lips.

"You frightened me. I wasn't expecting you to be here yet," she whispered as she climbed in. When Helen had finished with the buggy that morning, she'd left it positioned so that anyone in the driver's seat would have an unobstructed view of the front of the house and along the north side, where her aunt had her bedroom.

"Did you put fresh flour on the outside of the doors like I told you?"

She nodded and then realized he couldn't see that in

the dark. "I did just as you suggested. I also put some in front of my aunt's bedroom door. Anyone who goes that way will leave footprints. He has to be getting out her window somehow, but for the life of me I can't see how he is getting up to it. There's nothing under it that he can climb up on. Even standing on his hind legs, he can barely reach the window ledge with his front feet. I'm beginning to think he flies up by flapping those long ears."

"Now you're just being ridiculous."

"What's ridiculous is sitting in front of my aunt's house in the dead of night spying on a dog."

"You can go back in if you want."

"And miss the sight of Clyde flying out an open window? No way."

"He doesn't usually show up at my place until three or four in the morning. That means we may have a long wait ahead of us. Some nights he doesn't come in all. Are you sure you are up to this?"

"I'm as eager to solve this riddle as you are." But was she? Having Mark arrive with Clyde in time for breakfast and then drive her to work was something she enjoyed, but she could hardly admit that to Mark.

"I suggest that we take turns watching while the other one gets some rest. I can take the first watch."

"That's very practical, but I'm not the least bit sleepy at the moment. Why don't I take the first watch?"

"Okay." He scooted down to rest his head against the seat back and folded his arms across his chest.

His wide shoulders took up so much room that Helen had to scoot over to put a little distance between them so that their arms and shoulders weren't touching. She soon realized that not touching him didn't help. His presence beside her in the dark left her nerves standing on end. She scooted farther away, but that made the door handle poke her hip. She huffed and scooted back an inch.

He lifted his hat from over his face. "Is something wrong?"

"*Nee*, I'm just trying to get comfortable."

"It's hard to sleep with you bouncing up and down on the seat."

"I'm not bouncing up and down," she snapped.

"It feels like it to me."

She rolled her eyes. "I'm sorry. I'll try to be still."

He lowered his hat over his face. *"Goot."*

Helen stuck her tongue out at him and then had to stifle a giggle. She couldn't remember the last time she'd been that childish or enjoyed such excitement.

"What's so funny?" he asked without looking.

"Nothing," she said quickly and folded her hands primly in her lap. If Mark wasn't uncomfortable with their close proximity, then she wouldn't be, either. She focused her attention on the silent house. A three-quarter moon rose behind her and cast long black shadows in the gray darkness. The slow progress of the moon across the night sky was the only way to tell the passage of time.

Twice, she jerked herself upright after starting to doze off. Finally, she gave in and shook Mark's arm. He sat up. "Did you see something?"

"Nothing but the inside of my eyelids. It's your turn to keep watch."

He leaned forward to look up at the night sky. "It must be after two. Get some sleep, if you can. I'll wake you if I see a dog gliding out the window with his ears outstretched."

"Please do." Now that Mark was awake, Helen realized she was no longer sleepy. She sat silent for a few minutes then leaned toward him. "Have you ever done anything like this before?"

"Nope."

"Me neither."

"I find it hard to believe that a woman desirous of an independent life hasn't done a little sneaking around after dark."

"I did my share of running around with my friends as most Amish teens do during their *rumspringa*."

"And where did the scandalous Helen Zook go?"

"To the movies. Twice, no, three times. I went to five or six barn parties, but I didn't care for the loud music and dancing the kids were doing. Where did you go when you sneaked away from home?"

"I never did."

She turned to face him. Her eyes had adjusted to the dark. "Are you serious? You never slipped out to attend a movie or a barn dance or to have your *Englisch* friends drive you to a party?"

"Nope."

"I never figured you for a square."

"I was the oldest in the family. I had a responsibility to be a role model for the younger ones."

"Your responsibility is something you take seriously, isn't it?"

"Absolutely."

"I wasn't so *goot*."

"Why doesn't that surprise me?"

She heard the humor in his voice and knew he was teasing. "I never did anything I was ashamed of back then. I gave it all up when I took my baptismal vows. Have you taken yours?"

"I have. Three years ago."

"Because you intended to marry the girl back home?"

He shook his head. "We didn't have an understanding then. I knew I was going to remain Amish and saw no reason to delay."

"Was there anything that you hated to give up?" She tried to imagine the stern young man he would have been. In truth, he probably wasn't a lot different from the way he was now.

"I didn't like giving up my education. I got permission from our bishop to attend business night classes at a local high school. The teacher there took an interest in me and did some private tutoring. She made sure I expanded my vocabulary. After that, I read extensively. I still do. I don't feel there is anything crucial that I have missed by being Amish. Being close to God is worth any sacrifice. What do you miss? Parties?"

"I had a cell phone," she admitted wistfully. "Four of my friends had them, too. We talked all the time."

"Do you miss your friends back in Indiana?"

"I miss them and my family. I was close to my mother and father."

"You aren't close anymore?"

"They took my sister's side. I was bitterly disappointed that they did. Rebecca told me a little about your family. It sounds as if your father disappointed you, too."

He was silent for so long that Helen thought he wasn't going to discuss it, but eventually he cleared his throat and said, "More than once."

Mark couldn't believe he was sharing that part of his life with Helen. Somehow, sitting in the dark made it easier to talk. He couldn't see the sympathy in her eyes, but he knew it was there. She cared about him as he cared about her. The tenderness she evoked in him was unlike anything he'd ever known. Was it possible he was falling for her? He pushed the thought aside and refused to examine it.

"Some people say talking about your troubles helps," she said softly.

"Some people are wrong," he quoted her own words back to her.

"A few of them are right. In what way did your father disappoint you?"

"It's ancient history. You don't want to hear it."

"Mark, you and I have become friends. You have helped me so much. I won't judge you or your family. If you want to talk, I'll listen."

He did want her to know, and that surprised him. "It's no dark secret. Many know my father is a failure in just about every sense of the word. He never could hold a job. He couldn't take care of my mother when she became ill. I was sent to live with anyone who said I could stay with them. Most people were very kind. A few were not. They saw me as an unpaid laborer, and I had to work very hard. Every time Daed dropped me off with a new friend or relative, I didn't know if he would come back for me. He'd be gone for months without sending any word. Then one day he would show up, and we'd be together for a few weeks before I was sent away again."

"That must have been terrible for a small child."

It soothed his soul that she understood. "Fortunately, when I was eight, he sent me to live with Isaac and Anna. That was the best thing that ever happened to me. I became a part of a real family. I saw how a mother and father could work together to provide for their children. I saw carefully laid plans brought to fruition by hard work."

"But you eventually went back to live with your father."

"He met and married a fine woman. The day I met my new mother, I met my new brother, Paul. We hit it off and became best friends. I have five younger sisters now, too, but it was years before I got over the fear that my father would send me away again. He still bounces from job to job, but Mamm has put her foot down. She won't move. Paul and I send money home for her and the girls. Daed is the reason I've got to make a success of my business back home."

"Are you hoping to impress him or prove that you can do what he never could?"

He shook his head. "You have it all wrong. If I am running a successful business, he will always have a job with me no matter how often he quits and comes back. Best of all, I will be living and working a short walk down the road from my family. My sisters will never have to worry about being split up and sent away if something should happen to their mother."

Helen leaned in and kissed his cheek. "Thank you for sharing this with me."

He froze in astonishment, glad she couldn't see how red his face must be turning.

She sat back. "You are a much better person than I am."

"I find that hard to believe."

"You wouldn't if you knew more about me."

He cleared his throat. "I told you about my past and my plans. Turnabout is fair play."

"I'm serious. I wasn't a nice person. I don't want to lower your opinion of me."

He wanted her to trust him enough to confide in him. "My opinion of you has gone from pretty low to fairly high in the space of two short weeks. I accept who you are now. Not who you were before. But if you don't wish to tell me, I understand."

Helen hesitated. Not because she didn't believe him but because she didn't like to remember the hurt she had caused. He waited patiently without saying anything else, so she asked God for strength and started speaking. "Do you remember me telling you that my fiancé announced he wanted to marry my sister a few weeks before our wedding?"

"I remember."

"That isn't the whole story. Joseph was considered an excellent catch in our community. His grandfather is our bishop. His father owns a prosperous farm, and Joseph was his only son." She wished she could gloss over the rest, but it was time to admit that she had been at fault, too.

"My friends and I were all smitten with Joseph. We were shocked when he bypassed us and asked my sister, Olivia, to walk out with him. Olivia is gentle and quiet. She's never said a bad word against anyone. She works hard and never complains, but she isn't the brightest person. She didn't do well in school."

"School grades don't determine a person's success in life."

"I know, but it was humiliating that my little sister was going out with the most eligible man in our district. I set out to take him away from her. I was coy, I used flattery, I put it into my sister's head that he really liked me and was just being kind to her. She believed me and stopped going out with him. I consoled him after telling him she wasn't in love with him. I made sure I saw him often. One day, he asked to walk out with me."

"That doesn't seem like the Helen Zook I know."

"The Lord has taken me down a peg or two since that time, and I deserved it. Eventually, Joseph proposed to me, and I had everything I desired. Then his mother became ill. Olivia went to help care for her. In the weeks that she worked for his family, Joseph rediscovered what a treasure Olivia is. He asked me to release him from his promise. I said no. Eventually, he got up the courage to take matters into his own hands. He told my parents and his grandfather, the bishop, that he could not in good conscience marry me."

"It was for the best."

"I know that now but I didn't then. Word of my humiliation spread quickly. The morning of their wedding, I decided to leave. I never told anyone where I was going. I wasn't sure Charlotte would take me in. When she heard my version of the story, she wasn't as sympathetic as I expected, but she let me stay for the summer."

"So you weren't in love with Joseph?"

"That's the irony of it. I grew to care a great deal for Joseph, and I prayed he would one day love me half as much as he loved my sister. The tears you saw me weeping on the bus were real. I was selfish and cruel, and I didn't deserve his love. I hurt two kind and gentle people with my false pride. I ran away rather than face what I had done. I left them to worry and wonder where I was rather than offering them the blessings they deserve. I did find the courage to write my parents and tell them where I'm staying. They haven't written back yet. So now you know."

"I don't think any less of you for hearing this story. You have recognized your flaws, and you seek to overcome them. You have shown compassion to Charlotte.

I've seen you work hard at your job and at your baking business. I'm pleased to call you my friend."

Mark was more understanding than she deserved. Her attempts to keep her feelings for him those of a friend were quickly coming undone. "Angela is a blessed woman," she whispered.

He looked away. "Angela has had a change of heart. She has ended our understanding."

"What? How could she? Why would she?" Helen's voice rose. He hushed her with a finger to his lips.

"Did she say why?" Helen whispered.

"She didn't give a reason in her letter to me. I heard from her father yesterday. He wrote to say she has not given him a reason, either. Only that she believes she made a mistake in agreeing in the first place. He says he will continue to try to persuade her to honor her agreement, but he considers I am at fault, too, for staying away and not securing her affections after all this time. He also says he will not sell me the land I need unless we are wed."

"You should go home and find out what's wrong. As a friend and as a woman, I'm telling you that you need to speak to Angela in person."

It wasn't the reaction he expected from Helen, but he wasn't sure what he thought she would say. "I will give some thought to your suggestion. It seems pointless to spend the money to travel now when I return for good in another month."

"You shouldn't delay."

Was she right? Without the property he wanted or the money he had paid to Angela, he had no option left but to start over from scratch. His well-thought-out plans had come to nothing. He was at fault. He saw that now.

He had neglected to consider Angela's needs in their arrangement, but rushing back to her wasn't the answer. Even if she changed her mind, he couldn't enter into a loveless marriage. It wasn't Angela he wanted by his side for the rest of his life. It was Helen.

Movement on the north side of the house caught his attention. Glad for the distraction, he sat up straight. "Something is going on."

"Can you see what?"

It was hard to distinguish things in the patchwork of shadows cast by the moon. "It looks like your aunt is sticking something out of her window."

"I think you're right. Is that a board?"

They watched in silence as Charlotte pushed a long plank out her window and let the end drop onto the grass. Mark realized what she was doing. "It's a ramp."

The words were no sooner out of his mouth than Clyde scrambled out the window and trotted down the plank. He took off at a run toward the Bowman house. Helen looked at Mark. "She lied to my face."

"Technically, she didn't. She said she did not open the front door or the back door for him."

Helen scrambled out of the buggy. "She lied by omission, and she has a lot of explaining to do."

"You talk to her. I'm going to try and intercept Clyde before he wakes the household."

"Take my bike."

"*Danki*, but my horse and buggy are just down the road."

Helen entered the house and went straight into her aunt's bedroom without knocking. Charlotte was pulling the outside board in through the wide-open window.

An identical board led from the window to the floor. Clyde had merely trotted up, over and out.

"Aenti, what do you think you are doing?"

Charlotte spun around with the slats in her hands. She crossed the room and slipped them under her mattress. "I'm making my bed dear. Is there something you need?" She tucked the sheet in and turned to face Helen.

"I need an explanation. Mark and I saw you let Clyde out the window."

Charlotte clasped her hands behind her back. "You did?"

"Why would you want to annoy the Bowmans like this?"

"Oh, I'm not trying to annoy the Bowmans. Anna is a good friend of mine. Clyde wanted to make sure Mark had an opportunity to spend time with you."

"Don't put any of this on Clyde. He's a dog. You, on the other hand, know better. Poor Mark has missed hours of sleep because of you."

"I'm trying to tell you it wasn't entirely my idea. Clyde likes Mark and you, too. He thinks the two of you belong together. I've merely been helping Clyde achieve his goal. He fancies himself something of a matchmaker."

"I don't care what Clyde thinks. Mark and I are friends, and that's all. He is leaving in a few weeks, and I will probably never see him again." The words tightened Helen's throat. She was going to miss him. She hadn't realized how much until this moment.

"How do you get him to go to the Bowman house every time he is loose?" Helen still couldn't believe her aunt had concocted such a scheme.

"I don't tell him where to go. I believe he is looking for Juliet, and I don't understand why he insists on stopping at the Bowman's tree unless it's to summon Mark."

"I'm ashamed of you, Aenti Charlotte. I don't know how I'm going to explain your far-fetched scheme to Mark without dying of embarrassment. A matchmaking dog. That's just ridiculous."

"Please don't tell that to Clyde. You'll hurt his feelings."

Helen shook her head in disbelief. She forced herself to use a milder tone. "Go to bed and get some sleep. I'll wait up for Mark to bring Clyde home."

"Are you angry with me?" Charlotte looked ready to cry.

"We'll talk about this in the morning."

Helen went to the kitchen and put the coffeepot on the stove. She wanted a freshly brewed pot ready when Mark returned. She had a feeling they might need it.

A half hour later, she heard the buggy pull up outside and went to open the door. Clyde came galloping in with his ears streaming back. He slid to a halt at her feet and looked up with a happy expression.

Mark's expression wasn't quite so happy. "What did she have to say?"

"It's all Clyde's doing. He fancies himself a matchmaker, and he gets you up so you can come spend time with me."

"She said that?" He rubbed a hand through his hair as he blew out a deep breath.

"She did and with a straight face. What am I going to do with her? I'm worried something is seriously wrong. Should I take her to see a doctor?"

"I don't know what to tell you. Maybe you should speak to Anna or Rebecca. Rebecca has nursing experience."

"Charlotte owes you and your family an apology if nothing else, but I will seek Anna's council. She has known Charlotte a long time. Do you want some coffee?"

"Sure."

Helen needed to do something. Mark moved to stand beside her. She pulled down the cups and started to hand him one but dropped it. They both tried to catch it, but it hit the floor and broke. Helen stared at the shattered pieces. "Do you think my unexpected arrival put too much stress on Charlotte's mind, or is Juliet's disappearance to blame?"

"Your aunt told Anna that she enjoys having you here. Maybe the loss of Juliet was too much."

Tears stung Helen's eyes and closed her throat, making it hard to speak. "I wish I knew what to do."

Mark drew her into a hug. "We'll figure it out. She'll get all the care she needs."

Helen rested in his arms with her head tucked beneath his chin. She'd never felt more comforted than she did at that moment. "I don't want to hurt one more person with my selfishness."

"You aren't." He slipped his hand under her chin and tipped her face up to meet his gaze. "You need to be strong for her."

"I don't feel strong."

"But you are. God placed you with Charlotte for a reason, and I think it was because she was going to need someone special."

"I'm not special."

He leaned close and rested his forehead against hers. "I think you are," he whispered.

His arms tightened around her. She knew he was going to kiss her.

# Chapter Thirteen

Helen's lips were a breath away from his. Mark wasn't sure how they had gotten so close to his, but the desire to kiss her was a great weight pressing him closer still. It took every ounce of strength he had to hold himself that breath away.

He had nothing to offer her. Not even a plan for the future. How could he begin courting her when she thought he should go back to Angela? Rather than fight a losing battle, he moved slightly to the side and kissed her cheek. The softness of her skin beneath his lips startled him and begged him to explore the contours of her face. She turned away, leaving him bereft in a swirling sea of confusion.

It wasn't friendship or a wish to comfort her that quickened his pulse and robbed the air from his lungs.

He didn't understand the powerful attraction she held for him, but he was starting to believe it was love. He stepped back and let his arms fall to his sides. With a little more distance between them, he was able to think coherently. "It's late. I should be getting home."

She knelt and began picking up the broken pieces

of the cup. "Please tell Anna and Rebecca that Charlotte and I will come by for a visit later this morning."

"I will." Should he apologize for kissing her? Maybe it was better to pretend the gesture was meant to comfort her. If she didn't say anything, he wouldn't, either.

"I won't be into work. I don't think Charlotte should be left alone. I hope you understand." She didn't look at him.

"Jessica can take care of anything that comes along. Let me know if you need something."

"I'm okay. We'll be okay. Clyde can sleep in my room for the rest of the night. You don't need to worry about a return visit."

"I was just getting used to him as my alarm clock."

She didn't smile as he hoped she would. She still hadn't looked at him. Rising to her feet, she carried the debris to the wastebasket and dropped it in. "*Danki*, Mark, for everything."

"I'll see you later. Get some rest now, and try not to worry about Charlotte."

She finally glanced his way and managed a shaky smile. "I'll do my best. Good night."

"*Guten nacht.*"

The urge to take her back in his arms sent him out the door, wishing he wasn't quite so strong but thankful that he'd come to his senses in time. How would he avoid giving in to the temptation to kiss her when he saw her every day? As he climbed into his buggy, he realized the answer was simple. He couldn't be alone with her. Or he had to convince her that she was the woman he wanted to court.

Everything he thought he knew about love had changed in the last few days. It wasn't a frivolous feeling. It was a deep and profound emotion that made his heart ache with the need to be close to Helen. He'd never be the same after tonight. He'd never look at her the same way again.

What was he going to do about it?

He had no idea how she felt about him beyond her friendship, but she professed to want an independent life, not marriage. Could he change her mind? Should he try, or would that destroy the very real friendship they shared? He wasn't sure what to do.

He had to have a plan.

Thunder rumbled in the distance as a sprinkle of rain began falling. He watched the light in the kitchen window until it grew dim and faded. The glow soon brightened the window near the back of the house, and he knew she had gone down the hall to her bedroom.

The wind rose, and the rain began in earnest, hitting the top of his buggy as the storm rolled in. He waited until Helen's light went out before he started for home. He had a lot of thinking to do and new plans to make. He'd never courted a woman before, but he intended to court Helen Zook. And he was going to need help.

Charlotte was as cheerful as ever the next morning when Helen entered the kitchen. She was scrambling eggs. "I made some coffee, if you want it. What would you like to take for your lunch today? We have some leftover meatloaf that would make a good sandwich."

"I'm not going to work today, so you don't need to make my lunch. I thought we should visit Anna today. You owe her and Isaac an apology."

"I guess I do, but Anna will understand. She knows about Clyde's talent." She carried the skillet to Clyde's bowl and gave him a portion of eggs before moving to the table and dividing the rest between her plate and

Helen's. The two women ate in silence. Helen was glad for that. She couldn't make idle chitchat if she wanted to.

She had been sure that Mark intended to kiss her. Why had he given her a peck on the cheek instead? Had she mistaken his intentions? Had the bold way she offered her lips to him disgusted him? It would be difficult to pretend she cared about him as a friend when he was so much more. The sensible thing was to avoid being alone with him in the future.

"What did you and Mark talk about for so long last night?" Charlotte asked, looking at Helen over the rim of her coffee cup.

"This and that. Nothing really. Chitchat mostly."

"Strange. I was certain I heard you talking about me."

Helen leveled a stern look at Charlotte. "Were you eavesdropping?"

Charlotte shook her head. "Absolutely not. I just happen to be in the hallway outside the kitchen doorway."

"Why were you in the hallway?"

"That's a silly question. I couldn't hear a thing in my room." She winked at Helen.

Helen had to smile at her confession. "Eavesdroppers rarely hear anything good about themselves."

"*They* say that's true, but I still don't know who *they* are. What time are we going over to see Anna?"

"After I do these dishes and wash a load of clothes. I don't have a single clean apron to wear. Everything is covered in flour."

"You will have to invest in some material to make more white ones. Flour won't show on them as much. I will go fill the washer for you. I think we are done with the rain, so you can hang them out on the line without a worry."

It took about Helen an hour and a half to wash her aprons and dresses along with several of Charlotte's in the surprisingly new wringer washer Charlotte had on her back porch. When the line of blue and mauve dresses and black aprons were fluttering on the clothesline at the side of the house, Helen hitched up the buggy and waited for her aunt to join her. She came out a few minutes later with Clyde trotting beside her.

It didn't take long to reach the Bowman house. Paul was outside and offered to take care of the horse, and the two women went in. Anna greeted each of them with a holy kiss on the lips, surprising Helen. The gesture was normally used at baptisms in Helen's congregation. It wasn't common practice to do it outside of a special occasion.

"Come in the living room and sit down," Anna said. "Rebecca and Lillian are here, too."

"Where is Mark?" Charlotte asked, taking a seat.

"He and Isaac are trying to decide the best way to take that old tree down. A limb broke off and hit the roof in the storm last night. I'm sure he'll be in soon." Anna took a seat beside Charlotte.

The silence stretched for an uncomfortable long minute until Charlotte turned to Helen. "Aren't you going to tell them how crazy I am?"

"You aren't crazy, Aenti," Helen rushed to reassure her. "But you have put this family through some uncomfortable nights by your actions. You need to apologize."

Charlotte chuckled and smiled at Anna. "Clyde has been matchmaking again."

"So I have noticed," Anna replied with a grin. She patted the dog sitting beside her.

Charlotte cast a sidelong glance at Helen. "My niece doesn't believe he has such a talent."

"Dogs can't be matchmakers. It's not possible," Mark said from the doorway. He entered the room and sat down across from Helen. She was glad to have him there.

"Actually, Clyde has something of a reputation for doing just that," Rebecca said gently.

Helen couldn't believe what she was hearing. "You can't be serious."

"Oh, she is," Lillian added. "I've seen it myself."

"You met Grace Yoder at the frolic, didn't you?" Charlotte asked.

Helen combed her memory. "The elderly lady in the wheelchair?"

Charlotte nodded and leaned forward in her chair. "Last year she was attending a wedding for one of our nice young couples. She was Grace Troyer then. I needed my hands free, so she offered to hold Clyde's leash. She tied it to the arm of her wheelchair. Clyde bolted across the lawn, pulling her behind him, and ran right into Silas Yoder. He ended up in Grace's lap as Clyde raced down the lane, pulling both of them. When he stopped and people caught up with them, Grace and Silas were sharing a great laugh. She said it was the most fun she had had in years. It wasn't two months before their banns were announced. Everyone was stunned except Clyde and me."

"It was a coincidence," Mark said with a dismissive gesture.

Rebecca gave a slight shake of her head. "We can name four other instances where Clyde's activities brought couples together who wouldn't normally have gone out with each other. They all married."

Helen rose to her feet and paced across the room and back. "This is ridiculous. Mark and I aren't meant to be a match."

"Clyde thinks so," Charlotte declared. "I might be a little crazy, but I usually understand what my boy is telling me."

Mark rose to his feet. "This is food for thought."

Helen spun to face him. "You can't be serious."

He headed for the door but paused to look back. "I have work to do. Since Charlotte is fine, perhaps you could come out to the shop and give us a hand, Helen?"

She caught the slight come-with-me nod he gave her as he opened the door. It was better than staying and listening to this nonsense. Besides, she wanted to hear his explanation of food for thought.

His aunt spoke up. "Helen, I wanted to ask you before you go if you would be able to work in the gift shop for a few hours a week from Wednesday? The family has been invited to a picnic with Fannie's family. It's her birthday, but I hate to close the shop. We have an Amish country tour bus scheduled to stop for refreshments that day."

Charlotte huffed and crossed her arms. "Tourists. There are more every day."

"They are *goot* for business, and we must show kindness to strangers," Anna said with a stern look for Charlotte, who rolled her eyes without commenting.

"I'd be happy to help out," Helen said, eager to be gone.

Anna smiled. "*Danki*, my dear."

"We'll see that Charlotte and Clyde get home later this morning," Lillian added.

Helen went out the door with Mark, forgetting for the moment that she wasn't going to be alone with him anymore. Once they were away from the house, she hurried to keep up with him. "You don't believe any of that, do you?"

He kept walking. "That a dog knows who should marry? Of course not. But Charlotte believes it, so we will play along to keep her happy, and she'll keep Clyde at home."

Helen stopped. "What do you mean play along?"

He turned to face her and hooked his thumbs under his suspenders. "We do what we've been doing. I'll come by for breakfast and give you a ride to work. I'll even go to the market with you. The difference will be that I, and the whole house, can sleep until a decent hour."

"I'm not sure about this." Wasn't spending time with him what she wanted to avoid?

"Let's give it a try. If it doesn't work out, we'll try something else."

"Okay. I guess I can do that for the few weeks you have left here." She tugged nervously on the ribbons of her *kapp*. She could pretend they were still friends for that long, couldn't she?

Mark almost shouted for joy when she agreed. He never would have believed his courting help would come from a dog. God had a wondrous sense of humor. Mark didn't have a new plan for his business yet, but he was willing to give the problem over to God to solve for the first time in his life. A great weight lifted from his shoulders.

Inside the woodworking shop, Mark began carving the intricate detail along the edge of the reproduction dresser while Helen went to work in the office.

An hour later, Mark looked up to see his uncle

watching him. He straightened. "Is there something you wanted?"

"I just like to watch a fine craftsman at work." He moved closer and drew his hands around the surface. "This is *goot* work, Mark. You are getting better all the time."

Mark took a step back. "I like to bring the beauty God put into the wood out for all to see."

"The understanding and respect you have for the piece shows. If you weren't so set on your own plan, I'd tell you to follow your heart and see where it leads you."

Mark frowned at his uncle. "I don't know what you mean."

Isaac laid his hand on Mark's shoulder. "You have a head for business, but you have the heart of an artist."

Isaac left the work area, leaving Mark to stare after him and ponder his words.

It wasn't until later in the afternoon that Helen left the office. He saw her coming his way and slipped her nearly complete spice rack beneath his table.

She turned her head first one way and then another to study the dresser top he had finished. "That's *goot*, Mark."

"I'm satisfied."

The smile she pasted on her face looked as if it might crack. "Have you decided what you are going to do about Angela?"

He took a deep breath. "I'm not going home to see her."

"Then you should write her a letter and explain how you feel," Helen stated firmly.

"She doesn't want to marry me."

Helen kept her gazed fixed on the dresser, avoiding his eyes. "You haven't even tried to change her mind. Have you told her you miss her and how much you look forward to the end of your time here? If you haven't said it in so many words, she doesn't know those things. A woman needs to know how a man truly feels about her in plain words. You can't leave her guessing."

What did Helen want to hear from a man who was falling in love with her? Who better to tell him than her? "What could I write that would change a woman's mind? What would you want to hear?"

Helen stared down at his tabletop. "We aren't talking about me."

He picked up a pen and took a clean sheet of paper from his top drawer. "Where do I start? *Dear* or *dearest*?"

She looked at him. "How do you usually start your letters?"

"I just use her name. 'To Angela, my sister in Christ.'"

"Then I would start with *my dearest Angela*."

"*My dearest*. All right, what else could I say that might win her over?"

Helen straightened the tools on his desk and lined them up neatly. "Tell her what is in your heart."

"Like what?"

"How do you feel when she isn't with you?"

He bent over the paper. "Every day that I am not with you is like living inside a dark cloud. How is that?"

"Nice."

"Just nice?"

"You can do better."

"You bring light to my world, to my heart and soul. My heart smiles every time I close my eyes and imagine your face. I dream that one day your heart will smile back at mine."

"That's beautiful, Mark."

"You like it?"

Helen cleared her throat. "I'm sure she will."

He bent over his paper again. "When I can't sleep, I look up at the moon in the night sky, and I wonder if you are looking at it, too. It comforts me to know you and I share something so lovely." He looked up. "What else should I say?"

"Tell her what she does that makes you happy"

"Everything you do makes me happy."

"Specifics are better."

He nodded. "I love the way you tap your foot when you are feeling impatient, and that cute pout on your lips makes me want to kiss you into a better mood."

Helen stepped back and put her hands in her pockets. "You have the idea now. No point in my eavesdropping any longer."

"Would those words make you come back to a man?"

She gazed at him. "Only if I knew that he loved me."

"How could you be sure of that?"

"By the way he kissed me." She looked away. "Go see her in person."

"Did you know Joseph didn't love you by the way he kissed you?"

"Maybe I did." She marched out of the room, letting the door slam behind her.

Mark sighed. How could he convince Helen of his feelings if she thought he wanted a different woman? How could he make her believe the truth?

He turned back to his work and noticed Paul standing a few feet away. How much had he overheard?

"I wondered what was wrong with you. Now I know," Paul said, coming to stand beside Mark.

"What do you think you know?"

"You're in love with Helen. *The moon in the night sky*, I may use that line myself."

"Helen was helping me write a letter to Angela."

"That's not who you were thinking of. I saw your face when you looked at Helen."

"Okay, I wasn't writing to Angela. I was trying to find out what Helen would want to hear from a man who's falling in love with her."

"Want some advice?"

"No. Yes." Mark raked both hands through his hair. "I had everything figured out, Paul. I had a way to build a business with Angela's father that would keep Daed working and provide security for our sisters so they would never have to be sent to live with strangers."

"Whoa." Paul leaned in to look Mark in the eyes. "Why would our sisters ever be sent to live with strangers?"

Mark shrugged. "Bad things happen."

"Like your mother dying?"

"That's right. And like your father."

Paul took Mark by his shoulders and gave him a gentle shake. "I know your dad shuffled you off to different places when he couldn't get work. Mamm told me about that, but you and I would never let that happen to our sisters. Would we?"

Paul slapped a hand to his chest. "I wouldn't let that happen. We are a family. We'll always be a family, and we'll always look out for each other. Isaac and Anna, Noah and Fannie, Samuel and Rebecca and their children, Timothy and Lillian, Joshua, Mary and Hannah, Luke and Emma, my mother and all our sisters and your father and the members of our church, not to mention our God in heaven who looks after all His children. You aren't alone, Mark. You aren't the only one responsible for what happens to us."

Mark wrestled with his need to be in control even

as he realized how fruitless his attempt had been. "But I'm the oldest son."

Paul straightened. "You might be the oldest, but you aren't the only one who cares. Is that why you were going to marry Angela? So you could go into business with her father?"

"It seemed like a good plan at the time. Fortunately, Angela has decided she won't marry me, but Helen thinks I can convince her otherwise."

"Well, your letter-writing exercise didn't help there."

"Thanks for that bit of useless insight. Tell me, how can I convince Helen she is the one I want and not Angela?"

"Knowing how stubborn Helen can be when she sets her mind to a thing, you shouldn't rush her. You two are friends. Continue to be her friend and pray her feelings grow into something more. I think she is already in love with you, but she isn't ready to admit it."

"I don't know. I don't have anything to offer her. No job, no business prospects. Nothing."

"What do you mean no job? I've heard Onkel Isaac tell you many times that you can stay here and work with him."

"It wouldn't be my business." Was that really so important anymore?

"That's where you're wrong. This is the family's business. You and I are already a part of it. We have been since the day we arrived."

Paul was right. God had been working on a plan for Mark's life without him even realizing it. Mark reached out and ruffled his brother's hair. "How did you get to be so smart?"

Paul playfully slapped his hand away. "Not because of anything my big brother taught me."

* * *

Helen was amazed at how easily she and Mark slipped back into old habits. He showed up for breakfast at Charlotte's three times the following week without Clyde bringing him. Sometimes she caught him staring at her with a look of longing on his face, but he would quickly look away and make a joke or tease Charlotte. On Friday, he accompanied her, along with her aunt and Clyde, to the farmers' market. Clyde and his clowning drew a crowd again, and Helen sold out of the dog biscuits before the evening was half over and took orders for another dozen packages. She was happy to stay busy because it kept her mind off how much she wanted to tell Mark about her growing feelings for him.

There was no point in denying it any longer. She was in love with him, but she couldn't say anything. She wouldn't. She had come between two people who belonged together once before and hurt them deeply in the process. She would never do anything to hurt Mark. She knew how much his plans and his family's security meant to him.

Charlotte still spent hours searching for Juliet each day. Helen had given up all hope of finding the raccoon, but Charlotte wouldn't. Clyde remained in her room all through the night and didn't bother the Bowmans again.

On Saturday, Mark helped Helen stock her unsold items in Anna's gift shop. He carried in two large boxes for her and then stood looking around. "Where do you want these?"

"I've been putting some of the breads and rolls beside the honey and jams Anna has for sale. I put the rest of the baked goods on the table at the back."

He removed several packages of bread from her box and handed them to her to arrange to her satisfaction.

"I think you should display the cookies, cake pops and dog treats beside the checkout counter. You'll get more impulse buys that way."

"You might be right." She set out the bread and headed toward the table Anna had set up for Helen's display. She moved behind the table to put a little more distance between Mark and herself.

Mark chuckled, and Helen dipped her head. She loved the sound of his laughter. "What's so funny?"

"You should have Clyde in here to point toward the dog biscuits and clown for people."

She shook her head as she put more of the goods on the table. "I don't think that's a wise idea. How many of Anna's customers would enjoy being knocked down by him?"

He planted his hands on the table and leaned toward her. She looked up and met his gaze. "Some fellas might enjoy having a pretty girl pushed into their arms. I did."

Helen felt the heat rush to her face. "I don't remember it that way."

Mark walked around the table and stood close beside her. Too close, but she couldn't move away. Every moment, it became harder to keep her feelings hidden and pretend she didn't love him. More than anything, she wanted to be held in his arms and feel the touch of his lips on hers.

"It was the loss of your cream horns that upset me." He picked up a package of them and began to unwrap it.

"Those are for sale," she said, but her voice cracked. She hoped he didn't notice.

"I'll pay for them." He took out one and bit into it but he made a sour face. "There's something wrong with these. They aren't sweet enough."

Had she made a mistake in the recipe? "Really?"

"Try a bite and see what you think." He turned the

pastry around so she could sample the other end but he still held it between his fingers.

She was forced to lean forward slightly. She took a quick nibble, then pulled away. "It tastes okay to me."

He used his thumb to brush away some crumbs at the corner of her mouth. She licked her lips to remove the tingle, but it didn't help.

"I remember them being much sweeter," Mark said softly as he cupped his hand beneath her chin and leaned toward her.

Helen closed her eyes as his lips touched hers ever so softly. Her heart soared with joy. Nothing could be sweeter than this. It was everything she dreamed of and more.

The next second, he drew away. She wanted to pull him back, to know that happiness again, but the bell over the door jingled as a customer came in, forcing her return to reality. She pressed her fingers to her lips as she stared at Mark. "I'm sorry I let that happen," she whispered hoarsely.

"I'm not." The tender look in his eyes was more than she could bear.

Helen fled, leaving the rest of her goods in the boxes.

Thankfully, she was able to avoid seeing Mark on Sunday except for brief glances during the church service. She didn't stay for the lunch, giving him no opportunity to seek her out. All afternoon and evening, she waited for him to come see her at home, but he didn't. In her mind, it was proof that the kiss had been a mistake.

When Mark didn't show up for breakfast the next morning, Helen was deeply relieved. She still had no idea how she could face him or what she would say. Taking a clue from his absence, she decided the best thing to do was to pretend it never happened.

When she reached the office, she learned he would be away on business for the next several days, and she breathed a sigh of relief. She wasn't at all certain she could pull off such a pretense.

On Tuesday, the mail carrier brought Helen the letter she had been both dreading and praying to receive. It was from her family. She carried the letter down to the bank of the river to read in private. Tearing open the envelope, she pulled out a single sheet of paper. There was one line written on it.

*Helen, Come home for we all love and miss you. Olivia.*

Tears poured down Helen's cheeks as she clutched the letter to her chest. She loved them and missed them, too. Her shame and her pride had kept her away, but her sister's words bound up the wounds of her heart. She could go home. Maybe there, she could eventually forget about Mark and the love she didn't dare admit.

The next morning, Helen was putting out packages of cookies and cake pops to replace the ones that had sold in the gift shop. The entire Bowman family, including Mark, had gone to a picnic with Fannie's parents to celebrate Fannie's birthday, making one more day that Helen didn't have to face him. She hadn't told anyone about her plans to return home, but she would have to do so soon.

The bell over the door jingled. Helen looked up to see who had entered. It was a tall Amish woman with a wary expression on her face.

Helen smiled. "Welcome to our gift store. Feel free

to look around. Be sure to ask me for help if you need it. Are you looking for something special?"

"I'm not shopping. I hoped you could tell me where I might find Mark Bowman. I've been to the house, but no one is there, and the business seems to be closed until later today."

"Mark and his family have gone on a picnic with the Erb family. It's a birthday party for their daughter, but he should back before long. Is he expecting you? I can give you directions to the Erb farm."

"Mark isn't expecting me. In fact, I'm sure he'll be shocked to see me. I'll just wait, if that's okay." She carried a small suitcase in one hand, and Helen wondered who she was.

"Of course. You are welcome to wait here, or you can go over to the house and wait there. The Bowmans won't mind. I'm Helen Zook. I'm a neighbor."

The woman smiled. "It's nice to meet you, Helen. I'm Angela Yoder."

Helen stared at her in shock. "From Pennsylvania?"

"I take it Mark has mentioned me."

"He has." What did Angela want? Why had she come all this way to see Mark when he was returning to Pennsylvania in another few weeks?

"I'm on my way to a cousin's wedding in Millersburg, and I had my driver stop here since I was this close. I wasn't expecting to wait. I can't stay long."

"I'm sure Mark will be delighted to see you."

"I hope so. I sure do hope so," Angela muttered more to herself than to Helen. "What has he said about me?"

"That you and he had an understanding but that you changed your mind."

Angela's laugh sounded flat. "I guess he has told you quite a bit. You must know him well."

"We're friends."

"That's more than I can say, and I'm going to marry him."

Helen's heart plunged to her feet. She should be glad for him, but all she felt was heartbreak. "Mark is a fine man. He is honest and hardworking. He will make a loving and comforting husband. He deserves to be happy, and so do you."

"I hope what I have to tell him will make us both happy."

Mark's letter must have convinced her to give him another chance. "His dream of a business back home means everything to him."

"I'm glad to know that."

Helen noticed the Bowmans' buggy turn in and stop. Mark and Anna got out, but Isaac and the others drove on. "Here he comes now."

The bell over the door jangled as Mark and his aunt entered. Anna pulled off her black traveling bonnet. "I'm ever so grateful that you kept an eye on things here, Helen, but you are free to go now." She went behind the counter and hung up her bonnet.

Mark had seen Angela. He looked frozen in place. Angela walked toward him. "Hello, Mark."

"Angela! What are you doing here?"

Angela glanced around nervously. "I wanted to see you. I've made a mistake. Is there somewhere private that we can talk?"

He glanced at Helen. She turned away to finish filling the shelf and to hide the tears pricking the backs of her eyes.

"Angela, if you will step across to the woodworking shop, I'll be over in a few minutes and we can talk in my office. I need to speak to Helen first."

"Okay." Angela glanced between them but went out the door.

"Don't keep her waiting, Mark. She came a long way. Your letter convinced her to change her mind." Helen moved farther down the counter.

"Helen, please. I want to tell you how much you have come to mean to me."

She turned around with a bright smile frozen in place. "Your friendship has meant the world to me, too."

"I think we both know this is more than friendship between us, Helen. I haven't forgotten our kiss."

Neither had she. She drew a deep breath and faced him. "I've had a letter from my sister asking me to come home. I'm going."

He frowned. "When did you decide this?"

"After I read my sister's letter. I've been very selfish. I didn't realize how much my leaving hurt everyone. I need to reconcile with her and the rest of my family."

"Then you'll come back?"

She saw the hope in his eyes and couldn't bear it. If he gave up his dream for her, she would always regret causing that. "*Nee.* Nappanee is my home. That's where I belong."

"What about Charlotte?"

"She is tired of having me in the house. She'll do fine. She has friends and the church to look after her."

"When are you leaving?"

"The soonest I can get a bus home is Saturday."

"What about us?" he asked softly.

She sighed deeply and turned to him. "You and I will always be friends. I hope you'll write and tell me how the business is doing and if your father is enjoying working with you."

He stepped up to grasp her shoulders. "I thought we had something special."

"We had a special friendship. I'm sorry if you thought it was something more. Go to Angela. You have everything you've dreamed of now." She pulled away and fled out the door before she could blurt out that she loved him.

Mark watched Helen leave as a wave of sorrow nearly brought him to his knees. He should have found a way to make her stay and listen to him. He should have told her sooner how much he loved her and how much he wanted her to be a part of his life. How could she not love him in return? How could she walk away? Bereft as much now as he had been as a child, he blinked back tears.

Maybe he shouldn't have kissed her.

No, if nothing else, he would have that one sweet memory to carry with him forever.

"I'm sorry, Mark." He'd forgotten Anna was still there until she spoke.

"She doesn't love me. Am I so hard to love? What's wrong with me?"

Anna came and put her arms around him, pulling him close to comfort him as she had when he was a small scared boy. "Many people love you. *Gott* loves you. Never doubt that."

"What should I do?"

"Give Helen some time and then go speak her, and tell her how you feel."

"How much time? You heard her. She's leaving on Saturday." What if she didn't love him? How could he face that?

Anna held him at arm's length. "Silly boy. You can

always buy a ticket to Indiana, too. These things happen in *Gott's* time. Have faith."

He closed his eyes. *Please, Lord, show me how to make her see that I love her.*

He gave his aunt a weak smile. "I reckon I should go speak with Angela."

"You do that. Close one door and perhaps a new door will open more easily."

Mark left his aunt's gift shop and crossed the parking lot to the woodworking shop. He found Angela seated in his small office. A faint frown creased her brow. She didn't look happy to see him. How had he ever imagined being married to her? "I'm sorry I took so long."

"I should have let you know I was coming."

"If you had, I might have been able to save you the trip. I won't marry you, Angela. Your father may keep his land and the money I have paid him if he feels I have broken our contract, but I love someone else."

Angela closed her eyes, clasped her hands to her chest and lifted her face to the ceiling. "Thank you, dearest Lord, for hearing my prayers."

Mark wasn't sure what to make of her words. "I thought you had come to tell me you would marry me."

She drew a deep breath and looked at him. "I did."

"Then I'm confused."

"Father has been pressuring me to accept you ever since I told you I had changed my mind. I finally gave in only to learn his insistence wasn't because he wanted me to be happy. He didn't want to return your money."

"Let him keep it."

She smiled. "*Nee*, for it is yours. This has been a lesson to my father on the sin of greed. We have not spent a penny of it. I have brought the full amount with me in case you did not wish to marry me."

She opened her purse, pulled out a bank draft and held it toward him. "Father wasn't happy to write this check, but he has seen the error of his ways."

Mark slowly took it from her. "Won't your father be upset?"

She grinned, giving him a glimpse of a woman he hadn't seen before. "I'm sure he will be, but I'm his only child. He'll forgive me in time. I'm on my way to my cousin's wedding and since you won't have me, I will be able to have a wedding of my own soon. My late husband's best friend, Anthony, has offered for me. Now I'm free to say yes. My father can't interfere or forbid it. Anthony is a good man, but he isn't fond of my father. He wants us to move to Colorado."

"Will you go?"

"Happily. Daed will be free to visit us whenever he likes."

Mark shook his head. "What would you have done if I had agreed to marry you?"

"Spent my life being a good wife to you."

"We would have both been miserable."

"Maybe, maybe not. Only God knows that, but He had a better plan for us. I have to get going. I have a driver waiting for me."

Mark stood and held out his hand. "I wish you every happiness."

She leaned in and kissed his cheek. "I pray the same for you. What will you do now?"

He would give Helen some time, but he was going to speak to her before she left Bowmans Crossing. "I'm going to follow my heart and see where it and God lead me."

# Chapter Fourteen

The following morning, Helen was on her way to tell Isaac about her decision and say goodbye to the people she had worked with in the shop. It would be hard to see Mark again, but she could bear it knowing things had worked out for him and he would be happy in the life he had worked so hard to achieve. Charlotte had insisted on coming with her to visit Anna again. Clyde, her ever-present shadow, lay on the floor snoring.

Helen heard the sound of a chainsaw as she approached the covered bridge. The sound echoed inside the bridge structure, making her horse twitch his ears nervously. Clyde sat up and began barking furiously. He struggled against the hold Charlotte had on his collar.

"What is the matter with you?" Charlotte asked the dog as she got a better grip on him. He squirmed harder.

When Helen came out the other side of the bridge, she saw Mark and his uncle standing beneath Clyde's tree. Several large limbs lay on the ground already. Paul was up in the tree itself with the chainsaw. She pulled her horse to a stop off the edge of the road to watch.

Paul, secured with a harness and rope, was cutting through a large dead limb that hung toward the river.

From her vantage point, she saw something the foliage of the tree had kept hidden until now. There was a large knot hole in the middle of the dead limb. To her amazement, a raccoon stuck its head out of the hole and then vanished back inside. "Aenti, did you see that?"

"See what?" Charlotte bent forward for a better view.

Helen had only a momentary glimpse of the animal. "I'm sure I saw a raccoon, and I think I saw a flash of pink on its neck."

"Do you mean you saw Juliet? The Lord be praised."

The raccoon's hideaway was about to plummet twenty feet to the ground. Helen leaped from her buggy waving her arms. "Stop! Wait!"

Clyde's struggles and yelping grew frenzied. He broke away from Charlotte and raced toward the men.

The workers didn't hear Helen's shouts over the loud buzz of the saw. She got out of the buggy and rushed down the steep embankment, struggling to keep her balance as she continued yelling. Clyde caught Mark's attention by jumping on him, but it was too late. The saw stopped as the huge limb toppled out of the tree, hit the ground and then rolled down into the river. Clyde raced after it and plunged into the water.

Helen stopped her mad dash and pressed a hand to her heart, certain that she had just watched Juliet's demise.

"Clyde, come back," Charlotte shouted as she followed Helen down the slope. "Mark, help him. Basset hounds are terrible swimmers. He'll drown."

Juliet scrambled out of the hole. She held a kit in her mouth. After pacing back and forth for several seconds, she left the log and began swimming for shore. Clyde tried to change direction and follow her, but he was struggling badly. When he went under, Charlotte screamed.

Mark rushed to the water's edge, pulled off his boots, threw his hat aside and dived into the water. He came up, swimming toward the spot where Clyde had vanished. To Helen's relief, the dog surfaced, although he was clearly fading. Mark reached him and tried to support him. It was all he could do to keep Clyde's head above water.

Helen saw a rowboat beached near the bridge. She raced to it, pushed off and got in. Rowing was not as easy as it looked, but she managed to turn the boat and headed toward Mark. She pulled alongside them, shipped the oars and leaned over to grab Clyde's collar.

"I've got him." As soon as she took his weight, the boat tipped dangerously.

"Don't let him pull you in," Mark shouted. "Can you swim?"

"I never learned."

"The time to learn is before you are in danger of falling into the river."

"Thanks for the tip," she said through gritted teeth. Her arms ached from holding Clyde's weight as he continued to struggle.

Mark grasped the rope at the bow of the boat and began towing it to shore.

They were within a few feet of the bank. Paul, Isaac and Charlotte stood on dry ground calling encouragement and instructions, but Helen was barely holding on. Clyde gave a sudden, powerful lunge. The boat tipped, spilling Helen over the side. She shrieked as she hit the cold water and sank. Seconds later, strong arms grasped her and pulled her to the surface. She came up choking and sputtering.

"I've got you. You're fine," Mark said calmly.

She clutched him tightly, afraid they were both about to die. "I can't swim."

"You don't have to swim, my love. Put your feet down. It's not that deep here."

She realized he was right. She could touch the bottom. Mark captured one of her hands and led her toward the shore. Clyde bounded out and shook himself off before lumbering to where Juliet was licking her kit. She greeted Clyde with a warning hiss, then relented and began licking him, too. Charlotte dropped to her knees to stroke Juliet's head. The raccoon reached up and patted her face. Charlotte was crying tears of joy.

Isaac and Paul reached Helen and Mark as they emerged from the water. "Are you two okay?" Isaac asked.

Helen nodded and sank to the ground. Mark sat beside her. She looked at his beloved face and wished he would take her in his arms. She loved him so much, but he belonged to Angela.

She let her fright turn to anger so she wouldn't blurt out her secret. "Mark Bowman, that was the stupidest thing I've ever seen a man do. That dog could have pulled you under. Was that the plan?"

He grinned at her. "I didn't have a plan. I just went with my heart. The boat was a better idea. *Danki*, my darling, but if we are going to live by this river, you and our children are going to learn to swim."

Her mouth dropped open. What did he mean? Before she could gather her scattered wits to ask, Anna arrived and draped a quilt around her. "You poor dear. Come up to the house and get out of those wet clothes before you catch your death."

Isaac pointed to the river, where the tree limb was

caught at the edge of the bridge and bobbing in the current. A second tiny raccoon kit had crawled out of the hole and was crying. If the limb became dislodged it would be swept downriver.

Mark looked up at Paul. Paul nodded. "Let's try."

Mark rose to his feet. Helen caught hold of his pant leg. "Try what?"

He loosened her hand and gave it a squeeze. "We need to rescue the rest of Juliet's family." He and Paul pushed the boat out and climbed in.

Helen scrambled to her feet and pulled the quilt more tightly around her shoulders. Anna steadied her with an arm around her waist. They all watched silently as the two men maneuvered the boat up beside the log. If it became dislodged, it could easily overturn the boat. Unable to reach the opening where two little masked faces were staring at them, Mark slipped over the side of the skiff and into the water. Helen pressed a hand to her mouth to keep from crying out.

Mark pulled himself in among the branches and reached into the cavity. One by one, he pulled out three babies and handed them to Paul. Before Mark could get back to the boat, the limb broke free of the piling and rolled as the current swept it underneath the bridge, taking Mark with it. Helen screamed.

# Chapter Fifteen

Helen dropped the quilt and ran toward the base of the bridge with Isaac and Anna close behind her. She heard Paul shouting for Mark. The tree limb bobbed faster in the swift current between the bridge pilings and disappeared from her sight. She closed her eyes. "Please, Lord, spare his life. I love him so much. Please be merciful."

She could hear Paul shouting, and then there was silence. She stared into the dark shadows under the bridge and prayed as she had never prayed in her life. Then she saw the bow of the boat emerging into the light. Paul was rowing with difficulty against the current. Finally, the rest of the boat appeared with Mark sitting at the rear.

Helen's knees gave way, and she sat abruptly in the grass as tears of joy and thanksgiving blurred her vision. Anna and Isaac helped her to her feet. "He's fine," Anna said. "He's fine. Praise God for His goodness." There was as much relief in her voice as there was in Helen's heart.

Paul beached the boat and both men climbed out. Paul scooped the mewing kits from the floor of the boat and carried them to their mother. She took each one, nosed it thoroughly and then licked it before she seemed satisfied. Helen had never seen her aunt looking so happy, as she gathered the new family into her apron.

Mark sat beside Helen and leaned close to whisper in her ear. "At least we know why he was always barking beneath the tree."

Nodding, Helen smiled at him. "He was trying to convince her to come home."

There was so much more she wanted to say to him, but she settled for whispering, "Thank you."

He smiled softly. "You're welcome."

Helen's gaze shifted to the house. "I hope Angela didn't see this."

"She's not here. She's gone to her cousin's wedding."

"Oh." She didn't know what else to say. All through the previous sleepless night she had practice telling him goodbye and wishing him well without bursting into tears. It would be impossible at the moment for tears were already gathering in her eyes. She blinked them back.

Clyde crawled close beside Charlotte, who was sitting cross-legged on the grass, and laid his head on her knee as he gazed at the pile of babies. Charlotte patted his head. "You will make a fine stepfather. Oh, what fun we shall have."

Anna made shooing motions at Mark and Helen. "Up to the house, both of you, and get out of those wet things."

Helen allowed herself to be shepherded up to the house, where she changed into clothing borrowed from Rebecca. By the time she came down to the living room, word of the morning's adventure had spread. Mark and

Paul were surrounded by the men from the workshop asking questions and shaking their heads in amazement.

Anna came out of the kitchen and stopped beside Helen. "Charlotte is anxious to get home and get Juliet and her family settled into a safer nest."

Helen had her battered emotions under control. She wanted to speak with Mark, to say her goodbyes but not in front of everyone. He looked up and caught sight of her. He made his way through his friends to her side. "Are you okay?"

No, she wasn't. Her heart was breaking, but she managed a half-hearted smile. "A little waterlogged. I'm going to have to wash my hair."

He grinned at her. "Then you're going be home this evening?"

"Most definitely."

His brother Joshua came in with his wife, Mary, and their daughter, Hannah. "I've been hearing that my cousin jumped in the river to save a raccoon. Is it true?"

Mark tipped his head close to Helen. "I'll be over to see you in a couple of hours. I have a lot of things to tell you."

He turned to his cousin, and Helen's smile faded. All she had to say to him was goodbye.

Mark couldn't wait until evening. It was only four thirty when he stepped onto Charlotte's front porch with a package under one arm. His heart was pounding in his chest. Could he convince Helen that he loved her? Would she give him a chance to prove his love, or was her mind still set on leaving? Did she love him even a little or was he only fooling himself? He loved her so much. The thought of going through life without her was unbearable.

He knocked on the door, but no one answered. Had she changed her mind about seeing him?

Clyde ambled around from the side of the house and woofed once. He turned around and went back the way he had come. Mark took it as an invitation to follow him. He hadn't been in Charlotte's flower garden during daylight hours.

He stepped through a white lattice arbor laden with fragrant red roses. Helen was seated on a white wrought-iron bench in the middle of a stone patio, surrounded by yellow and purple irises. She hadn't seen him. She was brushing her unbound hair. She looked to be enjoying the feel of the warm sun on her face. Her wheat-blond hair glistened in the sunlight and shimmered like liquid gold with each stroke of her brush. He sucked in his breath as he realized she was truly a pearl beyond price, but her beauty wasn't the reason he loved her. He loved every complicated and fascinating part of her mind. Every giggle, every frown, every sigh. He wanted to have and to hold her for all eternity. If she loved him.

Clyde nudged the back of Mark's knee. He looked down at the dog. "I'm going, I'm going."

Helen must've heard him for she opened her eyes and turned her head toward him. The happiness he saw in her beautiful eyes left him speechless. How could he have imagined spending a lifetime with a wife he didn't love?

Helen quickly looked away as the joy in her expression turned to sadness. His confidence slipped. Maybe she didn't love him.

She looked up and shook her hairbrush at him. "You're early."

"Shall I go away and come back later?"

"*Nee*, you should come and sit beside me."

"I reckon that's the best invitation I'm liable to get all day."

She scooted over to make room for him. He sat down, suddenly tongue-tied and nervous. She fiddled with the brush in her hands and avoided looking at him. Clyde decided to sit on the bench beside her, forcing Helen to scoot closer to Mark.

Knowing the dog was on his side, Mark's courage returned. "I brought you something." He handed her the package.

She took it from him, held it to her ear and shook it. The rattle of glass made her eyes widen. "What is this for? It's not my birthday."

"I'll explain in a minute."

"What is it?"

"Open it and see."

She quickly tore off the brown paper wrapping and gasped. Gently, she ran her fingers over the figures of Clyde in various poses, sitting, rolling over, sleeping, even flying with his ears out straight, all carved in relief into the dark walnut doors. She opened the doors and pulled out one of the dozen empty spice jars.

"I didn't put the labels on because I didn't know what spices you would want," he said quickly, hoping she liked it.

She tucked the jar back in place and closed the doors. "Mark, this is beautiful. But why?"

"I'm hoping it's an engagement gift. Helen Zook, will you do me the honor of becoming my wife?"

Her mouth dropped open. "You can't mean that. You're going to marry Angela."

"I'm not."

"You aren't? What about the land and the business?

You've spent years working to fulfill your plans. I don't understand."

"The good Lord has opened my eyes and made me see that my plan wasn't His plan for me. You are if you will have me. I'm not much, but I promise to be a good and loving husband. Will you marry me?"

"You're not going to marry Angela?"

"*Nee*, I'm not."

"You're not going to start a business with her father?"

"Nope."

Her eyes widened as his words sank in. "Why?"

"Because I love you. Do you…do you care for me at all?" He held his breath.

"Oh, Mark I love you, too. I can't believe this is happening. I have been rehearsing how to say goodbye without falling apart."

"God willing I will never hear that speech." He laid the spice rack aside, pulled her close and kissed her as every fiber of his being shouted with joy. After a long interval, he pulled away to look into her eyes.

"I love you, Helen Zook. I think I fell in love with you when you smashed those delicious cream horns into my chest."

She covered her face with her hands and laughed. "I was absolutely humiliated that day. The look on your face did not say *I love you*."

He took her hands in his. "What does the look on my face say today?"

Tenderness filled her eyes. "It says everything I have always wanted to hear."

He swept back a lock of her hair. "Does it say 'I think you are beautiful?'"

She tipped her head to the side to study him. "I believe it does."

He gently cupped her face and ran his thumb across her lips. "Does it say that I'm dying to kiss you again?"

She tipped her head slightly. "I don't see that in your eyes."

"Then I reckon I had better show you." He bent forward and gently kissed her.

She sighed against his lips. He turned to gather her in his arms and draw her close. Her arms circled his neck, and he thought his heart might explode with the love that expanded inside him. Her lips were soft and yielding beneath his. He'd never know a sweeter moment in his life. He kissed her eyelids and her cute nose and the pulse beating in her throat.

When she finally drew back, he knew without a doubt that this was the woman God meant to be his wife. "I didn't know I could love someone so much," he whispered.

"It came as a surprise to me, too," she said with a smile. "God has been good to us."

"What is your answer, woman of my heart?"

Helen grew somber as she gazed at the man she loved. "In answer to your earlier question, *ja*, Mark Bowman, I will be pleased to become your wife. This morning you said that we will raise our children by this river. Have you decided not to return to Pennsylvania?"

"I've been working on a new plan, but I'm going to need some help with it."

"I'm always willing to give you *my* point of view."

He kissed the tip of her nose. "Even when I don't want it, I know. This time, I want it. I've taken some inspiration from you. You love baking, and it shows in what you produce. The part I like best about building furniture is carving. I'm a good carver. I think I can become a master carver in time. Adam Knepp, my uncle's master carver, is willing to teach me. My uncle says I have the gift. Bowmans Crossing is drawing more tourists every year. I think a bakery beside the gift shop can become a paying proposition in two or three years with the right baker in charge."

"Me? You want me to have my own bakery?" She shook her head sadly. "We don't have the money for that."

"When I told Angela I couldn't marry her, she gave me back the money I had paid to her father. She was hoping I wouldn't take her back. Her father pressured her into saying that she had reconsidered and that she was willing to go through with our arrangement, but she wanted to marry someone else. She didn't come because of the letter you thought I wrote her. I never sent it. I was writing it to you. I wanted to hear what it would take to make you love me."

Helen laid a hand on his cheek. She was glad he hadn't sent Angela that letter. "Are you sure about this? You dreamed of owning your own business there for so many years."

He covered her hand with his and turned to place a kiss on her palm. "God has given me a new dream. One that will change and grow over time as He blesses us with children and grandchildren."

"I like the sound of that."

He kissed her temple. "So do I. When can we wed?"

"As soon as the banns are announced is fine with me," Helen said and leaned toward him for another kiss.

"Nonsense," Charlotte declared from her bedroom window. "Fall is the time for weddings. You don't want folks wondering why the rush. We have so much to do to get ready. Are you finished wooing yet?"

"Not yet, Charlotte," Mark said sternly. "Stop eavesdropping, and shut your window."

"How rude. Helen was right about you." She slammed the window sash down with a bang.

Clyde woofed. Mark looked over at him. "Get lost. I've got this."

The dog jumped down from the bench and trotted around the corner of the house.

"Now, where was I?" Mark asked, gathering Helen close once more.

She tapped her lips with one finger. "I think you were here."

"I believe you're right."

Helen thrilled to the touch of his lips on hers and proceeded to kiss him with all the passion in her heart. God had indeed been good to them.

* * * * *

# THE AMISH NANNY'S
# SWEETHEART

## Jan Drexler

To my dear aunt, Waneta Bundy,
who sowed sunshine wherever she went.

Soli Deo Gloria

Therefore whosoever heareth these sayings of mine, and doeth them, I will liken him unto a wise man, which built his house upon a rock:

And the rain descended, and the floods came, and the winds blew, and beat upon that house; and it fell not: for it was founded upon a rock.

And every one that heareth these sayings of mine, and doeth them not, shall be likened unto a foolish man, which built his house upon the sand:

And the rain descended, and the floods came, and the winds blew, and beat upon that house; and it fell: and great was the fall of it.

*—Matthew* 7:24–27

# Chapter One

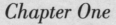

*LaGrange County, Indiana*
*February 1938*

"You're sure you want to do this?"

Judith Lapp grinned at her brother-in-law, Matthew Beachey, as she climbed into the buggy. "I've been looking forward to going to a Youth Singing for years. Why would I refuse this chance now?"

Matthew's grin echoed hers as he turned the buggy onto the road leading to the Stoltzfus family's farm. "That's just what your sister would say."

As the horse trotted down the snowy road, the cold February air pressed close inside the buggy. Judith pulled her shawl more tightly around herself and tucked the heavy lap robe under her legs. A shiver made her teeth chatter, but she didn't care. All those years growing up on the farm near Shipshewana, she had never gone to a Singing. Of course, she hadn't been old enough to go until the last few years. Even so, she and Esther would never have gone if their older brother, Samuel, had had his way. Living at the edge of the Amish community, just like she had when their father had been alive, Judith had never felt welcome among the young people her own age.

But then, last fall, their lives had changed. Samuel had met Mary. The couple had wed in September, and Esther had moved next door to live with Mary's sister and their aunt. Judith had joined them until she moved to Matthew and Annie's home last week to help care for their growing family. Not only was she delighted to become reacquainted with Annie after their years of separation, her oldest brother, Bram, lived in the same community, and she was learning to know him again, also.

A tingling started in Judith's toes and she tapped them on the buggy floor to warm them. Matthew's shoulders were hunched, and he had pulled his chin into the collar of his coat like a turtle.

Dear Matthew. It had been his idea for her to live with him and Annie after the twins were born. Such wiggly, red, crying babies! Judith's job was to fix meals and care for Eli, her eighteen-month-old nephew. She shivered again, but whether it was from the cold or happiness, she couldn't tell. She had to pinch herself every morning to convince herself that her new life wasn't just a dream.

Matthew turned the horse into the Stoltzfus farm lane and Judith leaned forward as they approached the large white farmhouse. A dozen or more buggies were lined up along the edge of the lane in front of the barn, the buggy shafts resting on the ground. Lights from the house shone onto the snow, and through the windows Judith could see a crowd of young people milling around inside the Stoltzfuses' big front room.

Her grin grew wider. These girls would be her new friends. And, perhaps, some evening a young man would ask to drive her home from the Singing. A fine, upstanding Amish man who was looking for a bride to share his life with. Finally, the night she had longed for was here.

The barn door opened and closed in a beam of light as one of the young men led their horse into the warm shelter. Ahead of them, silhouetted against the lantern light from the barn, someone walked up the lane toward the house with his hat perched on the back of his head the way an *Englischer* would wear it.

"Is that Guy Hoover?" She nudged Matthew's elbow. "I know I've seen him before."

"It looks like it might be. He lives with the Masts on the farm across the road from us."

"That's right. He brought some milk over on Friday." His smile had been enough to make her like him right away. "I don't remember seeing him at meeting this morning, though."

"He was there, but the Masts left before dinner. David said one of their cows wasn't doing well this morning, and he wanted to get back to her."

Judith smiled at the young man as the buggy passed him. He might have returned her greeting, but she couldn't tell with his face wrapped to the eyes in a wool scarf.

"I'll be back to pick you up at ten thirty," Matthew said as he pulled his horse to a stop at the end of the walk leading to the house.

"What if some fellow asks to take me home?" Judith couldn't resist teasing Matthew.

"Tell him he'll have to wait. It's my privilege tonight." He helped her take the robe off her lap as she slid the buggy door open. "Have fun."

"I will," she said, but her attention was on the icy walk leading to the kitchen door.

Guy reached the back step the same time she did.

"It's sure cold tonight, isn't it?" His words were muffled by his scarf.

"*Ja.* Very cold." She shivered, anxious to get into the warm house.

He pulled the scarf down, revealing a pleasant face and ready smile. "Do you remember me? Friday I saw you when I brought milk to the Beacheys." He spoke in a mixture of *Englisch* and *Deitsch* words, turning his sentence into a jumble.

"For sure, I remember." She remembered how his brown eyes had widened and then crinkled into a grin when she answered the door.

"In a hurry, you were..." He stumbled on the *Deitsch* words and switched to *Englisch*. "You were in a hurry on Friday."

Judith changed to *Englisch*, too, as she reached the door. "You didn't stay long, either."

Guy opened the wooden storm door and followed her into the washing porch. "You surprised me. I didn't know anyone but Annie would be there."

"And then Eli was crying..."

"Those babies were, too."

Judith unwound her scarf from her neck. "They always cry, but I don't mind. There is nothing sweeter than a new baby, and the twins make things twice as much fun." She glanced through the glass window of the kitchen door. The room beyond was crowded, and even though she longed for its warmth, she wished she had an excuse to stay here and continue visiting with Guy. She wondered why he didn't seem comfortable speaking *Deitsch*, but how could she ask that question?

Suppressing a shiver, Judith settled for a smile. "It was nice seeing you again."

Guy unwrapped his own scarf with one hand as he held the door open for her, then she was swept into the crowded kitchen.

Two girls stood between the door and the big kitchen stove, talking with each other, but turned to greet her.

"I'm so glad you came," one of them said. "We met at church this morning. I'm Waneta Zook."

"*Ja*, Waneta, I remember. It's so good to see you again."

"This is my friend Hannah Kaufman."

"I saw you at meeting," Hannah said. Her smile was friendly and welcoming. "You came with Matthew Beachey, didn't you?"

"He's my sister's husband. I came to live with them last week." Judith started to say how thankful she was that Matthew and Annie had opened their home to her, but Hannah's face lit up.

"You've come to help Annie with the twins? What fun!"

Judith smiled as she untied her bonnet. "They are so sweet, but all they do is eat, cry and sleep. Annie keeps busy with them while I watch Eli and take care of the house."

Waneta led the way to a back bedroom where Judith laid her shawl on top of a pile of other shawls and coats on the bed and set her bonnet on a table. She felt to make sure the hairpins were still holding her *Kapp* secure and ran her hand down her skirt to smooth out any wrinkles, then she followed Waneta and Hannah into the big main room. She found a spot against the wall with the other girls and watched the group of boys lounging along the opposite side.

Hannah leaned close to speak into her ear. "After the singing, I'll have to introduce you to my brother. He's that handsome one over there."

Judith looked in the direction Hannah indicated. The young man was tall, and as good-looking as Hannah said. He glanced in her direction as he talked with some other boys who gathered around him, but Guy caught her attention as he stood off to the side, staring at her. He wore the same plain clothes that the other boys wore, but somehow, he looked out of place.

Before she could ask Hannah if she knew Guy, one of the older boys announced that it was time for the Singing to begin. As the girls took their places on one side of the long table in the middle of the room, the boys scrambled to sit across from the girl of their choice. Judith watched to see who would sit across from Waneta. The spot remained empty until a tall young man came in late.

"That's Reuben Stoltzfus, Waneta's beau," Hannah said, whispering into Judith's ear. She giggled as a young man sat across from her.

"Who is that?" Judith whispered back.

"Reuben's brother, Ben."

Hannah looked everywhere except in Ben's direction. Judith didn't dare look to see who had taken the seat across from her. She had never had much to do with boys, since she and her sister Esther hadn't attended the Singings in their home district of Shipshewana. She didn't know if she should say hello, or if she should acknowledge his presence at all. She watched Hannah, who finally looked across the table at Ben, blushing as she gave him a smile.

Judith dared to look at her partner. She drew a breath of relief when she saw it was Guy. His dark brown eyes crinkled as he grinned at her. She could only give him a brief smile before she looked down at her lap. The boys chose to sit across from a girl they were interested in, according to what Annie had told her about the Singings. But was Guy interested, or had he sat there because no one else did?

She took a songbook from the stack that was passed along the table and dared to meet his gaze again just as a voice called out the first song number. She fumbled with her book until she found the right page, knowing he was watching her all the time. The group started singing and she struggled to join in the unfamiliar tune. She glanced up again and was relieved to see that he was concentrating on the songbook.

Holding her book in front of her face, Judith squeezed her mouth shut tight to keep from giggling. She was at a Singing, and a boy was sitting across from her. So, this was what it was like to be grown up. She dared to peek at Guy again, but he was still concentrating on the book in front of him. She suppressed a little quiver that went from her middle all through her, then turned her eyes back to the words of the song. It was a hymn, but not one from the hymnal they used on Sunday mornings, the *Ausbund*.

The tune became more familiar as they started the second verse and she joined in. As she did, she could hear a clear tenor humming the tune without singing the words. It was Guy. He frowned at the book in his hands. If he didn't speak *Deitsch* well, perhaps he couldn't read it, either. Judith lost her place in the song as she let her imagination fill in the empty pieces of Guy's story without success. She would just have to get to know him better if she wanted her questions answered.

\* \* \*

Guy Hoover couldn't believe that the seat across from the new girl had remained open long enough for him to claim it. But now, he told himself, he had to quit staring at her. It didn't matter if she was the prettiest girl he had ever seen. She would think he was some kind of fool if he didn't get hold of himself.

Running a finger inside the too-tight neckband of his shirt, he stared at the songbook in his hands. He hadn't wanted to come to the Singing tonight. He hadn't been to one since Hannah Kaufman had laughed at his attempt to talk to her in Pennsylvania Dutch. Three months had passed since then, but the sting of her rejection had kept him away from any gathering of the community's young people. Tonight, though, Verna Mast had pushed him out the door.

"Go have some fun," she had said. "David has you working so hard all through the week that you deserve to spend some time with folks your own age on a Sunday evening."

Folks his own age, yes, but the fellows treated him like the outsider he was. They knew his past, that his pa had abandoned him at the orphanage. That he was an unwanted mongrel, not worth their bother. That he was only a hired hand.

David and Verna had never made him feel that way, though. They were good people.

He sneaked a glance over the top of his songbook. Judith's soft blue gaze, as soft as her voice had been as they talked outside, met his, then dropped to her book.

Looking down at his own music, Guy gave up trying to sing. He could speak a little bit of the Pennsylvania German, but not enough to follow the words on the pages. He knew the tune, though, and hummed along with the singers while his mind wandered.

He let his thoughts drift to the first time he had seen Judith. David had sent him to the Beachey home with a pail of milk and he had knocked on the kitchen door the same as every other time. But when Annie's sister had opened the door...

Guy felt a foolish grin slide over his face and glanced across the table just in time to see Judith's red face before she lifted her songbook to hide it. His grin took over. With some planning, he might be able to talk to her some more before the end of the evening. Perhaps he would even be able to walk her home.

At that thought, his stomach churned like a windmill. Judith sat next to Hannah, and he could imagine what Hannah was saying about him. Why couldn't folks let the new girl get to know him on her own, without gossiping?

After the group had sung several songs, Elizabeth Stoltzfus announced that refreshments were ready. Guy noticed that several of the fellows were coming out of the kitchen with cups of punch for the girls. This would be his opportunity to talk to Judith, but he saw that Luke Kaufman was already at her side with a cup. As he offered it to Judith, she smiled up at him.

Luke Kaufman.

Guy pushed away from the table and made his way to the kitchen. If she was interested in Luke, then she would never even look at him.

As he reached the table filled with sandwiches, John Stoltzfus thrust a plate toward him. "Glad to see you here tonight, Guy."

Guy nodded at the older man, the father of Benjamin

and Reuben. John had always welcomed him whenever he was in the Amish community.

*"Denki."* Guy switched to English. "Thank you for hosting the Singing."

"Of course." John spoke in English, too. "You know that whoever hosts the morning church services also hosts the Youth Singing in the evening."

"All the same, thanks." Guy took a thick sandwich spread with ground ham and then one with egg salad.

"Don't miss the pie," John said. "Elizabeth makes the best pumpkin pies."

"I know." Guy slid a piece of pie onto his plate, then moved around the table to stand next to John, out of the way. John's wife, Elizabeth, was the best cook he knew of, other than Verna. "I'll probably have seconds if there are any pieces left."

John grinned and clapped him on the shoulder. "I'll keep one back for you, if you'd like. Although you look like the Masts' table has been agreeing with you."

Guy nodded as he took a bite of the ham sandwich. He had worked for David Mast every summer since he was nine, and those summers had filled his winter dreams with memories of Verna's delicious cooking. When he turned eighteen last year and could no longer live at the Orphan's Home, David had offered him a regular job, including room and board. He had jumped at the offer.

"Verna's cooking is a sight better than—" Guy stopped. He didn't need to remind John or the others in the kitchen of where he had lived most of his life. "Her cooking is delicious."

The short refreshment break was nearly over, and while Guy finished his first piece of pie, the kitchen emptied as the others drifted back into the front room.

John cut a second helping of pie for him, and Guy couldn't refuse.

"How are things going? David speaks highly of your help on the farm."

Guy raised his eyebrows as he swallowed a bite of pie. "You wouldn't know it to hear him some days. It seems I can't do anything right."

Especially yesterday. He had driven the wagon too close to the corner of the shed and had spent the rest of the afternoon whitewashing the scraped siding.

John grinned. "I'm sure my boys think that about me, sometimes." He shrugged. "But how else will you learn to be a good farmer?"

Guy stared at the plate in his hand. Is that what David was doing? Teaching him to be a farmer?

"I'm not sure that's what I want."

John scraped the last crumbs of his pie into a pile with the back of his fork. "Don't be too quick to decide. Ask for God's direction."

Guy nodded. "Sure." Ask God. That's what Verna would tell him.

"Meanwhile, soak up all you can from David's teaching. You never know when those skills will come in handy, whether you stay on the farm or not."

"Yeah, you're right." Guy took his plate to the sink. He didn't know how long he'd be living with the Masts. David had never said anything about him staying on past this year. But then, he never had the other years, either.

"David loves you like a son. You know that, don't you?"

Guy glanced at John as he went back into the front room to join the Singing again. He had gone over this time and again in his head, ever since the first summer he had stayed with the Masts. David and Verna seemed to like him, but after all these years, they had never adopted him, and he knew why. He wasn't Amish. He wasn't good enough for them.

Judith leaned away from Luke until her back touched the wall. His hand rested next to her head as he loomed over her. She had to look up at an uncomfortable angle to see his face, but it was worth it. Luke Kaufman was one of the cutest boys she had ever seen and popular with the other fellows.

"How long will you be staying with Matthew's family?" Luke's blue eyes held hers in a steady gaze as he took a sip of punch.

"Quite a while. At least until the twins are a few years old, I think."

He glanced away as a girl's laughter rose above the conversations in the room, then focused back on her.

"Did you leave a lot of friends behind in Shipshewana?"

Judith shook her head. She and Esther hadn't done much socializing before their brother Samuel got married.

Luke leaned even closer. "Not even a boyfriend?"

"*Ne*, no boyfriend." Judith felt her cheeks flush hot. Were all boys this bold?

"Then you'll have to let me be your first beau." He smiled, but his eyes smoldered. "I'll take you home from the Singing tonight."

Judith pressed her lips together to keep from giggling. Luke leaned even closer to her, making her even more nervous, but she couldn't move away with the wall right behind her. "You must already have a girl you're interested in." She turned her punch glass in her hands, not daring to take a drink. She was shaking so much inside that she would spill the punch down the front of her dress, for sure.

He shrugged. Even his shrugs were smooth and self-assured.

"No girl to speak of." He lifted one of her *Kapp* strings with his finger. "Not now."

She couldn't stop the nervous giggle from escaping again. "Then, there was a girl?"

"No one special." Luke breathed the words as he leaned even closer. He smelled of soap and something else that Judith couldn't identify. Something smoky and bitter. His gaze slid from her eyes to her mouth and her stomach flipped over.

Someone clapped their hands to get everyone's attention. "It's time to take your seats." Reuben Stoltzfus's voice carried over the rest of the sounds in the room, but Luke didn't move.

"Let me take you home tonight. Meet me at the end of the lane."

Judith found herself nodding, but then remembered her promise to Matthew and turned the nod to a shake.

"I can't. Matthew said he was coming for me."

"When he sees that you've already gone, he'll understand."

Judith shook her head again and ducked under Luke's arm to head back to her seat. "*Ne.* Matthew said that he wanted to take me home this time."

"I'll get my way." He tugged on the *Kapp* string again and gave her a heart-stopping smile. "Count on it."

As Judith slid into her seat next to Hannah, the other girl grabbed her hand.

"I saw you talking to Luke. Did you like him?"

Judith glanced down the table toward Luke. He was laughing with the fellows sitting on either side of him. Their conversation during the break had been unsettling, but she wasn't sure why. She hadn't had much experience talking to boys.

"He is nice, I guess."

Hannah squeezed her hand. "I knew you'd think so."

Reuben called out the number for the first song, and the group had nearly finished it before Guy took his seat again. He looked in her direction, then at his songbook. Judith kept watching him. He stared at the book, but didn't join in the singing.

The next song was a fun one. Each verse was about two people who had a hole in their bucket, and at the end it repeated the lines from all the previous verses. By the time they reached the twelfth verse, everyone was laughing so hard they couldn't keep singing. Everyone except the young man across the table from her.

After the rollicking fun, someone suggested a quick break. Judith stayed in her seat this time, not wanting to be cornered by Luke again.

A few minutes later, a cup of punch appeared on the table in front of her. She looked up to see Guy smiling at her.

*"Denki,"* she said.

He made his way around the end of the table to his seat and took a drink of his punch. Judith leaned toward him, keeping her voice low so the others wouldn't hear their conversation.

"Why didn't you sing with us?"

Guy rubbed the side of his nose. "I don't talk *Deitsch* well, and I can't read it."

"So why did you come to the Singing?"

"I don't know." He looked miserable.

"You have a nice voice. I heard you humming along with us earlier."

A shadow of a smile flashed at her. "Do you mind if we speak English?"

She switched languages, just as he had. "No." She gave him a mock frown. "But you won't improve your *Deitsch* if you don't use it." She laid her hands on the table and leaned closer to him. "Why don't you know how to speak like us?"

"I wasn't raised here——"

Before he could finish his sentence, the next song was announced. This one was a round, and it took concentration for Judith to keep up with her part. Half of her thoughts were on Guy, though. How could he not know *Deitsch*?

At ten o'clock, the singing was over. Luke and some of the other boys rushed out the door, but the girls stood in groups to chat. With a half hour to wait for Matthew, Judith started helping a few of the young people who were collecting the songbooks.

She had picked up a small stack when she met Guy coming around the other side of the table with his own hands full of books.

"I'll take those for you," he said.

Judith handed him the books she had gathered. "You're speaking English again."

Guy shrugged. "The Penn Dutch is too hard. Everyone here understands English, so why should I learn it?"

"You'd fit in with the other fellows better. Don't you want that?"

"I'm not sure they want me around."

"You should give it a try." Judith stepped closer to him. "All you need is someone to teach you."

He glanced around, then ducked his head toward her. "Could you teach me?"

He was serious, his eyes locked on hers, waiting for her answer.

"I'm not sure I'd be a very good teacher, but I could try."

"Maybe we could get together this coming week?" He grinned. "If you can ever get away from those babies."

Judith frowned. Did he dislike children that much? "Those babies are the reason I'm here, and I don't want to get away from them."

"C'mon, I was only teasing." His cheeks turned red.

Judith grinned back at him. "I'm glad you were, because I love Annie's children. All three of them."

"So, when can we start the lessons?"

"I'll have to check with Annie, first."

He nodded and thumbed at the corners of the songbooks in his hand. "I saw you talking with Luke Kaufman earlier. Is he taking you home?"

If any boy was taking a girl home, it was supposed to be a secret, except for the girls who had steady beaus, like Waneta. Even Judith knew Reuben would be taking her home. But Guy looked at her with such intensity when he asked the question that she had to give him an answer.

"No." She shook her head. "He asked, but Matthew is coming for me."

"Whew," Guy said. "I'm glad."

He picked up a few more songbooks that someone had left on a chair and Judith followed him. If he was asking to take her home, he had a strange way of doing it.

"Why are you glad?"

"No reason." He gave the books to Benjamin Stoltzfus, then turned back to Judith. "Except that maybe I can get a ride with you and Matthew?"

He wiggled his dark eyebrows up and down as he asked, and Judith found herself laughing at him.

"For sure, you can. Matthew will be here at ten thirty." She glanced at the clock. "I had better get my bonnet and shawl. Meet you by the back door?"

"Yeah. I'll wait for you there."

As Judith went toward the kitchen, she glanced back. Guy had picked up the end of one of the benches, ready to help Benjamin carry it out to the church wagon. After talking with Luke at the break, she had been breathless and feeling a little bit like she was dabbling in deep, unknown waters. But that exchange with Guy…it had been more like talking to a friend she had known for a long time.

Hannah was in the bedroom, putting on her bonnet. Her black shawl was already wrapped around her shoulders.

"You're ready to go home?" Judith asked, reaching for her own bonnet.

*"Ja."* Hannah peered into a small, round shaving mirror fastened to the edge of the towel rack on the washstand, pinching her cheeks to bring some color into them. "Luke asked me to remind you that he'll be waiting for you at the end of the lane." She turned to Judith with a smile. "He has a brand-new courting buggy and can't wait to try it out."

"But I told him that Matthew was coming for me. I don't need a ride."

Hannah laughed. "No girl ever needs a ride!" She grasped Judith's hand. "My brother is looking for a wife, and I have a feeling you're just the girl he's been waiting for. If you step carefully, you and I could be sisters before you know it."

Judith withdrew her hand. "I'm not ready to be married. This is my first Singing, and I want to get to know other people before I settle down to one fellow."

Hannah picked up a pair of mittens from the bed and pulled them on. "If Luke is set on you, there will be no changing his mind."

"I'm still not going to let him take me home. Matthew asked to be the one to do it on my first night out, and I want to go home with him." Judith found her own mittens tucked in the folds of her shawl. "Besides, Guy Hoover is going to ride with us."

Hannah faced her. "Guy Hoover? You don't want to get involved with him."

"Why not?"

Hannah shook her head, her face set in a frown. "He isn't one of us. Never has been, and he never will be. He's an outsider." She turned toward the door, then gave one last shot. "He doesn't belong here."

Judith's fingers chilled as if she had plunged them into a snowdrift. Hannah's animosity toward Guy was shocking, and not what she had expected from her new friend.

If Guy was an outsider, that explained why he didn't know *Deitsch*. Judith tugged her mitten on. New friend or not, Hannah was wrong. She would do everything she could to help him feel welcome in the community.

## Chapter Two

Spring was in the air on Tuesday morning as the week-end's cold spell gave way to warmer breezes and fitful sunshine. Guy turned the team at the end of the field, then threw the lever to start the manure spreader's gears as they made another pass. When David had given him this early-spring job of fertilizing the fields, Guy had chosen to do these acres first. Why? He grinned to him-self as he drove the horses toward the fence on the other end. Because from here he could watch the Beacheys' farmyard across the road.

He had only seen Judith once since the Singing two days ago. Just a glimpse, but he knew she was there. Ever since he had said goodbye to her when Matthew let him off at the end of the Mast lane that night, the only thing on his mind was to see her again.

Judith. Even her name sang in his mind.

He shook his head at himself, frowning. Why would he think he had a chance with her? The prettiest girl around, and new in the community, to boot. The boys were going to buzz around her like bees in a flower garden.

Guy turned the horses at the other end of the field

and started back across. There, finally, he was rewarded with the sight of a figure in a blue dress and black shawl. She carried a basket and headed toward the chicken house. And disappeared. He hadn't even seen her face, so he knew she hadn't seen him.

After two more trips along the length of the field he saw her again. This time, she had let the shawl slip back from covering her head and held it loosely around her shoulders. She carried a basket full of eggs in her other hand as she picked her way along the wet path to the house. With her white *Kapp* gleaming in the bit of sunshine that had made its way through the cloud cover, she was a lovely sight. Blue eyes, he remembered. Dark blue and thoughtful. She dodged a mud puddle with a graceful step, hurried the rest of the way to the house and disappeared behind the closed door.

He stared at the door. Hannah Kaufman had brown eyes, full of laughter and beautiful. At least, he had thought so until he found out the laughter was at his expense. He had no business getting mixed up with an Amish girl, even though Judith seemed kinder and friendlier than Hannah. He didn't belong here, and he wasn't planning to stay. If Pa showed up—

"Guy! What in the world are you doing?"

Startled by David's shout, Guy slammed back to reality. The horses had pulled the spreader off the straight track he thought they were on and were headed toward the barn.

"Sorry!" he called, and waved in David's direction as he guided the horses back to the middle of the field. At least no one would notice his distraction, the way they would if he had been plowing. He shook his head as he thought about the ribbing he would have gotten if the crops had grown in crooked rows.

He finished the field and headed toward the barn to pick up another load of manure. Without a word, David met him at the manure pile and started shoveling. Guy joined him, eyeing his expression to gauge his mood.

David was a good boss, and had always been more than kind to him, but even David could get riled. He expected the best work from Guy, just as he expected it from himself. Mistakes were always fixed, sloth was never tolerated and attention to the task at hand was demanded. Guy had broken that last rule too often, and he waited for David's reprimand.

It came when the spreader was filled and ready for the next field.

"You weren't driving the team back there, they were driving you." David leaned on his shovel, his gaze on the front acres. "What were you thinking about?"

Guy shot a glance toward the Beachey house. The first thing he had learned that summer when he was nine, his first summer with the Masts, was that David could always tell when he tried to skirt the truth.

"I saw that new girl come out of the house."

David let the shadow of a grin show. "I guess a girl is a fair distraction for a fellow your age, but don't let it happen again. When you're driving a team, they need your full attention."

Guy climbed onto the seat of the spreader and clicked his tongue as a signal to the horses. He didn't have a view of the neighbor's house from the back field, but his mind went off on its own thoughts, anyway. Keeping the team on track, he focused on the fence post at the far side.

David had taught him that if he picked a point and kept his eye on it, his path would always be straight and true. Almost everything David taught him had more than one meaning. He had made it clear that Guy needed to have a goal for his life and to keep his eyes on that. He was an eddy in a stream, David had complained. Always doing, but never going anywhere. But Guy just couldn't find that centering point.

When the horses reached the fence post, he turned them around and lined up the next goal, the crooked tree by the farm pond, just beyond the fence.

At nineteen years old, he still had no idea what he wanted out of life.

No, that was wrong. He knew.

He had known ever since Pa had taken him to the Orphan's Home on his fifth birthday. He still remembered the green suit Mama had made and how the wool had made his neck itch. He remembered the smell of the Home. The putrid odor that lingered in the dormitory rooms and drifted down the stairs. The crying that echoed in the hallways.

"I'll come get you when I find work," Pa had said as he crouched in front of him, smoothing the collar of the green suit. "It may be a while, but they'll take good care of you here." And then Pa had patted his shoulder and left, trotting down the sidewalk back to the old dusty black automobile.

Guy had waited for his return, and the years of aching emptiness had about killed him.

He knew what he wanted out of life. He wanted a father who never left his boy behind. He wanted a mother who didn't die. He wanted his family.

But that was a dead-end dream.

The next time Pa had come back, on an early-spring day three years later, he had smelled of alcohol. A woman had been with him.

"Dressed in floozy clothes," Mrs. Bender, the matron at the Home, had said with a sniff.

The fancy woman had taken one look at him and poked Pa in the shoulder. "That ain't your kid. He looks nothing like you."

Then she had leaned close to Guy, grabbing his chin and turning it one way and then the other. "Nothing like you."

She had released his chin from her icy stick fingers and lit a cigarette, walking toward the shiny burgundy-colored car waiting by the road. "It's him or me, Sugar Daddy," she had called over her shoulder as she climbed into the front seat.

Pa had shrugged his shoulders, his eye on the woman and the car. "She won't be around long, and then I'll be back for you." He had straightened his striped jacket and settled his hat more firmly on his head. "You see how it is, don't you, Sport?"

Pa had come by to visit a few times after that, showing up every couple of years. Twice he'd had different fancy women with him. Another time he had shown up on foot, dressed in torn clothes and dusty shoes that were cracked and showing Pa's bare feet through the peeling leather. Every time, he had left with the same promise of coming back to get him. Guy only needed to be patient until Pa's ship came in.

But Guy had learned that Pa's promise was nothing but straw. Easily made, easily broken.

The horses had stopped with their noses at the fence, and Brownie turned his head to look back at Guy.

"All right, all right. Hold your horses." Guy shook off the memories and grinned as he turned the team around to start the next pass down the field. Horses holding their horses. If he'd still been at the Home, he'd have told that joke to the other boys as they shivered on their cots waiting for the lights-out call to drift up the long stairway. But he no longer belonged there. Too old for the Home, he was on his own.

He looked at the big white house at the edge of the barnyard. David and Verna's place wasn't home, either, no matter how welcome they tried to make him feel. He wasn't theirs and never would be. He didn't really belong anywhere.

The memory of Judith's quiet glance sent a cool stream of peace through him. Maybe, just maybe, she could help him belong. The Penn Dutch lessons should help him become more comfortable in the community. Maybe he could put down roots here. Buy a farm. Raise a family. He let his thoughts flow to a home and family like Matthew Beachey's, with a girl like Judith as his wife and children growing along with their love for each other. Guy shook his head with a laugh. That dream was far beyond the reach of an outcast like him.

Judith turned the ham frying in the cast-iron skillet then checked the potatoes with a fork. Dinner was nearly ready, and just in time. She could see Matthew heading toward the house for his noon meal.

"*Ach*, Judith, you're a blessing!"

Annie stood in the kitchen doorway, rocking and bouncing as she held a fussy Viola in her arms. Or was it Rose? Judith couldn't tell the two babies apart yet. They both looked like Annie, with wisps of red curls growing on their soft, pink heads. Meanwhile, Eli squirmed, trying to get down from his perch on her left hip.

As she set him on the floor, she waited until he had his balance before letting him go on a headlong dash toward his mother.

"You never told me what a job it is to try to cook with a toddler underfoot." Judith opened the oven door to check on the green bean casserole. She had quickly learned that this dish was one of Matthew's favorites.

Annie knelt to put her free arm around her son. "And soon enough there will be three of them running around the kitchen, all wanting to help." She smiled as she pulled her son close and kissed his cheek.

Judith took four plates from the cupboard and set them on the table, watching Annie. Even though her sister hadn't slept much last night, with the babies awake and crying at all hours, Annie still kept her good humor. Her face looked tired, though, and Judith was afraid she might fall asleep at the dinner table.

"When I put Eli down for his nap, I'll take care of the girls so you can get some sleep this afternoon."

Annie's eyes widened. "Would you? I don't remember when I last slept for more than a few minutes at a time."

Matthew's feet stamped in the porch outside the kitchen door, Judith's signal to finish setting the table.

She smiled at Annie as she laid the silverware next to the plates. "I'd love to take care of them for a while. Tiny babies are so sweet."

Annie cooed at Viola, who was still fussing. "They are sweet, but exhausting." She kissed Eli's brown curls as Judith lifted him into his tall stool at the table. "I don't know what I would do without you here."

Judith pulled out a chair so Annie could sit down next to her son. "If I wasn't here, someone else would help you. There are plenty of girls in the church who would have been glad to come."

"Did you get to know any of them at the Singing

on Sunday evening? I didn't have a chance to ask you about it yesterday."

Judith drained the potatoes. She was serving them boiled, since she hadn't had time to mash them. She added a lump of butter to the pot and shook salt and pepper over them.

"I had met Waneta Zook at the morning service, and she introduced me to Hannah Kaufman. There were others there, but I don't remember all of their names."

She set the green bean casserole on the table and put the ham on a serving plate. Just as Matthew came in, still damp from washing up on the porch, she dumped the potatoes into a dish and set it on the table. She sliced a loaf of bread while Matthew greeted his family, then she put it on the table and stepped back to evaluate her work.

"*Ach*, the peaches. I forgot to get them from the cellar."

"It's all right," Matthew said, pointing to her chair. "I'm too hungry to wait for them."

After the prayer, and when Judith had gotten the peaches and put them on the table, she sat down next to Eli. Annie had cut up some potatoes and a few green beans and put them on his plate, but they were already nearly gone, so Judith cut some ham into bites for him.

"What were you girls talking about when I came in?" Matthew asked, taking a second helping of the casserole.

"Judith's first Singing. I was asking if she had made any new friends."

Matthew grinned across the table at her. "I thought I saw a couple boys buzzing around her when I picked her up."

Judith felt her face heat. "I had a great time, and I

hope I can go to the next one. Waneta Zook is such a nice girl."

"Guy Hoover seemed to think you were pretty nice, yourself." Matthew teased her as much as he did his wife.

"Guy is nice," Judith said. "He was easy to talk to." Not like Luke Kaufman. She spooned a few peach halves into her sauce dish.

"What did you think of our young people?" Annie asked. Matthew had finished eating, and Annie handed the baby to him.

"I'm looking forward to getting to know more of them. Reuben Stoltzfus kept everything going, and we sang some hymns, and some new songs I had never heard before." Judith buttered a slice of bread and cut it into pieces for Eli. "I didn't know it would be so much fun."

When they had all finished eating, Matthew read from the *Christenflicht*, the book of prayers that sat with his Bible on the edge of the table, then went back out to work. By that time, Rose was fussing in the other room and Annie went to care for both babies. Judith washed the dishes while Eli played with a spoon and pot on the floor. After a few minutes, Annie came back to sit at the table while she ate another dish of peaches.

"The girls are both asleep," she said, licking her spoon. "I put them in their cots in the front room."

"That will be fine." Judith finished the dishes and sat with her sister for a bit of a rest. "I'll put Eli down in a few minutes, and you'll all have a nice long nap."

Annie scraped the last of the peach juice from the bottom of her dish and Judith put it in the dishwater she had saved.

"I don't suppose we have any cookies?"

Judith cringed as she got them from the top of the icebox. "I should have remembered to get them out earlier so Matthew could have some." Eli climbed on her lap to eat his, leaning against her and watching his mother.

"He can have his when he comes in before the afternoon chores," Annie said, brushing a crumb off her skirt. "And now that it's just us, tell me about the boys."

"Boys?"

"I'm sure you met more boys than Guy Hoover. Which did you like best?"

Judith thought about Luke's blazing blue eyes, squirming a little as she remembered how small she had felt as he had loomed over her. "What do you think about Luke Kaufman?"

Annie leaned her chin in her hand. "He's very popular with both the fellows and the girls, but I'm not sure that's a good thing."

"Why not?"

"I've seen young men like that put too much store in what others think of them. Pride can be a real danger."

Judith nodded, taking the remains of Eli's cookie out of his hands before he dropped it. He was sound asleep.

Humility was a sign of a true Amish person, but falling into the sin of pride was too easy.

"What about Guy?" Annie said, munching on the last half of her son's cookie. "He seems like a nice young man."

"He asked if I would teach him *Deitsch*. Do you know why he doesn't know the language already?"

"He didn't grow up Amish. He's been working for the Masts since before I married Matthew and moved here. It wasn't until last year that he moved onto the farm, though."

"Why? Did he live with his parents before?"

Annie shook her head. "He's from the Orphan's Home. He doesn't have any parents, except for the father who took him to the home when he was a little boy."

"He's part of the community, though, isn't he?" Judith pushed away the memory of Hannah's face when she claimed that Guy would never be more than an outsider.

"Verna hopes he will choose to be baptized and join the church. If they had been able to adopt him, it would have been much easier for him, and them, too. They have no children of their own, but they love Guy and treat him as a son."

"Does he want to join church?"

"I don't know. It isn't something that happens often, you know, an outsider joining the church. That's why it would have been easier if David and Verna had been able to adopt him when he first started spending his summers with them as a young boy."

"Why didn't they adopt him then?"

Annie stifled a yawn. "I think Verna said his father never signed the papers to release him. But if you teach him *Deitsch*, it will make it easier for him to fit in. When do you think you'll start the lessons?"

"I was thinking about some evening this week."

"That sounds fine. After supper, the twins go down for the night, and so do I. Once Eli is in bed, your time is your own." Annie pushed back from the table. "I'm going to lie down. Are you sure about taking care of all three children this afternoon?"

Judith tipped her chin toward the sleeping Eli in her lap. "Of course I am. I'll wake you if I have any problems."

Annie made her way to her room as Judith carried Eli upstairs to his bedroom across the hall from her own. She laid him on the bed and removed his shoes before she covered him with a warm quilt. She looked out the window as Eli shifted in his sleep, settling into what she hoped would be a long nap. This window faced the road and the Mast farm on the other side.

She wasn't lonely, but Annie was busy with the babies, and Judith missed the hours she and Esther, her other sister, had spent talking when she was still at home. She needed a friend, and Guy promised to be a good one. At least, she thought he would be from the little time they had spent together.

Guy was right. He needed to learn *Deitsch* and she could teach him. She had a picture book she had brought to read to Eli, and she could use that to teach him a few words. A warm feeling spread when she thought of the hours they would need to spend together as he learned her language. Their friendship would deepen, and perhaps turn to… Judith felt her cheeks heat in the chilly room.

She frowned, keeping her thoughts stern. There would be no romance during her lessons with Guy. He wanted to learn, that was all. She shouldn't jump to conclusions. Besides, he wasn't Amish. It didn't matter how attractive or friendly he was, she could never let him get any ideas about wooing her.

Unless he was planning to join the church.

Judith gave her upper arms a brisk rub to chase the chill away, then checked to make sure Eli was covered and warm in his bed. As soon as she found a moment, she would walk over to the Mast farm and see when Guy wanted to start his lessons.

Guy had just finished the afternoon milking and was carrying the warm pails to the dairy in the corner of the barn when Judith opened the door.

"Verna told me you were here, but she thought you'd still be milking."

"I just finished, even though the ladies aren't done eating yet." Guy pointed an elbow toward the two cows still munching on their supper of timothy hay. "It's a surprise to see you here."

"I came over to ask you something."

Judith followed him into the dairy and watched in silence as he set the milk on the bench, then shrugged off his barn coat and hung it from the hook on the wall. He watched Judith from under the shock of hair that always fell over his eyebrows as he started assembling the cream separator. He tried to catch her eye, but she seemed distracted. She stepped forward to help him sort the dozens of rings and filters, chewing on her bottom lip.

"Well?" Guy set the filters in their place and attached the big onion-shaped hopper on the top of the cream separator.

"Are you serious about learning *Deitsch*?" She handed him the clean steel buckets that would hold the separated milk and cream. Guy started the slow, heavy crank, getting the separator up to speed before he poured the milk into it.

"Of course I am." He lifted the first pail and poured steaming milk into the hopper. "At least, I am if you're going to teach me."

Judith leaned on the table, watching until the twin streams of milk and cream came out of the spouts and into the waiting buckets.

"I'll be happy to do it, if you really want to learn. You'll need to speak and read *Deitsch* well if you're going to join the church."

Guy poured the second pail of milk into the top

of the separator, then continued cranking at the slow, steady speed the machine required. The look in Hannah Kaufman's eyes as she laughed at him last fall still stung. The only reasons to learn Penn Dutch were so he wouldn't be laughed at and so he could fit in better with the crowd. He hadn't thought about joining church. Becoming one of them.

"I don't need to join the church to fit in around here, do I? The other guys my age haven't joined."

"Some of them have."

Glancing at her face, her pink cheeks told him that he had been too blunt. She was disappointed in him.

"It just isn't for me." He tried to make his voice sound casual. The pink had spread to the end of her nose.

"You don't have to join church," she said, clearing her throat. "But being able to understand what folks are saying will make living in the community easier. Like when you go to the Singings or to the church meetings."

He cranked the separator in silence. She wasn't laughing at him. It seemed like she really wanted to help him. The bonus was that getting Judith to teach him Pennsylvania Dutch meant they would spend time together. Time he could spend learning to know her, getting close to her. Becoming a friend.

"When would we do this?"

Her face brightened. "I thought we could get together after supper, unless you still have chores to do then."

"Naw, David gives me the evenings off." He let the separator slow as the last of the milk emptied out of the hopper. "Were you thinking of starting tonight?"

"We can begin tonight, but it's going to take more than one evening. It will take weeks for you to pick up the basics."

That brought a grin he couldn't hide. Weeks spent

in Judith's company? He set the pails of skim milk and cream aside and put the empty milk buckets under the separator's spouts. He dumped a bucket of hot water into the hopper and let it pour through all those disks and filters, rinsing out any milk that lingered.

"Okay, I'm game."

*"Wonderful-gut!"* She started for the door. "I have a children's book we can use to begin with. Come over after supper, when Eli is in bed for the night. Around seven o'clock."

Judith smiled then, her joy catching him by surprise. She truly wanted to do this, which meant only one thing. She liked him. He felt his own smile spreading across his face.

"I'll be over after supper, then." He grinned. "It's a date."

As Judith let the door close behind her, Guy went back to his work, but the grin slid off his face. He was looking forward to spending time with Judith, but what was he expecting to get out of learning that Penn Dutch stuff? It was one thing to live with the Masts and work for them. It was something completely different to become one of them.

He pushed away the warm feeling that started whenever he thought of belonging here. Truly belonging here. That would never happen. He had learned long ago not to get his hopes up. The Masts, as much as they seemed to like him, had never really made him part of their family. It seemed if you weren't born Amish, you'd always be an outsider.

Besides, when Pa came for him...

Guy shook his head, chasing the stale hope away.

Once the room was clean and tidy, ready for the morning's milking, Guy picked up the small pail of cream, leaving the skim milk to feed to the hogs the next day.

If David and Verna had adopted him when he was younger, it would be different. He would have learned the language, grown up with the other boys like Luke Kaufman and been a true part of the community. But that hadn't happened, and it wouldn't. Judith was wrong. He would never be Amish.

# Chapter Three

That evening, Guy showed up at the back door right at seven o'clock. He was grinning when Judith opened it, but the smile disappeared when he saw Eli hanging onto her skirt.

"Am I too early?"

She shook her head. "You're right on time. I've just had one of those days." She picked up her nephew and led the way into the kitchen. "Eli didn't sleep well last night, and then had a short nap this afternoon. Annie says he is getting some new teeth."

Guy took a seat at the table where she had set a plate of cookies and a glass of milk for each of them.

"I didn't know you were going to feed me," he said, glancing at the book she had also laid on the table.

"My brother was always hungry for a snack, no matter how soon it was after a meal. I thought you might be the same way."

Eli laid his head on her shoulder, watching the strange man in their home.

"I'll never turn down a cookie." Guy reached for one, then stopped with his hand hovering over the plate. "Why is he staring at me?"

Judith shifted Eli on her lap. "Probably because we're speaking English. He doesn't understand what we're saying." She held a cookie in front of the little boy. *"Gleischt du Cookie?"*

Guy laughed as Eli put the cookie in his mouth. "I guess I don't need Dutch lessons, after all. I know you just asked him if he wanted that cookie."

Eli held the bitten cookie toward Guy. *"Cookie?"*

"I'll get my own, thank you." Guy held a cookie up and looked at Eli. "Cookie."

Judith frowned at Guy. "You should only speak *Deitsch* during your lessons."

He winked at her. "Then how will Eli ever learn how to speak English?"

She had to smile back at his brown eyes twinkling in the lamplight. She pushed the book toward him.

"I thought we could use this to learn some of the names of common objects…"

He halted her speech with a raised hand. "I'm not going to do this if you're going to talk like a school-teacher."

"All right. No schoolteacher talk." She opened the book in front of her and Guy scooted his chair closer to her. So close that she could feel the warmth of his forearm resting on the table between them. She tightened her left arm around Eli.

The first page had a drawing of a boy holding an apple. "I know what that says," Guy said. "Apple. The word sounds the same in both Dutch and English."

"You're right, *Appel* sounds the same. But what does the whole sentence say?"

Guy stared at the words with a frown. "I don't know."

Judith read the words. *"Der Buh gleicht der Appel. Er esst der Appel."*

"Wait. You're going too fast."

"I thought you said you could read it." Judith grinned as his face grew red, then she regretted it. She squeezed his arm as she leaned toward him. "I'm sorry. I don't mean to laugh at you."

He regarded her with those brown eyes. "I don't like to be teased, but I know you didn't mean any harm." He looked down at her hand, still resting on his shirtsleeve. "I do like the way you apologize, though."

The twinkle was back.

*"Cookie?"* Eli asked, looking up at her.

*"Ne.* No more cookies."

Eli pointed at the book. *"Appel?"*

"He's got it right," Guy said. "He's a smart kid."

*"Er ist schmaert."*

"That's what I said."

"So say it in *Deitsch. Er ist schmaert.*"

Guy repeated after her, then pointed at the book again. "Read this again, slowly, and I'll try to catch it this time."

Judith read the sentences again, one word at a time, and Guy repeated each word after her.

"Now, what does it mean?" he asked.

"It means, 'The boy likes the apple. He eats the apple.'" Eli relaxed against her, his eyes heavy. "I'm going to take him up to bed. You practice those sentences while I'm gone."

By the time Judith returned, Guy had turned to the next page, where the picture showed the same boy petting a cat.

"Don't get too far ahead, now."

"But I'm smart, just like Eli. I can read this one, too."

Judith sat in her chair, leaning back with her arms

folded, doubting that he could read any of it. "Go ahead. Let me hear you."

Guy recited a few words, but the only one she recognized was "cat." She shook her head, trying to keep a stern look on her face.

"Sorry, that wasn't right. Let's go back to the first page."

They worked together until Guy could read the sentences with the correct pronunciation, and then she had him recite the different verb forms until the cookies and milk were gone.

Guy ran his fingers through his hair. "Can we stop now? I feel like I'm back in school."

"In a way, you are. It isn't easy learning a new language. I remember my first days at school when we could only speak English. I had older sisters and brothers who spoke it a little at home, but I was still lost." Judith closed the book. "That's enough for tonight, though." She looked at him. "Do you think you learned anything?"

He rolled his eyes. "I'll be saying 'I like apples, you like apples, he likes apples' in my dreams." Then he caught her gaze with his. "But yes, I learned something."

Judith shifted in her seat. He was staring into her eyes. "What did you learn?"

"Amish girls can be awfully pretty."

Her face burned, remembering that Matthew was in the next room, reading a magazine, and could hear every word. "I'm sure you noticed that before. There are a lot of pretty girls around here."

"Not as pretty as you."

"You're flirting with me."

Guy leaned his chin in his hand, elbow propped on the table. "Of course."

"But you came over for your *Deitsch* lesson, not to flirt."

"The lesson is over now, isn't it?"

Judith couldn't keep a giggle from erupting, even though she covered her mouth. He leaned back in his chair, grinning. When he lifted his eyebrows in an exaggerated way, she giggled even more.

"You're going to get us in trouble," she said between gasps for air.

"I'm not doing anything. You're the one making all the noise." He raised his eyes and pretended to whistle.

"Stop it."

He wiggled his eyebrows at her and she nearly fell off her chair, she was laughing so hard. She grabbed his arm. Unable to speak, all she could do was shake her head.

Guy took her hand and leaned toward her. "I'll only stop if you do one thing."

She hiccupped as the giggles subsided. "What?"

"Let me kiss you."

All silliness disappeared at his words. "You can't be serious," she whispered, hoping Matthew hadn't heard what he said.

The twinkle had left his eyes as his gaze focused on hers with their faces inches away from each other. The only sound was the clock in the front room ticking away the seconds.

Guy drew back and smiled. "Naw, not really." His rough fingers caressed the hand he still held. "But someday? Maybe?"

She couldn't look away from his warm brown eyes, soft and hopeful in the lamplight.

"Maybe," she said. "Someday."

Just then the clock struck eight and Matthew's feet hit the front-room floor with a thud. He cleared his throat to make sure they had heard him.

"That's my signal to head home." Guy rose and took his coat and hat from the hook by the back door. "Thanks for the lesson. When do we get together again?"

"Is tomorrow night too soon?" Judith opened the back door for him. "We could meet together most evenings, and that will help you learn quicker."

"I'll be looking forward to it." Then he gave her one last wink as he put his hat on and let himself out the door.

Judith's knees shook as she leaned against the door, but she couldn't keep from smiling. In spite of the awkward moment when he had asked to kiss her, it had been a fun evening. The hours until tomorrow night stretched in front of her.

Matthew looked in from the front room. "Guy went home?"

"*Ja*, for sure." Judith picked up the plates and glasses and took them to the sink. "He understood your signal that it was time for him to go."

Matthew grinned. "I have to practice pushing suitors out. I can't imagine what it will be like when Rose and Viola grow to courting age. Thanks for letting me practice on you."

He left as Judith washed and dried the few dishes. Courting? Is that what Matthew thought she and Guy were doing? Is that what Guy thought they were doing?

She hung the dish towel on the rack over the stove. There would be no courting from Guy until he said he wanted to join the church, and that wouldn't happen until he knew *Deitsch* a lot better than he did now.

\* \* \*

Guy shoved his hands in the waistband of his trousers as he trudged down the Beacheys' farm lane toward the road and the Masts' farm. He shouldn't have done that. Shouldn't have asked for a kiss. Judith wasn't that kind of girl.

Pa would have done it, though. At least, he figured Pa would have gone ahead and kissed her. The girls Pa had brought around would expect him to act like that. Girls like the one in the floozy dress with a bright smile that looked like brittle painted porcelain. Girls that had hung on Pa's arm and ignored the boy Pa had come to see. The girls that had kept Pa from taking Guy away with him.

Pausing at the end of the lane, Guy looked back at the quiet house he had just left. There was nothing brittle about Judith. When she'd held Eli on her lap and smiled at the little boy, something had tugged at his heart. A long-forgotten memory of his own mother? All he remembered were soft kisses and gentle hugs. Had she held him with the same joy he had seen in Judith's face when she held Eli?

He bent his head against a northeast wind promising snow in the morning. It looked like the brief warm spell they had enjoyed was over.

When he reached the house, he let himself into the kitchen quietly, but David and Verna were still up, sitting at the table. They both turned as he entered.

"Did you enjoy your time with Judith?" Verna held out her arms to him for the quick hug she gave him every time he came into the house.

He gave her a kiss on the cheek and sat in his chair. Verna passed a plate of cookies toward him.

"We had a good time." He grinned at the memory

of Judith's laughing fit. "I'm going over again tomorrow night."

Verna gave David a look and folded her hands in her lap. Guy knew what that meant as well as David did, and waited for the talk Verna wanted them to have.

David cleared his throat. "Are you, um, interested in Judith?"

Guy looked at Verna's worried face and back at David. "She's a nice girl, but we're not dating."

The older couple exchanged looks again.

"Then why are you spending so much time together?" Verna's voice was laced with worry.

"She's teaching me Pennsylvania Dutch."

David leaned over the table. "You've never wanted to learn it before. What makes the difference now?"

Guy shrugged. "I feel left out of the other fellows' conversations. They speak Dutch when I'm around, even though they know I don't understand it well. I guess I just want—" His voice faltered. What did he want?

Verna took his hand. "You want to be part of the community? You want to join us?"

"It's a little late for that, isn't it?" A pounding started in his ears. "It would have been different if you…" Should he say it? He had never asked why the Masts had chosen not to adopt him.

David's fist clenched, his head bowed. "It would have been different if we had been able to call you our own son." His eyes were moist as he looked at Guy. "If we had been able to adopt you when you first came to us, then you would have grown up speaking *Deitsch* and knowing our ways. But we only had you a few months a year, and then you went back to the world."

Verna squeezed his hand, her voice a whisper. "That

was so hard, every fall, sending you back to the orphanage."

"But why didn't you adopt me? Other kids from the Home were adopted."

David swallowed and exchanged glances with Verna again. "Your father never relinquished his family rights. He never released you to be adopted."

Guy frowned, bitterness rising up in his throat. "So he just left me at the Home."

"Don't think too harshly of him," Verna said.

"Forget it." Guy pushed back from the table. "All he's done is ruin my life."

"Guy, don't let this fester." David folded his hands in front of him. "You need to forgive him and go on with your life. The fact that you're learning *Deitsch* shows that you're ready to become part of our church, doesn't it?"

"I don't know what it means." Guy sighed. "I hate not belonging anywhere."

"You belong here." David took Verna's hand. "You belong with us. We love you as if you were our son. You'll always have a home here."

"But I'm not really your son. I'm just a farm hand. I'm not Amish, and I never will be."

Verna sniffed as the three of them sat in silence. David's head was bowed, his eyes closed. A different kind of bitterness filled Guy. Not the anger at Pa, but regret that he had caused the old couple pain.

"If you feel that way," David finally said, "there isn't anything we can do about it." He looked up and met Guy's eyes. "The decision is up to you. You can be our son, or you can be our hired hand. We'll still think of you as nothing less than one of the family."

Guy glanced at Verna's bowed head and the couple's clasped hands, then headed upstairs to his bedroom.

His bedroom.

He padded over to the dormer window in his stocking feet. That first year, when he was nine, this had become his favorite spot. David had built a small chest for him and set it under the window, and Guy had spent hours sitting here, gazing out at the house across the road, watching the birds, looking for foxes in the moonlight... At the Home he had nothing, but here, everything he looked at was his own. He sank down on the chest and drew his feet up, crossing his legs as he looked around the room as if seeing it for the first time.

His bed. His dresser. His chest that had held all the treasures he couldn't take back to the Home. This was his refuge.

On the bad nights at the Home, he would lie in his narrow cot and dream of this room. Summer and freedom couldn't come soon enough. Every year, David and Verna had welcomed him...home...as if they had missed him as much as he had missed them.

Had he ever thanked them? He had spent so much time waiting for Pa to keep his promise that he had neglected what he had here with David and Verna.

The Masts had never made any promises other than to love him, and even tonight they reaffirmed that promise.

But Pa had never kept his promises, and it was time Guy faced that fact. Pa's promises had broken as easily as spring ice on a mud puddle. Why hadn't he seen the truth sooner? He had wasted time and energy waiting for...

A sigh escaped, ending in a sob. He bent his head on

his knees and closed the door on that place in his mind that had held fast to a straw promise all these years.

On Wednesday morning, during the twins' nap, Annie made bread while Judith ground ham for Matthew's favorite sandwiches. Judith had brought Eli's blocks into the kitchen, and he sat under the table, playing with them.

"I didn't stay awake long enough to say hello to Guy last night." Annie turned the dough out onto the bread board and started kneading it. "Did you two have a good time?"

"We did," Judith said, smiling at the memory of how silly they had been. She paused the grinder to cut some more of the ham into the smaller chunks that would fit into the hopper. "But Guy didn't seem to want to learn anything. He kept saying it was too much like school."

"I thought you said he wanted to learn *Deitsch*. It seems like he would apply himself to the task if he really wanted to."

Judith's face grew warm at the memory of the look in his eyes when he said he wanted her to kiss him. "Maybe learning *Deitsch* isn't what he really wants."

Annie stopped her kneading. "Do you think he's interested in you?"

"He shouldn't be, should he? I mean, he hasn't joined church, and I'm not going to keep company with anyone who isn't at least considering it."

"Maybe you can be a good influence on him."

Judith fed more pieces of ham into the grinder and turned the crank. She didn't want to get her hopes up about a future with Guy. Not yet. Not until she knew he wanted more than just a fun time together.

"What do you know about the Kaufman family?"

She had turned away from Annie, but heard the small disapproving sound she made.

"I've already told you what I think about Luke."

"But what about the rest of his family? Hannah seems nice." Judith chewed her lower lip. Hannah was very friendly to her, but her comments about Guy made Judith cautious about a true friendship with her.

Annie put the ball of dough into a bowl and covered it with a clean, damp dishtowel. "Let's see." She washed her hands at the sink, staring out the window at the winter-brown fields still covered with snow in the shady places. "Luke's father has a large farm between here and the county line. Their family has lived in the area since the middle of the last century. They were some of the first Amish settlers who came to Indiana from Pennsylvania."

"And they're well liked in the community?"

*"Ach, ja."* Annie sat on a chair at the kitchen table.

Eli held a block out for his mother to see, then pounded it on the floor. "Block, block, block." Then he looked at Judith and grinned.

She grinned back at him. She was growing to love this little boy more each day.

Annie sighed and stretched her back. "The Kaufmans have been leaders in the church for years, according to what Matthew has told me. Luke's *daed* is one of the deacons. Why are you asking about them?"

Judith leaned her back against the kitchen shelf, facing her sister. "I think Luke is interested in me."

"What makes you think that?"

"The way he acted at the Singing. He singled me out to talk to, and he wanted to take me home. Hannah said his courting buggy was new, so I know he wanted to show it off to me."

"Would you welcome his attentions?"

Judith stared out the window. Luke was handsome, and the family was well established, according to what Annie said. But could she face the future with Luke, knowing how uncomfortable he made her feel? That might change as she got to know him. After all, he had the means to support her and a family, and there was no question about his *daed's* commitment to the Amish faith.

Luke was the kind of suitor she had always dreamed of. A man who could change the course of her life.

Judith sat in the chair facing Annie, wiping her hands on a towel. "I don't want to end up like *Mamm*, working too hard and never having enough."

Annie's face paled. Eli climbed into her lap with a block in each hand, and she made room for him, but her brows puckered. "You mean you don't want to marry someone like our *daed*? You want someone who can provide well for you?"

"I don't want to sound ungrateful or that I'm not honoring *Daed's* memory...but I didn't like him very much."

Annie grasped her hand. "You and Esther had it the worst of all of us, I think. I remember that his drinking became a lot worse after *Mamm* died."

Judith nodded. "I only remember him being angry those last few years, and we could never please him." She pressed her lips together before more complaints about *Daed* slipped out.

"I don't blame you for wanting a different kind of life." Annie squeezed her hand, then released it to help Eli slide off her lap and onto the floor again. "But they were happy once. *Mamm* really did love him."

"Before he started drinking."

"She loved him, even then."

Annie fell silent, and Judith watched Eli stack one block on top of another. Annie was right. Their parents had loved each other at one time. But was love enough to make a happy marriage?

"Still, I don't want to end up poor and living on the edge of the family and community."

"There's nothing wrong with being thankful for what the Good Lord provides," Annie said, her voice quiet.

"But don't you think a marriage has a better chance of being happy if there's enough money to live on?" Judith went back to the meat grinder. She had ground all the ham and she needed to wash the grinder before the gears became crusty and hard to clean. "The Kaufman family is well-to-do, from what you said."

"But Judith, just because Luke's family has a good farm doesn't mean he would be a better husband than anyone else."

"Don't you think it's worth getting to know him better?"

Annie shook her head. "He's broken more than one heart already."

Judith let Annie's comment settle in her mind. She didn't have enough experience to tell what kind of man was the right one to marry, but Annie and Matthew seemed happy together.

She sat down at the table again, next to her sister. "How did you know Matthew was the right man for you to marry?"

Annie smiled. "First of all, he made me laugh."

Judith grinned, remembering nearly falling off her chair the evening before.

"But most important, he showed me how much he loved me."

"You mean he whispered mushy poems in your ear?" Judith wrinkled her nose at the thought of some boy's moist lips next to her ear, breathing words of love.

"*Ne*, nothing like that," Annie said, laughing. She sat back in her chair and looked at the ceiling as she went back in her memories. "He remembered that I like the piece of cake from the very middle of the pan and always made sure I got that one. He let me win when we played games with his brothers and sisters. He always gave me his hand to help me in and out of the buggy."

Annie leaned forward, cupping the top of Eli's head in a loving caress. "Matthew has always put my needs and our family's needs before his own comfort. He works hard to provide for us and never complains."

They sat together for a few minutes while Judith thought about Annie's description of her husband. A swelling rose in her throat…a longing for someone to cherish her in that same way.

A cry from one of the babies drifted from the bedroom. "I think someone is hungry again." Annie started toward the kitchen door, then turned back to Judith. "Don't go chasing Luke. He's not the man I'd want my baby sister to marry."

Judith smiled, hoping to reassure her sister. "Don't worry. I'll be careful."

She let the pieces of the grinder soak in warm, soapy water while she chopped onion, celery and pickles to mix into the ham spread.

"Me?" Eli said, tugging on her skirt.

"For sure." Judith lifted him into his chair at the table and spread some of the ground ham on a bit of cracker. "What do you think?"

Eli opened his mouth and she popped the bite in, then

he scrunched up his face into a smile. He nodded and patted his tummy as he swallowed. "More? Eli more?"

Judith prepared another cracker for him, grinning as he opened his mouth like a little bird.

"You love ham spread as much as your *daed* does, don't you?"

"*Da?*" Eli held his hands up. "*Da* here?"

"He's working now, but he'll be in for dinner."

Eli kicked his feet against the chair. "Go *Da*. Down. Go *Da*."

Judith glanced out the window. The weather was cold and cloudy, but it hadn't started snowing yet.

"After I finish my work, we'll go out and see what *Daed* is doing." She wiped off the little boy's hands and put him back down with his blocks, then started washing the dishes.

As the suds swirled around the parts of the meat grinder, she considered Annie's words. She thought Matthew was the perfect husband. Guy seemed to come close to that ideal, the way he made her laugh. But he was only a hired hand with no prospects, and she wasn't about to live the rest of her life as the destitute wife of a man who wasn't even Amish.

# Chapter Four

Guy shifted his feet, waiting just inside the kitchen door for Verna to get ready. She had asked him to carry a basket to the Beacheys' this morning for the quilting, but first she had taken her time putting the donuts in the lined basket and covering them with a towel. Then she had disappeared into the back bedroom. He finished his second donut and reached for a third, careful to replace the towel covering the warm treats.

Leaning against the doorframe, he savored the donut as he thought about Judith. After a week of Penn Dutch lessons, Guy felt a bit overwhelmed. Too many words sounded the same, and even though she tried not to, Judith often giggled at his mistakes. But she was a good teacher, and he was learning little by little.

Even Verna was in on the game. She had stopped talking to him in English as soon as she had learned about the lessons. That was frustrating, but no matter how much he pretended he didn't understand her, he had to admit that he knew more now than he had that first evening. At breakfast, Verna had asked what he wanted on his toast, and he had been able to ask for and get apple butter. A few days ago, he thought he had asked for apple butter, but Verna had given him a dish of applesauce.

Was his Dutch good enough to ask Judith to go with him to the next Singing?

"Are you ready to go?" Verna asked as she came back to the kitchen, setting her bonnet in place. She wore her thick black cape and her heavy winter shoes.

Guy missed some of the words in her question, but caught the meaning. "*Ja*, for sure."

Still munching on his donut, he took the heavy basket in his other hand and followed her out of the house and down the lane toward the road.

"Even with that sharp north wind, you can tell spring is coming," Verna said, lifting her face toward the sunshine.

"It smells…" Guy struggled to come up with the word he wanted. It was one of the new ones on the vocabulary list Judith had given him the night before. He made a guess. *"Frish?"*

*"Ja*, fresh." Verna took a deep breath. She pulled her cape closer around her and hurried down the lane. "But chilly."

Stuffing the last bite of the donut into his mouth, Guy pulled his chin down into his coat and followed her.

Buggies were coming from both directions on the road, all heading toward the Beacheys' house.

"This is the first quilting at Annie's since the twins were born," Verna said as he caught up with her. "Everyone is coming to see the babies, so there will be a crowd." She lifted her hand and waved to a buggy full of women coming from the north. "There is Annie's sister Esther with the ladies from Shipshewana. Judith will be glad to see them."

Guy walked behind Verna as she headed toward the

door and followed her in, holding his hat in his hand. As he set the basket on the kitchen table, he searched for Judith in the crowd of women. When he finally found her, she gave him a quick wave and headed in his direction.

She said something, but he couldn't catch the words. He shook his head and pointed to his ears, feeling more uncomfortable by the minute as he realized he was the only man in the entire house.

Judith grabbed his sleeve and led him out to the washing porch. It was sheltered from the breeze but not heated.

She shivered. "You can't stay here."

"*Ja*, I know." He licked his lips. "I wanted to ask you if—" Now that it came to it, he found his knees shaking. "If I could take you to the Singing on Sunday night. I don't have a courting buggy, but we could walk. It's only at Deacon Beachey's, in the next mile." He cringed as his sentence drifted from Dutch to English.

Judith's face took on a slight frown. "I will walk there with you, but this doesn't mean we're going together."

Guy gave up on the Dutch. "You mean, it isn't a date."

"That's right. I'm not ready to keep company with anyone, but I'll be glad to walk with you. As a friend." She put her hand on the doorknob, ready to join the others in the kitchen. "Matthew is out in the barn. I'm sure he'd like some manly company today."

"Yeah." Guy put his hat back on.

Judith opened the door, disappearing into the sea of *Kapps*, and anything he might have said was lost in the noise.

He stood back to let another group of women into the house, then he headed toward the barn. He thought he had been clear, that he wanted to take Judith to the

Singing, but had he said it wrong? Or maybe he had misunderstood their evenings together when he thought she liked him. Maybe Matthew could solve the puzzle.

Guy found Matthew in the barn loft, forking clean straw down into the horses' stalls. He cupped his hands around his mouth and called up to him. "Hello!"

Matthew peered over the edge of the loft. "Guy. Good to see you. I'll be down in a minute."

Three more clumps of straw drifted down into the stalls, then Matthew came down the ladder and shook Guy's hand.

"What brings you here today?"

Guy grimaced, trying to catch Matthew's words. It seemed that everyone was bent on making sure he learned the Penn Dutch.

"I carried a basket over for Verna." He grinned as a phrase came to him. "The house is packed with chickens."

Matthew rubbed his chin. "Chickens?"

"Chickens. *Ja.* A house of chickens. Talking."

"I see. You mean it's a hen party in the house."

Guy shook his head, giving up. He switched to English. "Yeah, that's what I mean. A hen party."

"You're right about that." Matthew sat on a bench and motioned for Guy to join him. "How are the *Deitsch* lessons coming?"

"I don't know if I'm ever going to learn this." Guy rubbed at a stain on his trousers with his thumb. "It's too hard, and I don't think I'm smart enough."

*"Du bischt schmaert."* Matthew grinned at him. "You are smart. Judith says you're picking it up quickly."

"But the words keep getting mixed up in my head. Like the chicken-house thing. Why couldn't I remember to say it right?"

Matthew shrugged. "Learning a new language is hard."

"But all of you speak two languages. Three, if you count the German the ministers use for Sunday preaching."

"We learned to speak *Deitsch* from birth. *Hoch Deutsch*, High German, isn't much different, and we've heard that from when we were babies, too. And we learn *Englisch* when we go to school, when we're still young. If I was trying to learn, say, French or something, I'd have a hard time, too."

"Maybe." But Guy doubted that Matthew would have trouble learning anything if he put his mind to it. "I have another question for you, though."

Matthew took off his hat, running his fingers through his hair. "Sure. What is it?"

"Why doesn't Judith want me to take her to the Singing next week?"

"Did she say she wouldn't go with you?"

"She said she'd walk with me, but not like if we were going together."

"You mean, she doesn't want to be more than friends."

Guy nodded. "I'm not sure she even wants to be friends."

"She does, but she's still young. She doesn't want to be tied down, yet."

"Going to the Singing with me won't tie her down."

Matthew stood, clapping Guy on the shoulder. "You might not think so, but Judith is different. Until last year, her world didn't go much farther than her back door. She wants a chance to be a girl and have some fun with the other young people." He picked up a broom and started sweeping up loose bits of straw. "Be patient with her, and let her take her time."

"Sure." Guy frowned. He could understand that Judith didn't want the others to think they were dating.

"I wouldn't worry about another fellow horning in," Matthew said as he swept the straw into a pile. "You have the advantage of seeing her almost every day. When the other boys start buzzing around, she'll remember who her friends are."

Guy waved a goodbye to Matthew as he started back toward the Mast farm and the chores waiting for him there. Matthew was right, as long as one of those friends didn't end up being Luke Kaufman.

Judith was at the door to greet Esther as soon as Guy went out to the barn. Even though it had only been two weeks since they had seen each other, Judith felt like it had been forever. Esther must have felt the same way, from the strength of her hug. But they couldn't linger, because Mary, Ida Mae and Aunt Sadie were right behind her.

"How does it feel, taking care of those babies all day?" Esther asked as she untied her bonnet.

"Annie has charge of the babies." Judith took Mary's cloak from her and put her hand out for Ida Mae's.

Ida Mae handed her shawl to Judith, then helped Sadie with her wraps. "I'm sure you get your turn at holding them and changing diapers, though."

Esther laughed. "I can just see Judith changing diapers."

"Then get ready to be surprised," Judith said. "Eli still wears diapers, too. And all of those diapers need to be washed every day."

Sadie moved past the girls, leaning on her cane as she went. She patted Judith's arm. "I know you're a *wonderful-gut* help to Annie."

Judith and Esther carried the cloaks and bonnets into the bedroom while the others went into the front room where the quilting frame was set up.

"Now that there's just us," Esther said, "you can tell me. How are you doing?"

Esther's eyes were fixed on Judith's face, concerned.

"You were right. It is a lot of work taking care of a house full of people and babies up to our ears." Judith smiled to relieve Esther's worries. "But Annie and I work together well, and we have a lot of fun in the midst of the work. I had forgotten how cheerful she is."

Esther smiled. "She's much happier since she married Matthew."

"And the babies make her even happier, if that could be possible."

"So, who was that boy you were talking to?"

Judith felt the blood rush to her cheeks. "What boy?"

"That handsome young man who headed for the barn as soon as we walked toward the house."

It was just like Esther to jump to conclusions. "He's the neighbor's hired hand. He carried a basket over for Verna."

"I know I saw him talking to you." Esther grinned. "I'd say you're sweet on him, the way you're blushing."

"He's a friend."

"Is that all?"

Judith looked straight into Esther's eyes, dark blue, just like her own. "*Ja*, that's all. I'm teaching him *Deitsch*, and so we've spent some time together. But I'm not ready to settle down to one boy. The Singing next week is only my second one, and I plan to have fun with the other girls."

Esther tapped a forefinger on her pursed lips as Judith's face turned even warmer.

"I think there's more to him than you're saying. Did he ask to take you to the Singing?"

Judith sighed, giving up. "How can you always guess my secrets?"

"Everything shows on your face." Esther pushed the pile of cloaks aside and perched on the edge of the bed. "Tell me all about him. What is his name? Where is he from?" She covered her mouth as an idea struck her. "He isn't one of those bachelors from Illinois or Ohio who has come to look for a wife, is he?"

Sitting next to Esther, Judith was determined to answer her sister's questions as quickly and simply as possible. "He's not from anywhere. He lives right here in LaGrange County. His name is Guy Hoover, and he works for the Masts."

"He has family around here, then?"

Judith shook her head. "He's from the Orphan's Home."

"What Amish family would allow a child to go to an—" Esther broke off, then whispered. "He isn't Amish, is he? I didn't think Hoover sounded like an Amish name."

Judith shook her head. "That's why he wanted me to teach him how to speak *Deitsch*, so he would fit in better around here."

"Then he must be wanting to join church?"

"Not from what he says, but who knows what will happen?"

"Are you going to the Singing with him? He asked you, didn't he?"

Judith picked a bit of lint off the quilt they were sitting on. "He asked, and I told him we could walk together, but we're not courting."

"Why not?"

"Two reasons." Judith ticked them off on her fingers. "One, he isn't Amish."

"But he could be, right?"

"I'm not going to keep company with anyone who isn't Amish."

"I would, if he was part of the community. It isn't much different than seeing an Amish boy who isn't baptized yet, is it?"

Judith shifted on the bed. She hadn't thought of that.

"Two, I'm not going to pay attention to only one boy. Not yet."

Esther nodded. "All right. I can understand that, because I feel the same way. I don't want to tie myself down just yet. There will be plenty of time for that later."

Judith laced her fingers around one knee. "Unless the right boy comes along. How is Thomas Weaver?"

"He still only has eyes for Ida Mae."

Ever since Ida Mae had moved from Ohio with Mary to live with Aunt Sadie, the most popular boy in the Shipshewana church had ignored all the girls except her.

"Have you gone to any of the Singings in Shipshewana, yet?"

Esther nodded. "We've had two since you moved, and both of them were a lot of fun."

"Does anyone special take you?"

Esther grinned. "You know how protective our brother is. Samuel made me promise to only ride with him for the first few times."

"Matthew insisted on driving me to the first one." Judith shifted on the bed so she could see Esther's face better. "But have you met anyone at the Singing? Anyone new?"

Esther shook her head, but her cheeks turned pink.

"It's the same crowd of boys that we always saw at church." She stood, heading for the bedroom door. "We had better get in to the quilting before we miss everything."

Judith hopped up and grabbed Esther's arm. "Not until you tell me his name."

"I didn't say there was anyone."

"Esther…"

"All right, but you have to keep it a secret." Esther chewed on her lower lip until Judith nodded. "It's Forest Miller."

"Forest?" The gangly fourteen-year-old had been the bane of Esther's existence when the two of them were in eighth grade.

"He's nicer than I thought he was a few years ago."

"Didn't you hate him when you were in school together?"

Esther shrugged. "He has changed and grown up." She smiled in a way Judith had never seen before. "And maybe I have, too."

Judith dropped her sister's arm and watched her walk away. Esther with a beau? Her eyes prickled as she thought of Forest, an earnest young man who worked on the family farm with his *daed*. As the only son, he would take over the farm when his parents retired, and he would do well. If Esther ended up marrying Forest, her future looked bright and secure.

Perhaps she should reconsider her vow to stay free from romantic entanglements. When Esther married, Judith would be the last one of the family without a husband, and that sounded like a lonely prospect.

A figure waited for Guy at the end of the lane on Sunday evening. He had tried to be early, but Judith had arrived at the meeting place before him. The air was cool, but not bitter, and Judith stamped her feet in the dusky light just after sunset.

"You're late," she called when he got close.

"I'm not. I checked the kitchen clock. I'm right on time, so you're early."

When he got close enough, he could see she was grinning at him, her eyes luminous.

"I don't want to be late to the Singing." She started down the road, leaving him to catch up. "I met some more of the girls at the Sunday meeting this morning, and I'm looking forward to seeing them again."

Guy lengthened his stride, pushing away the familiar gnawing ache of being left behind. "Wait up. We planned to walk together, remember?"

"Then hurry up." She turned midstep and walked backwards. "And you're supposed to be speaking *Deitsch*, remember?"

Jogging the last few steps, he fell in beside her as she faced forward again. "*Ja, ja, ja.* I know. But it's hard."

"It will only get easier if you practice."

Guy caught her arm. "If I promise to stick to *Deitsch*, will you slow down and walk with me?"

"I don't want to be late. Everyone will notice if we come in late together, and we don't want them pairing us off."

"Why not?" A warm feeling filled Guy's chest as he thought of the jealous looks he would get from the other boys if that happened.

"Because we're not together."

As she hurried ahead, he took her arm again and made her walk at a slower pace. By his side. Her arm yielded to the pressure and she matched her steps with his. "We could be."

She looked at him, tilting her head to see past the edge of her bonnet. "But we're friends."

"Yeah. We're friends. What's wrong with that?"

Judith looked to the crossroads they were approaching. The clip-clop of a horse sounded from ahead, coming toward them, the buggy silhouetted against the dusky gray sky as the horse turned onto the road toward Deacon Beachey's.

"Nothing. Except…"

Guy stopped in the road and turned her toward him, forgetting all about speaking Penn Dutch.

"Except what?"

She chewed on her lower lip, not meeting his eyes. "Except that, well, I don't want people to think we're more than friends."

That gnawing ache started again and his stomach clenched. "I'm not good enough for you? I'm not Amish?"

Judith hesitated just long enough for his clenched stomach to spiral toward his feet.

"No, no, of course not." She glanced at him, then away again. "It's just that this is all so new for me, and I want to make friends with both the boys and the girls. If they thought we were a couple, then everyone would leave us to ourselves."

Guy couldn't answer. He didn't know her well enough to figure out if she was telling the truth or just trying to make him feel better.

"Come on," she said, tugging at his arm. "Let's keep walking."

He fell into step beside her. "So which girls have you met?"

"I like Waneta Zook. She's so friendly and kind."

Guy nodded. "Her brother Elias always makes me

feel welcome, too. But he doesn't come to the Singings here. He has a girl in Clinton Township he likes, so he goes over there."

"And then there are Mandy and Rebecca Stoltzfus. I found out this morning that my sister-in-law Ellie is their older sister. So that makes us sisters, too, doesn't it?"

A twinge of jealousy surprised Guy. Jealous of Judith? He looked at the side of her bonnet, wondering how she made friends so quickly. They crossed the road as they turned at the corner. Elam Beachey's house was just ahead on the left.

"Anyone else?"

"There's Hannah Kaufman. She's been very friendly. And this morning I met her sister Susan."

"And you already met her brother Luke."

"*Ja*, I've met Luke…" Her voice trailed off.

"What do you think about him?" Guy heard a hard edge to his question. He knew his own opinion of Luke. They had never been friends.

"He's nice."

Such a safe answer.

"I saw you talking with him at the last Singing."

"He brought me some punch, and he wanted to take me home."

"He isn't the kind of fellow you want to spend a lot of time with."

She looked at him. "Why not?"

Guy had a slew of reasons, starting with the rakish smile Luke's face always held when he talked about girls and ending with the disdain in his voice whenever Guy was around. But that was his opinion, and he didn't want to gossip.

"He just isn't the type for a girl like you."

They had reached the Beacheys' lane, and buggies crowded the narrow space, making it impossible to walk side by side.

He slowed to let Judith walk in front of him, but first, she looked straight at him. "You have no idea what kind of boy is right for me, Guy Hoover. I'll make my own decisions about that."

She hurried on, meeting some other girls who had stepped out of buggies and were walking up to the house. Guy stood in the crusty leftover snowbank beside the lane, watching them. Judith was wrong. He knew her well enough to know that Luke was not the right boy for her.

He waited until Judith and the other girls had gone into the house, then followed a group of boys in. The kitchen was crowded and hot, but the front room was spacious. Someone had already cracked a window open to keep the air fresh, and the walls that had been moved out of the way for the morning's service were still off to the side. The young men were lined up along the far wall, waiting for the girls to come in and take their seats, and Luke Kaufman was with them, surrounded by a few friends.

As soon as Guy stepped into the room, Luke spotted him and beckoned him over.

"Look fellows," Luke said. "It's the *Englischer*, trying to be Amish again."

Guy didn't answer. He never answered Luke. In the past, he had a hard time understanding him, but his Dutch must be getting better. He not only understood the words Luke used, but the mocking tone behind them.

"Leave him alone," Benjamin Stoltzfus said. "Guy can come to the Singings. He comes to church, doesn't he?"

"Only because old man Mast makes him."

The back of Guy's neck was on fire. It was one thing for Luke to ridicule him, but to speak of David Mast in that tone was unfair.

"He doesn't make me come."

Luke's eyebrows shot up. "The *Englischer* speaks." He looked around the circle of onlookers. "Be careful what you say, boys. It seems he understands *Deitsch*, after all."

Benjamin pushed out of the group, clasping Guy's shoulder and propelling him toward the table.

"Let's find our seats. The girls are beginning to sit down."

"Did you hear what he said about David?" Guy shrugged Benjamin's hand off. "He needs to know he can't talk about folks like that."

Benjamin stopped, facing Guy. "He's just trying to rile you up, don't you see? He'll keep prodding you until he gets you sent home. Is that what you want?"

Unfamiliar words skipped over Guy's understanding. "Say it in English. What is he doing?"

"Trying to get you to start a fight, and you don't want that."

Guy glanced at Luke's mocking face, still holding court with the group of boys.

"*Ne*, I don't want that." He slipped back into *Deitsch*. "*Denki*. I'm glad you stepped in."

"No problem. That's what friends do, isn't it? Look out for each other?"

Benjamin's words sent an unfamiliar warmth through Guy's middle. He watched as Benjamin slipped into the chair across from Susie Gingerich. He had never thought he'd have friends among the Amish. Too often he only saw the laughing faces and Luke's mocking grin, but maybe he spent too much time worrying about Luke's opinion instead of noticing fellows who were being friendly. Judith had reminded him about Elias Zook earlier, and now Benjamin Stoltzfus. Maybe he could fit in with this crowd.

Guy scanned the girls taking their seats, watching for Judith, but just as he saw her take a chair, Luke pushed past him and sat across from her. Guy finally found an empty seat across from a girl he didn't know. She blushed and giggled, whispering to the girl next to her, but he ignored her, glancing down the length of the table toward Judith.

Her face flushed as she glanced toward Luke, then looked down at her lap. She bit her lower lip, then stole a glance at Luke again before looking in Guy's direction. Judith smiled at him, then opened her book as the first song was announced. The smile was friendly, in spite of Luke's presence. Maybe she still considered him a friend, after all.

# Chapter Five

Judith sipped a cup of punch during the break, standing on the edge of the group of girls. Listening to Hannah's story of their pig, which had escaped from its pen yesterday, only took half of her attention while she watched the group of boys across the room. It seemed that Luke was telling the same tale as his sister from the laughs he was getting from his audience.

"*Mamm* was furious by the end of it," Hannah said. "The old sow ran right through the clean wash on the line. The rope broke and she dragged all the sheets through the mud. *Mamm* had to do all that laundry over instead of getting the garden plowed like she wanted."

"How did the pig get out?" asked Waneta.

"My sisters and their families were visiting while the men were at the mud sale over in Granger, and one of the kids opened the gate."

Hannah laughed, but the rest of the girls looked at each other. Judith knew what they were all thinking. If one of their nephews or nieces had done such a thing, there would have been trouble. And what had Hannah been doing while all this was going on? She hadn't said a word about helping her *mamm*.

"If I had been your *mamm*," Waneta said, "I would have made the kids wash the dirty clothes."

"Not them. They won't do anything unless their *daeds* are around." Hannah shrugged. "That's the way it is with kids, isn't it?"

Judith was glad when Waneta changed the subject.

"Are any of you coming to the quilting at our house this week? *Mamm* and I are putting my quilt top in the frame, and I can't wait for all of you to see it."

"Is it a special quilt?" Mandy Stoltzfus grinned at Waneta. "I heard Reuben talking to *Daed* about buying the farm next to ours sometime this year."

Waneta's face turned bright pink, but couldn't hide her smile. "Of course, it's a special quilt."

Mandy nodded knowingly at the rest of the girls. "It's the pattern Reuben picked out."

"Maybe," said Waneta, laughing along with the rest of them. "You never know."

The group of boys had broken up, some of them heading outside and some heading to the kitchen for more refreshments. Luke walked straight over to Judith and her friends.

"What are you girls talking about?" He winked at several of them, but his gaze finally rested on Judith.

"Quilting," said Waneta.

Susie Gingerich stepped closer to Luke's side. "Hannah was telling us about the pig that escaped at your place yesterday. What were you boys laughing about?"

Luke grinned. "What do boys ever talk about?"

"Hmm…" Susie tapped her chin with one finger. "Either horses or girls."

"This time it was both."

"And here I thought you were laughing at the same story we were," Judith said.

Luke caught her eye, his grin changing to a soft smile just for her. Had she been wrong about Luke? He didn't seem as intimidating tonight as he had before.

As Deacon Beachey called the young people back for the next round of songs, the girls scattered to their seats, but Luke moved closer to Judith.

"I hope you'll let me take you home tonight."

In spite of Luke's tall form between her and the rest of the room, Judith's gaze was drawn toward Guy, standing off to her left, his brow pulled down into a frown. She turned away from him and looked up at the handsome boy in front of her. Luke's eyes smoldered as he watched her.

Her insides squiggled, but she couldn't let Guy's worries rule her life. "I'll let you give me a ride."

A movement at Judith's right caught her attention. Guy had come a step closer, still watching her with Luke, frowning even harder.

"Meet me at the end of the lane, then. We'll leave during the next break."

"You're not staying until the end of the Singing?"

Luke lifted her *Kapp* string and rolled it between his fingers. "Not if I get to take you home."

She nodded, then slipped around him to take her seat just as the first song was announced.

The songs followed one after another, Judith singing along with the others automatically. All she could think about was the coming ride home. What would she talk about with Luke? She hardly knew him. Her stomach turned with an uneasy wrench. Maybe she shouldn't have accepted his invitation, but what could it hurt? Perhaps after this ride home, he would stop asking her.

Judith glanced across the table at Luke, catching his grin. Her gaze drifted down to Guy. He wasn't frowning anymore, but he stared at her, his songbook lying on the table. Irritation rose as she looked away from him and turned the pages to the next song as it was announced. Was Guy so jealous of Luke that he couldn't even have fun at the Singing? He was assuming a lot about this friendship between them if he thought he could tell her who she could spend time with.

As the next verse started, Judith risked a glance down the table again. Guy had his book in his hands, singing with the rest of the group.

When the song ended, Luke nudged her under the table with his foot. She looked up to see him mouthing the words, "Don't forget." She nodded as he left the table.

During this second break, instead of dividing into groups of boys and girls, some of the young people paired off, just like they had at the first Singing she attended. Judith started toward the back bedroom where she had left her cloak and bonnet, but when she reached the narrow hallway, Guy was at her side.

"You're leaving already?" He didn't bother to attempt speaking in *Deitsch*.

Judith backed against the wall as another girl slipped past them. "I have a ride home, and he's leaving now."

"Luke is taking you home?" Even though he kept his voice low so their conversation wouldn't be overheard, Guy's words were harsh.

"That isn't your concern."

"Yes, it is. I heard some of what he was saying to the other fellows about you, and you shouldn't go with him."

Judith stared at him. "What do you mean? Luke was talking about me?"

Guy looked around, but the rest of the crowd was leaving them alone. No one was close enough to listen. "He said he was going to steal a kiss from you tonight, and one of the other boys even dared him that he couldn't."

Judith's cheeks exploded with heat. "Now I know you're lying to me, Guy. No Amish boy would do that."

His brown eyes widened at her words. "I would never make something like this up. I told you before, Luke isn't the kind of boy you want to spend time with."

"And you aren't the one to tell me who I can see and who I can't. I don't belong to you, Guy Hoover."

Judith turned to go into the back room, but Guy grasped her elbow. "Judith, don't do this."

She wrenched her arm out of his grasp and hurried into the bedroom. She searched among the cloaks on the bed for hers, blinded by the tears that filled her eyes. Guy had been such a good friend, but why was he acting this way tonight?

Hannah Kaufman came into the room, smiling when she saw Judith.

"So, you're leaving early, too?"

Judith grabbed her shawl and threw it around her shoulders, leaning down to wipe her eyes when Hannah wasn't looking.

"*Ja.* I have a chance to ride home instead of walking, and he's leaving now."

Hannah settled her stiff black bonnet over her *Kapp*, her eyes twinkling. "I know who is taking you home. Luke said he would take you or nobody tonight."

Judith smiled, willing the uneasy feeling in her stomach to leave. "Is anything around here a secret?"

"Not when it comes to my brother." Hannah put on her shawl and tugged her mittens over her hands. "But if you want to know who I'm riding with, my lips are sealed."

Hannah slipped out of the room by a rear door Judith

hadn't seen before. She followed and found herself in the backyard. Hannah had run ahead, but Judith could see through the darkness well enough to follow her until Hannah climbed into a waiting courting buggy.

Judith made her way toward the road, where another open buggy sat at the side of the lane, the black lacquered sides shining in the moonlight. Luke jumped down as she approached.

"I'm glad you came." He reached for her and helped her into her seat. "I was afraid you changed your mind."

"I told you I'd come, and I keep my word."

Luke settled himself close to her and picked up the reins. "So do I, Judith. So do I."

He clucked to his horse and they started down the road.

Guy paced into the kitchen of Deacon Beachey's house, then back into the main room, hoping he had been mistaken. But no, Luke Kaufman had left. He glanced at the bedroom door again, where Judith had disappeared. How long did it take her to put her wraps on? She had been in there for at least five minutes.

"You're missing out on the pie."

Benjamin Stoltzfus held two plates in his hands, each with a big piece of cherry pie on it.

*"Denki,"* Guy said as he took one of the plates. He took a bite, glancing at the door again.

"What are you doing?" Benjamin took a bite of his own pie. "Did your girl disappear?"

"I don't have a girl." Guy swallowed the last bite of his pie, sorry that he hadn't taken the time to enjoy it. But his mind was on Judith.

"Then who are you sitting with?"

Guy shrugged. "I don't know. I didn't ask her name."

"You aren't jealous because Luke sat with Judith, are you?"

"Not jealous. Just worried. I don't see Luke anywhere around."

Benjamin scraped the last bit of his pie off the plate with the side of his fork. "He often disappears during the second break, especially when he's taking a girl home." He licked the last smear of cherry juice off his fork. "My *daed* would give me a good talking-to if I tried a stunt like that."

A girl came by with a tray for the dirty dishes and Guy added his to it. "I don't think David would know if I left early or not."

"He would find out. Deacon Beachey would tell him."

"But what would David do?" Guy gave up trying to find the *Deitsch* words and switched to English. "It isn't like he's responsible for me or anything."

"That doesn't mean he doesn't care." Benjamin's voice was quiet, and his gaze was thoughtful as he watched Guy. "The problem with Luke is that his *daed* doesn't seem to care what he does with his time. I've heard him say that his *daed* treats him like an adult and lets him run his own life."

Guy shrugged. "What's wrong with that?"

"Luke doesn't have the wisdom to make decisions on his own. It's like he's running his horse toward a river and ignoring the warnings that the bridge is out. Sometime, he's going to make a mistake that will wreck his life or someone else's." He rubbed the back of his neck with one hand. "I'm just thankful I have a *daed* who cares about me enough to keep me from doing stupid things."

"Don't you resent it sometimes?"

"Yeah, sometimes." Benjamin grinned. "But then I see what happens to fellows whose fathers don't keep an eye on them, and I'm glad *Daed* is holding the reins for a few years, yet."

Nathan Zook walked up to Benjamin then and they started talking in *Deitsch*, but Guy didn't try to follow their conversation. He was too busy pushing back the bubble of resentment that always appeared when one of the fellows mentioned his father. What would his life have been like if Pa hadn't left him in the orphanage? Would he have been there to help him grow up? Or would he have been one of those fathers Benjamin mentioned, the type who didn't care what their boys did?

He would have liked to find out, but it was too late now. Frank Hoover wasn't coming back.

Nathan nudged him with an elbow. "Did you hear what I said?"

"Sorry, I was thinking about something else."

Benjamin laughed and Nathan grinned. "You mean Judith Lapp?"

Guy grinned back at them, their friendly teasing dispelling his gloom. "Maybe."

"The break is almost over, and Luke isn't anywhere around," Nathan said. "I'm sure Judith would like you to sit in his seat for the rest of the evening."

"You don't think she left with him?"

"She's smarter than that, isn't she?"

Guy glanced toward the bedroom door again. "I hope so."

Nathan and Benjamin went back to their seats as Deacon Beachey called for the next round of singing. The door to the back room opened, but the only people to emerge were two girls Guy didn't know. Beyond them, the room was empty. He ground his teeth when he spied the other door on the far wall, remembering Luke's words from the beginning of the evening. He must have convinced Judith to leave with him, and she'd slipped out during the break. Guy had no idea how long she had been gone, but he knew the risks she was taking. Luke had bragged that he would do more than steal a kiss from her. His innuendos had made the boys in the group laugh, but the thought of what Luke might have in mind for Judith tonight made Guy's stomach turn.

Slipping out of the room just as the singing began, Guy went through the kitchen to the washing porch where he had left his coat and hat. He shrugged on the coat as he ran down the steps to the patchy snow. The yard was quiet. He trotted down the lane toward the road, but didn't see anyone. Stopping at the end of the lane, he fastened his coat and snugged his hat down. At least in Luke's bragging, he had let his destination slip out. Guy started jogging down the road toward Emma Lake, a favorite place for courting couples.

Judith shivered in the night air, even though Luke's shoulder against hers was warm. Slowing his horse to a walk, he circled her shoulder with one arm.

"Are you cold?"

"A little."

Luke's breath warmed her cheek as he pulled her closer. "We'll have to see what we can do to warm you up."

Judith searched her mind for something to talk about. "Did…did you go to the sale in Granger yesterday with your *daed* and brothers?"

"Naw. I don't have to worry about stuff like that yet."

She shifted in her seat, trying to put a little distance between them.

"I thought you would want to be part of looking for new horses for your farm."

He shrugged. "*Daed* takes care of that. I won't have to concern myself with the farm until he's gone."

"Don't you want to learn about it? It will be yours one day, won't it?"

"There's time enough for that later." He tightened his arm, pulling her close again. "First I have to find a wife, don't I?"

Judith swallowed. He couldn't think she was interested in marrying him.

"Do you have someone in mind?"

"You, of course."

His arm slipped off her shoulder and settled around her waist. The horse turned south at the intersection instead of north.

"Luke, you turned the wrong way. I live in the other direction, up that road."

"I know that." Luke's hand wormed under her shawl and he shifted even closer. "But I thought we'd go the long way around, past Emma Lake."

"I'd rather go home. It's getting late."

"Not that late. We have plenty of time." He urged the horse into a faster walk. "The lake is beautiful on a night like this. We can take a few minutes to stop and look at the moonlight shining on it."

Judith looked up at the clouds scudding across the sky. The horse turned at the next intersection.

"The moon has gone behind those clouds."

"That doesn't matter. We won't really be watching the lake while we're there, will we?"

"What else would we do?"

Luke's laugh was low. "We'll find something to keep us busy."

He urged the horse to a trot and turned again after a half mile. Ahead of them, Judith saw the dark water of a small lake. Luke slowed the horse down to a walk again and draped the reins over the dashboard. He turned toward her on the seat, still holding her around the waist. With his free hand, he untied the ribbon holding her bonnet on and pushed it back. She rescued it from falling to the floor of the buggy.

"What are you doing? Leave my bonnet alone."

He pinned her arm between them and caught her other hand. "You know what I'm doing. It's what you wanted when you said you'd ride with me tonight."

"I don't know what you're talking abou—"

Her words were cut off when he caught her mouth with his wet, slobbery lips, pushing against her until she was off-balance. With both of her hands caught, Judith used the only other weapon she had. She swung her foot against his leg, catching him in the tender calf muscle with the toe of her shoe. She wrenched her hands free and pushed at him until he fell back and she jumped out of the buggy.

"Don't ever try that again, Luke Kaufman." She held her bonnet close to her chest, trying to catch her breath. "I'll… I'll tell everyone what you tried to do."

Luke was bent over, massaging his leg. "And I'll tell everyone that you led me on." He spat on the ground near her feet. "No one turns me down. No one. You'll be sorry."

"I don't think so."

"Fine. Have fun walking home."

Luke slapped the reins on his horse's back harder than he needed to and the horse jumped into a trot, leaving Judith standing by the side of the road.

Judith stamped her foot and turned around to walk

home. But as she took the first few steps, her anger at Luke faded. The road stretching before her was unfamiliar, and the night was dark. The wind had picked up, tugging at her shawl.

Ripples covered the black, oily surface of the lake and lapped against the shore along the roadside. From the woods across the water came the hoot of an owl. A night bird trilled in response. Judith backed away and started down the road, hoping she was heading the way Luke had brought her.

They had turned so many corners after they left the Singing that she wasn't sure where Matthew's farm was. Putting her bonnet back on, Judith hugged herself, trying to stay warm. She kept walking. Maybe she would come to a farmhouse, and they would know how to help her get back to Matthew's.

Judith shivered as she walked, the cold air seeping beneath her shawl. She wiped her mouth on the back of her mitten, but the clammy feeling of Luke's lips remained. One thing she knew: she would never accept a ride home from Luke Kaufman again.

She stumbled over a rock and stopped. A lane led off the road to the left, straight as an arrow between two fields and disappearing into a stand of trees. Beyond the trees, a barn roof was silhouetted against the cloudy sky. As the breeze blew the clouds from in front of the moon, she could see the outline of a house in the trees, but there were no lights. No welcoming lantern glow seeping around the window shades.

Indecision planted her feet at the muddy edge of the farm lane. Judith chewed her lower lip as she considered her choices. To go down that lane might help her find someone who could give her directions to Matthew's farm, but the dark house looming in the shadowy trees made her shiver from more than the cold breeze.

On the other hand…she looked around at the empty road, the silent lake she had left a half mile behind her, and the clouds scudding across the sky on the rising wind…there wasn't another house in sight. Not far beyond her was a T-intersection, where she would need to decide to turn right or left.

She glanced down the lane at the house again, and chose the open road. She would take her chances on another house.

At the intersection, Judith turned right. When Luke had headed toward Emma Lake instead of Matthew's, he had taken her south, so she would go north. Her steps faltered. Or was this road leading her west? Or east? In the distance, the lights of an automobile lit up the dark sky, reflecting off the low-hanging clouds. Judith made her decision. She didn't want to be caught alone on a dark road by any *Englischers*, so she reversed her direction, hoping this road would take her somewhere safe.

# Chapter Six

As the first cold raindrops pelted his shoulders, Guy hunched into his black wool coat, wishing he was in Verna's warm kitchen. Or back in the room crowded with young people at the Singing. Or in the Masts' barn, milking the cows. Anywhere but jogging down a gravel road in the dark and the rain, chasing after Judith. He was a fool to follow her. She had to have known what she was getting into when she went with Luke. If he found them, he wouldn't be welcome company.

His foot slipped and he slowed to a walk, breathing hard. Emma Lake was ahead, the slow, heavy raindrops plopping onto its dark surface. From here, he couldn't see Luke's rig. Of course, when the rain shower started, Luke wouldn't have wanted to stay out in his open courting buggy. He had probably taken Judith on home and was sitting in the warm, dry kitchen, munching on cookies and flirting up a storm. Guy pulled his collar closer to his neck.

The quick shower let up as the wind pushed the clouds to the east. The moon came out, giving Guy a better view of the lakeshore. No one was there.

He should just walk home. Judith didn't want him

around, and didn't want his advice. He should just forget about her and her beau. Isn't that what a friend would do?

*Ne*, he thought, snorting when the word came into his mind in *Deitsch*. *Ne*, that's not what a friend would do. He couldn't shake off the feeling that Judith was in trouble. But where was she?

Guy started jogging again, keeping to the center of the slick mud-and-gravel road. Perhaps he should check at Matthew's and see if Luke had taken her home. If Judith wasn't there, he'd keep looking. It was all he could do.

Not all he could do, David would say. He had often said that the solution to a problem, to any problem, was to pray. But what David didn't know was that God didn't listen to Guy's prayers. He had discovered that long ago. But this time he would be praying for Judith. Maybe God would listen to a prayer for her.

Guy slowed to a walk again as he reached the T-intersection west of the lake. He had come from the north a few minutes ago, making his way to the lake. He hadn't run across Luke's buggy on the way, but Luke could have taken a roundabout way to spend more time with Judith. They might not have reached the lake yet. Perhaps he was coming from a different direction.

Leaning on his knees while he let his breathing slow to normal, Guy looked up the road and down. He looked up into the sky with patches of stars showing through the disappearing clouds.

"Left or right, God? Which way should I go?"

Guy waited for an answer. A flashing star. A pillar of fire. Anything.

A cow bellowed from somewhere to his left, but no sign from God. He looked up the road again, toward the north. There was no sound. Nothing moved. He looked south. Something might have disturbed that cow to make it bellow like that. Guy turned south and started jogging again.

Before he reached the end of the mile, he gave up jogging, his side seared with pain. He walked, breathing hard as the discomfort eased. He stopped again, listening for any sound of a buggy. He had never heard such a quiet night.

At the next crossroads, he saw someone walking ahead, just cresting a rise, a shadow against the stars, a couple of hundred yards ahead. The person might have seen something, even if it wasn't Luke's buggy. He started jogging again as the shadow disappeared over the hill. As he came up the rise, the clouds gave way at last, and the moon shone with a clear light. Ahead of him, leaning against a fence post, was the person he had been following. As he came closer, he recognized her.

"Judith?"

She jumped and faced him. "Guy? What are you doing here?"

"I followed you. I didn't think I'd ever find you. What are you doing walking, so far from home?"

He closed the space between them, catching her in his arms.

"I'm so glad you found me." She hiccupped and buried her face in his shoulder. "I don't know where I am. Luke drove in circles. And it's such a dark night, and the rain was cold…"

Guy wrapped his arms around her as she trembled, trying to control her sobs.

"Shh. It's all right, now. I'm here." He let her cry for a few minutes while his irritation with Luke grew. "Judith, where is Luke? Why are you here alone?"

That stopped her crying. "I don't know, and I don't care." She pulled back from his embrace and wiped her cheeks. "You were right about him. I should have listened to you."

A surge of hot anger went through Guy. "Why? What did he do? Did he hurt you?"

Judith shook her head. "It was so stupid. He thought he could get away with kissing me." She sniffed. "Oh, Guy, it was awful. So wet and slobbery. Like a cow licking my face."

Guy nearly laughed at her description, but choked instead. He was glad his face was shadowed so she couldn't see his reaction. "I hope you told him off for being so fresh."

"I kicked him right in the leg. And then I got out of the buggy and he drove away."

"He left you in the road with rain coming?" If Luke had been here right now, Guy would have done a lot more than kick him in the leg.

Judith sighed, a sob catching her breath. She leaned against the fence post again. "I didn't know which way to go." She rubbed her forehead, her shoulders slumped. "I'm so tired."

"Don't worry. We're near Bram's farm, and I can borrow your brother's rig to take you home."

She hiccupped. "That would be wonderful. All I want to do is get dry and warm."

"Come on, then." Guy tucked her hand in his elbow and started back toward the crossroads. He hoped she was up to the walk, even though Bram's farm was less than a mile away. Judith would be welcome there, that was for sure.

She walked in silence beside him, stumbling once in a while.

"Are you sure you are all right? Do you want to wait here while I walk ahead and get the buggy?"

She clutched at his elbow. "*Ne*, don't leave me. I can walk. Just don't leave me alone."

Guy stopped and turned her toward him, tucking a finger under her chin and tilting it up. The moonlight shone on her bonnet, but her face was in shadow. If he could see her expression, maybe he'd know what to say.

"I would never leave you alone."

She tilted her head, as if she was seeing him for the first time. "You wouldn't, would you? Even if I had kicked you."

Guy grinned at the thought of Luke's sore leg. "I wouldn't give you any reason to kick me."

Judith nodded.

"And I would never leave you alone to find your way home."

"I know."

She didn't move. Their cloudy breaths mingled in the cold, damp air between them, and Guy leaned closer, her dark eyes in the shadowy depths of her bonnet drawing him in.

"If I kissed you," he said, his voice catching, "it would be only because you wanted me to."

"If I let you kiss me," her breath spanned the inches between their lips, "I don't think it would be anything like Luke's kiss."

Guy stroked her soft cheek with one thumb. "I would make you forget all about Luke and his kiss."

She smiled and he could feel a dimple form beneath his thumb. Pa's fancy girl, the last one he had brought to the Home, had had a dimple. The girl had clung to Pa's arm, pulling him back to the car as he had waved at Guy.

*I'll be back*, Pa had called. *Watch for me. I'll find a job we can work on together.*

One more wave and then Pa's attention had been on the girl with the dimple, the waiting boy forgotten.

Guy stepped back, the mood broken. Judith deserved to be treated better than how Pa treated the fancy girls he hung around with. She deserved someone better than another Luke.

"I need to take you home. Bram's farm is just down this road, the first one past the bridge."

Did he sense disappointment as she turned to walk on? He tucked her hand back in his elbow and started on the last leg of their walk together.

Even though Bram and Ellie's house was dark when Judith and Guy walked up the lane, Bram opened the door quickly at their knock.

From inside the house, Ellie's voice called, "Who is it, Bram?"

A match scratched on the stove top as Ellie lit a lamp. Bram pulled Judith into the kitchen, her big brother's grasp on her arms as strong and comforting as Guy's. Her knees started shaking. She was finally safe and in a familiar place.

"It's a couple of drowned kittens from the looks of them."

Ellie peered around Bram's shoulder. "Judith! Come in here and get warm."

She set the lamp on the big kitchen table and pulled a chair out. Judith sank into it, every bone weary and sore. And cold. She couldn't stop shivering.

Bram built up the fire in the kitchen stove while Guy pulled off his wet coat and hat.

"You two got caught in the rain?" Bram asked, feeding the growing fire with kindling.

"Something like that." Guy watched Judith in the lamplight as she untied her bonnet, his brow wrinkled with concern. "We were on our way home from the Singing, and your house was the closest after we got caught in the rain. I hoped to borrow your rig to take Judith home."

Judith's teeth chattered.

"Take your shawl off," Ellie said, helping Judith ease the wet wool off her shoulders. "Are you soaked through?"

Judith shook her head. "*Ne*, just my shawl and bonnet." She lifted one foot. "And my shoes."

"Come in the bedroom with me, and I'll loan you a pair of warm socks."

Following Ellie's waddling form through the kitchen and into the bedroom, Judith shivered again. Her shawl had been wet, but at least it had held a little warmth. Ellie lit the candle on top of the dresser and pulled a knitted throw from the back of a small chair, her movements awkward. The newest addition to their family was due to arrive sometime very soon.

"Here," she said as Judith sat on the chair, "wrap up in this while I find some dry stockings for you."

Judith pulled the warm blanket around her shoulders and relaxed against the chair back.

"And here," Ellie continued, bending down to open a dresser drawer. "These are a pair of Bram's socks. Take off your shoes and stockings, and slip these on."

As Judith removed her stockings, she held her toes for a minute. They were ice cold.

"How did you get caught in the rain, anyway?" Ellie

sat on the edge of the bed, facing her. "Our house is pretty far from Deacon Beachey's."

Now that Judith was getting warmer, the memories of her ride with Luke came flooding in. Her nose prickled.

"I made an awful mistake."

Ellie sat on the edge of the bed and waited for her to go on.

"Luke Kaufman wanted to give me a ride home, and I said he could, even though I had gone to the Singing with Guy."

"Luke?" Ellie said. "He's kind of wild, isn't he?"

Judith nodded. "I guess I didn't realize what that really meant."

Ellie took her hand. "Did he do something on the way home?"

"First, he drove all around until I was lost, and then we ended up at the lake."

"Emma Lake? That's at least three miles from here."

A shiver ran through Judith. But she couldn't tell if it was from the cold or remembering the dark lakeshore.

"Then he tried to kiss me."

Ellie nodded. "Some boys think they can get away with anything. Did you let him?"

"It was awful." Judith wiped her lips with her free hand, feeling his wet mouth again. "I don't think I like kisses."

With a laugh, Ellie leaned forward and hugged her. "Someday the right boy will kiss you, and then you'll find out how sweet they can be."

Judith leaned her head on Ellie's shoulder, suddenly sleepy now that she was getting warmer. As she closed her eyes, she saw Guy's face, handsome and ruddy in the moonlight, close to her own, and the way his eyes had flicked to her mouth. She had thought he wanted to kiss her, out there in the dark, but he hadn't. Would his kisses be sweet, the way Ellie said?

Ellie gave her another squeeze, then stood up slowly, leaning backward and pushing herself up with one hand.

*"Ach,"* she said, smoothing her hand over her swollen stomach, "I'll be glad when this wee babe is finally here. Then I'll be able to put it down in its cradle instead of carrying it with me all the time."

Judith glanced at the waiting cradle in the corner of the room. "Is the baby awfully heavy?"

Ellie smiled as she rubbed her back. "It isn't so terrible. But I can hardly wait to see the little one."

"It won't be much longer, will it?"

"It can happen any day now." Ellie kneaded her back with her fist as she led the way back to the kitchen. "Any day."

Ellie made them all some hot tea to drink, and they sat on the chairs Bram and Guy had brought near the stove. Judith hung her wet socks on the line behind the oven so they could dry.

The conversation turned to the Singings that Ellie had attended before she married her first husband.

"Did you ever have a beau other than Daniel?" Judith asked, cupping her hands around her mug of sweetened tea with milk.

Ellie shook her head, her eyes focused somewhere over Judith's head. "Daniel was my only beau. He was handsome and kind. And such a good father." She smiled at Bram. "Almost as good a father as you are." She turned to Guy. "He was an orphan, too."

Guy cleared his throat. "You mean he lived at the orphanage?"

"He came from Ohio to live with his aunt and uncle

when his parents died. They are Hezekiah and Miriam Miller, who live in our *Dawdi Haus*, now. He was only fourteen years old, and it was very hard for him. He lived with the Millers until we married. They were a second set of parents for him, and the three of them needed each other."

"Well, he needed a home, I know that." Guy turned the mug in his hand. "But why did they need him? To work on the farm?"

Ellie sipped her tea. "The Millers had never had children. Daniel coming to them was a gift. He gave them a reason to continue building up the farm. A reason to work for the future." She smiled, her eyes focused on her hands as she looked back over the years. "Miriam says that Daniel was the child of her heart, and his coming to them was the greatest blessing God could have given them. And Daniel's children—" she paused to take Bram's hand in hers "—and our new son or daughter, are the light of their old age."

Guy frowned as he drained his mug. "We should get going. It's late, and Matthew will be wondering where Judith is."

"I'll drive you both home," Bram said. He put his mug on the drainboard next to the sink. "You know, I had never thought about it before, but David and Verna are a lot like Hezekiah and Miriam. You're the son they never had, just like Daniel was for his folks."

"Not really," Guy said. His frown deepened.

"Why not?" Judith retrieved her dry stockings and slipped them on.

"I don't belong to them, I just work for them."

"That's not the way David thinks of you," Bram said. "I've heard him tell the other men how glad he is that you're living with them full-time now, rather than going back and forth to the orphanage."

Judith slipped her feet into her damp shoes as Guy and Bram went to the barn to hitch up the horse. Why didn't Guy see how much David and Verna loved him? It was almost as if he pushed away any idea that he belonged here in the community. If it hadn't been for his *Deitsch* lessons and attending church with the Masts, she wouldn't think he had any interest in becoming Amish at all.

Ellie dipped some hot water out of the stove reservoir into a dishpan.

"Let me wash the cups for you."

Ellie shook her head. "I'm not sleepy. I'd rather be up and doing something until Bram gets back." She rubbed the small of her back with one hand.

"Are you feeling all right?"

"It's only the wee one making himself known. I think he might be making his appearance tomorrow or the next day, the way I'm feeling."

"What if you need help while Bram's gone?"

"Don't worry about me," Ellie said, shooing her toward the door. "If I need someone, I can send Johnny to the *Dawdi Haus* for Miriam."

"If you're sure…"

Ellie laughed. "I'm sure." She settled Judith's damp bonnet over her *Kapp*. "But Judith, are you sure?"

"About what?"

"Luke and Guy. It seems like you're caught in between the two of them."

"Not anymore." Judith tied her bonnet under her chin. "I thought Luke was nice looking, and he is popular, but he isn't the boy for me."

"But is Guy?"

Judith looked toward the barn, where Guy was leading the horse out, hitched to the buggy and ready to go. His only thought through the entire evening had been for her. Making sure she was safe, making sure she was taken care of. Even when she had pushed him away, he didn't abandon her.

"I don't know." Judith gave Ellie a quick hug goodbye. "But he's given me a lot to think about tonight."

Ellie caught Judith's sleeve before she stepped away. "He seems to be a kind and thoughtful man. Someone who will be a good friend for you."

Judith glanced toward Guy, waiting to help her into the buggy. Ellie was right. Guy had been a good friend tonight. Her words from earlier in the evening echoed in her ears. Had she really told Guy she didn't want folks to see them as a couple?

As she stepped into the buggy, her hand in Guy's for balance, she met his look. Those eyes, so gentle and comforting, lit a warm fire inside her.

She sat next to Bram, and Guy squeezed into the seat on her other side. He laid his arm along the back of the bench, his hand barely touching her shoulder. But at the same time, she felt safe and protected.

*Ja*, he was a good friend. Someone she could trust.

A light was shining from the kitchen windows when they arrived at Judith's house. The ride had been silent, with Judith sitting next to Guy in the front seat, and he welcomed the pressure of her shoulder against his side as his arm along the back of the seat made room for her to sit close to him. He had hoped that she'd lay her head on his shoulder, but she stared straight ahead.

"Looks like Matthew is up and waiting for you," Bram said as he pulled the horse to a halt by the kitchen door.

Judith stifled a yawn. "Or Annie is up with the twins."

That question was answered as Matthew opened the door wide and trotted down the steps toward them before Guy could help Judith from the buggy.

"Judith? Is that you?"

"You didn't have to wait up for me." Judith stood next to Guy. "We got caught in the rain and ended up at Bram's."

Matthew leaned into the buggy. "I appreciate you bringing Judith home, especially since it's so late."

"Being late is partly our fault," Bram said. "We got to talking while their wraps dried and kept them too long."

"How did they end up at your place? That's out of the way if they were walking between here and my folks' place."

Guy shifted his feet when Bram fixed his gaze on him. He had been responsible for Judith, but she had ended up walking nearly all the way to Topeka.

"It's my fault," he said, blurting the words out. "I should have brought her straight home."

Judith stepped between Guy and the older men. "*Ne.* Guy had nothing to do with me ending up so far from home. If he hadn't come to find me, I would still be out there in the dark and lost. I'm sorry I caused you so much trouble, Bram."

"It is no trouble. Ellie hasn't been sleeping well lately, and I know she enjoyed the company."

"Everything is all right at your place?" Matthew asked.

"She's doing well. She thinks we'll be meeting our little stranger soon, though."

Guy knew that was as close as the men would come to discussing Ellie's condition.

"Then you need to get home. I appreciate you giving these young folks a ride." Matthew shook hands with Bram, then closed the buggy door.

Matthew stepped back as Bram drove away and turned to Judith. "Morning will be here before we know it, and I need to turn in. I know Annie will want to hear all about your adventure tomorrow, but I'm just glad you're home now, and safe."

Judith nodded. "I'll come in a minute."

As Matthew went into the house, Judith wrapped her arms around herself. The night air was brisk as a breeze started blowing.

"You should go in, too," Guy said, turning her toward the door. "It's late, and you're cold."

"Come into the washing porch with me." Judith tugged on his hand. "I'm not ready for sleep, and I want to talk to you. We'll be out of the wind there."

She was right. The washing porch was quiet and snug, even if it wasn't warm. Judith closed the door against the chill and sat on a bench, patting the spot next to her. When he sat, she looked at him, her smile barely visible in the dark.

"All the way home from Bram's, the only thing I could think of was how silly I was to go with Luke." She spoke in English, and Guy was glad he didn't have to work to understand her. "I don't know why I did it, except that it sounded like fun. And Hannah has been encouraging me to get together with her brother, so I thought I'd give him a chance."

"Hannah likes to interfere where she isn't wanted." Guy didn't want to think about Hannah and girls like her.

"She isn't mean about it though, is she? She's always been nice to me."

Guy rubbed at his chin. "She's thoughtless more than mean." He scratched the whiskers growing on his cheek. Hannah's carelessness about his feelings last fall had hurt, no matter what her intentions had been. "But she's blind where her brother is concerned. All the fellows knew he intended to see how far he could get with you tonight. He wanted to take advantage of your inexperience."

Judith was silent for a moment, and when she spoke, her voice was strained. "Why didn't you warn me?"

"I tried, remember? But you didn't listen to me."

She grasped his hand. "I'm sorry. I thought you were just trying to run my life, but instead you were only protecting me."

Guy closed his fingers over her cold hand and reached for the other one. Clasped in his larger ones, they would warm quickly. "Of course I was trying to protect you. You went to the Singing with me, and Matthew trusted me to watch out for you."

"I was wrong about Luke."

"What do you mean?"

"I assumed that I could trust any of the boys in our church. I should be able to, shouldn't I? I thought he would watch out for me, just like Matthew would or you would. But he didn't."

Guy thought about the fellows he knew from town and the Home. He wouldn't trust any girl with them if they were alone on a dark night. He stroked the back of her hand.

"One of the things I like about you is that you look for the good in everyone, but not everyone is good."

"But Luke's father is a deacon." Judith pulled one hand from his grasp and untied her bonnet.

"That doesn't make Luke so good that he won't succumb to temptation when it comes."

"Like a girl who is trusting enough to accept a ride home with him." Judith stood and paced the length of the porch. "I actually thought he was going to bring me home. How stupid could I be?"

"Not stupid." Guy leaned against the wall and watched her walk back and forth. "You aren't stupid." He stood and caught her arm as she walked past the bench again. "You are new to this whole thing. The Singings, fellows being interested in you, flirting, all of it." He turned her toward him, wishing he could see the expression on her face in the shadows. "You'll learn, and someday you'll ride home with a boy who actually takes you home instead of trying to take advantage of you."

Judith sighed and leaned against him. "But how will I know which boys I can trust and which ones I can't?"

He tightened his arms and held her close. "Ask me. I know most of the fellows and can give you advice." His stomach turned when he thought of someone else talking with her the way he was now. He couldn't think of boys he trusted, except perhaps Benjamin Stoltzfus or Nathan Zook.

"*Denki*, Guy. You're a good friend."

As she went into the house, Guy lingered on the porch, fastening his coat before walking across the road to his warm bed. Judith was looking toward the future with more confidence than he had. She would go out with those boys and perhaps end up marrying one of them. He could see her standing next to Nathan Zook in a few years, a toddler at her knees and a baby in her arms. Happy and content.

And where would he be? Guy shoved his hat onto

his head and let himself out into the night. He tucked his chin into his coat and skirted a puddle. Who knew? Still working for David, most likely, and waiting for something that would never happen.

# Chapter Seven

"Why are Mondays always so busy?" Annie, with a baby in each arm, pushed a pile of laundry across the washing porch's floor toward Judith with her foot.

"Well, first of all, it's washday." Judith took a shirt from Eli. He was trying hard to help, but the job would have gone smoother without him handing her the soiled clothes one item at a time.

Annie shifted one of the twins to face front as the baby grew fussy. That one must be Viola. She was always wanting to see what was happening around her, while Rose was more likely to be content watching whoever held her.

"*Ja*, it's washday, but that doesn't explain why things are always in a kerfuffle on Mondays."

Judith grinned at her. "Or it could be because you didn't get much sleep last night. I heard you up with one of the twins soon after I got home."

"Both of them." Annie sighed and jiggled the babies, soothing Viola's fussing. "First Rose woke up, and then before I could get her fed and changed, Viola was crying. Sometimes I feel like I get nothing else done except feeding them and changing their diapers."

Judith watched Annie's expression soften as she leaned down to kiss Viola's red curls and swallowed a sudden longing that had appeared from nowhere. A longing so strong that her throat filled and her eyes grew moist. Such a simple gesture, but one that showed the intimate bond between mother and child. She shook her head and turned back to the next shirt Eli handed her, not wanting to stare.

She smiled at her nephew. "But you wouldn't trade them for anything in the world, would you?"

"*Ja*, that's for sure. Sometimes, when I should be sleeping, I just sit and watch them, amazed at the wonder of babies."

That brought Judith's thoughts to her sister-in-law, and the mysterious labor she might be experiencing at this moment.

"Guy and I stopped at Bram and Ellie's last night. She said she expects their little stranger to arrive any day now."

"I haven't had an opportunity to ask you how the Singing went. Did you have fun?"

Judith's cheeks warmed as she put the rest of the load of clothes into the washtub. Eli had found the handle to the wringer and was busy trying it out. "Most of it was a lot of fun."

"Most of it?"

"Matthew didn't tell you?"

Annie shook her head. "He was out and doing chores by the time I woke up this morning. We haven't had a chance to talk."

Judith had been glad when Matthew didn't mention anything about the previous night at breakfast, but she thought he had already told Annie.

"There was a bit of a problem. I got caught in the

rain, and Guy took me to Bram's to dry off and borrow their buggy."

Annie stepped closer as Judith scrubbed a shirt on the washboard. "You went to Bram's? How did you end up all the way down there?"

Judith told her the story of Luke and how she ended up alone on a strange road. "I was so embarrassed. I hope the story doesn't get out to everyone."

"No one will hear it from me. But how did Guy know where to look for you?"

"I'm not sure. He was suddenly there, and I never asked him. I was so glad to see him." Judith stopped her scrubbing and looked at Annie. "But you don't need to worry. I won't be accepting a ride from Luke Kaufman again."

"I hope you'll let Guy bring you home from now on."

"Or someone else. Guy said he would let me know which of the boys I can trust."

Annie didn't answer but chewed her bottom lip as Judith ran a shirt through the wringer and dropped it in the basket with the other clean clothes.

"What is wrong?"

"Guy said that? Why? I thought he would have wanted to bring you home himself, not make way for another fellow."

"We're friends, and that's the way I want it to be. I appreciate his willingness to help me, but he knows that I'm not looking for anything more from him."

Viola squirmed and Annie started rocking from one foot to the other with a bouncing motion, a habit Judith had seen in other young mothers. It worked, though, and Viola's fussiness eased.

"I'm not sure that Guy thinks of you as just a friend."

Judith stared at her, the wringer forgotten in midturn. The memory of how his eyes had darkened when she'd thought he might kiss her last night flashed through her thoughts. "What makes you think that?"

It was Annie's turn to grin at her. "I see the expression on his face when he thinks no one is looking."

Feeding the next shirt into the wringer, Judith started turning it again. "Now you're imagining things. Guy is just the boy across the road."

"That you spend a lot of time with."

Judith put the last shirt through the wringer. "Only because of his language lessons."

"Are you sure that's all it is?"

As she picked up the laundry basket to take it outside to the clothesline, Judith caught Annie's gaze. If she was going to have any peace, she needed to squelch Annie's speculations once and for all.

"Of course that's all it is. Guy and I are friends. Nothing more."

Judith let the wooden door slam, Annie's giggles echoing behind her. Picking up the first shirt, she shook it with a snap, then reached up to pin it to the clothesline. As she did, her gaze wandered across the road to the Mast farm. Looking for Guy? She shook her head and concentrated on jamming the pin down on the shirt's shoulder. Where was her determination to find a boy from a good, Amish family? One who would be able to offer her the security and comfort *Mamm* had never enjoyed?

Guy was a friend. Only a friend.

As she bent down to pick up the next shirt from the basket, her gaze went across the road again. Two figures stood in the barnyard, one a few inches taller than the other. That one must be Guy. David grasped Guy's shoulder as they walked behind the corner of the barn, their heads bent together as if they were deep in conversation.

Annie had been right about Luke, and she might be right about Guy. Security and a good name would be nothing without love. The kind of love Judith saw between Annie and Matthew, and Samuel and Mary. Even last night, she had seen that same love between Bram and Ellie.

Would she and Guy ever share that kind of love? Judith stared at the Mast farm as if the empty barnyard held the answer.

"I didn't ask you how things went at the Singing last night." David held the wagon tongue as Guy fitted the new bolts into place.

"It went fine." Guy finished replacing the bolts and picked up the pieces of the old, worn ones to put in the scrap bucket.

The older man ran a hand over his beard. "You got in later than I thought you might."

"Judith had some trouble getting home, so I stayed to make sure she made it all right."

"Trouble?"

Guy leveled a look at his boss. He didn't want to betray Judith's confidence, but he could use some advice. He gave David a brief account of what had happened the night before. "I did the only thing I could think of, and took her to her brother's place."

"You did right, son." David gave his shoulder a squeeze as they walked toward the machine shed next to the barn. "Bram is a good man and would make sure she got home safely."

"I tried to tell Judith not to accept a ride home from Luke, but she wouldn't listen to me. How can I convince her I know what I'm talking about?"

"After last night, she might trust your opinion more."

Guy tossed the broken pieces of the bolts in the air a few inches and caught them again. "Sometimes I get the feeling she thinks of me like a younger brother. I don't know if she'll ever listen to me."

"You're her friend, aren't you? You are earning her trust."

Guy couldn't think of how to answer. Every time he thought he might want her to be more than a friend, the sound of Hannah's laughter echoed in his ears.

"Yeah," he said, switching to English. "Yeah, we're friends."

David stopped in the doorway, facing him. "Verna and I started out as friends, sitting across the aisle from each other in school. Some of the best marriages start out that way." He grinned. "Should we look for a courting buggy for you?"

His stomach dipped down and then up again. A courting buggy?

"If I bought a courting buggy, it would be the same as putting a sign on my back saying Bachelor Available. Looking for a Wife."

David laughed, then set to work on the new milking stool he was making. "You're probably right. A courting buggy would declare your intentions to the world." He held up the three legs of the stool he had sanded and finished yesterday, checking them against each other. "It would also tell the world that you're thinking about joining church."

"It would, for sure." Guy tossed the old bolts and washers into the scrap bucket.

"And you're not ready for that?"

Leaning on the workbench, Guy watched David whittle the end of one leg of the stool to match the others. "I never put much thought in it." He flicked at a little pile of sawdust. "I've always assumed that when my pa came back, I'd go off with him."

"Do you still think he will?"

After the years of broken promises? "I don't think he'll ever ask me to go with him. Not after all this time. I'm not sure he'll even show up again."

David fitted one of the legs into the hole he had drilled in the bottom of the stool. "You've put a lot of faith in your father over the years. I've seen you waiting and watching for him. One of your first summers here, you'd perk up every time an automobile drove by the farm, hoping it was your dad coming for you."

Guy glanced at the older man, but David was concentrating on getting the angle of the leg right. "I remember that. Pa had stopped by the Home in April, just before my twelfth birthday." Guy ground his thumb into the little pile of sawdust he had created, pressing it together. "He had promised he'd be back before school was out. He said he had a job out West somewhere, and I could come with him."

It had been another broken promise.

David dipped an old brush in the glue pot, swirled it in the hole and set the leg in place. "People will always disappoint us. That's why we should be wary of putting our faith in them. Even the best of men will let us down eventually."

Guy snorted. "You've got that right."

"God, on the other hand, will never let you down."

God again. Even when he had prayed last night, God had remained silent.

"What about when things go wrong, or people die, or accidents happen?"

David set the second leg in its place. "We have a knack for expecting something different than what God promises. He never promised our lives would be easy, and He never said we would always be happy. What He does promise is that when troubles come, He will be with us." He looked Guy in the eye. "He has never left you or forsaken you."

Guy couldn't meet David's gaze. He swept the little pile of sawdust away, remembering the silent emptiness after Mama died. "It has sure felt like it sometimes."

David sighed as he set in the third leg. Once it was in place, he gave each of the legs a final thump with the mallet, then set the stool upright on the workbench.

"Life is a lot like this stool." David took a bit of sandpaper and rubbed the seat. "What would happen if I had given it only two legs? Or one leg?"

"I wouldn't want to sit on it."

"I wouldn't, either. But that's what we do when we try to live without God and a community of believers." He pointed to the legs, one at a time. "God's Word, the Bible, is the first leg, and the community, the church, is our second leg."

"And the third?"

"That's us. All by ourselves we're like a one-legged stool. We can get by, but it's precarious. So God has given us the church for support and help."

Guy stared at the stool. He knew what it was like to only have yourself to depend on.

"Folks don't have to belong to a church, do they? There are other groups, like the Lion's Club or the Odd Fellows that have halls in town."

"Run by men, for men. Social or civic clubs aren't the same as a church, and aren't built on the foundation of God's Word. A man of faith lives by prayer and the Word of God."

David ran his hand over the stool, then applied the sandpaper to a rough spot on the edge.

"When I think of all three of the parts of my life, the church, God's Word and myself, I can see how everything works together. And all three parts are connected to God Himself." David brushed off the seat and put the stool on the dirt floor. "Try it out."

Guy sat, feeling the stool's support, even on the uneven floor. "It will work fine for milking the cows."

David grinned. "It works fine for your life, too. I urge you to think about joining the church, Guy. Not for me or for Verna, but for yourself. For your future."

As David turned back to the workbench, putting away his tools, Guy took the new stool into the milking parlor. Was David right? That joining the church would give him a future?

Guy grabbed the manure fork and started cleaning out the aisle behind the milking stanchions. Every time he considered his future, he only saw emptiness. If Pa would come, then he'd know what to look forward to. A life like he had before Mama died, with someone he belonged to.

Carrying the loaded fork to the manure pile, he paused to gaze out the open door at the bare tree branches against the blue sky. Ever since Mama died and Pa left him at the Home, he had been waiting. Even knowing that Pa wasn't likely to keep his straw promises, he couldn't give up completely.

Guy turned and shoved the fork under the soiled straw again. Fat chance of that happening.

But until he was sure, until he knew for certain, his feet were stuck in the mire of doubt. There was no moving forward until Pa came back.

## Chapter Eight

By Tuesday morning, Judith felt rested after her late night on Sunday. She fixed scrambled eggs for breakfast, with sausage patties and biscuits, hurrying to have the meal on the table by the time Matthew finished with the morning chores. Annie wanted to start clearing out the third upstairs bedroom today, in anticipation of Rose and Viola using it in a few months. The room had been used for storage since Annie and Matthew's marriage, and it promised to be a lengthy project.

Before Judith put breakfast on the table, Bram drove into the yard. He jumped from the buggy and pounded up the porch steps, not taking the time to knock.

"Where's Annie?" He strode into the kitchen, his uncombed hair framing his flushed face.

"She's with the twins." Judith stirred the scrambled eggs then turned to pick up Eli, who had taken refuge behind her skirts at Bram's loud entrance. "What's wrong?"

Bram turned to her, half laughing and half panic-stricken. "It's Ellie. The baby is coming and she's... she's..."

Annie appeared in the other door, a twin in each arm. "The baby is coming? Is anyone with her?"

"Miriam is there, but she wants you and Judith, if you can come. Ellie wanted her *mamm* to be there, but Elizabeth has gone to her sister's for the day."

Annie placed a calming hand on their brother's arm. "It's all right. Ellie has gone through this before, and she'll be fine. Go out to the barn and tell Matthew that Judith and I are taking the children to your house for the day and that his breakfast will be in the oven for him."

She laughed as Bram stumbled out the door. "First-time fathers! I remember the state Matthew was in when Eli came." She turned to Judith, her eyes lit with joy. "I suppose we had better get ready. I'll pack diapers and extra clothes for the children if you'll finish Matthew's breakfast. It's going to be a long day!"

As Annie rushed out of the kitchen, Judith jiggled Eli in her arms. "You get to play with Danny today. That will be fun, won't it?"

Eli grinned a drooling smile, his fist stuffed partway into his mouth. "Danna, Danna!"

"That's right." Judith set him back on the floor and stirred the eggs once more. She took the plate of sausages she had already cooked out of the warming oven and added some of them to the skillet, then covered the skillet and put it into the oven. "Danny will be happy to see you."

"Blocks?" Eli ran toward the front room. "Blocks."

Judith grabbed three biscuits from the covered basket and split them open, laying a sausage patty inside each one. She took a fourth biscuit for Eli and cut a sausage patty into bites for him. At least they could eat some breakfast on the way to Ellie and Bram's. In just a few minutes, Annie was back in the kitchen and they were ready to go.

As Bram's horse, Partner, trotted down the road at a faster pace than Judith was used to, she handed the biscuit sandwiches around.

Bram shook his head at the offer. "I can't eat anything."

"You need to," Annie said, leaning forward from the backseat. "You need to keep your strength up."

"All right." Bram's growl sounded like Samuel as he stuffed the biscuit into his mouth, driving one-handed.

"And Bram," Annie added, "don't worry so much. Everything will be fine."

Bram shook his head again and urged the horse to trot even faster. "You didn't hear her. I think she must be dying, the way she was moaning."

Annie patted his shoulder. "That's how it is for women. And after the baby comes, she'll forget the pain because of the delight of seeing her little one."

Judith stared out the window. From what Bram was saying, Ellie must be having a terrible time, but Annie didn't seem worried at all. The woman's part in dealing with babies was a mystery to her, even after growing up on a farm. Judith hugged Eli as he sat on her lap and she jiggled the basket that held little Rose. The baby yawned, her eyelids drooping as the steady movement of the buggy put her to sleep.

When they arrived at the farm, Bram pulled up at the back door, jumping out to help Annie and Judith take the children in. Johnny, Judith's nine-year-old nephew, met them at the door.

"How is your *mamm*?" Bram asked, his eyes on the closed bedroom door at the other end of the big kitchen.

"*Grossmutti* Miriam won't let us in." Johnny swung

the door open and stared at the folks Bram had brought with him.

"That's all right," Annie said, taking charge. "You and your *daed* need to go take care of the horse, and maybe you can find another task to keep you busy for a while."

Johnny frowned. "I want to stay here with *Mamm*."

Annie shooed the two of them out the door. "I know you'll find something to do. Don't come back in until we call you."

Johnny planted his feet on the floor. "But I'm hungry. I haven't had breakfast yet."

"I'll make something and bring it out to you," Judith said. As much as she was curious about what was happening in the bedroom, she'd much rather make herself useful fixing meals and taking care of the little children while Annie helped Ellie.

"Coffee cake?" Johnny's hopeful grin made her smile.

"I'll see what I can do."

With Bram and Johnny gone, Annie placed the sleeping twins in their baskets on the table and headed into the bedroom. She paused with her hand on the doorknob.

"Have you ever helped with a birth, Judith?"

Judith shook her head.

"We're going to need boiling water, so keep a kettle on." She hesitated, looking worried for the first time that morning. "Will you be all right with all of the children?"

"Susan will help me, and we'll be fine." Judith loved her sweet niece, and at seven years old, Susan was the perfect little mother with young ones.

Annie disappeared into the bedroom and Judith took

Eli into the front room. Susan was there, playing with three-year-old Danny.

"*Hallo*, Susan."

The little girl grinned at her from the floor, where she and Danny were building with blocks. "*Hallo*, Auntie Judith."

"I'm going to make some breakfast. Will you be able to play with both Danny and Eli while I bake some coffee cake?"

"For sure." Susan scooted over to let Eli take her place on the floor, then stood to whisper in Judith's ear. "We're going to have a new baby."

Judith grinned at the excitement in Susan's voice. "I know. Isn't it wonderful?"

"Do you think it will be a boy baby or a girl baby?"

"Either one would be *wonderful-gut*. Which one do you want it to be?"

Susan's face grew serious as she watched her little brother and Eli play. "I think a boy would be nice, because then he can play with Danny." Then she turned to Judith, her face pensive. "But is it all right if I really want a little sister?"

Judith laughed and gave Susan a hug. "I don't blame you for wanting a little sister. I'm Annie's little sister, did you know that?"

Susan's eyes grew big as she considered this. "But you're a grown-up."

"I haven't always been a grown-up. Once I was little, like Rose and Viola."

Susan shook her head. "I don't remember that."

Judith bit her lip to keep from laughing again. "I don't remember it, either. I'm going to be in the kitchen with the babies. Be sure to call me if you need anything, all right?"

Susan nodded and went back to supervising the boys' play. Judith peeked into the twins' baskets when she reached the kitchen, then found a large bowl to use for mixing the cake.

As she put the cake in the oven, a sharp cry came from the bedroom, then the lusty yell of a newborn baby. It seemed that Annie had arrived just in time.

The door opened and Miriam, Ellie's elderly aunt, came out with a basin. "We're ready for some clean water to wash the wee babe." Her face was one big smile, and the midmorning sunlight streamed through the window, making her hair shine in a silvery shimmer.

"Is Ellie all right? Can I tell Bram?"

Miriam nodded as she poured warm water into the basin. "She's a beautiful little girl, with dark hair just like Susan's." The older woman gripped Judith's arm. "Give us a few minutes to tidy things up, then Bram can come in. Ellie's already asking for him."

As Miriam went back into the bedroom, Judith ran out the back door to find Bram, flying as if she had wings. No matter what Ellie had gone through, she was blessed with a baby girl. Maybe this business of becoming a mother wasn't such a scary event, after all.

Later, after the baby had been swaddled in soft cloths, Ellie lay in the bed resting and holding her new daughter. Judith leaned on the doorframe of the cozy bedroom with Eli in her arms, while Miriam and Hezekiah leaned against the wall on the other side of the bed. Bram had brought the other children in to meet their new sister, and at the sight of Susan's glowing face, Judith's eyes grew moist. The love in Bram and Ellie's family was apparent, and so was their joy at the arrival of this new little one.

"What is her name?" The question came from Johnny, and Danny echoed it.

"What's her name, *Memmi*?"

Ellie looked at Bram and he cleared his throat. "We thought a good name for her would be Margaret Ruth, after her grandmother, my mother. We'll call her Maggie for short."

Annie smiled as she stroked the top of the baby's head. "That's a fine name, Bram, and our *mamm* would have loved it. Little Maggie Ruth."

March came in like a lion on Friday, with a storm that left a foot of snow on the ground. But the next day, the sun shone brightly, turning the spring air balmy. Judith sat in the wagon bed with Guy, while David Mast and Matthew rode on the high wagon seat. Matthew had replaced the wagon's wheels with sled runners that morning and had hurried her out the door before she'd even cleared breakfast away.

"So the snowstorm means there's more sap in the trees?" Judith asked Matthew. She still didn't understand why everyone was in such a hurry or why they needed her help.

Matthew spoke over his shoulder. "Cold nights hold the sap back, so the storm we had slowed things down. But this sunshine and warmth means the sap will be shooting up the trees faster than a cottontail running from the hounds. My folks need all the help they can get to collect the sap."

"Their sugar bush must be a large one."

"Last year they made more than three hundred quarts of syrup."

"Annie has a jar in the cellar. I wondered where she had gotten it." Judith could still taste the delicious syrup she had eaten with her fried mush for breakfast. No wonder Matthew was excited. "I've never helped with a syrup harvest before, but it sounds like fun."

"The sap only runs like this for a short time, so we need to bring it in while we can." Matthew turned the horses at the corner, the harnesses jingling. "And we don't harvest syrup. We take the sap from the trees and that's boiled down to make the syrup."

The ride to the Elam Beachey's farm was short. Judith had been to the farm last week for the Singing, but this morning Matthew drove past the farm lane to the wood lot beyond it. As he drove into the woods, following a narrow track, Judith smelled wood smoke. The horses went around a thick clump of trees and a shack appeared, with smoke and steam pouring from the chimney. The yard around the shack was crowded with Matthew's brothers and some older boys, with Elam, Matthew's *daed*, standing on a stump in the middle of the group, assigning chores.

After welcoming them with a wave, Elam went on.

"We have four sleds now, with Matthew's, so we'll have four teams. Four people with each sled, and *Mamm* and I will work here in the sugaring shed, boiling sap."

"Wait here," Matthew said as he jumped off the seat. "I'll get some cans and a barrel for our sap."

As Guy helped Matthew load the big wooden barrel into the back of the sled, Judith watched the other three sleds head into the woods. Matthew rushed to the wagon seat as soon as he could, and drove into the woods, taking a different route than his brothers had.

"Why the hurry?" Guy asked.

Matthew laughed. "It's a competition every year, to see which of us brothers can bring in the most sap. I've won every year so far, but those nephews of mine are getting older. Manassas and his two boys are bound and determined to win this year, but I think we'll beat them."

When he stopped the wagon, the four of them jumped down. A bucket sat at the base of most of the trees, under a little trough that was stuck into the trunk. Clear liquid dripped from each little spout.

Guy pulled on Judith's sleeve. "Come with us. David is going to show us what we need to do."

He grabbed two empty milk pails out of the back of the sled and followed David to the first tree. The bucket was nearly full.

David stepped into the deep snow at the base of the tree. "First, take anything out of the sap that doesn't belong there."

"What kinds of things?" Judith peered into the bucket.

David snatched a brown leaf from the surface of the sap. "Leaves, like this one. Later in the season, you might find bugs floating in it."

Judith hoped that she wouldn't need to help when the weather grew warmer.

David went on. "Pour the sap into your pail, then re-place the bucket under the spout."

Judith crowded close to Guy to watch. "The sap looks like water. Not like syrup at all. Are you sure this is a sugar tree?"

David nodded and moved to the next tree. "It doesn't turn into syrup until it's been cooked down. That's what Elam and Sarai are doing at the sugar shack."

Judith took her pail and went to another tree. The work was simple enough, but her milk pails filled so quickly that she was heading back to the sled after every two trees. Before she had finished a dozen trees, Matthew called to them.

"We've filled our barrel, so I'll head back to the sugar shack."

As Matthew drove off, David pointed out a smaller tree, away from where Judith and Guy had been working. "When I got to that tree, the bucket was empty. Can you see if the hole needs clearing out? I'll go around and see if there are any others that need attention."

Judith watched Guy take the little trough out of the tree. He broke a dead twig off a larger branch and poked it into the hole. He kept poking and wiggling the stick until the sap started flowing, carrying a few wood chips along with it.

"That should do it," Guy said, straightening up. "Listen to the sap ring on the bottom of the bucket."

All around them, drops of sap fell into the buckets they had emptied, filling the woods with a pinging noise.

Suddenly, a sharp crack rang through the woods, followed by a cry. Without a word, Guy ran through the soggy snow toward the sound. Judith ran after him. This was the direction David had gone.

Guy stopped at the edge of a small gully, next to a creek. David lay in the snow below him, his face white.

"Be careful." David held his hand up in warning. "The edge gave way under me, and that's why I fell."

"There's the problem." Guy pointed to a broken tree trunk. Snow had been shaken off and the jagged edges showed where it had broken under David's weight. Guy tested it by stepping on it, and the log cracked underneath him. "This log has rotted through."

He jumped down to where David was still lying in

the deep snow. The older man's eyes had closed. Guy knelt next to him, then shot a glance at Judith.

"Go get help. Quick."

Judith turned and ran back through the woods, not stopping until she reached the sugar shack. Matthew and Elam were emptying the barrel on the back of Matthew's sled, while one of his brothers waited for his turn to unload.

"Help!" Judith shouted, trying to catch her breath. "There's been an accident."

All the men turned toward her, the sap forgotten.

"Who?" Matthew asked, grabbing his team's bridles and turning them to head back the way Judith had come. "Where?"

"David." Judith couldn't speak, she was breathing so hard. She pointed with one hand into the woods. "Guy is with him. He said to hurry."

Matthew's brother Manassas jumped onto the sled and pushed the empty sap barrel off the back as Matthew urged the team to go as fast as they could through the wet snow and mud. Elam jumped on, too, and Matthew's nephews followed, running in the packed snow of the trail.

Sarai, Matthew's mother, had come out of the sugar shack at the commotion and grasped Judith's arms before she could strike out after them.

"Don't try to follow them. I'll need your help here."

Judith nodded, and the tears she had held back started falling. Her last glimpse of Guy's face haunted her, full of fear and a deep sorrow. David had been lying still. Too still.

Melting snow seeped through the layers of clothing Verna had made him wear, and Guy was glad he had listened to her. If he was getting wet and cold, sitting here beside David, how cold must the other man be? Since Judith had gone for help, David hadn't moved. Guy had to look closely to make sure he was breathing, but David had lost consciousness and was lying on his back beside the gurgling stream, as still as death.

"Hurry, hurry," Guy muttered. A prayer? Maybe. He swallowed a threatening panic, tasting the bile. He had to remain calm. He had to think clearly to help David.

The older man's face was white above his graying beard, his eyelids partially open. Guy leaned closer. David couldn't die. He couldn't. What would Verna do without her husband?

Guy grabbed the end of his leather glove in his teeth and pulled it off. Touching David's white cheek with the back of his hand, he felt a bit of warmth. The injured man's breathing was shallow, but he was alive. His breath whooshing out in relief, Guy sat back on his heels. What would he do without David's guidance in his life? The old man had to survive this.

Guy bit his lip. David should have reacted to his touch. Before Judith left to get help, he had been awake. He had talked to them, so the fall hadn't knocked him out. Something was terribly wrong.

Grasping David's hand again, Guy leaned close to the still form. "Don't leave me, David." There was no movement.

After too many breaths, too much time, the sound of horses and the jingle of harness echoed through the woods. Then Matthew's head peered over the embankment.

"What happened?"

"That dead log gave way underneath him."

Manassas and Elam joined Matthew, and Elam slid

down the slope, landing next to Guy. "Has he been unconscious the whole time?"

Guy thought he understood the question asked in *Deitsch*. "*Ne*. He was awake when Judith and I found him. He warned us to be careful so we wouldn't fall, too."

Elam felt David's face the way Guy had. "David," he said. When David didn't respond, he called again, louder and with more force. "David! Can you hear me?"

David's eyes fluttered, then opened. He took a deep breath and let it out, then closed his eyes again.

"David," Elam called again. "Talk to me. Do you hurt anywhere?"

A groan was the only answer. Guy felt a bubble of panic rise in his chest. Why didn't David wake up?

Elam's expression was determined rather than scared, and Guy took a breath. If Elam could stay calm, so could he.

"David, try to move your arms."

"He moved one earlier," Guy said.

David's hands twitched. "Cold. I'm cold," he said.

Elam frowned. "Move your legs next. First the left one."

David's left knee raised slightly, then fell back to the ground.

"Now try your right leg."

During the pause that followed, Guy's fists clenched and unclenched. No movement. Then David groaned.

"It looks like his right leg might be broken," Matthew said.

"My hip," David whispered. "Hurts."

Guy glanced at Elam's face. The other man frowned as he stroked his beard.

Finally, he stood. "We need to get him to the house,

and we need the doctor. His hip might be broken, or his leg. Either way, we need to handle him carefully."

"Just tell us what to do, *Daed*," Matthew said, speaking for all of them.

"All right. You boys go for the doctor. Take my buggy and hitch Storm to it. He's fast and spooks easy, but you can handle him."

The boys ran off before Guy could even gauge their reaction to their grandfather's trust in them.

"Manassas, we need something to use for a stretcher. There's a ladder in the sugaring shed that will work. And tell *Mamm* to send some blankets."

Manassas took off at a run, following his sons, while Matthew turned the sled around, ready for the journey back to the house. Guy didn't move from David's side.

"Will he be all right?"

Elam locked eyes with him for a long minute. "That's in God's hands. We'll do the best we can to keep from hurting him more than he is already, but it's going to be tricky."

When Manassas got back with the ladder, the four of them worked together to move David's inert form from his cold bed in the snow to the makeshift stretcher. Underneath him was the rocky stream bed, covered in stones. Blood had seeped from a cut on David's head and covered a large rock. Guy swallowed at the thought of David falling onto it with no warning.

"Careful now, boys," Elam said. "Keep your movements steady."

By the time they reached the Beacheys' house and laid David on the bed in a downstairs bedroom, the doctor had arrived. Guy pressed against the wall of the little room, giving the doctor as much space as he could, but refused to file into the kitchen with the others. Judith stayed with him, slipping her hand into his.

As Guy watched the doctor examine David, Judith's grip tightened.

"He'll be all right," she said, standing on her toes to whisper into his ear. "Everyone in the kitchen is praying for him, and the doctor knows what he is doing."

Guy squeezed her hand. Her encouraging words flowed through him, easing the tightness and strengthening him. The doctor continued to work in silence while Guy waited. Judith leaned against him and he encircled her shoulders with one arm. He needed her here, with him. As David's white face remained still, fear drummed in his heart. If not for Judith's presence, the earth would be rocking beneath his feet.

After the boys brought the doctor, they had gone again to fetch Verna. Her voice, strong and sure, drifted into the room before her, like waves pushed by a boat in a quiet lake.

"Doctor," she said. "How is he?"

The doctor stood, stuffing his stethoscope into his black bag. He glanced at Guy, then focused on Verna.

"He has had a bad fall, and some bones might be broken. He also suffered a blow to his head, and it concerns me that he remains unconscious. There could be some internal bleeding."

"Can we take him home, doctor?" Verna asked.

"Not for some time, I'm afraid," the doctor said. "We can't risk moving him."

Verna seemed to age several years at the doctor's words, and reached one shaking arm toward Guy. He went to her, willing his strength to support her. She shuddered slightly as he took her in his arms, and she rested her forehead against his shoulder.

"Do whatever needs to be done, doctor," Guy said, feeling Verna nod in agreement as he spoke the words.

The doctor's eyebrows raised. "And you are…?"

Guy felt the pressure of a weight on his shoulders. He took a breath, holding Verna with a tight grip.

"I'm…"

"Our son," Verna said, her hand on his chest, looking up at him. "Guy is our son."

# Chapter Nine

Guy woke to the delicious scent of bacon frying, and for a long, comfortable minute he lay still, absorbing the fragrance. Only his nose was out of the covers, and he let his mind drift until the events of the past two days crowded into his consciousness and tugged him into a groggy wakefulness. Kicking the covers off, Guy rolled until he sat on the edge of the bed, his head in his hands.

David. After the morning chores were done, he needed to go to the Beacheys' to see how David was doing and to take Verna the things she had asked him to fetch.

That thought brought him fully awake. He should be alone in the house, but who was frying bacon? That aroma hadn't only been in his dreams.

After he dressed, he tiptoed down the stairs in his stocking feet, trying to talk himself out of his worries. No thief would take the time to fry bacon. Perhaps Verna had come home, after all. Perhaps David was well again, and life could get back to normal.

He reached the bottom of the stairs and peered around the corner into the kitchen. Judith was there, working at the stove, with Eli sitting at the table eating a slice of bread. As Guy stepped into the room, Eli saw him and grinned. Judith still had her back to him. She had put the bacon on a plate on the stove to keep warm and was cracking eggs one by one and dropping them into the hot pan. The bacon grease sputtered as they hit and Guy's stomach growled.

Guy leaned against the doorframe, watching her. He had taken Verna's work for granted. Her meals were always delicious and on the table right when he and David came in from working around the farm, a methodical efficiency born of long years of practice. Judith worked with as much efficiency, but her movements expressed the grace of a dancer, her skirt swaying, each movement choreographed to perfection as her tasks came together in a meal just for him.

When she turned to set the table, she saw him, but didn't pause in her work.

"I see the sleepyhead has finally appeared. I thought I would have to do the barn work as well as make the breakfast."

The cows. Guy had slept through milking time. Why hadn't their bawling woken him up earlier?

Pushing past Judith, Guy glanced at the frying eggs with regret. "I need to get to the barn. Keep my breakfast warm, if you can."

"Don't worry. Matthew already milked and put the cows out in the pasture. He left the separating for you to do, and the rest of the chores. But you can do those after you finish eating."

"Matthew did that? Why?"

Judith shrugged as she slid the eggs from the frying pan onto a hot serving platter. "That's what neighbors do when there's a need. He knew you returned home late last night and thought you needed the rest." She put the eggs on the table along with the platter of bacon, then reached into the oven for a stack of hotcakes that had been keeping warm.

She pointed to the chair next to Eli. "Go ahead and sit down. I'm not going to eat all this food by myself."

Guy sat, and without a word, they both bowed their heads for the silent prayer. But he couldn't pray, not with Judith sitting across the table from him and Eli staring. His thoughts kept drifting to David and Verna, the responsibilities of the farm. How they were depending on him. He was even beginning to understand why the farm was so important. It was their home and their life.

He squeezed his eyes tight, trying to banish Verna's echoing voice, but the thought still swirled. To the doctor, she had referred to him as their son, but he wasn't a son to anyone but Frank Hoover. He had no home. No life of his own.

Eli stirred, restless at the length of the prayer time, but Guy wasn't done. A fleeting thought, perhaps a prayer, ran through his head. That God would see fit to give him a place where he belonged. A family. A future.

He shook his head, sitting back in his chair as he opened his eyes. That was a pipe dream, like all the others.

As Judith put one of the fried eggs on Eli's plate, Guy let his gaze feast on the breakfast she had prepared for him. He hadn't asked her to do it. He hadn't even considered that she might. But she had thought of him and his needs and had put them before her own.

*"Denki,"* he said, turning his spoon over and back again. He couldn't look at her. "I'm sure you had plenty of your own work to do instead of making breakfast for me." He cleared away a tickle that had appeared in his throat.

"I was hungry, too, and Eli hasn't had his breakfast

yet." Judith passed the plate of eggs to him and took hotcakes for herself and Eli. "I knew that Verna was at Deacon Beachey's." She cut Eli's hotcake into bites for him. "And bachelors are notorious for fixing themselves poor meals."

"You can say that again." Guy reached for the hotcakes. "I ate dinner at the Beacheys' yesterday, but only had some bread and cheese for supper last night."

He piled a half dozen hotcakes on his plate, spreading a generous smear of butter on each one. As the golden stream of maple syrup flowed onto the stack, his eyes blurred. Would maple syrup always remind him of David's accident? And what if he wasn't better this morning? What if…?

Half blinded by his watering eyes, Guy set the little glass pitcher down before he spilled the syrup.

"Is everything all right?" Judith paused with a forkful of eggs partway to her mouth.

Guy wiped his forearm across his face. "*Ja*, I'm all right. The maple syrup just reminded me of David."

"How is he doing? We didn't get over there to see him yesterday."

He knew that. He had expected Judith to come, but the long hours by David's bedside had dragged on without her. There were visitors, folks from the church who had heard of the accident and came to offer their support and help, but no Judith. No calm presence to hold him up under the strain.

"The doctor said he's doing as well as we can expect. He woke up and talked to us for a while, but spent most of the time sleeping. The doctor said that was a good sign."

"I'm glad."

Guy looked up to meet her smile.

"I missed you yesterday."

"I spent the day at Bram's. With the new baby, I knew Ellie would need help with the other children."

He ran his fingers through his hair. The irony wasn't lost on him. A new baby's cries filled one home, while at Deacon Beachey's, the day had felt like a deathwatch.

"That's good. Everyone is all right?"

With that simple question, Judith's enthusiasm bubbled up. Guy finished his hotcakes and his eggs, and was down to the last piece of bacon while she talked nonstop about the baby and the other children, and who knew what else.

"And you'll never guess what they named her."

Her words drifted into the swirl of thoughts he had been wading through while she talked. The worry about David, Verna and the farm kept breaking through so that he hadn't kept track of everything she had said.

"What they named who?"

Her face turned bright pink as she glared at him. Without another word, she washed Eli's hands and face and set him on the floor to play. Then she grabbed the empty dishes off the table and dumped them into the dishpan. Seizing the dipper from above the stove, she took the lid off the reservoir and started ladling hot water into the pan.

He watched her stiff shoulders as Eli came over to him, oblivious of his aunt's mood.

"Up?"

Guy absently took the little boy on his knee and let Eli pull on his suspenders.

"Horses." Eli said, pushing on Guy's stomach to get his attention. "See horses?"

"*Ja.* I'll take you to see the horses."

Guy stood up, Eli in his arms. He took a step toward Judith but thought better of getting too close.

"Did I do something wrong?"

Her glare could have peeled paint.

"I'll take Eli out to see the animals, then I'll bring him in before I start the chores." He took a step toward the door as she turned back to shaving soap into the dishpan. "I appreciate the breakfast. More than you know."

He helped Eli put on his jacket and grabbed his hat from the hook. Glancing at Judith's rigid back, he regretted whatever he had done to make her angry. If he knew more about women, he might know what to do to bring back that peaceful feeling that had reigned during breakfast.

"Come on, Eli." He took the little boy's hand. "Let's go see the horses."

Pausing before taking the final step out of the kitchen, he tried one more time.

"I'll be heading over to Deacon Beachey's as soon as the chores are done. Do you want to come with me?"

"*Ja*, I would like to." Her voice was tight with strain. "I'll have to ask Annie if she can spare me, though."

"That's good." In his relief, he slipped back into English. "That's real good. I'd like to have you with me."

Her shoulders relaxed and she glanced over her shoulder. "And I'd like to be there with you." Then she smiled at him.

He whistled as he grabbed Eli's other hand and swung him down the steps to the ground. Giggling, the boy ran ahead toward the barn and Guy ran after him, catching him just as he stumbled on the rough ground and swinging him around.

Clutching Eli close again, Guy covered the rest of

their path to the barn like a galloping horse, making the boy laugh with every jolt.

Even if it took David months to recover from his fall, and even if nothing else right ever happened again, Judith's smile would see him through.

Later that morning, Judith peeled potatoes and carrots in Sarai Beachey's kitchen, preparing them to go into the chicken pie Ruthy and Waneta Zook were making. Judith hadn't gotten to know Waneta's stepmother well yet, but as they worked together, Judith appreciated her quick smile and her willingness to work while Sarai took a much-needed rest.

"We are so thankful that David is doing better today," Ruthy said. She boned the stewed chicken faster than Judith had ever seen anyone do that task.

"Do you know if he'll be able to go home soon?" Judith put the diced vegetables into a pot to cook before she added them to the pie filling.

"The doctor said that once he sets the broken leg and puts a splint on the hip, he will be able to be moved." Ruthy strained the broth from the stewed chicken. "It's good that the Mast farm is a short distance. The move will be hard on him, as it is, but they won't try it for a few more days."

Waneta looked up from the piecrust. "He won't be able to work on his farm, though, will he?"

Ruthy shook her head. "Only God knows when he will be recovered enough to work again."

"It's a good thing he has Guy to help him, isn't it?" Waneta eased the crust into the large baking pan. They were expecting to feed more than twelve people for the noon meal with all the neighbors who had come to visit David and help collect the sap and boil it off. "If it was only David and Verna on that farm, they would have a hard time of it."

Judith dumped the potato and carrot peelings into the slop bucket. "But the church will help, won't it? I heard the men talking about a work day to get the crops planted."

Ruthy nodded. "There are still the day-to-day chores that need to be done, though. That responsibility is too much for Verna, so Waneta is right. Having Guy around to help is *wonderful-gut*."

With this talk of Guy, Judith's stomach took a turn. Just when she thought their friendship was growing into something more, he had to prove himself just as infuriating as any man could be. He had let her make a fool of herself this morning as she talked on and on about baby Maggie Ruth and Bram's growing family. Why she had smiled at him as he had taken Eli to see the horses, she had no idea. Just because he'd said he wanted her to come to Elam and Sarai's with him? That one kind offer wasn't enough to make her forgive him for ignoring her, even if he had made Eli happy with the trip to the barnyard.

While Ruthy took the dishpan off the wall and started filling it, Judith decided to start a batch of gingerbread for dessert. The soft cake would be a welcome end to their meal. As she looked through the cupboards to make sure all the ingredients were on hand, Waneta joined her.

"What kind of cake are you planning to make?"

"I thought gingerbread would be good. The molasses will make it sweet, but I can't find any ginger."

Waneta opened another cupboard. "Here are the spices." She picked up one of the small cans and read the label. "Cream of Tartar." She looked at each of the containers, one by one. "Does Guy like gingerbread?"

Judith fetched the can of lard from the cupboard next to the sink. "I'm not sure if I care if he likes it or not."

Waneta found the ginger and set it on the counter next to the mixing bowl. "Why not? I thought you were good friends."

She kept her voice low, and Judith was glad. Guy was in the next room with Verna and David, and she didn't want him to suspect that they were talking about him.

"We are. I mean, we were." Judith broke some eggs into a small bowl and whisked them with a fork. "But this morning I was telling him about spending yesterday at Ellie and Bram's, and he didn't listen to me at all."

"Reuben will do that, too. I think he just doesn't hear me sometimes."

Ruthy shaved soap flakes into the dishwater and swirled them around with her hand, waiting for them to dissolve. "You need to be patient with Guy. David's accident is a shock for everyone, but for him and Verna most of all."

"That's right," Waneta said, scooping the lard into the mixing bowl. "He has a lot on his mind. You'll learn to gauge his moods and know when he's ready to listen and when he isn't."

The whisking fork slowed in Judith's hand. Gauge his moods? That's how *Mamm* had lived with *Daed* all those years, and how she and Esther had treated Samuel after their parents were gone. Every day they had tiptoed around their brother, not knowing what kind of mood he was in or how he would treat them. If that was what living with a man was like, then it wasn't for her.

A soft knock at the back door drew her attention. Levi Zook stood in the doorway, his hat in his hand and a shy smile on his face. "Ruthy, I'm going over to David's with Guy, Bram and Matthew to see what needs to be done on the farm."

As Ruthy dried her hands, Judith happened to see the glance that passed between her and her husband. A private look. A loving look. No tiptoeing around Levi's feelings. It was the same look she had seen pass between Bram and Ellie after Maggie Ruth's birth and the same look she saw often when Matthew and Annie were together. Many words were held within those looks. Private words that only the couple understood.

Perhaps her family's example wasn't the way all couples lived. After all, she had seen those same private looks pass between Samuel and Mary since they got married last year.

Maybe gauging a man's moods had less to do with avoiding his anger and more to do with knowing how to make him happy.

Levi stepped into the doorway of the bedroom where David was and said something to Guy. As the two men headed out the door, Guy glanced at Judith. His face was hopeful, his eyebrows raised. Waiting. Apologizing? She smiled and he broke into a grin before he followed Levi out the door. She turned back to her work. If she remembered right, Guy had said he liked anything sweet—and especially gingerbread.

Guy followed Levi out of Deacon Beachey's house with a light step. David seemed to be recovering, and Judith had smiled at him. Twice. It seemed that whatever he had done to put her off had been forgiven.

Matthew drove the four men to David's. As they rode, Matthew talked about the work that needed to be done.

"Has David started his plowing, yet?"

Guy shook his head. "We were going to start this week."

"That will be the first thing, then." Matthew turned the horse north at the intersection.

"Does he have his seed?" Bram asked. "Do you know what his plans were?"

"He said something about planting sorghum in the lower field and buckwheat in the field next to the pasture. The upper fields, between the house and the road, are being planted to corn this year."

"What about the mint fields?"

Guy whooshed out a sigh. The mint fields along the creek bottom at the back of the farm were a mystery to him. "That's part of the farm I know nothing about. I know we cut the mint last August, but I don't know if he does anything with the crop in the spring."

Last spring, he had still lived at the Home and only worked for David a couple of days a week. It wasn't until after his eighteenth birthday in May that he had left the Home and David had hired him on as a farm hand. In the ten months since then, he had begun to feel the rhythm of farm life, but this was his first spring to work with David full-time. He wasn't ready to step into the older man's shoes, that was for sure and certain.

Matthew let out a thoughtful grunt. "I remember David saying something about checking out the fields after the spring rains. Last year he had to replant some of the areas along the creek bank. We'll have to keep that in mind once May comes."

"You don't think he'll be able to work by then?" Guy looked from one man to another, but none of them met his eyes.

Bram cleared his throat. "David is suffering quite a

bit, and the broken bones will keep him laid up for a long time. If he recovers—"

"If?"

"You heard what the doctor said, that his hip is broken."

"But broken bones mend, don't they?"

Bram rubbed his knee with one thumb, not looking at Guy. "*Ja*, for sure they mend, but David is an old man, and he may not be able to work again."

Guy stared at the fields they passed, but didn't see them. David not able to work? The man had always been the first to the barn in the morning, the first to get to work when Guy was lagging behind. When the doctor said David would survive, Guy had never thought that he wouldn't be able to get back to normal.

They rode in silence until Matthew turned into the farm lane. The barn rose ahead of them, on the right, and the house was on the left. Guy's throat closed as he looked at them, strong and steady. Well cared for. And his responsibility. Could he run the farm without David? He was just a kid. At least, he felt that way. He didn't have what it took to run a big farm like this. Especially not to David's standards.

As they got out of the buggy, the other men surveyed the neat barnyard and well-kept grass lawn around the house.

Levi clapped him on the shoulder. "It looks like you're caring for things the way David would want you to."

Guy noticed a loose screw on the door to the milking parlor and the chicken house that David had wanted him to whitewash this week. The others might not have noticed those details, but David would have. "I don't think I would ever keep this place going the way David does."

"You don't have to do it alone," Bram said as he led the way into the barn. "You have the church to help out."

Inside the granary, Guy showed the others where David had stored his seed for the planting season. The lead-lined bins were clean and free from vermin.

"The plow and harrow are all set for the spring." Guy led the way into the machine shed across from the granary where the equipment stood ready, the metal plow-shares glowing in the dim light.

"It looks like all you need is a dry day like today," Levi said, leaning down to test the edge of the plow.

"We should be ready. David and I have been cleaning and sharpening the equipment all winter." Remembering the hours he had spent with a whetstone brought tears to Guy's eyes. David had leaned over him, showing him the right angle to hold the stone, the right pressure to wield to hone the perfect edge.

"I know the harnesses don't need any work," Matthew said, interrupting Guy's thoughts. "David always keeps them in fine shape."

The men wandered out into the barnyard again, and Levi walked over to the empty field between the house and the road, on the north side of the long farm lane. The snow from last week's storm had melted in the warm spring weather they had had since then.

"What is he doing?" Guy asked.

"Checking the soil," Bram said. "That's one thing I've had to learn as I've begun farming on my own. Hezekiah taught me what to look for, but I don't quite have the knack yet. Someone who's been farming for years just knows when the soil is right. It needs to be dry enough to plow, but not so dry that the wind will draw all of the moisture out of the soil when you turn it."

Matthew looked up into the sky. "Doesn't look like

we'll be getting any rain the next few days. The high pressure seems to be holding."

Guy gazed up into the clear blue sky. He didn't see anything.

"Now I know you're all pulling my leg. You can't tell what the weather is going to do any more than Levi can feel when the soil is ready. You make it sound like farming is full of old wives' tales and old timers' signs." He grinned, waiting for them to laugh at the joke.

Bram grinned, but no one laughed. "It might seem that way, but where do you think the signs and tales came from? Experience is what a farmer relies on, and if you're smart, you'll pay attention and learn for yourself."

Guy stepped closer to Matthew. "So, tell me how you know it won't rain tomorrow."

The shorter man leaned back on his heels, his eyes on the trees rising behind his house across the road. "Look over there at the tree tops and tell me which way the wind is blowing."

The breeze was light enough that Guy couldn't feel it on the ground, but the ends of the branches swayed slightly against the sky. "They're hardly moving, but I'd guess the wind is from the northwest?"

Matthew nodded. "And after the snow went through over the weekend, the wind was from the northeast."

"And cold," Guy said.

"Today it's turned to the northwest, which means fair weather ahead. When the wind turns to the south, you can expect a storm, or at least rainfall." He turned to Guy. "A wise farmer keeps track of the weather. Makes notes on the calendar or in a journal. The direction and strength of the wind, the amount of rain. Some even have a barometer and keep track of the air pressure. When the barometer goes down, you know rain is coming."

As Matthew, Levi and Bram discussed the best time to start plowing David's land, Guy hung back. A heavy weight pressed on his shoulders and his stomach soured. Why hadn't he paid more attention when David went on endlessly about soil and manure and seeds and hours of sunlight? With one misstep, David was laid up and now the responsibility of the farm fell on Guy.

He took a step back from the others, but they didn't notice. Panic sent a bitter taste to his mouth. He swallowed. What could he do? He couldn't stay here. He would mess things up, everyone would see that he didn't know what he was doing and...worst of all... David would know how inept he really was.

"Guy!"

He focused on Matthew, who was gesturing to him.

"Come over here. We need to make plans."

What had Bram said? Guy wiped the back of his neck with one hand. He wasn't alone in this. The church would help. That community that David had talked about the day he made the three-legged stool.

The weight lifted a bit as he joined the others.

# *Chapter Ten*

On Wednesday, after her chores were done, Judith took Eli to the Masts' to help Guy ready the house for David's return home on Thursday. The doctor had given Guy and Verna a list of changes that needed to be made for David's comfort, including moving a bed into the front room. And after living as a bachelor for nearly a week, Judith knew Guy would need help with household chores before Verna came home.

Judith let Eli run down the lane to the Masts' house in front of her. He stopped every few feet, bending over to pick another dandelion growing in the fresh, green grass alongside the buggy tracks, then took off again, running in his stiff-legged, toddler way. When he had gathered three or four of the yellow flowers, he came running back to her.

*"Die Blumm."* Eli opened his sticky fist and held them up to her. *"Blumm."*

*"Denki*, Eli. The flowers are beautiful."

He grinned and ran off again, stopping to pick another flower every few steps. By the time they reached the Masts' back porch, her hands were full of dandelion blossoms.

Guy must have seen them coming. He opened the door and stepped out just as Judith was laying the mass of yellow flowers on the back step.

"Verna will be glad to see those," he said. Catching Eli in a hug, he sat on the top step with the little boy on his knee. "She loves dandelion tea. I've heard her talking of it often."

"I think Eli has picked enough flowers for a dozen cups of tea." Judith sat on the step next to him. "And I see you've been practicing your *Deitsch*. You only used two *Englisch* words in that sentence."

Guy held up one of the flowers. "What are these called, then? I only know them as dandelions."

"I've heard them called a couple different things, but I've always called them *pusteblumm*. Because when they turn white, you puff on them to scatter the seeds."

"I get it." He twirled the stem, switching to *Englisch*. "Puff flowers. I can just see you as a little girl, picking all the white balls and blowing the seeds everywhere."

"My sister Esther calls them *buddah blummen*." She held one of the flowers under her chin. "Because if you see yellow on your chin when you hold the flower like this, that means you like butter."

"So, butter flowers." Guy grinned. "I can tell you like butter."

Judith snatched the flower away from her face, knowing from the heat in her cheeks that she was blushing. "What do you call them?"

He made a face. "Weeds. The headmaster at the Home wanted the grass in the lawn to be without any weeds, so one of our chores was to dig up the dandelion plants every spring."

"I've never heard of someone wanting to get rid of them. The flowers are good for tea, and the leaves are yummy greens cooked with bacon and vinegar, and the roots are good for medicine."

"I know. But the headmaster made up his mind, and we had to obey."

Something in Guy's tone drew Judith's gaze. He still jiggled Eli on his knee, giving the boy a pony ride, but his eyes were shadowed, as if he was looking into the past.

"What was it like, growing up in the Orphan's Home?"

He shook his head. "You don't want to know."

"In one way, I suppose it could be fun to have so many brothers and sisters. A big family."

"It wasn't like that." His voice was quiet, but with a hard edge. "We weren't children. Not like Eli or the other children you know. We were property." He swallowed, his Adam's apple bouncing down and up. "The headmaster hired us out to whoever was looking for a boy or girl to work for them."

"But the families who hired you, like the Masts. They were good to you, weren't they?"

Guy shook his head. "Not all of them. The summers that I was seven and eight, I was hired out to a farmer who treated me worse than the headmaster." He held Eli tightly and stopped the pony ride. "I remember one time when the rooster fell in the well. The farmer had to get it out before its carcass poisoned the water, so he sent me down there. He tied a rope to my foot and lowered me headfirst."

Judith scooted closer to him as he passed a hand over his eyes, as if he was trying to erase the memory.

"He didn't hear me yell when he had lowered me to the surface of the water, and I nearly drowned before he hauled me up again."

Guy shuddered, then gave Judith a weak smile. "I've been deathly afraid of water ever since. When I came here, I thought the headmaster had made a mistake. This place was too nice."

"The Lord God led you here to a family who loves you." The shadows in Guy's eyes faded as she spoke. "How old were you?"

"I was nine that first summer. David and Verna gave me a room in the house. My own room with a real bed instead of a cot in the lean-to or a pile of straw in the barn. Verna made new clothes for me and fed me the best food I had ever eaten. The best part was that David never whipped me."

Judith's stomach turned. "Were you whipped at the other place?"

"And at the Home." He chuckled, but the sound was more of a sob than laughter. "The headmaster believes that boys need to have evil beaten out of them." He shrugged. "I don't know if he's right or not. But I do know that I was always happiest during the summers when I was here." He looked at the barn and outbuildings. "David and Verna hired me every summer after that, and I'm grateful."

Judith could see that little boy in her mind. A young Guy, about the same age as her nephew Johnny. What would a life like that drive a boy to when he grew up?

"You must be glad that David asked you to work here, then, and be part of their family."

Guy frowned as he flicked at a spot of mud on his knee. Eli leaned against his shoulder, sucking his thumb, his eyes heavy.

"I'm glad they made room for me, but I don't know how long it will last."

"Why wouldn't it last? Why would you go anywhere else?"

He shrugged. "One thing I've learned is that noth-

ing lasts forever. People come and go out of our lives
for one reason or another, so I've learned to take life
as it comes. Someday David will quit farming and sell
out, or he'll hire someone else with more experience
than I have, and I'll have to find a new job. That's just
the way it is."

Judith stared at him. His words put a cold space between them as if he had reached out and pushed her
away with his hand. "You can't think David and Verna
would do that to you. I heard Verna talking about you
at the quilting a couple weeks ago. They love you and
are so grateful you are living with them and helping
them. And with David's accident, they need you now,
more than ever."

"Yeah. Sure. That's what they all say. That's what
Pa said, too, but where is he? Forgotten all about me,
I expect." He drew Eli closer in a casual hug. "I'm on
my own and always will be."

"You aren't alone."

"Not now. I appreciate the church, Matthew and all
them, and their willingness to help on the farm while
David recovers. But it won't last. There will come a
time when they don't need me, and then I'll move on."

Judith laid her hand on his forearm, trying to close
the gap between them, but his muscles were tense beneath his sleeve. Hard and unyielding.

"Don't you want to stay? To become part of the community? To have a home?"

His arm jerked away and his jaw bulged, but his eyes
grew moist. She scooted closer to him.

"Why do you fight against it if you want it so much?"

Guy shifted Eli to her lap and stood. "Who said I
wanted anything?" His eyes glittered with unshed tears.
"I'm just looking out for myself, that's all. I don't need

you to feel sorry for me, and I don't need anyone's help. You got that?"

He stalked toward the barn, not looking back, even when Eli began to cry. Judith felt like joining her nephew. Guy could have slapped her in the face and it would have hurt less. She jiggled Eli to stop his crying and bent close to his ear.

"Should we go in the house and find a nice, quiet place to lie down? Would you like that?"

Eli nodded and wrapped his arms around her neck, his innocent love a healing balm for her sore heart.

Guy took three steps into the barn before he remembered the work he needed to do was inside the house instead of out here. But his only thought had been to get away from Judith. He heard Eli's crying end and turned to watch Judith comforting the boy. Her head bent over his brown curls as she talked to him, then she wrapped him in her arms as he clung to her, safe and secure.

Judith rose and went into the house, but the scene clouded over as tears filled Guy's eyes. He let them fall, leaning his head against the solid wood of the doorframe. He had shut her out and pushed her away just as much as he had shoved Eli off his lap and onto hers. But why?

Because the feelings she brought out stopped his very breath. He dug his fingernails into the oak beam as the pain of those feelings overwhelmed him. If he could be little again…if he could see Mama again…if he could feel safe again…

He tore his thoughts away. He was a grown man, not a child. His life was laid out in front of him. A stark and lonely track with no end.

What was it about Judith that upset his well-ordered life? Before she'd come along, he had been happy.

Well, maybe not happy. But he could work, laugh and enjoy David's company and Verna's cooking. But now that he knew her, it was as if her steady blue eyes looked right into him and saw the scared little boy who needed a friend.

She made him long for things that would never happen. Things like a home. His own family. A…a wife. A partner in life. Someone to love and to love him. Someone who wouldn't leave him behind.

How could something he wanted so badly hurt so much?

So he had pushed her away when she awakened those longings in him again. But the hurt only grew worse until it felt like someone had sucker-punched him and left him gasping for breath.

"Please, God." The words came out as a whisper, barely passing over his lips as he breathed out. "Please, God, show me how to make the pain go away."

The pain eased, and in its place came the need to see Judith. To be with her. To patch things up.

But what if she was mad at him? What if she had gone home already?

He stuck his head out the door with that panicked thought, but there she was. She had left Eli in the house and was gathering the discarded dandelion blossoms into one of Verna's mixing bowls. Relief washed over him.

Walking across the barnyard to the porch, he waited for her to lift her head. To notice him. But she had turned away as she retrieved the blossoms that had fallen off the porch. He stopped a few paces behind her and cleared his throat.

Judith turned to him, looking worn out. "Eli was so tired, I put him down to sleep in the bedroom." She took a step closer to him, peering at his face. "Are you all right? You look like you might be ill."

He rubbed at his eyes, wiping away the last remnants of the tears, but he was sure tell-tale redness would remain.

"I'm fine." He took the bowl of dandelions from her. "I was out of line, back there."

"What does that mean, 'out of line'?"

"It means that I acted poorly. I treated you badly."

She didn't speak. If Guy had any doubts that his attitude had hurt her, they were silenced now. He had wounded her sorely.

"I was a real jerk."

She smiled then. "You were a *nah*. A fool."

*"Ja. Ich voah der nah."* He had been a fool, all right. A fool to think he could ever survive without seeing her smile.

Judith led the way into the kitchen as he followed.

"Why did you act that way, then?" she asked. "We were only talking."

Guy gazed out the kitchen window. Could he open his heart to her? She needed to know what she did to him. She put the bowl of dandelions in the sink under the spout. Guy pumped water for her as she thrust the blossoms below the surface, letting the excess drain off.

"I've haven't had a home for years."

She started to speak, but he stopped her.

"I haven't had a home since my mother died, when I was five." Her eyes fixed on his, and he could feel them boring deep into his soul. "I want…no, I need what you have. A family, friends. A future. But every time I think it's within my grasp, something happens to take it away." Pa's face flashed for an instant, then it was gone. "So I'm afraid that if I join the church, or if I reach out to accept the home David and Verna want me to have, it will melt like a snowflake in my hand."

Judith leaned closer and he stopped pumping, letting the last of the water run into the basin.

"So you want it, but you're afraid to want it."

His eyes grew damp again. "I want it so badly that it hurts." He turned toward her. "And you. You make me want it even more."

She swirled the blossoms in the water, watching the spiral of yellow.

Guy bent down, catching her gaze. "I like you a lot, Judith."

He didn't just like her. He needed her like a thirsty plant needed rain. He needed her to fill that empty place.

She smiled, not looking at him. "I like you, too."

"Would you...would you be my girl?"

"You mean that I'd only talk to you at the Singings? And only ride home with you?"

When she put it that way, Guy felt her softness sliding away from him. The empty place ached.

"But you want to spend time with other fellows." He backed away. He had spoken too soon.

"Guy, I don't want to see other boys. Not really. I just want..." She bit her lip as her voice trailed off.

"What do you want? I'll do anything."

"I just want to be sure that my future will be secure. That I'll always have a place in the community with my family." She looked at him, her expression serious. "Anyone who courts me has to want the same thing."

The aching feeling flared until his joints burned. Didn't he want that, too?

Or did he? If Pa came by right now and offered Guy a chance at a life together with him, wouldn't he jump at it?

His breath whooshed out. He hadn't been aware that he'd been holding it.

"I don't even know what I want." He swept his hand in the air, taking in the table where he had eaten so many meals, the front room beyond the door where he had spent so many evenings with David and Verna, the staircase leading to his room upstairs. "This and the Home are all I know, but I feel like there's something else out there…"

"Life with your father." Judith's voice was flat as she supplied the answer for him. "The father who may never return."

Guy nodded his head. Even though Pa's promises might be made of straw, they'd been strong enough to hold him captive in the past. Trapped until he knew for sure if Pa would ever come back or not.

Judith woke up early on Saturday, the big work day at the Masts' farm, after what seemed like a sleepless night. So many chores pressed in on her mind that it felt like she'd been making lists in her head all night. Finally, long before dawn, but while the waning moon was still high in the sky, she got up. Lighting the candle she kept on the table by her bed, she found an old envelope and the stub of a pencil and wrote out every item she needed to do before going to David and Verna's in the morning. Finally, she blew out the candle and settled under the covers to get a bit of sleep.

But it didn't work. Even in her sleep, she dreamed of peeling potatoes until the peelings overflowed the dishpan and spilled out through the kitchen door.

Finally, she opened her eyes. The sun was nearly up and there was light enough to see. Now she could start on that list and get plenty done before Eli woke up.

Judith sat at the table in the quiet kitchen and started peeling the potatoes she had washed and sorted the previous night.

Matthew had helped to bring David home on Thursday, and the older man was comfortably settled in the front room. David had asked to be there, rather than the bedroom, so he could be in the center of things. Guy had moved the spare bed into the room, and then had gone to town to purchase the special mattress the doctor had recommended. And Guy had altered the bed so that the top half could be raised or lowered and David could recline or lie flat.

Thinking of Guy brought a smile and her peeling slowed. She liked Guy. He was strong and clever and… and he was a friend she could talk to about anything.

But that was all. A special friend. He said he wanted her to be his girl, but she didn't want to go any farther than friendship until he was ready to commit to being part of the community.

Sighing, she reached for another potato. Some days, she felt like he was already part of the church, but then other times it was like he stood on the opposite side of a fence, looking in, but ready to flee like a skittish horse.

Judith put the third peeled potato into the big pot of clean water and eyed the waiting pile. Nearly thirty pounds waited to be peeled, washed, cut and boiled. Then mashed, buttered and seasoned. Then kept warm in the big pans until dinnertime. Meanwhile, she still needed to make the noodles. She tackled the next potato. At least she wouldn't have to make all this food by herself. Perhaps the other ladies would get to Verna's in time to make the noodles. Several had told Verna they were bringing chickens to stew. They would make a half-dozen pans of chicken and noodles, her favorite dish.

As Judith started on the next potato, someone knocked on the door and walked into the kitchen before Judith could dry her hands.

"Judith? Annie? Am I too early?"

Waneta carried a laundry basket covered with a towel.

"*Ach, ne.* I'm the only one up, but I've started on the work already." Judith took the basket and set it on the counter. "Is Ruthy with you?"

Waneta shook her head. "I came along early while the others finish the chores at home. I thought you could use some help with all the folks you're expecting to feed today."

Judith gestured toward the pile of potatoes. "I can, for sure and for certain. All I can think about is how much there is to do, and how little time before noon."

Waneta hung her shawl on an empty hook. "When you see what I brought, you'll stop worrying." She uncovered the basket to reveal a mound of fresh noodles. "*Mamm* and I made them yesterday. She said we might as well make them early and get the chore out of the way."

"She's right." Judith got a dishpan for Waneta's potato peelings. "And I'm so glad you came. We have at least an hour before Eli wakes up, so we can visit while we peel these potatoes."

"I know what we need to talk about first. We haven't had a chance to talk in private since Luke took you home from the Singing." Waneta found a knife in the drawer and sat down at the table. "You need to tell me about you and Luke and Guy." She paused, a narrow peel already hanging from her knife. "Have you chosen one of them?"

"I don't have anything to say about Luke." Judith tackled her own potato, trying to make her peelings as narrow and thin as Waneta's. Her earlier peelings had been thick with the flesh of the potato, which was wasteful, and she worked quickly to hide them under the new batch.

"Why not? I thought he was sweet on you."

"He thought he was, too. But I set him straight."

Waneta leaned forward. "What do you mean? You have to tell me everything."

"I'm not going to gossip." Judith concentrated on the end of her potato and the peeling dropped into the pan in her lap, almost as neat as Waneta's. "But Luke and I found that we don't have a lot in common."

"I thought he would be perfect for you." Waneta sounded disappointed as she resumed her peeling. "He has always said he wanted to marry the prettiest girl around, and when you showed up at church that first Sunday, I saw the way he looked at you."

Judith shook her head. Her? Pretty? "You've got it wrong. Luke was only interested because I was new. Besides, he isn't the type of man I'm looking for."

"What type is that?"

"Someone kind, and willing to work hard, and cute. A good Amishman."

"It sounds like you're describing Reuben, but you can't have him." Waneta sent her a mock frown and Judith laughed.

"I'm not describing Reuben."

"Then it must be Benjamin, Reuben's brother."

Judith shook her head and kept peeling.

"My brother Elias?"

"I've never even met him."

Waneta started in on another potato. "That's right." She sighed. "I suppose you want to keep it a secret for now. But when you're ready to tell someone, you'll tell me first, won't you?"

Judith grinned at this girl who had become a friend so quickly. "I'll tell you right after I tell my sisters."

Waneta laughed. "That's fair enough."

They worked in silence for a few minutes, then Waneta asked another question.

"Are you still teaching *Deitsch* to Guy Hoover? You were pretty upset with him the other day. Are you two friends again?"

Judith studied Waneta's face, but there wasn't any hint of teasing or that she thought Guy might be a special friend.

"He appreciates the community helping out with David's farm work today. He mentioned it several times when Annie and I were visiting David and Verna yesterday."

Waneta pulled some potatoes closer to her from the dwindling pile. "He's always been so standoffish. But since you've been teaching him, he hangs around with the other fellows more."

"I think he feels more comfortable with them now that he can speak our language better." Judith took another potato and changed the subject. "Is there anything new going on in your family?"

"Can you keep a secret?"

Judith laughed at Waneta's eager face. "Is it a secret you can tell?"

"It isn't that kind of secret, and everyone is going to know soon, anyway."

"I think I can guess. There's going to be a new baby at your house."

"How did you know?"

"It was something Ruthy did while we were at Deacon Beachey's the other day. She put her hand on her back, like she felt a twinge there. I've seen my sister-in-law Ellie do that same thing many times." Judith smiled, remembering the soft look on Ruthy's face when she did it, as if she was carrying a treasure only she knew about.

"I need to be careful around you," Waneta said. "You'll discover all my secrets even before I know about them." She grinned. "My brothers want the next baby to be a boy, but I hope Grace can have a sister that's close to her in age."

Waneta's youngest sister, Grace, was the prettiest baby Judith had ever seen, with curly black hair and dark blue eyes. "Grace doesn't look anything like the rest of you, does she?"

"That's because Grace had a different mother and father than we do. Her mother was *Mamm's* best friend, but she passed away when Grace was born. So we adopted her."

"Even though there were already ten children in your family?"

Waneta nodded. "Like *Daed* says, there's always enough love for one more."

Always enough love for one more. That sounded like something Verna would say. How different would Guy's life have been if they had been able to adopt him?

How different would her life be if Guy had grown up in the church, like Benjamin Stoltzfus or Nathan Zook?

No questions. No wondering about the future. She glanced sideways at Waneta reaching for another potato. As sure of Guy as Waneta was of Reuben.

Her life would be perfect. No less than perfect.

# Chapter Eleven

"It's a fine day, isn't it?" Verna set a plate piled with hotcakes in front of Guy. "The folks should be showing up soon, so eat your fill. You need your strength."

"How many do you think will be here?" Guy poured maple syrup over the stack of steaming cakes.

"I wouldn't be surprised if the whole church came." Verna poured coffee into a mug she had set on a tray for David. "That's the usual way of things. When someone is in need, the community steps in to help."

As Verna scrambled eggs at the stove, Guy cut into his stack of hotcakes and took the first bite. Light. Fluffy. Sweet. Just the way he liked them.

"Several of the women will be coming, too."

Guy took another bite, enjoying the warm feeling brought by the anticipation of seeing Judith soon.

Verna went on, speaking over the sizzle of bacon frying and the scrape of her spatula in the frying pan. "We'll be working on the noon meal all morning long, so don't think you can come in here to grab a snack anytime you want."

He grunted a response, his mouth full of hotcakes and his mind lingering on Judith. Would she smile at him in front of everyone? Or would she ignore him, insisting that they were no more than friends? Tradition dictated that no one should know he was sweet on her, but Guy wasn't one to stick to tradition.

"We'll be making donuts for a snack for you men, so you won't go hungry."

She brought two plates of eggs and bacon to the table. Setting one in front of Guy, she put the second on the tray. Next came two dishes of stewed prunes: one for the table and a second for the tray.

"When you're finished with your breakfast, will you take David's tray in to him?" Verna patted his shoulder as she took his empty hotcake plate. "He said he wanted to talk to you before the men arrived this morning."

Guy swallowed the last of the sweet prunes and set his plate of eggs on the tray next to David's.

"*Denki*, Verna. Breakfast was good," he said as he carried the tray into the front room.

David was sitting up in bed, leaning against the support Guy had made for him. He was dressed from the waist up, and Verna had helped him with his morning routine of combing his hair and shaving his upper lip, leaving his beard growing long and full as the Amish did. Guy laid the tray on David's lap, then sat in Verna's chair with his plate.

"It smells good," David said, taking a deep breath that ended in a cough.

Guy frowned while David bowed his head in a silent prayer. The doctor had warned them to watch for a cough that could easily turn to pneumonia in a bedridden patient.

"Do you need me to prop you up further? Will it help to be more upright?"

The older man shook his head, waving him away.

"I'm fine like this." He picked up his fork and took a small bite of the eggs. "Do you have a plan of what work you'll be doing today?"

Guy shrugged. "Matthew and Bram have it pretty well laid out. I thought I'd just do what they tell me."

David picked up his coffee, blowing across the steaming liquid before taking a sip. "This is our farm, Guy. The others will be here to help, not to do the work for you. You need to be the one to organize the men and plan the day."

Setting his fork on his plate, Guy looked at David. "Me? I'm just the hired help. I don't know what needs to be done, or when, or how. All of the others have a lot more experience than I do."

"But they don't know the fields the way you do. And you—" Another cough interrupted David's words. "And you're more than just hired help. You're acting for me today."

Guy ate a slice of bacon in three bites, then finished his eggs. Step into David's shoes? Him? There must be another way.

"Maybe we could move your bed outside so you could supervise. You could be there to answer everyone's questions…" His words trailed off as David shook his head.

"I'm not up to that, and you know it." He shifted slightly in his bed and grimaced with pain. "I'm tired." He leaned his head back against the pillow. "So tired."

His eyes closed and Guy stood up to leave him alone.

As he lifted the forgotten tray from David's lap, the older man's eyelids fluttered. "I'm counting on you, Guy." He laid a cool, dry hand on Guy's. "I can't be out there, but you can. And you can do this, son. I know you can."

As David drifted off to sleep, Guy carried the tray back to the kitchen. Verna shook her head, clucking her tongue as she scraped David's uneaten breakfast into the slop pail.

"He'll be all right." Guy ducked his head to kiss her on the cheek. "He just needs to rest and recover."

He swallowed as he thought of that cough. David was going to get well. He had to.

Grabbing his hat from the hook, he stepped out into the barnyard and looked up at the sky. The same as David would do first thing every morning.

Guy ran his thumbs along his suspenders. Okay, so he hadn't checked the sky earlier, when he had come out to do the milking. But he'd get in the habit eventually.

He tilted his head up again, this time taking a good look. A gentle breeze blew from the northwest, and the light, wispy clouds didn't seem to move at all. A quiet morning with the sun shining in a blue sky. A dry day ahead, and cool weather. Perfect for getting the work done that they needed to do. He went into the barn, checking the plow and harrow. He ran his hands along the harnesses, feeling for sticky spots that would betray a dirty harness or weak places in the leather. Everything was ready.

Going through one of the big box stalls, Guy opened the back door and whistled for the draft horses. He would hitch up all six of them today to plow the south front field. One of the other fellows could follow him with their team and a harrow. Meanwhile, another pair of men could do the same with the north field. The day's plans ordered themselves in his head as he mentally assigned men and teams to the various fields and different tasks. If all went well, they might even be able to get the buckwheat planted in the back field behind the house. Planting the sorghum and corn would have to wait a few weeks, until the soil was warmer.

The horses came into their stalls, eager for their oats and the work they knew was waiting for them. As they ate, Guy groomed each one, paying special attention to their shoulders and backs, where the weight of the harness would press. He checked their feet for any stones that might have gotten lodged in their hooves while they were out in the pasture, then fastened a lead rope to each halter. After they had eaten, he'd lead them to the trough for some water, then back into the barn to harness them up.

As he fastened the lead rope to Penny's halter, she lifted her nose from her empty feed box and nudged him, looking for another treat. He laughed and gave her a piece of carrot, just as he had the other horses. She munched the carrot slowly, watching him with one eye. Then she winked, as if to say, "We know you can do this work. You're not alone."

Guy laughed at his fanciful thoughts, then smiled as he heard the first team coming toward the barn along the lane. Penny was right. He had the whole community to help him work today. Confidence flowed through him as he headed out to the barnyard to greet the visitors.

By the time Judith and Waneta finished peeling the potatoes, Eli was awake and the day started in earnest.

Breakfast was quick, with fried potatoes, ham and scrambled eggs. Waneta ate with the family, helping Annie care for the babies while Judith dealt with a fussy Eli.

"The children know things are different this morning, with the work day and all." Annie sighed, holding baby Rose to her shoulder and patting her back.

Matthew finished his breakfast and rose from table. "I need to hitch our team, then I'll be heading over to the Masts'."

*"Da,"* shouted Eli, dumping his plate onto the floor with a crash. "I go with *Da!*" He squirmed in his chair, pushing at Judith's hands as she tried to keep him from falling, and Viola joined in the mayhem with a screaming cry.

Waneta's face grew red as she tried to suppress her laughter while comforting Viola. "Now this sounds like home when Grace is out of sorts!"

"Eli, stop that crying right now!" Judith kept her voice firm and the little boy stopped his wiggling. He leaned back in his chair, tears rolling down his cheeks.

"I go with *Da*." He reached his hands out toward Matthew, his voice pitifully sad.

"Not right now, Eli." Matthew picked up his son, holding the sobbing boy in his arms. "You'll come later, with Judith and Waneta. Until then, you help take care of your sisters." Eli cried louder, but Matthew set him on the floor next to Judith. "Do as I say now. I will see you later."

When Matthew shut the door behind him, Eli ran to it. *"Da! Da!"*

Judith went to him, lifting him in her arms. "You need to obey your *daed*, and crying won't change anything." She got a towel and wiped his face. "But you can help me with the potatoes, and we'll go hitch up the buggy in a little while."

"Horse?" Eli's tears stopped at Judith's promise of the work that lay ahead of them.

*"Ja*, you can help me with the horse." Judith grinned at him until he smiled back, then set him down, satis-

fied that he was over his tantrum. He loved Summer, the
buggy horse, more than any other animal on the farm.

Meanwhile, the twins were quieting down as Annie
and Waneta fed them, changed their diapers and put
them down for their morning naps. Judith washed the
breakfast dishes, then she and Waneta loaded the potatoes and noodles into the buggy. Eli sat on the buggy
seat with Waneta while Judith hitched up Summer.
While she worked, Eli sang a little song to the horse.

Waneta jiggled him on her lap as Judith climbed into
the buggy and picked up the reins.

"I don't know what song he was singing, but he was
enjoying himself."

Judith laughed. "Eli sings the same song to Summer
whenever he's around her, and she seems to like it. She's
always calm and gentle with him."

"They have a special friendship, then." Waneta
smiled as Judith drove across the road and up the Masts'
lane. "Much like you and…" Her voice trailed off, waiting for Judith to fill in the blank.

"You aren't going to tease me into telling you anything, so you may as well give up trying."

Waneta giggled and leaned down to speak in Eli's
ear. "You can tell me, can't you? Who is Judith's special friend?"

Right then, Eli spotted Guy standing in the middle
of the Masts' barnyard with Matthew, Bram and a few
other men. Judith's stomach flipped at the sight of him,
then fell when Eli bounced on Waneta's lap and pointed.

"Guy!" He looked at Waneta, then back at the men.
"Guy! *Da!*"

"*Ja*, Eli. There's your *daed*." Judith ignored Waneta's
pointed looks as she guided the buggy to the hitching
rail by the back door of the house.

Verna's kitchen was fragrant with frying dough as Judith and Waneta brought in the basket of noodles and big pot of potatoes. The kitchen was crowded and noisy, with women talking as quickly as their fingers flew. Three women sat at the table, boning cooked chickens, while two others worked with Verna at the stove, frying donuts. Judith pumped a pail of water at the sink and poured it into her pot, then set the potatoes on the back of the stove to start cooking.

"Here," said Verna, dusting a tray of fresh donuts with cinnamon and sugar. "You girls can take these out to the men." She handed one tray to Judith, another to Waneta and another to Hannah Kaufman. "I'll take care of Eli." She handed the little boy a donut and settled him on a chair.

"Hannah, it's good to see you," Judith said, as she started out the door with her donuts. "I didn't know you were planning to be here."

"*Daed* said we had to come." Hannah's pretty face was marred by a pouting expression. "I'd rather stay home and sew on my new dress."

"What color is it?" Waneta asked, walking next to Hannah toward the barn.

Judith followed them, not listening to their conversation as she searched the groups of men for another glimpse of Guy. But if Hannah was here, that meant Luke had come, too.

"Just what I was waiting for." Luke's voice came from her right, where he was lounging against some straw bales with a few other boys.

Putting a smile on her face, trying to be friendly, Judith held the tray of donuts toward them. "Would you like some donuts? They're fresh."

The boys didn't hesitate, but took three or four each.

Luke waited until they cleared away, then grabbed a few for himself.

"They're fresh, are they?" He grinned at her. "Just like you?"

Judith turned away, meaning to take the rest of the donuts to the barn, where she could see her brother Bram through the open door.

"Wait a minute." Luke grabbed her arm. She spun toward him to keep her balance. "Maybe I want some more of those."

"You have plenty. I'm going to take these to the men in the barn."

"If you stand here, I'll save you that trip."

Judith looked at the half-filled tray in her hands. "You don't mean you're going to eat all of these, do you?"

In reply, he picked up four more donuts and handed them to one of his friends. "We will, but mostly I want to talk to you."

"We don't have anything to talk about."

"I still have a bruise from where you kicked me."

"I wouldn't have kicked you if you hadn't—" Judith suddenly remembered their audience and lowered her voice to a whisper. "If you hadn't done what you did."

Luke backed away, holding his hand to his chest with a dramatic gesture. "You wound me. I didn't do anything to you."

Judith felt her cheeks burning. "I'm not going to argue with you about it. Take the donuts if you want them so I can go back to the house for more."

"Is anything wrong here?"

At the sound of Guy's voice behind her, Judith's knees went weak. He couldn't think she was talking to Luke because she chose to, could he?

Luke's mouth twisted as he took a step toward Guy. "What's going on here is none of your business, *Englischer*."

He made the term sound like something you'd find on the barn floor.

Guy's face reddened, but his voice was steady when he turned to her. "Are you all right?"

She nodded, and turned to continue into the barn. "I just gave Luke and his friends some donuts. I'll take the rest to the men inside."

Judith had only taken a few steps when she heard the sickening sound of a fist hitting flesh.

One of Luke's friends yelled, "Fight! There's a fight!" Turning around she saw Luke on the ground with Guy on top of him, pressing his head into the gravel with one hand.

"Have you had enough?" Guy said, holding a handkerchief to his nose.

"Let me up!" Luke's yell was muffled, but his anger gave it a deadly tone.

Guy backed off just as the other men ran up.

"What's going on here?" John Stoltzfus shouldered his way in between Guy and Luke. "This is no time or place for a fight. You should both be ashamed of your actions."

Luke crab-walked away from Guy until a couple of his friends helped him stand up. "He started it," he said, pointing at Guy. "We were talking and he...he punched me."

Everyone looked at Guy. The handkerchief he held against his nose was soaked with blood.

"Is this true? Did you strike Luke?"

"I only pushed him to the ground." Guy's face was stormy, and he avoided looking at anyone.

"He punched me," Luke said, turning to his friends for confirmation. They all nodded.

"The outsider attacked him. I saw it," one of them said. Judith couldn't remember his name.

John looked at Guy with a frown. "This is a serious matter. We don't solve our differences with violence."

When Guy didn't say anything, Judith pushed forward. "This is silly. Look at Luke. He doesn't have a mark on him, and yet Guy's nose is bleeding. It's apparent that Luke is the one who hit Guy."

John looked from one young man to the other, then turned to Judith. "Did you see what happened?"

Judith's breath caught. She shook her head. "I was on my way into the barn." She gestured toward the barn door. Donuts had fallen from her tray when the fight started and were strewn in the dirt.

Turning to Guy, John's frown deepened. "Do you have anything to say?"

Guy's face grew even darker as he took two steps back, then turned and stalked toward the house.

John caught Luke's arm as he turned to go, too. "This isn't over, young man. Your *daed* and I will need to discuss this."

He let him go then, frowning at Luke's jaunty step. Judith stepped back as Luke passed her.

John raised his voice as he addressed the crowd around him. "Let's get back to work. There's still plenty that needs to be done."

Guy disappeared around the corner of the house, away from the kitchen and the group of men in the barnyard. Judith longed to follow him, but she couldn't get the sight of him cruelly pushing Luke's head into the gravel out of her mind. She hugged her elbows, undecided. What had really happened between Luke and Guy?

\* \* \*

Guy strode around the corner of the house, heading somewhere. He didn't care where, as long as it was away from Luke Kaufman. At the back of the farmhouse, shielded from the barnyard by a lilac bush, were the old cellar steps. Shaded and cool, this spot had often been his refuge when he was a boy and had done something to make David mad.

He slumped on the third step, where his head was even with the ground, and leaned his head against the cool stone side of the stairway. Cautiously, he pulled the handkerchief away from his face. At least the bleeding had slowed. He pressed the side of his nose, but didn't feel the tell-tale pain of broken bones.

Luke's punch had taken him by surprise. At the Home, he had always been expecting a fistfight from any of the boys there. But here? Among the Amish? He had let down his guard.

Guy dabbed at a trickle of blood. He wouldn't make that mistake again.

But the worst was the expressions on the faces of the people who had gathered around. They had all believed that he had punched Luke, when all he had done was try to keep the bully from hitting him again. It hadn't been hard to throw Luke off balance, but once he had Luke on the ground and helpless, the fool had said it again. He had called Judith the name that had started the fight in the first place, and it had been all Guy could do to control his temper and keep himself from grinding Luke's face into the gravel.

He turned his handkerchief until he found a clean spot, then held it to his nose again, waiting for the bleeding to stop.

Fighting wasn't allowed among the Amish. He knew

that. Someone would be in trouble, but it probably wasn't going to be Luke.

Even Judith had to see how useless her defense of him had been. Luke's friends would lie for him, and Guy would be blamed for the fight. And what would happen then? David and Verna had been good to him, but would they allow him to stay on after this? Not if the whole community was against him.

Sounds filtered into his hiding place from the fields. Someone had organized the men into teams and sent them into the fields to plow and harrow. The day's work was going on without him. He wasn't needed after all. David had been wrong.

Guy dabbed at his nose again. His face felt tight and sore, but the bleeding had stopped. He'd probably have a black eye for days...and have to explain to David how it got there.

He shifted so his back was against the rough, cold stone. His mood was spiraling downward into a black hole, but he didn't care. John Stoltzfus hadn't believed him, and he was a minister. His opinion counted among these people.

And Judith... He had seen the look on her face. His fight with Luke had disgusted her. Maybe she had feelings for the bully after all.

Guy started to shake his head, denying that thought, but the motion sent a shooting pain from his nose to the back of his skull. He leaned against the stone wall again, seeking relief.

He sure had burned some bridges today. No one in the community would want him around. His job was gone, since David and Verna wouldn't want him on the farm. Any friendships he thought he might have...they were gone, too. He closed his eyes, imagining the reception he'd get the next time he showed his face around the other men. The cellar steps were a refuge, but someone would find him here. He had to go someplace until the workday was over and the farm was empty. He couldn't work with any of those men now.

Guy peeked over the edge of the stairwell, across the buckwheat field toward the woods along the river at the back of David's farm. If he could get across the field without being seen… Or if he was seen, he could say he was going to check on the mint or something. He stuffed his handkerchief in the waistband of his trousers and stood up.

"There you are!" Verna came around the lilac bush and stood with her fists at her waist, holding him in her gaze.

Guy's stomach turned as if he had eaten a rock that wouldn't settle. He hated to disappoint David, but the thought of disappointing Verna made him sick.

"I've been looking for you. The men have gone on with their work, and with you no place to be found. What has gotten into you?"

"There was some trouble—"

"We heard." Verna grabbed his suspender and pulled him up the step. She reached up to pull his chin around. "And you have quite the black eye coming on, there." She turned toward the back door. "Come along. David wants to talk to you."

The stone turned on end, but he followed. Looking over his shoulder across the buckwheat field, Guy put his thoughts of leaving on a shelf for now.

David waited for him, lying flat on his bed. The only sign that he was in pain was his pale face and the fixed set to his jaw. When David gestured toward the chair nearby, Guy sat down.

"What is this I hear about a fight?" The older man's tone was hard, but his expression spoke of grief and shame.

Guy swallowed. "I didn't start it."

"Luke says you did."

Guy fixed his gaze on the quilted edge of the blanket covering David's legs. "He said something about Judith, but it wasn't true."

"So you hit him?"

Anger turned the stone to lava. "Is that what you think? That I'm that outsider who can't learn to live like all of you? That the first chance I get I strike out at someone because that's the way I am? Some kind of sinner?"

Tears stood in David's eyes. He reached for Guy's hand and Guy gave it to him. The old man's hands were dry, leathery and tough. Guy's eyes grew moist, too.

"We are all sinners, Guy. There is nothing you can do that can't be forgiven."

For some reason, Pa came to Guy's mind. Any man who would abandon his own son was a sinner, for sure. But Guy hadn't done anything wrong.

"I didn't hit Luke. He hit me, then I tried to keep him from hitting me again."

"I want you to tell me the truth. Luke says you hit him first, and he has witnesses that agree with him."

"You don't believe me, do you?" Guy stood and shoved his hands in his waistband.

"I want to, Guy." David looked tired. "I want to. But the witnesses don't agree with what you've said."

"But I told you what happened. I didn't lie to you."

David coughed, a hollow, racking cough. "Remember, Guy," he said, his voice raspy. "A man of faith lives by prayer and the Word of God."

Then he coughed again. Guy turned toward the kitchen door to call Verna, but she was already coming with a hot compress.

"Lift him up, Guy. Just a bit, so he isn't lying flat."

She opened David's shirt and laid the compress on his chest while Guy made the adjustments to the bed. He slipped up the stairs to his room while Verna was occupied.

He slumped on the chest by the window, drawing his feet up. This was the end. If David believed Luke's lying friends instead of him, there was nothing left for him here.

Finding a clean handkerchief in his drawer, Guy wrapped some socks and another handkerchief in it and gathered it into a bundle. He took the few coins he had and added them.

Looking out the front window, toward the road, he saw the teams of men working in the front fields. Out back, another team would still be working the buckwheat field. But at noon, everyone would be coming to the house for dinner. He walked to the side window and opened the sash. The side porch roof was just below him, and from there he could drop to the ground. He'd just have to wait until everyone was occupied on the other side of the house.

He cracked his door open and listened for sounds of dinner being served. His stomach growled as the tantalizing aroma of chicken and noodles drifted up the stairway. He would miss dinner, but he couldn't risk going downstairs. He'd just have to go hungry.

Judith's voice rose above the other sounds from downstairs. Somehow, he would get word to her. Let her know where he was.

He ignored the itching eyes that warned him of the

tears that were about to fall. He didn't even know which direction to head. Maybe he could try the factories in Goshen or in South Bend. Once he got a job, then he could write to her.

Guy turned his back and leaned against the wall. He was just kidding himself. There were no jobs around. The other fellows his age from the Home had disappeared to the West, riding the rails because they might be able to pick produce in California. But he had seen just as many men riding the rails east. Or south. Chasing the next rumor of a job.

As the dinner bell rang, Guy grasped his bundle and started for the open window. He paused, waiting to hear the sound of Judith's voice one more time, but he couldn't distinguish hers from the others in the crowd. She would probably hate him for not saying goodbye, but it couldn't be helped. He was sure she hated him anyway for the part he'd played in the fight with Luke, whether she thought it was his fault or not.

Guy stuck one foot out the window and let it dangle while he pushed his shoulders and the bundle out. He stretched his foot to reach the porch roof, then climbed the rest of the way out of the window. He glanced back at his room, then across the fields toward the woodlot. The trees in the distance blurred.

It wasn't too late, was it? Could he go back?

The sound of voices and laughter drifting to him from the other side of the house hardened his resolve. He didn't belong here and he never would.

## Chapter Twelve

By Monday, Judith still couldn't understand what had happened. Keeping Eli company while he played with his blocks after dinner gave her plenty of time to think. Too much time to remember.

When Guy hadn't shown up to eat with the rest of the men during the work day on Saturday, Verna had told her not to worry. Guy had been upset about the row with Luke, but had had a talk with David and everything seemed to be fine. It wasn't until after the dinner dishes were done and the men were back in the fields, that Verna asked her to take a tray to Guy in his room.

She had knocked on the door, and when there was no answer, she assumed he was asleep. She opened the door to take his tray in to him, but he wasn't there.

Judith blinked back tears and smiled as Eli knocked over his stack of blocks, giggling at the fun.

Absently, she helped Eli stack up the blocks again, but it was like someone else was playing with her nephew while she stood at a distance, watching.

Where could Guy be? The bedroom window had been open, but that was the only sign that he'd left.

"Ran away," Matthew had said Sunday afternoon,

after he came home from visiting David. "Verna said he took a few things and was gone."

"But he'll come back, won't he?"

Judith hadn't been able to believe that Guy would disappear without a word to anyone, but he was gone. It had been all anyone talked about during the fellowship dinner yesterday after church. Matthew had volunteered to do Guy's chores, as well as his own, but he wasn't happy about the extra work.

But where was Guy? And when would he come back?

Eli knocked the stack of blocks over again and laughed. He clapped his hands, waiting for her to join in. But Judith doubted if she'd ever feel like laughing again.

When Eli yawned, Judith reached for the wooden box Matthew had made to hold the blocks and started putting them in.

"It's time for your nap."

*"Ne."* Eli frowned, shaking his head.

When Eli was being stubborn, she found she could easily distract him by inviting him to do something else with her.

"Show me how neatly you can put the blocks in the box," Judith said.

She counted as he stacked them, maneuvering them so they would fit. Once all the blocks were in the box, Eli pushed it toward the toy shelf in the corner of the front room.

"Cookie?" He tugged at her sleeve. "Cookie?"

Judith shook her head as she picked him up. "We just finished dinner, and you had a cookie then."

He rested his head against her shoulder as she walked toward the stairway.

"Cookie?" The word was slurred, and she knew he had his thumb in his mouth.

"After your nap."

As she passed the kitchen, Judith saw a movement at the kitchen door. Guy was on the porch, waving to her through the window. She motioned him in, then took Eli up to his bed. By the time she took his shoes off, he was sound asleep and she flew back downstairs.

"Guy!" She whispered his name as she stopped in the doorway.

She hadn't been imagining it. He was here, sitting at the kitchen table. His face was drawn, with whiskers like bristles on his chin. The left side of his face was bruised, especially under his eye, and his nose was swollen. His clothes were filthy, with mud caking the legs of his trousers. He looked terrible. But he was the best thing she had ever seen.

He didn't move as she slipped into the chair next to his.

"Where are Annie and Matthew? Are we alone?"

Judith nodded. "Annie is taking a nap with the twins, and Matthew is working at his *daed's* today." She rested her hand on his arm and leaned toward him. "Are you all right? We've been worried about you. Where have you been?"

He shrugged. "Here and there."

"Are you hungry?"

Guy gave a raspy *"Ja,"* so she took the loaf of bread from the counter and brought it to the table with the crock of butter. She sliced the bread and he took it as soon as she spread the butter on it.

"Mmm." He grunted and nodded as he chewed. "This tastes good."

"When is the last time you ate?"

He still hadn't looked at her, but watched the bread in his hand as if it would disappear. "I only had a few coins, and I used that on Saturday to buy some bread and cheese at the store in Emma." He stuffed the remaining part of his slice in his mouth and talked around it. "I almost didn't even go there. I thought I might see someone I knew."

Judith cut another slice of bread and buttered it. While he ate it, she went to the cellar and got the rest of the summer sausage they had eaten for dinner, along with a jar of canned pears. When she came upstairs, Guy was at the sink, pumping water into a glass. As she put the food on the table, he leaned with his back against the sink and took a long drink of water, watching her. He filled his glass again and sat back down at the table.

"You must think I have terrible manners." He took the sausage from her and sliced some for a sandwich.

"I think you're hungry."

"I was."

When Guy caught her gaze with his and smiled, Judith felt a laugh bubble up inside her. She slipped her hand into his as he took a bite of his sandwich.

"I'm glad you're all right. I've missed you."

He squeezed her hand. "I've missed you, too."

She opened the jar of pears.

"Don't bother with a bowl," he said, taking the jar from her. "I'll just eat them this way." He fished in the jar with his fork until he speared a pear half.

"Have you seen David and Verna? Do they know you're back?"

Guy put the jar down and took her hand again. "I'm not back, Judith. I just had to see you before I leave for good. I didn't want to leave without saying goodbye."

"What do you mean, you're not back?" Judith

switched to *Englisch* to make sure he understood her. "You're here. All you have to do is walk across the road and you're home."

His face grew red and he moved his gaze away from her. He picked up the fork again and chased a piece of a pear around in the juice. "I can't go back there."

"Why not? You should see David and Verna. They're worried sick about you."

Rubbing his forehead with one hand, he closed his eyes. "They're only angry because I'm not there to do the work for them."

"That isn't true. Matthew said—"

"I don't care what Matthew said. I don't care what David thinks." Guy pushed his chair back from the table. "I don't care what anyone in this whole Amish community thinks."

"Shh." Judith glanced toward the hallway and the bedroom door beyond. "Don't wake Annie." Her head throbbed. When she saw him at the door, she had assumed that everything would go back to normal, that he would make things right with David and Verna. But it was like he still faced Luke, ready for a fight.

"I don't even care if I wake up Annie." Guy's voice was gruff, but his words were quieter. He leaned his forearms on his knees and caught both of her hands in his. "I only care what you think, Judith. I feel like the whole world is against me right now, but I know you aren't. You have to understand that I have to get away. Start a new life somewhere else."

Leave? Judith drew her hands out of his grasp and leaned back in her chair. He couldn't mean what he was saying.

"You can't leave David and Verna...the church..." She pulled her bottom lip between her teeth as the thought of what he was giving up sunk in. "Guy, this is your home."

"I don't have a home."

The memory of Verna's face on Saturday when Judith had told her Guy was gone told a different story.

"David and Verna love you. You're part of their family. David is so sick—"

Guy's head shot up. "What? Is he worse?"

Judith's eyes blurred. "I thought you knew, but I guess you couldn't. Verna asked Matthew to bring the doctor out on Saturday evening."

"It's his cough, isn't it?"

She nodded. "The doctor says he's getting weaker." She took her handkerchief from the waistband of her apron and blew her nose. "They love you, and they need you. Now more than ever."

Guy didn't speak, but glanced toward the door.

"If you won't go home for yourself, go home for them. They've given you a job when no one else can find one. Verna has fed you and mended your clothes. David has taught you everything he knows. You owe them."

"David was mad about my fight with Luke. How can I work for a man who doesn't trust me?"

"Haven't you listened to what I'm telling you?" Judith rose and paced the length of the kitchen. "David doesn't care about the fight. He cares about you. If you don't think he trusts you, then you have to show him that he can." She came to a stop in front of Guy and leaned over him, her fists at her waist. "All you've done by running away is prove that he can't trust you. You've disappointed him."

Guy's head hung lower. "How can I face him?"

Judith knelt so she was looking into his eyes. "Just tell him you're sorry. Ask for his forgiveness."

"It can't be that easy."

She thought back to when her brother Samuel had changed last summer, after he met Mary. He had apologized to both her and Esther. "Asking for forgiveness is hard, but when you love someone, giving it is the easiest thing in the world."

Rubbing his hand across his face, Guy winced when he pressed too hard on his bruises.

"Go," Judith said. "If you don't talk to David now, you may never do it."

Guy swallowed, then nodded. "The worst he can do is throw me out, right?"

Judith stood when he did, and when he hesitated, she nudged him toward the door. "He won't throw you out. Go over there and see."

Guy stepped onto the porch and looked back at Judith. She gave him a nod and an encouraging smile. He hooked his thumbs in his suspenders and set his face toward the road.

The girl didn't know what she was talking about. She hadn't seen David's face on Saturday. Hadn't seen the disappointment etched in the deep lines around his eyes.

When had David gotten so old?

Stopping at the edge of the road while a blue Studebaker rumbled by, Guy shifted his shoulders. He had everything planned out, but somehow, once Judith started talking, it had all gotten shifted around again.

He couldn't face David and Verna, but he couldn't leave them alone again. Judith was right. He owed them. He had to stay with them until David was well again… or until David decided to sell the farm. They had opened their home to him when he had nothing, and the least he could do was to pay them back by being the farm hand they needed.

The Studebaker had pulled to a stop a few yards down the road, and now the gears ground as the driver shifted it into reverse. The dust rose around Guy as the car slid to a halt in front of him.

"Well, well, well." The man inside took off his hat and swiped his forearm across his dusty face. "You've grown up."

Guy swallowed, recognizing the man he had been longing to see. "Pa?"

Pa opened the door and stepped across the road to him, grasping him by both arms. "You sure are a sight for sore eyes. When the Home told me where you had gone, I never hoped that you were still here." He pulled on one of Guy's suspenders. "Workin' for the Bible thumpers, eh? And dressing just like them, too." He grinned. "But now I've found you."

Pa had come for him? Guy felt his own grin answering his father's. Finally, Pa had kept his promise.

"I haven't seen you for a while, Pa. Where have you been?"

Pa looked up and down the empty road, then thumbed over his shoulder toward the car. "Get in and I'll tell you all about it. We can't stand here in the middle of the road."

Guy trotted around the car to the passenger side and slid into the front seat. The leather seats were worn, but comfortable. Guy ran a hand along the fine woodgrain of the dashboard. The car wasn't new, but she had been taken care of.

"She's a nice-looking car, Pa."

The gears ground as Pa put the car into drive and

started down the road, much faster than any horse and buggy ever traveled.

"She's something, isn't she?" Pa patted the steering wheel. "A real looker. But she's hot, and I have to get rid of her."

"Hot?"

Pa glanced at him sideways. "You know. Hot. Stolen."

Guy's insides went cold. "Why did you steal a car?"

Pa shrugged, resting his right wrist on the top of the steering wheel. "Had to get outta town. It'd be unhealthy for me to stick around, ya know?" He looked in the rearview mirror and drummed the fingers of his left hand on the bottom curve of the wheel.

Guy's stomach turned as Pa popped over a bump, bottoming the chassis on the rough road. "What town was that?"

"You've never heard of it. A little place west of here, just south of Chicago." Pa snickered. "I was a guest of the kind citizens until yesterday morning."

Pa made a quick right into an overgrown lane through a patch of woods and eased the car along until they were out of sight of the road, then he cut the engine. He rolled down the window and leaned out, listening.

"Sure is quiet here." Pa pulled a packet of cigarettes out of his pocket and popped one out with an absent gesture. His face held no expression as he kept listening.

"Pa—"

"Shh!" Pa held out a warning hand, freezing in place. "Do you hear that?"

Guy heard nothing but the sound of a car driving along the gravel road they had just left. "It's just another car."

"It could be the Feds. That's a V-8. I'd recognize the

sound of one of their roadsters anywhere." As the car went on north past their hiding place, Pa relaxed and struck a match to light his cigarette. "They've been following me for two days, but it looks like I gave them the slip this time."

Guy shifted in his seat. They were in the woods that belonged to Old Man Ryber, David and Verna's *Englisch* neighbor. Guy had learned early on not to trespass on his land.

"Why are they following you?" Guy waved off the cigarette Pa offered him.

Pa put the packet back in his coat pocket and regarded Guy with narrowed eyes as he blew out a stream of smoke. "You've spent too much time among these hicks, boy, or else you're plain stupid." He flicked some ash off the cigarette out the window. "Do I have to spell it out for you? I'm on the lam. On the run. One step ahead of the coppers. You get it?" He slumped back in his seat and drummed his fingers on the steering wheel again.

Guy looked out his window so Pa wouldn't see the disappointment that had to show on his face. This wasn't what he'd expected of his reunion with Pa. The man hadn't changed at all, with one wild story following the next. He'd tell Guy he was the lost prince of Russia if he thought it would get him something.

Pa finished his cigarette and ground out the burning stub in the ashtray between them. "This is the way it is, boy." His tone softened, and Guy braced himself. "I need your help. I have to ditch this car and find a place to hole up for a while. If you're still working at that Amish farm the Home told me about, it'd be the perfect place. The Feds would never think of looking there."

Drumming his fingers on his knee, Guy looked at Pa. "What do you mean?"

"I figure you've got it pretty good, right? I mean, those Amish are pushovers. You can just tell them your Pa has come to stay for a while and that they need to keep quiet. If they get out of line, I can handle them." Pa thumbed his hat back on his head. "You'll do this for me, won't you boy?"

It wasn't a question. It was an order. Pa had always been the one in charge.

Guy knew what would happen if he took Pa to David and Verna's. He would take over the house, blustering about until he got his way. As frail as David was, this could be the end of him. And what would David and Verna think of the boy they had taken in? After they'd... loved him and taken care of him. He owed them, just like Judith had said. He couldn't let a liar like Pa into the house and into their lives.

He shook his head. "I can't, Pa. It wouldn't work."

Pa's face grew hard. "Make it work."

Guy's pulse raced as he tried to think of a reason not to do what Pa wanted. "They have folks over. All the time. Someone would say they saw you."

"Just tell them not to let anyone into the house. That's easy enough."

Shaking his head, Guy slid his hands between the leather seat and his thighs to keep them from trembling.

"Then folks would know something was wrong. And David is sick. The doctor comes to see him almost every day."

Pa's hand fell on Guy's shoulder. "Then think of somewhere else. Maybe that house you were coming from when I spotted you."

"They're Amish, too. The same thing—" His voice squeaked when Pa's heavy hand closed on his shoulder.

"Then think. There has to be somewhere I can hide."

Guy scanned his memory for something. Anything to solve Pa's problem.

"The mint still." Relief washed over him when the little building along the river flashed into his mind. "It's at the back of the Masts' farm, and it isn't used anymore. No one would know you were there."

"Okay. Let's go."

As they got out of the car, Guy hesitated. The blue car with the black top gleamed under the trees that were barely leafed out. "You're just going to leave this here?"

Pa ground another cigarette under the toe of his shoes. "You're right. Someone will find it and report it. You'll have to get rid of it."

"Me?"

"Yeah. Just take it somewhere north or east. Anywhere out of the county, or even up into Michigan."

"How would I get back?"

Pa glared at him. "Use your head, boy. Or your thumb. You'll find your way back." He slung his jacket over his shoulder where it dangled from his finger. "Now, show me that still."

"Guy has shown up back at the Masts'," Matthew said as he came in the house for supper that night.

Judith poured the boiled potatoes into the strainer and dropped a dollop of butter into the pot to let it melt. "I know. He was over here this afternoon and talked to me about it."

"I thought I heard voices while the babies were sleeping," Annie said. She was sitting at the table holding

Rose and supervising Eli as he put a spoon at each place. Viola was still napping.

"We didn't want to wake you, but I'm afraid we got a little loud."

Annie shook her head. "Don't worry about it. I was just resting, not sleeping." She reached out a hand to guide Eli to the next plate. "How did you find out, Matthew?"

Matthew finished washing his hands at the sink and dried them with the towel Annie kept hanging next to it. "I stopped by to milk the cows on my way home from the folks' and he was in the dairy, running the cream separator."

"Did he say where he had been?" Annie asked.

"Not a word." Matthew glanced at Judith. "Did he tell you anything this afternoon?"

Judith shook her head. "Only that he thought he might leave our area, but I convinced him he needed to stay."

"I'm glad you did," Matthew said. "David and Verna need him now more than they ever have before."

"That's what I told him. I'm glad he has come home." Judith set the potatoes on the table with the rest of the food and sat down. "I think I'll go over to see how Verna is doing after supper and take a pie."

"How Verna is doing?" Annie smiled at her. "Are you sure you aren't going over there to see someone else?"

Judith shrugged, ignoring the heat rising in her cheeks. "If I happen to see Guy, that would be all right, too."

Once supper was over and the dishes washed, Judith left Eli playing happily with his *daed* and walked across to the Masts' farm, carrying one of the dried-apple pies she had made during the afternoon. The quarter moon rode high in the twilight sky and the first star was shining at the horizon. The barn was dark and quiet, but light shone from the kitchen windows and the front room. Verna answered the door as Judith knocked.

"Judith, dear," the older woman said as she ushered her into the kitchen. "What a surprise."

Handing her the pie, Judith hung her shawl on the peg next to the door. "I thought David might like a treat."

"If he'll eat anything, it will be pie." Verna sighed as she put the pie on the cupboard shelf. "The doctor says to give him anything he wants to eat, but he just doesn't have an appetite."

"Did it make him feel better to see Guy again?"

"Guy came home, but he won't talk to David or me. He even ate his supper in the barn. He said he had too many chores to do."

Judith chewed on her lower lip. "When I saw Guy this afternoon, I thought he was on his way over to talk to David and straighten things out."

"I wish he had done that. I don't know what the boy is thinking."

"Where is he now? I can take him a piece of pie."

"He said he was going out to the barn to take care of something." Verna cut a slice and slid it onto a plate as Judith put her shawl back on. Verna covered the plate with a towel and handed it to Judith, then held her back with a hand on her arm. "You'll find out what is bothering him, won't you? We don't want to lose our boy."

Judith tried to smile. "I'll try my hardest. But if he doesn't want to talk, I'm not sure what more I can do."

Verna nudged her toward the door. "If he talks to anyone, it will be you."

The barn was still dark as Judith started across the

yard. The sky had gone completely dark while she had been in the house, and there was still no sign that anyone was in the barn. No light shone through the windows or filtered through the spaces around the doors. Judith stopped, unsure. Spring peepers sang their evening song, and in the distance, an owl hooted.

"Guy?" Her voice sounded thin in the evening air.

"*Ja*, I'm here." He came from the river, walking along the lane that skirted the pasture. By the time he reached her, he was out of breath. "What are you doing here?"

"I brought some pie for Verna and David and thought I'd bring a piece out to you. Verna said you were working in the barn."

He took the plate from her and walked with her to the porch where they sat on the steps.

Guy held the plate up and took a deep breath. "Apple pie?"

"*Schnitz* pie. Made from dried apples."

He took a bite. "Didn't you want a piece?"

"I had some with my supper." Judith could see his face clearly in the moonlight and the lamplight from the kitchen window, now that her eyes had adjusted to the dark. "What were you doing down by the river?"

He didn't answer, but took another bite.

"Was one of the cows loose or something?"

Laying the empty plate next to him on the step, he laced his fingers around one knee as he chewed. "*Ne.* I was just down there," he finally said.

"Doing what?"

He glanced at her, then stared into the dark shadow of the barn. "Nothing you need to worry about."

As soon as he said that, worry crept in.

"Verna said you didn't talk to David."

Guy picked up a stone and rolled it between his fingers. "By the time I got here, I had to do the chores."

Judith left that alone, too. He'd had plenty of time after he left her to talk to David before chore time.

"How is David feeling today?"

After another glance her way, he threw the stone across the barnyard. "Why all these questions? Can't we just talk?"

"But you're not talking." She stood, ready to go home. "Something happened this afternoon, didn't it?"

He didn't answer.

"Why were you afraid to talk to David?"

"I'm not afraid."

"But you didn't talk to him. You didn't ask him to forgive you."

"Forget it. Just forget it."

Judith stared at him. When he had left Matthew's this afternoon, it had seemed like everything was going to be all right. She had thought she'd convinced him to mend the fences he had broken on Saturday and reconcile with David. But now he seemed like a stranger, the outsider he always said he was.

"What are you keeping from me, Guy?"

No answer. He picked up another stone.

She turned her back on him and started down the lane toward home, waiting for him to call after her. Waiting for him to follow her. But there was nothing except the sound of the peeping frogs.

# Chapter Thirteen

Guy jerked to wakefulness with the rooster's crow early Saturday morning. He had fallen asleep on a pile of clean straw in the barn after Judith left the night before, not wanting to go into the house until David and Verna were asleep. But he had dozed off while waiting.

As he sat up, a quilt fell from his shoulders. He fingered it, recognizing the black-and-purple pattern of the quilt Verna had made for him years ago. She must have brought it to the barn last night and covered him with it. He could imagine the look on her face when she found him sleeping in the straw.

But he didn't care. Standing, Guy folded the quilt and left it on the straw pile. It didn't matter how Verna cared for him, because Pa was back now, and everything had changed.

Yesterday afternoon he had been exhausted, and Pa had taken him by surprise. He had actually believed that whole story about the car and Pa stealing it. Guy chuckled to himself as he headed down to the dairy to milk the cows. Pa had always been a great one for tall tales, and this had to be one of his biggest.

This morning, he and Pa would make their plans.

Real plans, with none of this fooling around and Pa's stories. With the car, they could head west to where there were jobs. He and Pa working together could make a good life for themselves. By the time he finished with the milking and the other barn chores, Verna was calling him for breakfast. He met her at the back porch and handed the quilt to her.

"You can bring my breakfast out here and I'll eat in the barn."

Verna crossed her arms over the quilt, holding the screen door open with her hip.

"You aren't some hobo coming around for a handout, Guy Hoover. You come right on in here and sit at the table." Her face was stern. "If you don't want my company, I'll eat in the front room with David. I want to be in there with him, anyway."

Guilt thrummed, but Guy ignored it. "It isn't that I don't want to eat with you. I just have so much to do and I don't want to take the time to clean up enough to come inside."

It was true, Guy thought, even if it wasn't his real reason for staying in the barn. Going inside meant he wouldn't have any excuse to avoid talking to David, and he wasn't in any mood for a lecture. Besides, Pa was waiting for him.

Verna disappeared inside the house, letting the screen door close with a slam behind her. She appeared a few minutes later with his breakfast on a platter. A mountain of fried potatoes, eggs and biscuits steamed in the cool morning air. Guy's mouth watered.

*"Denki."* He took the platter from her. "I'll set the plate on the porch when I'm done."

"Go on with you," Verna said, waving him away. "Get done what you need to get done." She handed him a bag. "Here are some more biscuits for your mid-morning. They'll keep you going with whatever you need to do."

As he grasped the bag, she held it for a second, until he met her eyes.

"Don't forget, Guy." Her voice quavered. "We do love you."

He dropped his gaze, his throat swelling. "I know."

She went back into the house and he brought the filled platter up to his nose. The aroma made his stomach growl, but Pa was waiting. With a last glance at the house, still trying to silence his guilt's rising tug, he started down the trail toward the river.

The mint still was in a little shed on a small rise along the low acres next to the river. In the old days, David had said, he'd extracted the mint oil himself and sold it for a cash crop each year. But that had been twenty years ago. These days, the mint was distilled at a big plant near Fort Wayne, and all David had to do was mow the field in the late summer and take his mint to the plant.

But the old still remained in the shed, and it had made a good overnight shelter for Pa. Everything was quiet as Guy approached and knocked.

There was no answer right away, but then the door opened. Pa leaned against the doorframe, yawning.

"What do you want, boy?"

"I brought some breakfast." Guy held up the platter with the rapidly cooling food.

Pa grabbed a potato between his thumb and forefinger and inspected it, then smelled it. "It isn't morning already, is it?" He popped the potato into his mouth and sat on an upturned log along the path in front of the shed.

"The sun's been up for hours." Guy set the platter on

another log and squatted next to it. "Here's a fork, and there's enough for two."

Pa took the plate onto his lap and shoveled a forkload of potatoes into his mouth. "You make this?" His words slipped around the potatoes.

*"Ne."* The *Deitsch* word slipped out before he thought. "Um, no. Verna did."

Pa downed a biscuit in one bite and half turned from Guy, shielding the plate while Guy's stomach growled again. Since it didn't seem Pa was going to share the food, Guy reached into the paper bag Verna had given him. A biscuit would have to tide him over.

"Now that you're here," Guy said, swallowing the buttery bite, "where are we going to go? Do you have an idea for a job?"

"That's why I came for you." Pa tilted the plate up and let the last of the crumbs fall into his open mouth, then handed the empty plate to Guy. "A fellow I met in Chicago has a job in Cleveland for us." He pulled a cigarette pack from his pocket, shook one out and lit it. "It's a two-man-and-a-boy gig, and I told him you'd be perfect." He looked at Guy sideways. "You've grown a bit more than I was expecting though. Not quite a boy anymore, are you?"

Guy cleared his throat. "I'm almost nineteen, Pa. I haven't been a boy for years."

Pa took a drag on his cigarette and looked out over the river that wound gently past the green mint field. Guy stood to stretch his stiff legs then sat on the log next to Pa.

"What kind of job is it? It seems that I can do more work now than I could as a boy."

When Pa didn't answer, Guy scooted closer to him.

"I thought we could go west, out to California. I've heard there's plenty of work there."

"Work? Picking vegetables and fruit? Boy, that isn't work. That's slavery." Pa waved his cigarette vaguely in the air. "I'm talkin' real money. Cash money." He leaned close to Guy, blowing smoke into his face, making Guy's eyes water. "Money is easy to get for a fellow who knows the ropes."

An uncomfortable turning started in Guy's stomach. "What do you mean?"

Pa shrugged, taking another draw on his cigarette before grinding it under the toe of his shoe. "You find a sap and play him. It's a game. No one gets hurt, and we get the dough."

Guy rubbed his sweaty palms on the knees of his trousers. He had heard all about confidence men from one of the fellows at the Home, and what Pa was describing sounded just like what they did. It sounded like Pa's story of being on the run might not be a tall tale, after all.

"I can't do anything illegal, Pa. I won't."

A grin split Pa's face, his teeth showing white against his unshaven cheeks. "Who said anything about it being illegal? We're just taking cash that's…extra. Some poor fools have more money than brains, and all we do is teach them a little lesson in how to be careful." He narrowed his eyes, inspecting Guy. "That job in Cleveland might work. We'll head over to Ohio after the heat is off."

"After the heat is off?"

Pa crossed his legs at the ankle. "The Feds. They'll give up looking for small potatoes like me and go chasing someone else. Once they've given up, we'll head to Cleveland." He punched Guy in the arm. "Just you and me, kid. How does that sound?"

Guy swallowed and stared at the river to keep Pa from seeing what he really felt. He didn't want to go to Cleveland. He wanted his pa back. His boyhood dreams mocked him. This wasn't the father he had longed for as he shivered in his cot at the Home on those long winter nights.

But even though this man wasn't the pa he had been waiting for, he'd stick with him. He wouldn't turn his back on his own. After all, to go with Pa and work with him was what he had been hoping for. It was what Pa had promised. Maybe somehow things would still work out. Maybe they could still be a family.

And he wasn't going to run out on Pa the way Pa had run out on him.

On Sunday morning, Judith ran up the stairs after breakfast. A trip home! That's what Matthew had proposed for this non-church day, and she and Annie had beamed at each other across the table.

"I'm ready to get out to see someone other than you two," Annie had said with a teasing grin.

"The twins are old enough to go visiting now, and I knew you'd enjoy the drive on such a fine spring morning." Matthew had smiled back at his wife, giving Judith the feeling she was intruding on a special moment between them.

As soon as Eli was ready to go, she sent him downstairs to help Matthew with the buggy while she took a few minutes to put on a fresh apron for the visit to see the folks at home. As she tied the apron strings, she went into Eli's room to fetch an extra pair of trousers for him, and the view of the Masts' farm through the window caught her eye. She leaned against the windowsill, scanning the lane and barnyard, but there was no sign of Guy.

She hadn't seen him since Friday evening, even though she had hoped he would walk over. But no. No word. No visit. Not even a trip across the road to talk to Matthew. It was as if he had forgotten she existed. Once again, the idea that something was wrong probed at her mind, but there was nothing she could do about it if he wouldn't talk to her.

The trip to Shipshewana seemed longer than she had ever experienced before. She shifted in her seat again, trying to make herself comfortable with Eli on her lap.

"You must be in a hurry," Annie said, looking over her shoulder at Judith and Eli in the backseat. "I thought Eli would be restless on such a long ride, but you're worse than he is."

Judith set Eli on the seat next to her, letting him stand to watch the horse through the windshield of the buggy while she held his hand to help him keep his balance. "You're right. I didn't know I'd be so anxious to get there."

"I know you miss Esther." Annie jiggled Viola gently as the baby fussed.

"I do. I've never been away from her this long. Even though we got to see each other at the quilting, it wasn't enough."

"I think you even miss Samuel."

The thought of their older brother brought a smile to Judith's face. "Even Samuel. It's nice to be with you all the time, and close to Bram in Eden Township, but I miss the Shipshewana folks."

Judith concentrated on sitting still for the rest of the trip while Annie and Matthew visited in the front of the buggy. Eli was content watching Summer, the buggy horse, even though he couldn't see more than her back and her two ears pointed forward.

When Matthew turned Summer into Samuel and Mary's farm, Judith could hardly wait until the buggy came to a stop at the new house that rose clean and white next to the lane before she was climbing out of the buggy. Mary came out of the kitchen door to greet them.

"What a wonderful surprise!" She took Viola from Annie and cooed to the baby as Annie jumped down.

Annie took Rose from Matthew's arms, then helped Eli out of the buggy. "I hope you don't mind a visit. I just had to come see you and Samuel today."

"Not at all." Mary stroked Viola's cheek with a finger. "Samuel and I had thought about coming to see you this afternoon, but we weren't sure if you'd be up to it."

"A visit with the family was the only thing I wanted to do today," said Annie. "I have to admit, I'm getting a bit of cabin fever staying at home."

"We'll have a nice long visit, then." Mary made a silly face at Viola. "Samuel is in the barn, Matthew. And Judith, I'm sure you'll want to go visit with Esther for a while. I'll give Annie a hand with Eli and the babies. Tell Ida Mae and Esther to bring Aunt Sadie over for dinner."

Judith didn't need any more encouragement, but started down the path toward Sadie's farm. The way was familiar; she had walked this path since she had been a child. Sadie had been their next-door neighbor all of Judith's life and had tried to help her and Esther with various things after *Mamm* passed away. She hadn't made much headway until Mary and her sister, Ida Mae, moved here from Ohio to help take care of Sadie last year. Not only had the two sisters become her good friends, but Mary even became her sister-in-law. Now Esther was living with Ida Mae and Sadie, helping to provide the care Sadie needed as she grew more forgetful with time.

Sadie's little house appeared through the trees. Judith heard voices as she approached, and when she came around the hedge she found the three women sitting in the spring sunshine.

Esther was the first one to see her coming. "Judith!" She ran to meet her, welcoming her with a hug. "How did you get here? It's so good to see you! Is Annie with you? Did you bring Eli and the twins? How long can you stay?"

Judith tightened her hug, drinking in the familiar feel of her sister's arms around her.

"Don't ask so many questions at once," Ida Mae said, joining them.

Judith gave Ida Mae a quick hug, then went over to kiss Sadie on the cheek.

"It's so good to see you," Sadie said. She put her hands on either side of Judith's face and looked into her eyes. "So good."

"It's good to be here," Judith said. She hadn't seen Sadie for a month, and she could notice the changes. Sadie looked older. Tired. Judith kissed the elderly woman's cheek again, then sat in the chair that Esther brought out from the house and set next to Sadie. "And to answer your questions, Esther, Matthew and Annie are at Samuel's, and I'm supposed to bring you all over there. Mary says we're to have a nice long visit."

"I can't wait to see the twins again," Ida Mae said. "Have they grown much?"

Judith nodded. "I can't believe how quickly they're changing. They are smiling more every day and taking an interest in everything that is going on around them. And Eli is so much fun."

"It sounds like you still enjoy being nanny for Matthew and Annie." Esther sat down next to Judith. "And how is everything else going? How is that boy who asked you to the Singing?"

"Guy?" Judith pressed the seam of her skirt between her fingers, the uneasiness still probing at her mind. "He's doing well." She cleared her throat, wanting to move the conversation away from her relationship with her neighbor.

"Didn't we hear that David Mast had a bad accident? And isn't that who Guy is working for?"

Judith nodded. "David is recovering at home, but isn't able to get out of bed yet." Judith's eyes grew moist at the thought. "We had a work day last week and the men got his fields plowed and harrowed, and planted the buckwheat."

"That's good. Is Guy able to keep up with the rest of the farm work on his own?" Esther leaned forward, interested in Judith's reply.

As she thought of how to answer Esther's question, Judith's throat grew dry. She twisted her fingers together, not knowing what to say.

"He seemed to be doing fine the day of the work frolic."

"What is wrong?"

Ida Mae's quiet voice broke into Judith's thoughts. She looked from one face to another. Sadie reached out to take her hand.

"I'm not sure. Guy had a fight with Luke Kaufman during the frolic, but I thought that was resolved."

"Until?" Esther laid a hand on her arm, prodding gently with her question.

"I don't know what happened, but suddenly he's different. Like a stranger." Judith sniffed. She wouldn't start crying. She wouldn't.

"Men worry about different things than we do," Ida Mae said. "Perhaps taking on the responsibility of the Masts' farm is too much for him."

Shaking her head, Judith thought back to the events of the past few days. "After he came to see me, he was going to talk to David and set things right. But for some reason…" Judith's mind went over the path Guy would have taken from Matthew's to the Masts'. The only thing that would have changed his mind about talking to David was if he had met someone on the road who talked him out of it. Or pulled his attention elsewhere.

"When I talked to him the other night, he seemed distracted by something." Judith wiped her cheek with the heel of her hand, concentrating. "He wasn't in the barn, like Verna thought. He was walking toward the barn from the direction of the river…"

"What are you talking about?" Esther asked. "You're rambling and making no sense."

"Never mind." Judith put a smile on her face, determined to think through this problem later. "Let's go over to Samuel's. I brought some ham salad to have for lunch, and Annie brought some fresh spinach from the garden."

As they gathered up the chairs to put them back inside the house, Judith's mind raced. Somehow, she would find out what Guy had been doing at the river.

By Monday morning, Guy could tell that Pa was in no mood to hide out in the mint shed any longer. He had never heard anyone complain so much about everything. The frogs were too loud, the mosquitoes were a nuisance and Guy never brought him coffee with his meals. Sometimes he wished Pa would just take his car and disappear…

But no. Guy shook his head at his own thoughts. He didn't want to go back to not knowing where Pa was. At least this way he had stopped waiting for Pa to show up. Now he could get his life started. The life he was meant to have with his own father, where he belonged.

After missing out on Saturday morning's breakfast, Guy made sure he ate part of the food Verna made for him before taking the plate to Pa. He was always careful to push the food around though, so Pa wouldn't notice some was missing.

When Guy carried his breakfast plate to the mint still, Pa was waiting for him. He grabbed the plate from Guy, almost causing it to spill.

"Be careful, boy. Watch what you're doing." He sniffed the plate. "Cold again, but I guess that can't be helped." He looked at Guy, his eyebrows raised. "No coffee?"

Guy shook his head.

"I'd give my eye teeth for a good cup of java." He shoveled an entire slice of ham into his mouth. "That's the first thing I'll find when I get back on the road."

Guy waited until Pa was finished eating and took his plate. "How will you know when it's time to go find work?"

"I have to know that the Feds have moved on." Pa wiped his mouth with his sleeve and took the last cigarette from his pack. "Go into town today, will you? Get me some more cigs and ask around. See if anyone has seen any cops." He struck a match and bent his head to shield the flame from the light breeze.

Pushing down his rising irritation with Pa's demanding ways, Guy watched the man beside him. He had looked forward to Pa's return for so long, but now that he was here, it was like Guy was the father and Pa was the wayward son.

"I have work to do this morning, but I'll try to get to town this afternoon."

"I'll get a list ready." Pa pulled on his cigarette as if he couldn't get enough of the stuff into his lungs. "There are some other things I need while you're there." Smoke poured out of his mouth as he spoke.

Guy headed back to the house, carrying the empty plate with him. He could imagine what would be on that list. Things a young Amishman wouldn't be buying, that was for sure. He'd have to avoid the store in Emma, where David and Verna usually shopped.

The path was starting to wear from his coming and going the past few days. If David hadn't been laid up, Pa couldn't have stayed hidden for long. But Verna never ventured this far from the house, especially with David as badly off as he was. The thought of David's gray face the last time Guy had seen him prodded at him. How was he doing now? As he reached the house, Guy hesitated. He could go in. Talk to David. Apologize for taking off the way he did. Apologize for...everything.

Guy set the empty plate on the back porch and went to the barn. He was in a hole, that was for sure. If he talked to David but didn't mention Pa, the old man would be able to tell he was hiding something. David had always known what Guy was thinking. He'd know something was wrong.

Wrong? Guy slumped against Billy's stall and the horse nudged him for the carrot Guy often brought. Yes, wrong. Pa being here was wrong. Hiding him was wrong. Even knowing about the shiny Studebaker hidden in the woods was wrong, especially if it was stolen, like Pa said.

And there was the problem. He couldn't trust anything Pa had told him. Broken promises and lies. That's all Pa had ever given him.

"Guy?"

Judith's voice echoed through the barn. She stood in the doorway, silhouetted against the morning light. Tension drained from his shoulders. He wanted nothing more than to take her in his arms. It had been too long since he had seen her. But the easy camaraderie was gone.

Ever since Pa had shown up.

"What do you want?"

She came closer to him. In the shadows of the barn, with the light streaming in the open doorway behind her, he couldn't see her expression.

"I just want to talk." She leaned against the stall next to him and stroked Billy's nose.

"Don't you have work to do?" Guy frowned at the gruff sound of his own voice.

"Annie took Eli and the twins to visit Matthew's folks today, so once I put the laundry on the clothesline, I have the rest of the morning free."

"And you chose to come over here? Why?"

Judith moved closer to him, pushing Billy's nose out of the way. Now he could see her face, and he had a sudden urge to run his finger along her soft cheek. Before Pa came, he would have. Now this secret stood between them.

"I know something is wrong." She faced him as she spoke. "You haven't been the same since the work day. First, you ran away from David and Verna because of that silly fight with Luke."

He shook his head. "I had forgotten all about that."

"But between then and when I saw you on Friday evening, something happened, didn't it?"

He couldn't answer, even when she leaned closer and the clean, fresh scent of her clothes teased his nose.

"I miss you, Guy."

Judith looked up at him, waiting. He missed her, too. He missed their friendship and the way she had of making him feel like he had a future here with David and Verna.

He gave in to the urge and ran his finger along the soft skin of her jawline. She leaned her cheek into his hand and he stepped closer to her. Close enough to slip his arm around her and pull her close. She turned her face toward him and received his kiss. Longing to lose himself in her, he deepened the kiss, pulling her closer. If he could have, he'd have stayed with her forever and never faced his pa or David again. Ending the kiss, he held her against him, tucking her head into his shoulder. She fit so well that she might have been made for him. Only for him.

After a few minutes, Judith drew back, holding his gaze with her own. "Tell me what's wrong, Guy. Let me help you." She rubbed her thumb over the whiskers on his chin. "Whatever it is, you don't have to face it alone."

Guy felt the truth of her words ring deep in his chest. It was the same thing Matthew had told him before the work day. But this…this was different. This wasn't about the Amish community, and it wasn't about family.

As he stared into Judith's eyes, he saw his reflection. Not a stranger, not an outsider, but part of her. And Judith was part of him. They belonged together, and knowing that ripped him apart, because he couldn't give up the dream of following Pa. The boy in him held fast to that dream, but the man reached for Judith. He needed to tell her, to convince her to come with him.

"You're right. Something has happened to change things. Pa showed up."

"Your *daed*?"

Guy nodded as she drew back, still watching his face.

"Where is he? What did David and Verna have to say about him?" She clutched his hand. "He isn't going to take you away from us, is he?"

Billy pushed against Guy's shoulder with his nose, impatient with him and waiting for his carrot.

"What if I did go with him?"

Tears stood in Judith's eyes. "And leave me? Leave your home?"

The pain in her voice was like a stab in his heart. He reached out, trying to bridge the chasm. "Come with me."

She turned from him. "You know I can't, and you shouldn't, either."

"But if I leave with Pa, we'll go somewhere. I'll find a job." He pushed the thought of Pa's job in Cleveland out of his head. "We'll make a new home, you and I."

"And your *daed*? The man who left you in the orphanage for all those years? The man who broke his promises to you?"

Guy slumped against Billy's stall, melting under her words.

"I won't go with you, Guy. You need to decide between me and him. Between a life on the road with that man or a home here with us." She spoke through her tears, her voice a hoarse whisper.

She walked toward the door, silhouetted once more against the bright spring sunshine.

"But I have to go." Hope rose when she paused in the doorway, and he pleaded once more. "I have to go with him. He's my pa."

"Then you've decided." She wiped her tears away. "Goodbye."

And she was gone.

## Chapter Fourteen

As Judith left the Masts' barn, she caught sight of Verna waving to her from the kitchen window. Judith waved in return, then walked as fast as she could down the lane. Away from Guy. How could he believe that anyone, even his father…especially the father who had abandoned him…was more important than their friendship? More important than the home he said he wanted?

Before she reached the end of the lane, a stitch in her side forced her to slow down. She paused to catch her breath, looking back at the house and barn. Guy wasn't coming after her, but she hadn't thought he would. The kiss he gave her had been a surprise, but it had made her hope that he'd made the right choice, that he was staying here with Verna and David.

But his choice was to leave, no matter how much it hurt her.

Since Annie was at Deacon Beachey's with the children, Judith didn't go straight into the house. The day was fine, but the blue sky grated on her. The weather should be cloudy and damp to match her mood. But even the songbirds ignored her, singing with melodies that would normally make her pause and listen. She went into the barn, banging the door shut behind her.

*"Hallo!"* came Matthew's call from somewhere above her in the high haymow.

"It's me. Judith."

She climbed up the ladder. Matthew was forking hay through the chute to the horses' mangers.

"You're back earlier than I expected." He leaned the pitchfork against a beam and beckoned to her. "I have something to show you."

On the far side of the stack, he parted the strands of hay, revealing Judith's favorite gray-striped barn cat, Belle, with a litter of newborn kittens.

*"Ach,* how sweet!" Judith sank to her knees next to the nest. Belle purred and reached her head toward Judith for a scratch. "Look how tiny they are! They must have been born this morning."

Matthew knelt next to her. "Belle thought she had hidden them well, the way mama cats do, but when I started moving the hay, I heard her meowing. We'll leave them here until the kittens are big enough to come out and play." He covered the little family up again and stood.

"How are David and Verna?" he asked, grabbing his pitchfork again.

Judith sat on the floor next to Belle's hiding place and stretched her legs in front of her. "I didn't see them. I went to the barn first to talk to Guy, and then…" She brushed a piece of hay off her skirt. "I guess I just forgot."

Matthew stopped his work and stared at her. "You forgot to see how David is doing? I thought that was why you went over there."

She didn't answer but brushed another piece of hay

off her lap. She should have gone to the house and talked to Verna first, but she had been more concerned about Guy than David. A hot tear trickled down her cheek and she dashed it away. She had to stop this crying.

"All right." Matthew waited until she looked at him. "Tell me what is wrong. If you didn't see David and Verna, it must be Guy."

Judith nodded. "What is it about boys? Why are they so…selfish and pigheaded?"

"I should feel insulted." Matthew thrust the pitchfork into the sweet-smelling pile and sat next to her. He stuck a piece of hay in his mouth and chewed on it. "But I think I understand. Guy did something you didn't like?"

How much could she tell Matthew? Judith sucked in her lower lip and watched him. He could be trusted, she knew that, but would he give her good advice, or would he take Guy's side?

"Guy's *daed* came back."

Matthew's brows raised. "When?"

"Friday. Guy has been keeping it a secret."

"He hasn't even told David and Verna?"

Judith shook her head. "And he wants to go away with his *daed* and live somewhere else."

Matthew threw the piece of hay off to the side and laced his fingers around one knee. "It's too bad that he wants to leave us. I know David was hoping Guy would be able to take over the farm one day."

It was Judith's turn to be surprised. "Does Guy know that?"

"*Ne*, and don't tell him. That is something David needs to discuss with him at the right time." Once Judith nodded her agreement, he went on. "Where is he thinking of going?"

She shrugged. "He didn't tell me."

"There's more to it, isn't there?"

Judith crumpled a piece of hay between her fingers. "I've always hoped he'd choose to stay here, to join the church."

Matthew sighed. "I know that's what David and Verna have prayed for, but I feel sorry for Guy. He has a tough decision to make."

"What do you mean? Guy is taking the easy way, going off with the father that he's been waiting for all his life. Now he can start living the way he's always wanted to." Her last words disappeared in a hiccupping sob.

"I've seen you and Guy together. That young man has it bad."

Judith blinked away her tears. "What do you mean?"

"He's in love with you."

"That can't be true. He's never said anything…" Except that kiss. That sweet kiss that had taken her by surprise.

"He might not even realize it." Matthew stretched his legs out, leaning back on his hands. "Don't you see the position Guy is in? Men can be fiercely loyal to their families, but sometimes they have to make a decision that is going to hurt the ones they love the most."

"I thought men always did whatever they wanted to and women just had to learn to accept it." Judith sniffed again. That was the way her *daed* had been and the way Samuel had been until he met Mary.

"Not always. A real man sacrifices everything for the ones he loves. That's why this decision must be agonizing for Guy. Do you think he wants to leave David and Verna?" Matthew put one hand on top of Judith's. "Do you think he wants to leave you?"

"You don't think he wants to go?"

Matthew shook his head. "Not the Guy I know. I think he has made this decision out of loyalty to his *daed*." He laced his hands around his knee again. "Instead of being angry with him, you could look for a way to help him."

"You mean I should help him leave?"

Matthew shook his head. "Give him a reason to stay."

All morning, as Guy went from one chore to another, Judith's final words rang in his ears.

She was right. He had made his decision. But if he didn't go with Pa, wouldn't he be doing the same thing Pa had always done? Putting his family second to what he really wanted?

If only Judith could see that.

When the time drew close to dinner, Guy put the tools away. If he was going to make that trip to town for Pa and get home in time for milking, he had to get going. He knocked on the back door.

"You're early," Verna said as she opened the oven door and slid in a chicken potpie. "I'm just putting dinner in the oven now."

Guy's mouth watered as the thought of Verna's delicious cooking filled his mind. "I'm going into town. Do you need anything?"

"Going to town on a Monday?" Verna went back into the kitchen and picked up a knife and a loaf of bread. The golden crust crackled as she cut thick slices.

Guy stepped closer to the kitchen door, still waiting on the porch. "*Ja*. It can't wait." Pa couldn't wait.

"You'll have your dinner first, won't you?" She turned from her work, watching him with narrowed eyes as if she was trying to figure out something. "Come and sit at the table for once."

He shook his head. "I have to get going. Can you put mine in a lard pail or something?"

"Do I hear Guy?" David called from the front room, his voice raspy and weak. The question ended in a cough.

Verna went to the doorway on the opposite end of the kitchen. "For sure, it is. He's going into town."

Another cough, then David said something that Guy couldn't hear. Verna beckoned to him.

"He wants to see you."

Guy swallowed, the taste of his guilt like bile. But he couldn't take time to talk to David now. Pa was waiting for him.

When Guy didn't move, Verna stalked across the kitchen and out on the porch. She took his arm.

"I don't know why you're acting this way," she said, tears standing in her eyes, "but it's time for you to decide to put someone else ahead of your own feelings. David is very ill, and worrying about you is likely to kill him."

Guy's face grew hot. "I'll see him later. I have to get going."

Verna leaned close to him, peering into his face. "Nothing you have planned is as important as saying hello to David. Just let him see you."

Everything in him wanted to do what Verna said, but Pa—

"Now, Guy. Or no dinner."

He knew the look on her face, and he couldn't go back to Pa without his dinner. He kicked off his work boots and hung his hat on the hook.

"I'll pack some lunch for you while the two of you are talking." Verna stood back to let him pass her, then grabbed his sleeve. "But don't say anything that will upset him, all right?"

Guy leaned down to give her a kiss on the cheek. He did it from habit, but as he caught a whiff of the rose-scented soap she always used, his throat filled. He would miss her when he left with Pa.

David was propped up in his bed with the wedge Guy had made. The old man's eyes were closed, his face tight with pain. As Guy paused in the doorway, David coughed again, a racking, dry cough. When it was over, he fell back against the pillows.

"You wanted to see me?"

Guy asked the question softly, but David's eyes popped open as he tried to turn in his bed to see him. Guy moved to Verna's chair in its place next to the bed, facing David.

"Guy." David reached out his hand and Guy took it. The skin was soft and papery, and the strong grip Guy expected was gone. "Where have you been?"

"Didn't Verna tell you? I've been keeping the farm going."

"*Ja, ja, ja*, I know you've been around the farm, but you haven't come to see me."

"I'm here now." Guy tried to keep his voice light, but David wasn't fooled.

"What has happened, Guy?"

David's grip clung, in spite of his weakness. Guy couldn't turn away, couldn't run. He glanced at David's eyes and was trapped by his gaze. This man was his boss. His teacher. His friend. The best...father he had ever had.

Guy dropped his gaze to the floor. To the toes of the wool socks that Verna had knitted during the winter. They had sat in this very room, the fire in the stove keeping them warm, Verna with her knitting needles and David rocking in his chair while Guy read aloud to them from the *Farm Journal* magazine or the weekly newspaper from LaGrange. This was his home. His family. How could he leave them?

His jaw tightened until it ached. The chasm yawned wide, reminding him that he couldn't stand with a foot on each side. He had to choose one or the other.

He had to stick by Pa, to prove to him that family was the most important thing, whether Pa thought so or not. If only...

His nose prickled and he rubbed it with his free hand. There was no use wishing Pa would be any different than he was.

"Nothing has happened," he said, giving David's hand a squeeze before he pulled free and stood up. "Nothing you need to worry about." He put a smile on his face and leaned over to straighten the blanket around David's waist. "I'm going to town this afternoon. Is there anything you need?"

Exhaustion showed in the tight lines at the corners of David's mouth. "I have a hankering for some licorice, if they have any. Ask Verna for a nickel."

"I'll look for it. If they are out, do you want some of those root beer barrels?"

The older man nodded, resting his head against the pillow. "*Ja*, that would be good."

Guy resisted the urge to kiss the old man's bare forehead. Instead, he squeezed his shoulder. "I'll be back in time for milking."

When he walked through the kitchen, Verna handed him the covered pail.

"I made some ham sandwiches, since you'll miss

out on the potpie. And the piece of bread on top is your favorite."

"Buttered, with cinnamon and sugar sprinkled on top?"

"*Ja*, for sure." Verna patted his cheek. "There's a napkin in there, too, and don't you go losing it."

"I won't."

"You'll have to drink water instead of milk." Verna's brow wrinkled as she thought of that.

"I can drink water, don't worry." Guy stepped into the porch and shoved his feet into his boots. "David said he wanted some licorice. Did you think of anything you need?"

"Some baking soda." Verna reached into the cupboard for the pint jar where she kept her coins. "A dime's worth will be fine. Here's a quarter."

"I'll bring you the change." Guy settled his hat on his head.

Verna waved away the idea. "Buy yourself a soda pop. You deserve a treat after working so hard."

Guy let the porch door swing shut behind him as he left before Verna could see his reaction. He didn't deserve a soda pop, or even the dinner pail he was carrying. He deserved to be shot. Or hung. Or at least put in jail for planning to leave them like this.

He went into the barn through the buggy shed, then out the back door and toward the little shed by the river, his stomach churning. Every step felt like he was wading through a mud hole.

The night Judith had gone home with Luke, he had asked God for help. Somehow, he had found Judith and been able to help her. Had that been God's answer to his prayer? Or had it just been chance?

Guy glanced at the sky as he walked. High, white

clouds floated overhead. He knew what David would say. He had heard it often enough: "A man of faith lives by prayer and the Word of God."

David was a man of faith, for sure and for certain. But was Guy? He put his hand on his middle, where the churning seemed to be easing.

"God, if You're there, help me feel better about what I'm doing. I don't want to leave, but I have to, don't I?"

The shed came into view as Guy got to the corner of the buckwheat field and descended to the edge of the mint fields. Pa stood next to it, waiting for him.

The churning came back with a vengeance.

Matthew's words echoed in Judith's mind as she cleaned up after the quick dinner she had fixed for the two of them. Matthew had gone back to his work in the barn and the house was empty.

"Give him a reason to stay?" She dried the plates and bowls while the pan she had used for the soup soaked in the dishwater. "How?"

She put the clean dishes away, glad that no one was in the house to hear her talking to herself. After she was done, she started up the stairs to fetch her sewing, but stopped halfway. Verna might know how to help her keep Guy at home, and she could see how David was feeling while she was there.

Verna answered the door as soon as Judith knocked.

"I saw you coming up the lane." Verna welcomed her with a hug and helped her hang up her shawl. "David and I are in the front room, and I could use your help."

"What can I do?" Judith hung her bonnet from the hook on the wall and followed Verna.

"I need to put a new mustard plaster on David's chest,

and I also need to change his sheets. Two pairs of hands will make the work go much easier."

Judith's mouth went dry. "But I've never made a mustard plaster before."

"There's no better time to learn. I'll show you what you need to do." Verna went to the table where she had been mixing a yellowish colored dough in a bowl. "This is flour and dried mustard mixed with warm water. It's a very simple remedy for chest congestion." She spread a wide strip of cloth on the table. "I need you to hold the edges of the cloth down while I spread on the paste."

Judith wrinkled her nose at the strong mustard smell but held the cloth until Verna had used all of the paste.

"Now we'll take it in to David." Verna folded the cloth so the paste was enclosed in a square envelope large enough to cover a man's chest. "We have to work quickly so he doesn't get chilled. I'll need you to take off David's shirt and undershirt, and then I'll put the compress on and we'll dress him again. I just need you to be an extra pair of hands for me."

Judith face grew hot at the thought of what Verna was asking her to do. "I can't undress your husband. It wouldn't be right."

Verna nodded. "Normally, it wouldn't be. But part of being a woman in this world is knowing how to care for the ill and infirm in your family." She lifted the plaster, holding it by the corners. "Someday you'll be a wife and a mother. I hope you'll never need these skills, but you probably will."

Judith's future suddenly looked very frightening as she followed Verna into the front room. "You mean I'll need to know how to do this, even though I may never use it?"

"You never know. But you'd hate to need this knowledge and not have it, wouldn't you?"

David was drowsing as he sat propped up in his bed. Verna caressed his forehead to wake him and he smiled when he saw her.

By the time the compress was applied and the bedding changed, David was exhausted. Verna tucked the blankets around him, then took his soiled clothes and bedding back to the kitchen.

"I'm glad you were here to help Verna," David said, grimacing as he shifted to a more comfortable position.

"How are you feeling?" Judith helped him straighten his pillows.

"The hip is healing, and my fever is staying down, so I hope we've passed the danger of pneumonia." David coughed. "But other than that, I'm feeling wonderful. I saw Guy today, and talking with him brightened up my day."

He coughed again as Verna came back into the room. She gave him a handkerchief and helped him lean over to cough as the mustard plaster started loosening the congestion in his chest.

"You must have seen Guy leave," Verna said. "He was going to town, and left not long before you got here."

"I didn't," Judith said. "I must have just missed him."

Her fingers grew cold. Had he gone to town, like Verna said, or had he already left with his father? When David said he had talked with Guy, a brief hope that Guy had changed his mind had flitted through her mind, but with this news…perhaps Guy had only been saying goodbye.

"He's a fine young man," David said, settling his head back against the pillows. "He thinks a lot of you."

Judith fingered her apron absently. Had Guy taken the buggy? Or had he walked? Was his father with him?

"He certainly does," said Verna. "He's going through a hard spell right now, but we keep praying for him."

"Praying for him?" Judith had heard folks say that, and she had prayed for others before, but she had never thought about what it meant. "You mean, you're asking God to make Guy act the way you want?"

*"Ach, ne!"* Verna covered her mouth at the idea. "We don't ask God to do what we want. We ask Him to do what He wants. As the Lord's Prayer says, 'Thy will be done.' And we hope that His will is for Guy to become a member of our church and our community."

"What if he doesn't become part of the church?"

David took Verna's hand in his. "Then that is as God wills it to be, and we submit to Him. But we will never stop praying for our boy." He ended with another fit of coughing.

Verna nodded, her mouth set in a grim smile. "The mustard plaster is working better today than it has the past few days. I think he's getting better."

David's coughing continued, but Verna didn't seem concerned as she supplied a clean handkerchief and rubbed his back.

Judith's thoughts went back to Guy. If Guy left with his father, that would tell her exactly how he felt about her. Even though Matthew was sure Guy loved her, and even with David's encouraging words, the truth would come out in Guy's actions. Any man who loved her had to love the Lord and His people first. He had to be willing to become part of the community.

But Guy had already made his choice. And if he was gone, then how could she convince him to stay?

As David settled back on his bed, he said, "I know

I'll never be able to work again, not the way I've always been able to."

He held up a hand as Judith started to protest. "It's the way of the world, Judith. Our lives are just wisps of fog in the moonlight. We get older, then we die and someone else takes our place."

David's face was calm. Relaxed. Secure. It was as if he was talking about planting a field rather than his own death.

He went on. "I've thought Guy would take over the farm when I wasn't able to work any longer, but I always thought we had a few more years left. With this accident, it seems it's time for me to retire and for Guy to have the farm. It will be a good place for him to live with his wife and to raise his family." He let his eyes close. "I just hope I'm here to watch his children grow."

His voice drifted off and Verna beckoned for Judith to follow her to the kitchen.

"Does his talk of dying worry you?" Judith asked as Verna indicated for her to take a seat at the table.

*"Ne."* The older woman's mouth quivered. "I don't want to lose him, but I don't want him to suffer, either. I keep praying that God will heal him, but some days it seems like he's only getting worse."

"He said that today was a good day."

*"Ja."* Verna's smile strengthened. "Guy talked to him for quite a while before dinner, and it made David happy to see him. I hope Guy decides to spend more time with him."

Judith followed a line of wood grain in the top of the table with her finger. When Guy left, it would break David's heart. Verna's, too. Couldn't he see that?

"I have been hoping that you would be the one Guy chooses to marry."

"We will have to wait and see what happens."

Verna covered her hand with her own. "I know he is restless. I've seen it even more during the past week. I can't help but think that something has gone terribly wrong for him, but he won't talk to me about it."

Judith shook her head. "Right now he isn't talking to me, either." Not since he had chosen his father over her and his family.

"Then we must pray for him. Constantly." Verna touched her *Kapp*. "We are always ready to pray as we keep our heads covered, so we can pray for our loved ones all through the day as they come to mind."

Judith turned her hand over so she could give the older woman's hand a squeeze. "I will pray for him. Always."

# Chapter Fifteen

As Guy drove the blue Studebaker into Goshen, the county seat of neighboring Elkhart County, he pushed in the clutch and tried to shift gears. A grinding sound growled from somewhere underneath the car and he cringed when folks turned to stare. Hunching down as far as he could behind the steering wheel, he drove past the courthouse and the bulletproof police booth on the corner.

Pa had insisted that he drive the Studebaker. "Take it and ditch it somewhere," he had said.

So Guy had taken it, but where in the world would he ditch it? And why? Guy couldn't believe that Pa would steal a car. It was more likely that he had made up that story, too. Pa was a liar, for sure. And probably a petty thief and con man. But to steal a car was crossing a line. Pa wouldn't go that far.

He parked outside the drugstore on Main Street, a block from the courthouse square, and read through Pa's list again. Cigarettes, chewing gum, sock garters, matches, hair pomade and a cake of bay rum shaving soap.

After purchasing the things on Pa's list, Verna's

baking soda and a ten-cent sack of licorice for David, Guy opened the door to leave. Two men inspecting the Studebaker made him pause in the doorway. One walked behind the car, writing on a notepad, while the other man leaned inside the vehicle, his head out of sight. Guy looked up and down the street and caught sight of the police box. At least help was nearby if these men were trying to steal Pa's car.

"Can I help you?" He tightened his grip on the box of items from the drugstore as his voice quivered.

The man with the notebook stepped onto the sidewalk next to him, flipping open the lapel of his jacket to show a shiny badge. "Who are you?"

"Guy Hoover." He took a step backward as the second man joined the first.

"Hoover, eh?"

The second man put his hands on his hips, drawing back his jacket just enough for Guy to get a glimpse of his badge and the shoulder holster he wore.

"We're looking for Frank Hoover." He moved so that he was on one side of Guy while his partner stood on the other side.

Guy backed toward the drugstore. "Frank Hoover?" Pa.

"Same last name as yours." The first man's smile didn't go past his mouth. "I don't suppose you know him, do you?"

The pieces fell into place. These were Feds. G-men. Guy had seen a movie a couple years ago with G-men and James Cagney, and these men looked and acted just like the cops in the movie. Was Pa a wanted man? Had he been telling the truth the whole time, after all? A stone sank in Guy's gut as the thought crossed his mind.

"I know him. He's my father. Has he done something wrong?"

The first man took the box from Guy and sorted through it while the second man stepped forward.

"I think you need to come with us."

"Where?"

The Fed grasped his elbow and started walking him down the street. "To the police station. We can talk there."

Guy tried to stop, but the man propelled him on. "Am I under arrest?"

"We just want to talk to you."

Folks stared as they walked the short distance to the police station, and Guy was glad he wasn't in Emma or Shipshewana where someone might recognize him. The Feds nodded to the police sergeant as they passed the front desk, then climbed a wide, creaking stairway to the second floor. The first man led the way into a room and motioned to a chair on one side of a table. The second man closed the door behind them, and then sat next to his partner across from Guy.

"I'm Murphy," the second man said, and threw a thumb toward his partner. "This is Sanderson."

Sanderson picked the items out of the box from the drugstore one by one. "Licorice. Hoover hates licorice." He glanced at Guy. "This must be for you."

Guy shook his head. "It's for a friend."

"Baking soda." The can rapped against the table. "Cigarettes. Chesterfields. That's Hoover's brand." The package hit the table as he pulled out the can of pomade. "Murray's. He's a man of habit, that's for sure."

Murphy leaned toward him. "Where is he? Here in Goshen?"

Guy shook his head in answer to the question as

Pa's lies and stories swirled through his head. He still didn't know which were true. Or were any of them true? The stone in his gut turned to ice. Perhaps all of them were true.

"Can you tell me why you want him? What has he done?"

Sanderson and Murphy exchanged glances.

"He hasn't told you?" Sanderson tapped his finger on the can of pomade.

The room closed in on Guy. What would Pa do if he was sitting here? Lie his way out?

David's voice echoed in Guy's head, "A man of faith lives by prayer and the Word of God." He sent a quick prayer up. Would God hear it?

He took a deep breath. Pa's way would only land him in jail, and he didn't have to ask himself what David would do at a time like this. More than that, he knew what Judith would want him to do. She would want him to be like David, not like Pa.

Guy looked at the two men in front of him. "Pa tells me a lot of things, and I never know if I should believe him or not. But he showed up at the farm where I work a few days ago after being gone for years."

"Did he tell you that car you're driving was stolen?" Murphy was making notes as he spoke.

"He said it was, but I thought he must be lying."

"And his escape from prison. He must have bragged about that."

Guy swallowed. "He said it was some city jail, and I thought sure that was another lie."

"Did he tell you he robbed a bank, along with another man?" Murphy's eyes drilled into Guy.

"Robbed a bank?" Guy shook his head, his feet growing cold. If these men were right, Pa was much worse than a con man, and Guy didn't know him at all. Suddenly the chasm he had been straddling was gone. Learning the truth about Pa made it easy to determine which side was the one where he belonged.

Sanderson slapped the table. "Quit fooling around and tell us what you know."

A firm, strong sensation flowed through Guy. He knew what he had to do.

"I'll tell you everything." Murphy and Sanderson leaned back in their chairs. "But what will happen to Pa?"

"I won't lie to you, kid." Murphy crossed his legs and thrust his hands into his pockets. "When we catch up with your old man, he'll go to prison for a long time."

Guy swallowed. He wouldn't wish prison on anyone, but Pa was a crook. And he was dangerous. The sensation strengthened. He had to do what was right, even if Pa was his only family. He couldn't help Pa escape the punishment for his crimes.

A lifetime of hopes and dreams, the anticipation of reuniting with his father and being a family again fell away like river ice melting on a warm spring day, disappearing into nothing. He bent his head, eyes closed. He never thought doing the right thing would be so hard.

Facing Murphy and Sanderson, he started at the beginning.

Judith took a shirt off the clothesline, folded it loosely and dropped it into the basket on top of the rest of the clean laundry. From this spot at the edge of the backyard, she could see across the road and up the Masts' lane. As far as she could tell, Guy hadn't come back from town yet, and it was almost milking time.

If she was right and he had left with his *daed*, what

could she do? Retrieving a few stray clothespins that had fallen to the ground, she lifted the basket and started back to the house. She would die an old maid, that's what she would do. Guy had made his choice, and it didn't include her or their faith. Ever since his father had shown up, Guy's future had been ruined.

She shook her head, picking her way through the yard to avoid stones with her still spring-tender feet. *Ne*, not ruined, but changed from what she had hoped for and dreamed of for him. He would never have a life here, at home in the community. They would never have a future together, and it was Guy's *daed's* fault.

*Ach*, here she was, letting hatred and resentment seep into her heart. She paused at the bottom of the porch steps and looked across the road once more. She would have to ask the Good Lord to forgive her wayward heart. The sun was lowering in the sky to the west, making the eastern sky a deep blue over the Masts' house and barn. It was a lovely farm, and the Masts were wonderful people. How could Guy leave them?

The sound of an automobile speeding along the gravel road made her move closer to the house. She opened the door to the back porch but lingered as the vehicle came nearer. The black car slowed to a stop at the end of the lane. Judith looked closer, risking discovery by the strangers as she leaned out to see Guy get out of the back of the car. He spoke to the men in the front seat before giving them a wave and heading up the lane toward the Masts' farm.

Judith set the laundry basket in the porch and waited until the car drove off before she followed Guy. She needed to be home in time to fix sandwiches for supper and to help Annie when she got home from her visit, but she had to find out where Guy had been and why he had come home in an automobile.

An automobile! The thought made her insides quiver.

She hurried along the grassy verge next to the lane, not wanting to run on the gravel. "Guy!" she called.

He waited for her to catch up, and they walked to the barn together.

"I can't stop to talk," he said, shifting the box under his arm. "I need to get the cows in for milking."

"I can help you. I saw you come home in an automobile. What is going on?" She followed him into the milking parlor.

Guy didn't look at her as he opened the gate to let the cows in from the pasture. "I went to town to get a few things, and some guys gave me a ride home. No big deal."

Judith gave each of the cows a measure of grain from the feed box while Guy washed their udders. As he sat on the stool to milk the first cow, she stood near him.

"When Verna told me you had gone to the store, I was afraid you had already left with your *daed*."

"Naw," he said, grunting as he stripped the last of the milk, filling the bucket. He set the full bucket out of reach of the cow's hooves and tail. "That's done with. Plans have changed."

Judith followed him to the next cow in line. "You mean you're not going? That's *wonderful-gut*."

"Maybe." The sounds of milk streaming into the pail stopped. "You can't talk to anyone about it, though." He resumed the milking, still not looking at her.

"Why not?"

"There's more going on than you know, and I don't want you involved in it."

Judith stood back as he finished the second cow.

When he said his plans were changed, she'd hoped they would continue the romance that seemed to be blooming. But Guy was being as hard and secretive as ever.

When he picked up the full milk pails to take to the dairy, Judith followed him. In the clean, whitewashed room, Guy lit the lantern hanging on the wall, then started assembling the cream separator. Judith stepped up next to him to help.

"If you're involved in something, I do want to know. This morning, I thought you had chosen your *daed* over me and your family. Now it seems you've changed your mind, but you still won't talk to me about it."

Guy sighed as he faced her. He put the last pieces of the separator together, then took her hands in his.

"Some things became clear to me today. I had been wrong about Pa, and I have to work to make things right."

"What do you mean? How can you make things right?"

"You can't tell anyone else what I'm going to tell you. Not until it's over."

Judith drew her hands back. "What are you talking about?"

"Pa is a bad guy. A crook. I've been talking to a couple agents from the FBI, and I'm going to cooperate with them so they can arrest Pa."

Judith shivered, even though the barn was warm. "You would turn your own father in to the authorities?"

A muscle clenched in Guy's jaw. "David is more of a father to me than that man has ever been. When I found out what Pa has been convicted of, and that he escaped from jail, I knew I would be wrong if I tried to help him." He smiled at her. "I thought about what David would want me to do, and the way was clear."

"Will it be dangerous?"

A shadow passed over his face. "The agents think it might be."

"Then I want to be there, too."

"No."

"What if something happens to you? I want to be there—"

"No. I don't want to risk you getting hurt." He ran his thumb down her cheek. "If something did happen to me, I'd want to know that you were safe." He started the crank on the cream separator. "But nothing is going to happen. The FBI agents and the police will make sure everything goes smoothly, so you don't have to worry."

Judith chewed her lower lip, watching as he poured the milk into the separator. No matter what Guy said, she had to be there. She would stay far enough away to be out of danger.

"When is this going to happen? And where?"

He glanced at her, eyes narrowed with suspicion. "Why do you want to know?"

"So I can pray for you. And for the police." And she would be praying.

"The agents will be here at sunset." Guy leaned into the crank, looking tired and worn as he turned it. "I'll come over to tell you when it's done."

Judith nodded. "I'll be waiting to hear."

After Judith went home, Guy carried the pail of cream into the house, along with the baking soda and licorice he had picked up at the drugstore.

"*Denki*, Guy," Verna said, lifting her cheek for his kiss. "You shouldn't have brought so much licorice for David, though. You'll spoil him."

"Don't you think he needs to be spoiled once in a

while?" Guy used a teasing tone that he didn't feel. His stomach churned at the thought of what he had to do after supper.

"Take it in to him. I've heated up leftover potpie for your supper." She laid a hand on his sleeve. "You will eat in the house with us tonight, won't you?"

Guy couldn't look her in the eye. "Not tonight. I have something else to do."

She dropped her hand and went back to the stove without a word. Guy pushed back the urge to tell her everything. She would know soon enough.

When he went into the front room, David was watching the western sky through the window.

"I brought your licorice."

David grinned. "You found some!"

Guy couldn't suppress his own smile at the pink tinge in the old man's cheeks. His breathing wasn't as raspy, either.

"The store had plenty, so I bought a dime's worth."

"*Denki*, son. This will be a fine treat after supper."

Guy put on a frown. "You'll share with Verna, won't you?"

David's brows lifted in surprise. "Of course. You wouldn't think otherwise, would you?"

"I know how you love this stuff."

David nodded, smiling. "But I love Verna even more."

Putting the bag on the table next to his bed, David said, "Are you going to tell me what is bothering you?"

Guy drew his hand over his face. David always could read his mind.

"I can talk to you about it tomorrow, but not now. Not yet." He stepped toward the door. "I have some things I need to do."

David's face wore a worried frown. "Take care, son."

Guy nodded and left. He picked up the plate Verna had fixed for him as he passed through the kitchen, and ignored her frown. She was just as worried as David, and he didn't blame them. But everything should be cleared up tonight. And once Pa was in FBI custody, then Guy would be free to mend the fences he had broken in the past ten days.

He stopped by the barn to collect the box from the drugstore and started toward the shed by the river. He had just enough time to give Pa his dinner and the things from the store before sunset. Enough time to ease Pa's feelings and to pretend that tonight was just like every other night.

"Been waitin' for you, boy," Pa said when Guy reached the shed. "I've been missing my cigs." He took the box and looked through it, inspecting each item. He tore open the package of cigarettes, shook one out and lit it before he reached for the plate. The warmed-over potpie smelled delicious, and Guy's stomach growled in response.

"How did things go in town?" Pa asked, his mouth full of food.

"Fine." Guy didn't trust his voice enough to say more.

"Got rid of the Studebaker?"

Guy nodded. "It's all taken care of."

Impounded in the police lot.

"See any Feds?"

Guy heard a crack in the undergrowth behind the shed, but Pa didn't react.

"Maybe. I saw a couple guys wearing suits."

Pa laid the plate down on an upturned log, the potpie only half eaten. He ground his cigarette out in the gravy and leaned his elbows on his knees.

"Did they notice you? Follow you?"

Shaking his head, Guy wiped away the sweat beads tickling his upper lip. "No, Pa. They didn't follow me."

Pa turned his head in the growing dusk, looking for all the world like a wolf sniffing out its prey. "You sure, boy?" His eyes bore into Guy. "I've always taken care of you, haven't I?"

Guy's stomach turned. "Pa, you put me in an orphanage."

"I made sure you had people to care for you. Give you clothes. Give you schooling. I did what I promised your ma."

"Yes, Pa."

"I promised her, even though you weren't my flesh and blood."

Guy's head snapped up. This was the worst lie of all. "That isn't true."

Pa went on. "Your ma had you before we even met. I let her tell you I was your pa, even though taking you on along with her was more than I had planned on." Pa shook another cigarette out of the package and put it between his lips but didn't light it. He spoke around it, his words muffled. "Your ma was one fine woman, though. A real looker."

A soft noise came from the dark underbrush toward the river, and Pa cocked his head, as if he was listening.

He leaned forward, speaking softly, and Guy found himself moving closer to him to hear the lies, drawn like a bird to a snake. "You were always in the way. Useless. Until now."

Pa grabbed Guy's arm and yanked him upward and around, securing him with a choke hold around his neck. He backed toward the shed, using Guy as a shield. Struggling to breathe, Guy clutched at Pa's arm.

"All right, you Feds. I know you're out there."

Through his blurred vision, Guy saw a gun in Pa's free hand.

"Come out where I can see you, or the kid gets it."

Guy got a grip on Pa's forearm, pulling it away from his throat long enough to suck air into his burning lungs. Murphy and Sanderson approached from the direction of the river, both of them holding guns. Pa tightened the grip on Guy's throat.

"Drop it, Frank," Sanderson said, coming forward with cautious steps. "You don't want to have murder on your conscience, too."

Pa—Frank—laughed. "You don't think I've killed before?" He shoved the barrel of the gun against Guy's temple. "What do you think happened to his ma?"

As if a door had opened, a scene from the past roared into Guy's consciousness. Mama screaming, prostrate on the floor, Pa standing over her, and Guy watching from behind the door. He was hiding, waiting for Pa to leave. Waiting to run to Mama so he could help her stop crying. Then Pa kicked with his heavy black boot, and Mama never cried again.

The realization of what Frank had done so many years ago exploded in Guy's brain. With a rasping cry, he threw his arm up, knocking Frank's hand away. The gun fired as he planted his heels in the soft ground and shoved backward, slamming Frank against the shed wall. Guy fell to the ground, his ears ringing. He rolled away from the shed and Frank. Shots from Frank's gun and the agents' guns flashed in the growing darkness, but Guy only heard soft pops muffled by the roaring in his ears. More men ran up, and one wrestled Frank to the ground.

Guy shook his head, trying to clear his ears, but the roaring hum continued. Murphy was in front of him, pulling him upright, his face contorted as his mouth moved. If he was talking, Guy couldn't hear. He grasped Murphy's outstretched arm and stood, but fell again. It was as if someone had tilted the ground under his feet.

As Frank was taken away, Guy closed his eyes, letting his head press into the soft ground, waiting for the throbbing to ease. Tears soaked into the grass, turning the dirt to mud.

# Chapter Sixteen

After a quick supper of sandwiches and canned fruit, Judith put Eli to bed. During the meal he'd fussed, refusing to eat anything but bread and butter.

"He didn't take his afternoon nap," Annie had said. "*Grossdawdi* Beachey took him out to the barn and he loved it. He had a lot of fun, but we're paying for it now."

"He'll fall asleep early, for sure." Judith had been glad, because her mind was filled with worry about Guy.

Now, as she left the house with the excuse that she was borrowing a sewing pattern from Verna, she glanced behind her at the western sky. The clouds glowed with orange and pink as the sun set, but the beautiful sight only added urgency to her worry. Guy had said something would happen at sunset.

Along the lane leading to the Masts' house, six police cars were parked. She walked past them, unease growing as she saw that they were empty. Where were the policemen?

Lamplight glowed from the Masts' parlor window, where Verna and David were probably wondering about the police, but Verna would stay with David, not wanting to leave him alone. Judith went to the barn, pushing the dairy door open. She listened, but there were no sounds other than a hoof stamping on the dirt floor, and all was dark. Guy had gone. But where?

Looking down the path that ran beside the buckwheat field, Judith hesitated. That was the direction Guy had come from when this started. His *daed* must be down by the river. She walked slowly, listening for any sounds, but even the spring peepers were silent. The hair on the back of her neck prickled. The evening was too quiet.

When she reached the corner of the buckwheat field, where the path sloped down toward the river and the mint fields, a movement at the corner of her eye made her duck down, crouching next to a fence post. She saw it again. A policeman was ahead of her, moving slowly toward a shed at the edge of the mint field.

The light from the setting sun was fading, and the scene in front of her became less distinct in the faltering light, but as she watched, she saw more men heading toward the shed with slow, stealthy steps. In the quiet, loud voices rose from the shed, and then a gunshot punctuated the dusky air.

Judith clung to the fence post as the scene in front of her exploded in gunfire and shouts. She couldn't distinguish one policeman from another with their uniforms, and she didn't see Guy anywhere.

Then silence fell again. Two men emerged from the confusion, supporting a handcuffed man between them. Once they'd gone by, Judith ran toward the shed.

When she saw Guy lying on the ground with two men standing over him, she started toward him, but a policeman caught her, holding her back.

"Let me go." Judith tried to pull out of his grasp. "I have to see him."

One of the men standing near Guy waved her over and the policeman let her go. "Do you live around here? Do you know where we can take him to get some help?"

Judith's hands trembled as she saw Guy lying motionless. She knelt next to him, afraid to touch him. "Was he shot? Is he hurt?"

"Nope. Not shot. He probably broke an eardrum when Hoover fired his weapon." As the man turned Guy over, a policeman shone a flashlight on him. Guy squinted his eyes against the bright beam.

"Judith?" His voice was loud, like he was shouting at her from a long distance. Blood trickled from his right ear.

"Can you hear me?"

"What?" He pointed at his ear.

"We'll take him to the house." Judith stood. "Was anyone else hurt? I heard a lot of gunshots."

The man helped Guy stand. "No injuries. Your boyfriend pulled off his part of the deal perfectly. Frank Hoover is in custody, and he'll be put away for a long time."

When they reached the house, Verna was waiting for them. Her eyes widened when she saw Guy being supported by the two *Englischers*.

"He can't hear anything," Judith said, "but otherwise he isn't hurt."

"What has happened? We saw the policemen come, but I couldn't leave David to find out why they were here."

"Everything is fine, ma'am. Guy helped us capture a dangerous fugitive, but that man is in custody now and we'll be leaving. Do you want us to call a doctor with our car radio?"

Verna shook her head. "We'll take care of him." She

took Guy's arm, and he put it around her, giving her a hug.

"We'll be on our way, in that case." The second man touched the brim of his hat in a kind of salute, then shook Guy's hand. "Thank you for your cooperation."

Guy nodded, still looking a bit dazed.

When the men left, Judith and Verna helped Guy into the front room and the soft chair in the corner. Judith explained to David and Verna what she knew about Frank Hoover and the arrest, but she left the details of Guy's involvement to him. Verna gave Guy a wet towel to clean away the blood that still trickled from his ear.

"You won't be able to hear well for a few days," Verna said in a loud voice, making sure Guy could see her mouth as she over-enunciated the words, "but the hearing should come back in your left ear. We'll have to wait and see."

Guy nodded, leaning back in the chair. He looked at Judith. "I told you not to come. I told you it was going to be dangerous."

"I stayed out of the way until it was over." She spoke loudly, like Verna had, and he nodded to show that he had heard her.

"I'm glad you're here now, though." He took her hand and squeezed it.

David sighed. "That's a good way for the evening to end."

Over the next two days, Guy slowly regained the hearing in his left ear.

When the doctor came to visit David, he examined Guy at Verna's insistence. Sitting at the kitchen table, Guy tilted his head, wincing as the doctor inserted something into the sore right ear.

"Whew." Doctor Bradley gave a low whistle. "You blew out that eardrum. Have you had any bleeding?"

Verna hovered over Guy. "He had some the first night after it happened, but I haven't seen any since then."

After looking in his other ear, the doctor sat in front of Guy and pressed his stethoscope against Guy's chest. "Any other problems? Coughing? Trouble breathing?"

Guy shook his head. "Why?"

"I'm trying to figure out what you did to end up with your ear looking like that."

"Someone fired a gun next to my head." Guy had told Verna and David part of the story, that he was present when the police arrested a fugitive, but he hadn't wanted to tell them everything until both he and David were better.

Doctor Bradley stowed his instruments back in his black bag. "I'm afraid the damage to this ear might be permanent, but the other one should be right as rain soon enough." He snapped his fingers next to Guy's right ear and then his left. "Can you hear all right out of your left ear?"

"It's a lot better today than it was yesterday."

"Take it easy while the right ear heals. And no swimming, either, or ducking your head underwater. Not until it heals completely."

Verna twisted her fingers together. "How is David doing, do you think?"

The doctor smiled at her. "You are one of the best nurses I've seen. The threat of pneumonia has cleared up, and the broken bones are mending. Now the hard part starts."

Guy took Verna's hand as her eyes widened, and he grinned at the doctor. "You mean that the hard part will be keeping him in bed now that he's feeling better, right?"

"That's right." Doctor Bradley shrugged on his worn overcoat. "He shouldn't get chilled, and he needs to remain quiet. He needs fresh air and sunshine, though, so when you can, open up the windows and move his bed so he can catch the afternoon light. In a few weeks, once the bones are mostly healed, we'll see about letting him sit outside."

After the doctor left, Verna wiped her eyes. "I've been so worried, but I didn't want to let David see."

"He's been pretty sick."

She shook her head. "You're the one I've been worried about."

"Now that David's feeling better, and I am, too, I'll tell you both what has been going on."

Facing up to the way he had treated David and Verna was one of the hardest things Guy had ever done. The three of them gathered in the front room as the afternoon waned, and he told them every detail of what had happened since the work day two weeks before.

"I should have realized that you have been my family more than Frank Hoover ever was."

Verna squeezed his hand. "What is done is done and past. You never need to question our forgiveness, and we hope you will forgive us."

Guy looked from Verna to David. "What do I need to forgive you for?"

David cleared his throat. "We should have spent more time looking into your situation. There must have been a way to claim that your father abandoned his rights, even if he never signed them away. We should have pursued any way we could to adopt you."

"Don't call that man my father." Guy forced the

words out through clenched teeth. "I hope he never gets out of jail."

"Guy." The one word brought Guy's eyes up to meet David's. "You must forgive him. Don't harbor that hatred. Frank Hoover is a man who has done unspeakable things, but if you can't forgive him the way you have been forgiven, then you will never be able to move toward your future."

The vision of Frank kicking his mother had replayed itself in Guy's mind over and over. The last couple of nights, ever since that distant memory had come back, he had even dreamed that he attacked Frank, saving his mother. How could he ever forgive that man?

"Don't forgive me, then," Guy said, staring at the floor. "Frank Hoover doesn't deserve forgiveness."

"None of us do." David spoke so quietly that Guy had to lean close.

"But you forgave me."

"Of course we did, because we love you. But I've also been forgiven by God for my sins because of our Lord and Savior, Jesus Christ. I couldn't truly forgive you unless I understood how vast my own sin is and how I've been forgiven."

Guy shook his head. "You don't have any sins. Someone like Frank does, but not you."

"We all have sinned and come short of the glory of God."

"That's from the Good Book, isn't it?"

"From Romans. Do you know what it means?"

Guy rubbed the side of his nose as he leaned his elbows on his knees. "I guess it means we're all sinners? But that can't be true."

"There was only one sinless man in all of history."

"Jesus."

"*Ja*, that's right. Every other man and woman is a sinner and needs to be forgiven. We are weak mortals, subject to committing sin knowingly and unknowingly."

"Then where is there hope?" Guy held his head in his hands. "We might as well all live like Frank, taking whatever we want."

Even as he said it, Guy felt a wrench in his heart. That wasn't the answer. That wasn't the way David lived.

"There is hope." Verna's words were soft but fervent.

David nodded. "There is hope in the blood of the Lord Jesus Christ. He died for our sins, so we could be forgiven. We take on His righteousness when He lives in us."

Guy swallowed. "So, if God forgives me…"

"When you belong to God, He looks at you and sees the sacrifice of Jesus. Your sins are forgiven. All of them. You no longer need to fear the penalty for your sins."

The penalty for his sins was much worse than what Frank Hoover was facing here on Earth. The orphanage made sure every child went to Sunday School, and Guy had heard of the destruction waiting for sinners. His knees trembled.

"How do I…" Guy swallowed. "I mean, what do I need to do?"

"Ask God to forgive you. Believe in what He has told you in His Word."

"That's all?"

"That's everything."

"And then what?"

"Then you belong to God. You are His."

Guy couldn't stop the prickling behind his eyes. He could belong to God. As bad as he was, as much as he had shrugged away everything David, Verna and the Sunday School teachers had tried to tell him about God, he could belong.

He felt the sudden urge to be alone. "Do you mind?" He stood, on his way to his room. "I need to…" What? Pray?

"Of course you do," David said. "Spend time talking with God. He will lead you in the way you should go."

"Story." Eli patted his bed, his way of telling Judith to sit with him. "Story."

"Only a short one." Judith sat, catching both of Eli's hands in her own. She leaned down to kiss his soft cheek. Her stories always helped him go to sleep faster. "What should the story be about?"

Eli's eyes lit up. "Horses."

Judith told him a story about Summer running in the meadow, looking for a kitten to play with. By the time Summer went to the barn for her supper, Eli's eyes had closed.

Sitting for a minute to make sure he was asleep, Judith let her mind and her gaze drift to the Mast farm. She had a good view from Eli's window, as the large white barn was lit with the golden beams of the setting sun. The scene was calm and peaceful on this Thursday evening, but Monday's events played through her mind once more. She hadn't seen Guy since that night, but he had sent word through Matthew that he was better today and would be over for his *Deitsch* lesson tonight.

He had been speaking only *Deitsch* in every conversation they had had lately, and rarely made a mistake. What more could she help him with? She grinned at the thought. It didn't really matter, when they could spend a quiet hour together.

A figure appeared at the side of the Masts' house, hurrying toward the lane. Coming to see her.

Judith rose from Eli's side slowly, but the little boy was sound asleep. She descended the stairs as quickly as she could, then let herself out the back door. Guy had just crossed the road and she met him next to the lilac bush at the corner of the house.

"Matthew said you might be coming tonight."

He grinned. "You must have been waiting for me. Are you that anxious to see me?"

"The last time we talked, you couldn't hear me. So, *ja*, I'm that anxious. How are you feeling?"

"Much better. Great, even."

Judith let the quiet of the evening settle in around them as she watched Guy's face. She had never seen him look so calm. So relaxed. As he stared at her, she realized that he was happy. More than happy. A deep peace smoothed over his features and lit his eyes with a glow.

"Do you really think you need more *Deitsch* lessons?"

He held out a copy of the *Ausbund*, the book of hymns they used at Sunday meetings. "I thought we could move to High German, so I could follow along with the singing on Sundays." As she took the book from him, he said, "Let's sit on the front steps as long as the light lasts."

He took her hand and led the way around the lilac bush to the seldom-used front porch. Sitting on the steps, they faced the same scene Judith had enjoyed from Eli's window.

Judith took the book and opened it. "You'll have to learn to read the old German script. It's quite different from the letters you're used to."

"*Ja, ja, ja.* I realize that. But to start with, just read one of your favorite hymns to me. We'll start there."

"Hmm." Judith leafed through the pages of the worn volume until she reached number thirty. "Many of the hymns talk about martyrs and their faithfulness, but I've always liked this one the best."

"Why?" Guy scooted closer to her, looking over her shoulder at the book.

Judith pointed at the page. "It's a hymn of praise in the midst of persecution. There's an introduction here that explains. 'This hymn was written by George Blaurock at Claussen in Tyrol with Hans from the Reve, who was burned in the year 1528.'"

"Burned?"

"Our ancestors suffered martyrdom in the old country. Many of them were burned at the stake for their beliefs, and the rest were finally driven out of their homes in Switzerland. They lived in Germany for a time but then came to America."

Guy's breath warmed her neck, his head next to hers as she read the first lines of the song, translating it into English as she read.

"Lord God, I will praise Thee from now until my end, that Thou gave me the faith by which I recognized Thee."

Taking the book from her, Guy ran his finger along the line of the text. "It really says that?"

"*Ja,* for sure." They held the book between them as she read the words in German and he repeated them.

Closing the book, Guy laid it on the step. He put his arm around Judith and held her close to him. "I'm glad you chose that hymn to read."

"Why?"

"That line about how God gives us the faith to recognize Him. It's what I've been feeling, but I didn't know how to put it into words."

Judith leaned her head on his shoulder. Across the fields, Verna lit the lamp in the front room, sending a warm glow into the twilight.

Guy went on. "Things have changed since I saw you on Monday. I understand some things a lot better now."

"Things about your *daed*?"

His head nodded, brushing against her *Kapp*. "*Ja*, and things about myself." He took her hand in his, stroking her fingers with his thumb. "I never thought of myself as someone who needed God. I would compare myself to someone else and always think that I wasn't as bad as that other person."

Judith waited for him to continue, pulling her lip between her teeth to keep herself from interrupting him. She knew…or she hoped she knew…what he was going to tell her next.

"But David showed me that it doesn't matter what I've done to sin against God, I'm just as much of a sinner as the next man."

His voice faltered and she turned to look into his face. "*Ja*, I know that I am, too. But God…"

Guy nodded. "*Ja*, but God forgives me, anyway. Like that hymn said, He gave me the faith to see Him, and to know Him."

He drew her close again and she relaxed against his strong shoulder. "I thought you looked different tonight. You're more confident, but not the way Luke is. He tends to talk himself into his confidence, but you've learned to rely on the Lord."

"I just needed a solid foundation under my feet, I guess. And now that I've found it, I don't have to live in the past. I have the future to look forward to."

Judith took a deep breath. "Are you still going to leave? Do you think your future might be somewhere out West?"

Guy kissed her *Kapp*, then leaned his cheek on her head. "*Ne*. I think my future is right here in my arms."

They sat together as the twilight faded softly away. Spring peepers sounded from the direction of the river, and a chill crept over the ground and up the porch steps.

"I could sit here all night with you," Guy said, planting another kiss on her *Kapp*, "but tomorrow is another work day. I'm going to visit the bishop in the morning to ask about baptism."

"Tell him that if he will be teaching a class soon, I'd like to join it."

Guy rose, pulling her up with him. "We could take the instruction together and be baptized on the same day. I'll tell Bishop we want to do that."

Judith nodded as he kissed her. Then he started back across the road, whistling a tune as he went. She watched until he disappeared into the dusk and sighed, hugging herself. A future with Guy Hoover sounded like the best future of all.

## Chapter Seventeen

When Guy went to ask about membership the next morning, the old bishop was wary of his intentions. He invited Guy into the *Dawdi Haus* where the elderly man lived alone, and asked him to sit at the table.

As Guy took his seat, Bishop leaned his elbows on the table. "It isn't a usual thing, for someone not born into the Amish church to become a member." The old man's eyes closed as he spoke, just as they did when he preached, as if the world around him was a distraction to his thoughts.

"I might not have been born here, but I belong here," Guy said. He leaned forward on the table, anxious for the bishop to understand. "The Lord God brought me here to be part of David and Verna's family. Now that I belong to God, I want to be part of the church."

Bishop's eyes opened at that, his bushy eyebrows raised. He steepled his fingers and leaned back in his chair. "Tell me how you know you belong to God."

As Guy related his conversation with David, and the conviction he'd felt as he realized the depth of his sin, the old man nodded. A smile passed over his lined features as Guy concluded.

"All is well and good, and I will be happy to help you take the steps toward membership. But one problem remains."

"Whatever it is, I'll take care of it."

"Luke Kaufman."

Guy felt heat rush to his face. As far as he was concerned, his fight with Luke was old news and in the past. Did he really have to face this again?

"When you take your membership vows, you are promising your life to the church. This isn't a social club that you can join one day and leave the next. The church is a body. A community of believers. We are to be holy and without blemish. If there are ill feelings between members of the community, the entire congregation suffers. Before we can admit you into membership, and even before you begin instruction for baptism, you must reconcile with Luke. There must be no division among brothers."

Before Guy left, promising to talk to Luke, Bishop set a week to begin the instruction. The classes would be held before the church services on Sunday mornings, during the first hour.

"There may be several who want to join the class, once I announce its formation."

"I know Judith Lapp would like to be part of it."

Bishop gave him a wink as he nodded. "I thought she would."

Instead of going straight home, Guy drove the buggy to the Kaufman farm. He had been there once before, last summer when the Kaufmans took their turn at holding the church meeting in their home, but he felt a new twinge of...jealousy. Or envy. The Kaufmans had three barns rising from well-tended fields and meadows. Brown-and-white cows grazed on lush grass, while a half-dozen Belgian mares drowsed in the midday sun, their foals lying at their feet with gangly legs sprawling. The house had been placed on a slight rise, surrounded by gardens and orchards. Everywhere he looked, Guy saw wealth. Compared to the Kaufman home, David's farm looked small.

His jaw clenched, and he worked it loose. It didn't matter how well-off the Kaufmans were, he needed to mend this rift between Luke and himself. As he turned into the farm lane, he breathed a prayer that Luke wouldn't take a swing at him again.

Tying Billy to the hitching rail outside the largest barn, Guy walked through the open door into the big bay. The roof soared above him, with high lofts waiting to receive this summer's hay. The walls were lined with stalls and the harnesses on racks in the tack room glowed with polish.

*"Hallo!"* Guy called. "Is anyone here?"

A noise came from one of the stalls, and Luke's head popped up.

"Guy Hoover?" Luke walked toward him, brushing straw off his clothes. "You're the last person I thought I'd see walking into my barn."

*"Ja*, well, I never thought I'd do this, either." Guy rubbed his chin. "I came to apologize."

Luke's eyes narrowed. "Why?"

"We shouldn't have had that fight during the work day, and I want to apologize for my part in it."

"What do you get out of it?"

Guy shrugged. "Nothing. It's just that I'm going to be taking baptism instruction, and I want to start with a clean slate." He glanced at Luke's face, but couldn't read his expression. "So, no hard feelings?"

Luke ignored the hand Guy stuck out to seal the deal and only stared at him.

"Baptism instruction? You're joining church?"

Guy nodded.

"Why?"

"Because I want to. I have to."

Luke barked out a laugh. "You want to marry that Judith Lapp, don't you? That's why you want to join church. You can't marry her unless you do."

Marry Judith? Down deep inside him, Guy felt a puzzle piece fall into place with a satisfying ease of pressure. Of course, he wanted to marry Judith. It had been a vague idea in the back of his mind, but now that Luke had put words to it, the idea became reality. He was going to marry Judith.

"*Ne*, that's not the reason." He took a step toward Luke, but halted when the other man backed away. "I've done a lot of thinking lately, and I've come to realize that I belong here."

"I heard about your *daed*. He was arrested by the police, wasn't he?" Luke's swagger was back. "Bishop will never let you join church, not with a *daed* like that. You're just like him, you know that. Bishop knows it, too. He won't risk letting an outcast like you into the church."

Guy's fists clenched, but he released the tension with a sigh. Pray. A man of faith lives by prayer and the Word of God. He must pray for himself. For Luke. He closed his eyes, all his thoughts focused on Luke and the destructive path he was following.

He opened his eyes. "Let me tell you a story, Luke." He motioned to a couple of stools near the doorway, where someone else had sat and talked in the shade of the barn, enjoying the breeze on a warm day.

Luke sat, but his movements were stiff, as if he expected Guy to strike out at him. But Guy leaned his arms on his knees and started his story from the beginning. He told Luke about his mother, about Frank Hoover and about the events of last Monday evening. He told Luke about his hatred of Frank, and how David convinced him that he needed to forgive the man he had once called Pa.

At the end of it, Luke stared at the barn floor. "I had no idea. I was a fool, riding on you and calling you names when you were going through all that."

"How could you have known? I didn't tell anyone about it."

"And here you are, asking me to forgive you, when it really should be the other way around."

Guy waited as Luke left his seat and paced back and forth across the open bay.

Luke stopped in front of him, pointing a belligerent finger. "If you think you're going to get me to go to baptism instruction with you, you're more of a fool than I am."

"That's not why I came here. I just thought maybe... well, maybe we could be friends."

Luke paced again, coming to a stop in front of Guy, his hands on his hips. "You know the other fellows would tease me, since I've always run you down in front of them."

Guy shrugged and Luke resumed his pacing.

The next time he stopped, his eyes glistened. "And I'm supposed to believe that you're going to forgive me after the way I've treated you?"

Guy shrugged again. "I have to. I've been forgiven, so I must forgive others."

Luke sat on his stool. "Why did you come here today?"

"To reconcile with you. To make things right."

"That's all?"

Guy nodded.

"Then you've got it. Things are right between us. No more fights. No more teasing."

Guy stuck out his hand and Luke shook it, then let go of him just as quickly. "I'm not going to promise I won't ask Judith out again, though."

Guy grinned. "I don't think you're going to have a chance."

Judith followed Eli along the lane leading to the Masts' house. Carrying a hot casserole dish wasn't easy when the little boy stopped every time he saw another dandelion.

"Eli, keep walking. We'll pick dandelions on the way home."

He held up his latest prize to her. "Flower. Pretty flower."

"*Ja*, very pretty." She balanced on one foot, nudging him toward the house with the other one. "But we need to give this casserole to Verna. She's waiting for it."

Eli headed toward the house again, this time at a run, and Judith hurried to keep up with him. Before they reached the side porch, Verna was there with the door open.

"*Ach*, what a pleasure to see you on such a nice spring day!" Verna leaned down to help Eli up the steps. "What brings you here?"

"I made a meal for you, and I thought I'd visit for a few minutes." She followed Verna into the kitchen and set the dish on the stove.

Verna lifted the lid as Judith put the dish towels she had been using to protect her hands on the counter and lifted Eli in her arms before he could do any damage in the clean kitchen.

"Potatoes and ham." Verna took a deep breath, then slid the casserole into the oven. "I haven't fixed anything for dinner yet, so this will be perfect. Come into the front room. David will want to see you and Eli."

David reclined in his bed, not quite in a sitting position. He smiled when he saw her.

"It's so good of you to come." He reached out and patted Eli's knee. "You too, young man. I saw you picking dandelions."

Eli opened his clenched fist and let a crushed dandelion flower fall onto David's lap. "Flower."

Picking up the wad of yellow and green, David inspected it. "*Ja*, for sure. That's what it is."

Judith sat down while David and Eli chatted about the flower. She hadn't seen any sign that Guy was at home, even though she thought he must have returned from his visit to the bishop by now.

"I think David is Eli's favorite person," Judith said. "He is always ready to come over here for a visit."

"He's my favorite boy," David said, smiling as Eli pulled the flower apart and gave him the pieces one by one. "How are folks at your place?"

Judith told about Matthew's farm work and the twins, who were already almost three months old. While she talked, she watched Eli, but also glanced out the window, wondering if Guy would be home soon. She would be able to see the buggy turn from the road into the lane from her vantage point.

"Guy went out early this morning," Verna said. "We expect him back any time."

Judith laughed. "I came over to see you."

Verna and David exchanged glances.

"For sure, you did." David gave Eli a small piece of licorice and grinned as Eli tasted it and made a face. "And we appreciate the company. But I've also seen how you are watching the lane for his return."

Judith's face exploded with heat and she knew she must be beet red.

"Don't let him tease you so," Verna said, patting Judith's hand. "It just shows that he's feeling better."

When Guy's buggy turned into the lane, Judith pretended not to notice. The conversation shifted to the weather, the sprouting buckwheat and when Matthew expected to plant his corn until Judith heard Guy come in the back door.

When he entered the front room, his grin widened when his eyes met Judith's, then he bent to give Verna a kiss on the cheek.

"Well, everything is set." Guy perched on the end of David's bed. "Bishop said he would announce the baptism class on Sunday, and we will start the next meeting day."

Verna and David looked at each other. Verna folded her hands in her lap and gave a nod in her husband's direction.

"*Ach*, what is it now?" Guy looked from one to the other. "I hoped to take a walk with Judith."

"Before you do," David began, "we want to talk to you about something."

"I should go." Judith stood, taking Eli in her arms.

"Stay, please. I think you'll want to hear this, too." David shifted his position, grimacing as he did. "Guy, I hope you know that we've always considered you to be our son."

Guy nodded. "I know that now, and I appreciate everything you've done for me over the years."

"I'll never be able to work like I did before the accident. That's something I've had to face over the past couple weeks." David reached for Verna's hand. "So, it's time to do something we planned years ago. As I retire, I want you to take over the farm."

Guy looked from David to Verna. "But I thought you would sell it, or give it to one of your nephews."

"Not when we have you to carry on after us."

"Why haven't you said anything before?"

David and Verna exchanged glances again. "We wanted to be sure you were committed to the farm and to our way of life."

Guy nodded. "I had always planned to go with... Frank Hoover, if he ever came for me."

"But now, I think you have a goal for your life. A future to plan for. The farm will do well for you and give you a living for you and your family."

Judith tightened her hold on Eli to keep him in her lap. Her eyes grew moist as she thought of what this meant for Guy. He would have a home and a family.

Guy cleared his throat, his own eyes glistening. "One more thing. I don't want to carry Frank Hoover's name." He met David's frown. "I've forgiven him, I think. At least, I've begun to forgive him. But I don't respect him, and he'll never be my father. Not the way you have been. If it's all right with you, I want to change my last name to Mast. You might not have been able to adopt me legally, but you did in all the ways that mattered."

Verna hiccupped as tears streamed down her cheeks. As she reached out to take Guy in her arms, Judith slipped out the door with Eli. This was a time for the family to be alone.

\* \* \*

During dinner, David and Verna helped Guy make his plans for the farm.

"We'll need to build a *Dawdi Haus*," David said. "Verna is ready to care for a smaller place, and I need to have a house I can get around in. I won't be able to run up and down stairs like I used to."

"But this is your home." Guy looked from one to the other. "And I can't live here alone."

Verna smiled. "I don't think you'll be alone very long." She gathered the empty plates to take back to the kitchen. "Judith will make a *wonderful-gut* wife for you."

As Verna left the room, David's grin made Guy laugh. "Is it that obvious?"

"I think I knew you two would be getting married when you first started going over there to learn *Deitsch*."

Guy glanced out the front window. All was quiet at the Beacheys' farm.

"I might head over to see if Judith can go for that walk, now."

David took a book from the table next to his bed and opened it. "She's probably waiting for you." He winked at Guy.

Guy left the house, whistling. The tune was one of the songs he had learned at the Youth Singings. He and Judith wouldn't be attending many more of those, if he had his way.

She must have seen him coming, because when he walked up the farm lane, she was waiting for him. Standing on the bottom step by the back door, one bare foot swinging through the long grass at the edge, she looked like a young girl. Guy drank in the sight with the sweet knowledge that she was his. His girl.

"Have you come to take that walk with me?" Judith smiled, the dimple in one cheek drawing him close.

"Are you free?"

"Everyone is napping in the house, and Matthew has gone to work the upper field."

Guy took her slim hand in his and led her around the back of the house. Passing the clothesline and the hedge of blueberry bushes, they reached the orchard. Matthew and Annie had a dozen fruit trees, and the spring blossoms filled the air with fragrance.

Stopping by an apple tree, Guy tried to keep his knees from shaking. Judith didn't seem to notice. Holding on to a sturdy branch with one hand, she swung around it, finally facing him with a smile.

"I think I'll always remember this day."

Guy ran his finger along the branch until he reached her hand. "Why this day, in particular?"

"Because of how your life has changed. Did you have any idea that David and Verna were going to give you their farm?"

He turned to look across the road at the white barn and house with the freshly plowed fields surrounding them.

"I never thought I could hope to find my home here."

"But it's true. I'm so glad for you."

Guy's shaking knees stilled. Now was the time. Now or never. He swallowed and stepped closer to Judith.

"You should be glad for yourself, too."

"Why?"

"If you want to, it can be your home."

Her smile disappeared and she ducked under the branch so that nothing was between them.

"What are you trying to say?"

Guy stroked the spot where her dimple had faded. Her expression was serious, waiting, anticipating.

"I don't want to live there unless you'll join me. I love you, and I want to spend the rest of my life with you."

The dimple was back. "I love you, too."

Guy's knees were shaking again, but he grinned. "Say that again. You were on the side of my bad ear."

She leaned close to his left shoulder, laying her hands on his chest. "I love you."

"So, what is your answer?"

"You haven't asked me a question yet."

He took her in his arms, holding her close, breathing in her fragrance. "You know the question," he said into her ear.

"I want you to ask it." Her whisper tickled.

"Will you marry me? Will you be my wife?"

Her hug nearly choked him. "*Ja*, you know I will."

Guy unwrapped her arms from around his neck. "You're sure?"

"You are the only man I want to spend my life with."

He bent his head to kiss her, and nothing else mattered.

# *Epilogue*

Judith fastened the suspenders on two-year-old Eli's trousers as he stood on the bed.

"Church today?" His face wore a puzzled frown.

"*Ja*, even though it is Thursday." She kissed his round cheek. "It's a special day."

"Cake?"

"*Ja*, there will be cake at dinner."

As he slipped off the bed and thumped down the stairway, Judith was drawn to the view from his window. Sunshine had turned the orange and red leaves into glowing flames of fire dancing in the September breeze. Across the road, the corn stood tall with the tassels beginning to turn harvest gold. Next to the white farmhouse stood the little *Dawdi Haus* that Guy had finished with the help of Matthew and Bram. David and Verna had moved into it last week.

The sound of footsteps on the stairway reminded Judith that she had plenty to do yet this morning, and time was flying by. As she crossed the hall, Esther met her at the top of the stairs with a hug and they hurried into Judith's room.

"Just think," Esther said as she helped Judith settle

a fresh *Kapp* over her hair. "It's September again. A year ago, we were helping Mary get ready for her wedding to Samuel."

Judith smoothed the white apron over her new rose-colored dress. "So much has changed in the last two years, hasn't it?"

The fragrance of chicken and noodles drifted up the stairs of Annie and Matthew's house. Pans of the simple meal were keeping warm in the oven and the scent made Judith's mouth water.

"You know who is getting married next, don't you?"

Judith nodded, rubbing her palms together. She wasn't nervous, so why were they damp?

"You think Ida Mae and Thomas are next?"

The corners of Esther's mouth twitched up in a little smile. "And soon only Sadie and I will be left. Two *maidles* living together."

Judith heard Guy's voice downstairs and her heart skipped a beat.

"You won't be a *maidle* for long. I thought you and Forest Miller were sweethearts."

Esther sighed. "He's been gone for the last several months, helping his *grossdatti* out in Iowa. Things have been bad there, with the drought."

"Has he written to you?"

"A couple letters. The last one came in June. It's been months since then, and I'm beginning to think he has found someone new."

"Or maybe he's just working hard."

Luke Kaufman came into the house, greeting Guy and everyone else with a loud voice. If someone had told her that Luke would become Guy's best friend, she would never have believed it. But they had grown close during the baptism class over the summer, and even

Luke's sweetheart, Susie Gingerich, had become good friends with Judith. They had spent many evenings together as the two couples courted.

Esther shook her head. "I think he has just forgotten me. But that's all right. Sadie can't live alone, and the Good Lord knows what He's doing." She smiled brightly. "I enjoy living with Sadie. Her house is pleasant, and the days are quiet."

More folks arrived and the buzz of the conversations downstairs grew louder. Judith chewed on her lower lip.

"You're doing all right, aren't you?" Esther peered into Judith's face. "You look a little pale."

"I'm fine." Judith swallowed. "Is my *Kapp* straight?"

"Of course it is."

"What about my apron? Are the ties even?" She stood up and turned around for Esther's inspection.

"You look wonderful. You're a beautiful bride."

"Then I guess it's time to go downstairs." Judith's mouth was as dry as if she had been eating chalk.

Esther paused with her hand on the doorknob. "You know *Mamm* would have loved to be here today."

Tears welled up. "Don't make me start crying. I may never stop."

Esther gave her a quick hug and started down the stairs. The furniture had been pushed back to open the lower floor enough to seat all the congregation from Eden Township as well as folks from the Shipshewana church. Faces blurred as Judith slipped into her seat on the front row.

Across the aisle, sitting next to Luke in the front row of the men's side, Guy glanced at her, his face as pale as death. She gave him a smile and he grinned back, his skin returning to its natural color.

Judith tucked cold fingers under her skirt and

watched the toes of her shoes, waiting for the service to begin. By the time the service ended in a few hours, she and Guy would be husband and wife, their lives joined together forever.

Her heart pounded until she glanced at Guy again. He smiled and gave her an assuring nod. Everything would be all right. She belonged to him, and he belonged to her. Forever.

* * * * *

# Save $1.00

## on the purchase of ANY Love Inspired® book.

Available wherever books are sold, including most bookstores, supermarkets, drugstores and discount stores.

✂ - - - - - - - - - - - - - - - - - - - - - - - - - - - - - - - - - - - - - - - - - -

# Save $1.00

## on the purchase of ANY Love Inspired® book.

Coupon valid until May 31, 2019.
Redeemable at participating retail outlets in the U.S. and Canada only.
Limit one coupon per customer.

**52616365**

## SPECIAL EXCERPT FROM

*Love Inspired*®

*With a new job at Big Heart Ranch, pregnant single
mom Hannah Vincent's ready for a fresh start.
But as she and her boss, horse trainer Tripp Walker,
grow closer, Hannah can't help but wonder if she's
prepared for a new love.*

*Read on for a sneak preview of*
Her Last Chance Cowboy *by Tina Radcliffe,
available March 2019 from Love Inspired!*

Hannah exhaled. "My point is that you should consider doing the 100-Day Mustang Challenge."

Tripp looked her up and down. The woman was a sassy thing for a stranger who'd only arrived a few days ago.

"You don't even know if you'll be here in one hundred days," he returned.

Though her eyes said she was dumbstruck by his bold statement, her mouth kept moving. "You don't believe I'm related to the Maxwells, do you?"

Tripp raised both hands. "I don't know what to believe." Though he tried not to judge, there was a part of him that had already stamped the woman's card and dismissed her.

"I am, and I'm willing to stick around to find out if it will help Clementine."

"Help Clementine?"

Hannah offered a shrug "We could use a little nest egg to start over."

"The prize money?"

"Sure. Why not? If I make it possible for you to train, maybe it would be worth some of the purse." The flush of her cheeks told him that her words were all bravado.

"What makes you think I'm going to win?" Tripp asked.

LIEXP47904

"I've seen you with the horses." She paused. "I know a winner when I see one."

He nearly laughed aloud. "So what kind of split are we talking about here?" he asked.

"Fifty-fifty."

Tripp released a scoffing sound. "In your dreams, lady. I'm the trainer and I'm paying for fees and feed and everything else out of my pocket."

"Sixty-forty?"

"More like seventy-thirty, and you have a deal." The words slipped from his mouth before he could take them back. What was he thinking, making a pact with a pregnant single mother who might very well prove to be a seasoned con artist? His mouth hadn't run off on him in years. Yet here he was, with his good sense galloping away.

"I, um…"

Despite his misstep, Hannah seemed reluctant to commit, and that stuck in his craw. Was she having second thoughts about his ability to win the challenge?

"What's the problem?" he asked. "Your bravado seems to be fading the closer it gets to the chute."

"Seventy-thirty?" She shook her head in disagreement.

"Are you telling me that you couldn't start over with fifteen thousand dollars? If you can't, then you're doing it all wrong, my friend."

"We aren't friends," Hannah said. Then she stood and walked over to his desk. She offered him her hand, and he stared at it for a moment before accepting the handshake.

"Deal," she said.

Tripp stared at her small hand in his.

The day had started off like any other. In a heartbeat, everything was sideways.

*Don't miss*
Her Last Chance Cowboy *by Tina Radcliffe,*
*available March 2019 wherever*
*Love Inspired® books and ebooks are sold.*

www.LoveInspired.com

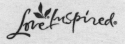

*Love Inspired.*

## Inspirational Romance to Warm Your Heart and Soul

Join our social communities to connect with other readers who share your love!

Sign up for the Love Inspired newsletter at **www.LoveInspired.com** to be the first to find out about upcoming titles, special promotions and exclusive content.

### CONNECT WITH US AT:

Facebook.com/groups/HarlequinConnection

 Facebook.com/LoveInspiredBooks

Twitter.com/LoveInspiredBks

LISOCIAL2018